D1424453

SUNKER'S DEEP

Also by Lian Tanner

THE HIDDEN
Ice Breaker
Fetcher's Song

THE KEEPERS TRILOGY
Museum of Thieves
City of Lies
Path of Beasts

Praise for *Sunker's Deep*

'Lian Tanner is a master storyteller. She weaves
complex, high action tales that are easy to read and
always fast moving and her fantasy worlds are so
detailed, they are completely believable. Like all
of Lian Tanner's stories, I just couldn't put *Sunker's
Deep* down.'
Kids' Book Review

'Tanner skillfully weaves the three plotlines together in
a tense narrative that not only explores the characters'
often conflicting motives but keeps pages turning…
fans will relish this return adventure.'
School Library Journal

LIAN TANNER

THE HIDDEN

SUNKER'S DEEP

ALLEN&UNWIN

SYDNEY·MELBOURNE·AUCKLAND·LONDON

For Deb, Pam &
Margie, with love

This edition published by Allen & Unwin in 2016

First published by Allen & Unwin in 2014

Copyright © Lian Tanner

All rights reserved. No part of this book may be reproduced or transmitted in any form or by any means, electronic or mechanical, including photocopying, recording or by any information storage and retrieval system, without prior permission in writing from the publisher. The Australian *Copyright Act 1968* (the Act) allows a maximum of one chapter or ten per cent of this book, whichever is the greater, to be photocopied by any educational institution for its educational purposes provided that the educational institution (or body that administers it) has given a remuneration notice to the Copyright Agency (Australia) under the Act.

Allen & Unwin
83 Alexander Street
Crows Nest NSW 2065
Australia
Phone: (61 2) 8425 0100
Email: info@allenandunwin.com
Web: www.allenandunwin.com

A Cataloguing-in-Publication entry is available from the National Library of Australia
www.trove.nla.gov.au

ISBN 978 1 76029 318 5

Cover and text design by Design by Committee
Cover illustration by Arden Beckwith
Set in 12.5/17 pt Bembo by Midland Typesetters, Australia
Printed in Australia by McPherson's Printing Group

10 9 8 7 6 5 4 3 2 1

www.liantanner.com.au

MIX
Paper from
responsible sources
FSC® C009448
www.fsc.org

The paper in this book is FSC® certified.
FSC® promotes environmentally responsible,
socially beneficial and economically viable
management of the world's forests.

CONTENTS

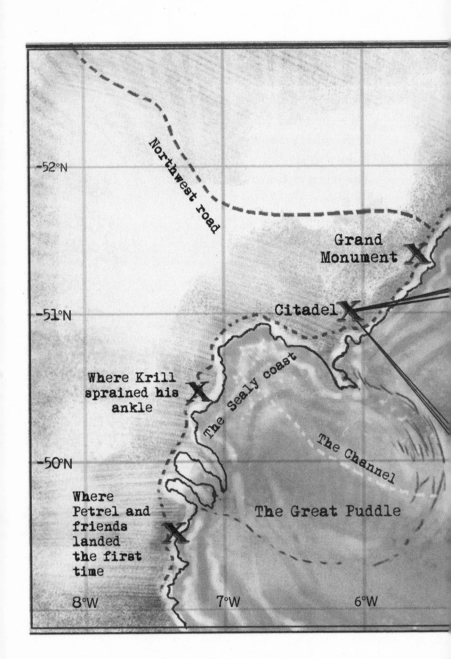

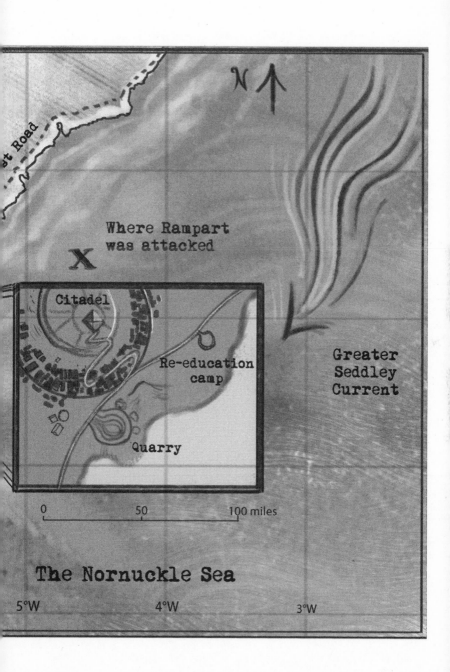

PROLOGUE

They came to the meeting shortly after midnight, separately and secretly. Professor Serran Coe was the first to arrive, and he greeted the other three with his finger to his lips. Not a word was spoken until they were in the basement, and even then, with the university abandoned above them and a dozen locked doors between them and the outside world, they were reluctant to name the things they were talking about.

'Has he gone?' whispered Professor Surgeon Lin Lin, a small, sharp-eyed woman with night-black hair.

Serran Coe nodded and a flicker of regret crossed his face. 'Two weeks ago. The ship sailed under cover of darkness.'

Ariel Fetch leaned forward, her long earrings tinkling. 'Did you give him the instruction? The one we agreed upon?'

'I built a compulsion into his circuits,' said Coe. 'It will come into play when he crosses the equator on the return voyage.'

'If there *is* a return voyage,' growled Admiral Cray, who was Lin Lin's husband.

The others began to protest, but the Admiral spoke over the top of them. 'Nothing is certain, and you cannot tell me otherwise. I have just learned that five of our best ships were sunk last night, and their officers murdered! By their own crews, mind you, who then deserted en masse to join the Anti-Machinists.' The Admiral's waxed moustache twitched in disgust. 'This whole thing is spreading quicker than anyone thought possible. There are even rumours that the government is teetering! And what do we four do about it? We run, we hide, we send a mechanical child to the far southern ice, hoping that one day he will return and be compelled to seek out—'

'Hush!' said Lin Lin, and her husband broke off his rant. The building above them creaked ominously.

'It is only the wind,' said Serran Coe in a tired voice. 'It has been rising all week.'

The Admiral grumbled, 'Look at us, jumping at shadows! Why are we not out there fighting the mobs?'

His question momentarily silenced the other three. Then Ariel Fetch sighed and said, 'You may be a fighter, Admiral, but we are not. And even if we were, we could not turn back the Anti-Machinists. Their time has come. All we can do is try to preserve as much knowledge as we can, so it is there when people want it again.'

'Pah!' said the Admiral. 'They will never want it again! They are fools and criminals—'

His wife interrupted him. 'Then you should be glad that we are leaving them behind.'

Her words fell like a blow on the tiny gathering. Serran Coe loosened his stiff white collar and said, 'You are going to do it? I thought you might change your minds. It is so – extreme.'

'Extreme it may be,' said Lin Lin, sitting up very straight, 'but I refuse to live under the rule of the Anti-Machinists, and I am not the only one who thinks that way. Besides, the medical papers we are taking with us must be preserved for the future. Even your mechanical child does not know everything.'

'When will you go?'

Lin Lin's calm voice gave no hint of what lay ahead. 'Another week, at least. It will take that long to gather family and friends.' She smiled wryly at her husband. 'Which means there is still time for a little fighting if you wish it, dearest.'

The Admiral took a deep breath through his nose – and let it out again. 'Nay,' he said. 'Nay, you are right. We must follow our plans to the very end. I just hope—' He scrubbed his fists against his knees until the blue cloth crumpled. 'I just hope it is worth it.'

Nine days after that meeting, Professor Surgeon Lin Lin and her people left. They told no one where they were going, and no one had the time or the inclination to ask; the government was on the brink of collapse and the city was in uproar.

Screaming mobs rampaged through the streets, determined to destroy the machines that they blamed for all the wrongs in the world. They smashed automobiles and typewriters, omnibuses and telephones. The police were helpless against them. The army, brought in by the collapsing government, destroyed its own gun carriages and joined the mobs. Everyone else, frightened and confused, barricaded their doors, telling each other that the madness *must* stop soon.

But they were wrong. The long harsh reign of the Anti-Machinists was only just beginning.

THREE
HUNDRED
YEARS LATER

Sharkey squinted one-eyed through the thick glass porthole. He was searching for scraps of metal – metal that'd be covered in weed by now, and colonised by barnacles, so that it looked no different from the rocks around it. But it was here somewhere, seventy-five feet below the surface of the sea, and he was determined to find it.

'Two degrees down bubble,' he murmured.

'Two degrees down, aye sir!' cried eleven-year-old Gilly, and she turned the brass wheels that tilted the little submersible's diving planes.

In the bow, eight-year-old Poddy's hands flew across the control panel, trimming the boat and keeping the direction steady as it sank. Further aft, Gilly's younger brother Cuttle braced his bare feet on the metal deck, waiting for orders to change speed. Pipes gurgled.

Dials twitched. Above the children's heads, the ancestor shrine maintained a silent watch.

'Ease your bubble,' said Sharkey.

'Ease bubble, aye sir!' Gilly turned the wheels the other way.

Outside the porthole, the green light that filtered down from above touched thick strands of kelp and a shoal of codlings. The throb of *Claw*'s propeller was like the beating of Sharkey's heart.

He straightened his eye patch and sang the last part of an old Sunker charm, under his breath.

'Below to find,
Below to bind—'

It must have worked, because almost straight away he saw something out of the corner of his undamaged eye. 'Starboard twenty,' he said.

'Starboard twenty, aye sir!' cried Poddy, and *Claw* began to turn.

When they were on the desired heading, Sharkey said, 'Midships.'

'Midships, aye sir!'

'All stop.'

'All stop, aye sir!' And Cuttle threw himself at the motor switches.

Gilly came for'ard, ducking past the periscope housing and wriggling around the chart table. 'Have you found something, sir?'

Sharkey wasn't sure, not really. But he always sounded confident, even when he had no idea what he was doing. 'Aye. There, where the kelp's thickest,' he said.

Young Poddy hooked her toe under the control panel and leaned back on her stool. 'Adm'ral Deeps *thought* you'd be able to find it, sir. And she was right!'

'Course she was,' said Sharkey, hoping that the strange-looking bit of rock really was scrap metal from the giant submersible *Resolute*, which had broken up somewhere near here ninety-three years ago.

'Has he found the boxes?' called Cuttle.

'Not yet,' said Gilly. 'But he will.' She bobbed her head in the direction of the ancestor shrine. 'Thank you, Great Granmer Lin Lin. Thank you, Great Granfer Cray.'

For the rest of the morning, *Claw* cruised back and forth through the ropy kelp, while Sharkey stared out the porthole, half-dizzy with concentration.

At the end of the forenoon watch, Gilly struck the bell eight times. *Ting-ting ting-ting ting-ting ting-ting.* 'It's midday, sir. We're due back on *Rampart* soon.'

'Mm,' said Sharkey. 'I want to find at least one of the boxes before we go.'

From the helm, Poddy said, 'You could ask Lin Lin and Adm'ral Cray where they are, sir.'

Sharkey said nothing. His fellow Sunkers venerated their dead ancestors, but at the same time they seemed to think that the spirits were like some sort of boat crew, and all he had to do was whistle and they'd come running.

Poddy glanced out the helm porthole. 'Look, sir, there's a dolphin! Maybe it's the spirit of Lin Lin! Maybe she's going to show you the boxes!'

Sharkey sighed in a long-suffering sort of way. 'Lin Lin talks to me when it suits her, Poddy. So does First Adm'ral Cray—'

The younger children bobbed their heads respectfully.

'—and *that* is just an ordinary dolphin.'

'Oh,' said Poddy, disappointed.

The dolphin swam idly away from them, and Sharkey watched it go. His eye flickered downwards. There was something—

'There!' he said. 'Port full rudder.'

'Port full rudder, aye sir!' Poddy's small hands brought *Claw* around, as smooth as sea silk.

'All stop.'

'All stop, aye sir!' shouted Cuttle.

'Hold us right there,' said Sharkey, and he gripped the lever that worked the retrieval device.

Like the underwater vessel that housed it, the device was called the claw. Sharkey pulled the lever back and it ratcheted out from the side of the little submersible and spread its talons. It wasn't easy to use with only one eye; Sharkey had to compensate for the fact that he couldn't judge distances very well since the accident. And he didn't want to wreck the box. Now that he'd found it, he was sure it'd be a good one, crammed full of surgeons' secrets with not a drop of water seeped in to spoil it.

Gilly eyed the chronometer. 'We're due back on *Rampart* now, sir,' she said.

Without looking up, Sharkey said, 'Send a message turtle. Tell 'em we'll be late.'

'. . . Aye, sir.'

There was no argument, of course. Discipline on the submersibles didn't allow for arguments. But as Gilly scratched out a note, and took one of the mechanical turtles from its rack, Sharkey knew what the middies were thinking.

He won't get into trouble. But we will, even though we're just following his orders!

It was true. Because of who he was, Sharkey could get away with being late, whereas the middies couldn't.

Still, that was their problem, not his.

It took him another ten minutes to juggle the box into the side airlock. As soon as it was secure, he murmured, 'Mark the position.'

Gilly squeezed past the ladder to the chart table. 'Position marked, sir!'

'Half-ahead. Take her up to periscope depth.'

As *Claw* moved forward again – the planes tilting, the bow rising – Sharkey sat back on his stool, pleased with himself. He knew what the other Sunkers would say when they heard about the box.

Sharkey can do anything. Sharkey can find anything. Sharkey's a hero, a future adm'ral, born on a lucky tide and blessed by the ancestors. Thank you, Lin Lin!

The submersible levelled out, and he grinned. 'Up periscope.'

There was probably no danger from their enemies, not so far from terra. But caution was drilled into the Sunker children from the day they could crawl. Gilly crouched, her face pressed against the eyepieces, her feet swivelling in a circle.

Halfway round, she stopped and rubbed her eyes. 'Sir, there's something strange in the Up Above. Like huge bubbles—'

Sharkey was already moving, snatching the periscope handles away from her.

'Sou'-west,' said Gilly.

The breath caught in Sharkey's throat. Gilly was right. There were three enormous white bubbles floating through the sky with woven baskets hanging beneath them! And figures leaning over the edges of the baskets, pointing to something below the surface. And lines tethering the bubbles to—

To skimmers! To a dozen or more skimmers with billowing sails and their hulls low in the water, following those pointing fingers with a look of grim purpose.

'It's the Ghosts!' cried Sharkey, and his blood ran cold. For the last three hundred years, the Sunkers had dreaded this moment. 'It's the Hungry Ghosts! And they've found *Rampart*!'

EARLIER THAT SAME DAY

As dawn broke, twelve-year-old Petrel leaned against the rail of the ancient icebreaker *Oyster*, staring into the distance. Somewhere over there, beyond the horizon, was the country of West Norn.

'Will there be penguins, Missus Slink?' she murmured.

'Probably not,' said the large grey rat perched on her shoulder. A tattered green neck-ribbon tickled Petrel's ear. 'But if my memory serves me correctly, there will be dogs and cats. And perhaps bears.'

'Bears is further north,' said Mister Smoke, from Petrel's other shoulder. 'Don't you worry about bears, shipmate. There's worse things here than bears.'

'You mean the Devouts?' asked Petrel.

'Don't frighten the girl, Smoke,' said Missus Slink.

'I'm not frightened,' said Petrel quickly. But she was.

For the last three hundred years, the *Oyster* had kept its course at the farthest end of the earth. Its decks were rusty, its hull was battered, and its crew had broken down into warring tribes and forgotten why they were there. All that had remained of their original mission was the myth of the Sleeping Captain, and the belief that the rest of the world was mad, and therefore best avoided.

But the Devouts, fanatical descendants of the original Anti-Machinists, had traced the *Oyster* to the southern ice, and sent an expedition to destroy the ship and everyone on board. Thanks to Petrel they had failed, and the Sleeping Captain had woken up at last.

The Devouts thought the *Oyster's* captain was a demon. But really he was a mechanical boy with a silver face and a mind full of wonders. He knew sea charts, star maps and thousands of years of human history. He could calculate times and distances while Petrel was still trying to figure out the question, and he could mend or make machines and lectrics of every kind. On his orders, the *Oyster* had left its icy hideaway and headed north.

'We are going to bring knowledge back to the world,' he had said.

The voyage had taken more than twelve weeks, with several engine breakdowns that had tested even the captain. But now Petrel was about to set foot on land for only the second time in her life.

She heard a rattling in the pipes behind her and turned to listen. It was a message in general ship code. *Shore party prepare to board the* Maw. *Signed, First Officer Hump.*

With the rats clinging to her shoulders, Petrel slipped through the nearest hatch and onto the Commons ladderway, which took her from Braid all the way down to Grease Alley. She ran past the batteries, which were fed by the *Oyster's* wind turbines, and past the digester, which took all the ship's waste and turned it into fuel.

And there was the rest of the shore party, making their way towards the *Maw*.

'Here she is!' boomed Head Cook Krill, in a voice that was used to shouting over the constant rattle of pots and pans. 'We thought you must've changed your mind, bratling.'

'Not likely!' said Petrel, putting on a bold front. 'Don't you try leaving *me* behind, Krill.'

'We would not go without you,' said the captain in his sweet, serious voice. '*I* knew you would come.'

Fin just smiled, his fair hair falling over his eyes, and handed her a woven seaweed bag.

'Ta,' said Petrel, and she smiled back at him, though her heart was beating too fast, and her mouth was dry at the thought of what lay ahead.

The *Maw* was an enormous fish-shaped vessel set to watch over the *Oyster* by its long-ago inventor. It travelled underwater, and the only way onto it was through the bottommost part of the ship. As the small party climbed through the double hatch, Chief Engineer Albie was giving last-minute instructions to his son Skua.

'No mucking around, boy. This is a big responsibility, taking the cap'n and his friends ashore.' In the dim light, Albie's eyes were unreadable, but Petrel thought she saw a flash of white teeth through his beard. 'You set 'em down nice and gently.'

It wasn't at all like Albie to be so thoughtful. By nature, he was a cunning, evil-tempered man who until recently had made Petrel's life a torment. But Petrel was so excited and nervous that she didn't think much of it. Not until later, and by then the harm was already done.

'Aye, Da,' said Skua.

'And come straight back when you've dropped 'em. You hear me?'

'Aye, Da. Watch your fingers, Da!'

There was a clang as the double hatch was clamped shut, and a moment later the *Maw*'s engines roared to life and the interlocking plates of its hull began to move.

Thanks to Albie's instructions, their passage towards land was smooth and uneventful. Skua brought them right up close to the headland, where the drop-off was steep, and they jumped onto the rocks without getting wet past their knees.

'I'll be back at noon,' said Skua as he stood in the mouth of the *Maw* tugging at his sparse red whiskers. 'Watch out for trouble, Cap'n. And the rest of you!'

His expression was suitably serious, but it seemed to Petrel that as he stepped back into the shadows, it turned into something else. A smirk, maybe. Mind you, that was normal for Skua, who smirked at everything, and once again she thought nothing of it. A moment later, the *Maw*'s huge mouth closed and the monstrous fish dived below the surface.

Petrel felt a tremor run right through her. *We're on land!* She took a cautious step forward, and the ground seemed to sway under her feet.

'Mister Smoke,' she hissed. 'The ground's moving!'

'Nah,' said the old rat. 'It's because you've been on the *Oyster* for so long, shipmate. It'll stop soon.'

Fin had been staring at the surrounding countryside with uncertain pride. Now he turned to Petrel and said, 'This is West Norn. What do you think?'

The landscape stretched out in front of them, muddy and inhospitable. There were patches of snow on the ground and the air was cold, though not nearly as cold as Petrel was used to. A few straggly trees were scattered here and there, with a bird or two huddled on their branches, but there was no other sign of life.

Petrel would've liked it better if there'd been a good solid deck under her feet and the familiar rumble of an engine. But she didn't want to hurt Fin's feelings, so all she said was, 'It's big, ain't it? Reckon you could fit the *Oyster* in its pocket, and it wouldn't even notice.'

Behind her, Krill said, 'What now, Cap'n? We head for the first village?'

The captain pushed back his sealskin hood and nodded. 'Once we have introduced ourselves, we will explain the workings of water pumps and other simple machines that will make their lives easier. We will find out what they want most, and go back to the ship for supplies and equipment.' He paused, his beautiful face gleaming in the early-morning light. 'Of course I will ask them about the Song, too.'

Krill scratched his chin until the bones knotted into his beard rattled. 'Now this is where you've lost me, Cap'n. I still don't understand this stuff about a song.'

'There is nothing mysterious about it,' said the captain. 'Serran Coe, the man who made me, must have programmed it into my circuits. As soon as we crossed the equator, I became aware of its importance.'

'But you don't know *why* it's important?'

'I know that it will help us bring knowledge back to the people. I know that I will recognise it when I hear it – the Song *and* the Singer. If I do not know more than that, it must be because my programming has been deliberately limited, in case I am captured.'

He pointed due west. 'Three hundred years ago there was a prosperous village in that direction. We will start there.'

★★★

Everything Petrel saw that morning was strange and unsettling. She was glad of Mister Smoke and Missus Slink, riding on her shoulders, and of Fin, who walked beside her naming the objects she pointed to.

'That is a fir tree,' he said. 'It does not lose its leaves in winter, like the other trees. That is an abandoned cottage.'

Petrel clutched the seaweed bag, which contained dried fish, in case they got hungry, and a telegraph device that the captain had built so they could talk to the ship. 'Folk used to live in it?'

'Yes.'

'What happened to 'em?'

'I do not know. They probably got sick and died.'

The mud slowed them down, and the village they were heading for seemed to get no closer. But at last Fin nudged Petrel and said, '*That* is a tabby cat.'

Mister Smoke's whiskers brushed Petrel's cheek. 'You sure it's a cat, shipmate? Looks more like a parcel o' bones to me. I can see its ribs from 'ere.'

My ribs were like that not so long ago, thought Petrel, and she took a scrap of dried fish from her bag and tossed it to the cat.

'Captain! Krill!' called Fin. 'If there is a cat, the village is probably close by. Beyond that row of bare trees, perhaps. But we should be careful. There might be Devouts.'

The captain nodded, and waited for them to catch up. 'That position accords with my knowledge. Mister Smoke, will you go ahead and see if there is danger?'

'Aye, Cap'n,' said the rat, and he leaped down from Petrel's shoulder and scampered away.

'D'you really think there might be Devouts here, lad?' Krill asked Fin. 'We're a good hundred miles or more from their Citadel.'

'They have informers everywhere,' said Fin. 'And there are always rumours that someone has found an old book, or unearthed a machine from the time before the Great Cleansing. The Devouts travel the countryside, trying to catch them.'

Petrel listened to this exchange carefully. Fin knew all about the Devouts. He used to be one of their Initiates, and had travelled to the southern ice with his fellows to destroy the *Oyster* and her crew. But Petrel, not knowing who he was, had befriended him, and bit by bit Fin had changed.

Now he's one of us, thought Petrel. *And we're going to find his mam.*

Her heart swelled at the thought. She knew that the main purpose of the *Oyster*'s voyage north was to bring knowledge back to a world that had sunk deep into ignorance and superstition. But as far as *she* was concerned, the search for Fin's mam, who had given him to the Devouts when he was three years old to save him from starvation, was just as important.

Mister Smoke returned with mud on his fur and his silver eyes shining. 'No sign of Devouts, shipmates. Village is quiet as a biscuit.'

Petrel looked towards the trees, feeling nervous all over again. 'But what about the informers?'

'The Devouts who attacked us down south know we weren't beaten,' said Krill. 'I reckon they could guess we might come after 'em. And what with all that engine trouble we had on the way, I wouldn't be surprised if they passed us and got here first. So we're not giving up too many secrets by showing ourselves to a few villagers, informers or not.' He cracked his knuckles thoughtfully. 'All the same, it won't hurt to take it slowly. How about I go in by myself, chat to a few folk, see what's—'

But the captain was already striding towards the village.

'Wait!' cried Krill. 'Cap'n! Wait for us!'

In the end, they entered the village in a tight group, with the captain's silver face hidden under his hood. For her part, Petrel was glad they were sticking together – and not just because of her fear of the Devouts.

For most of her life she had survived by pretending to be witless. Shipfolk had called her Nothing Girl, and believed that she couldn't talk. Then the Devouts had attacked, and Petrel had spoken up at last, to save the *Oyster*.

Since then, she had grown used to speaking her mind, to proving over and over again (to herself as much as anyone else) that she was *not* Nothing. But that was on the ship, where everything was as familiar and comforting as her own two hands.

This was different. This was *land*, and these villagers were strangers. She already felt out of place. *What if they take one look at me and decide I'm not worth talking to?*

To take her mind off such an ugly possibility, she whispered to Fin, 'Wouldn't it be good if your mam was right here, in the first place we stopped?'

'She will not be,' said Fin. 'Look! There are the cottages!'

'They're small,' said Petrel.

'And *dirty*!' Fin sounded shocked. 'I knew people's lives were hard, but I had forgotten—'

He broke off, and they all stared in dismay at the little settlement. The cottages were made of earth and reeds, with more reeds for the roofs. Most of them leaned one way or the other, and the ones that didn't lean slumped in the middle as if they could no longer be bothered standing upright. The snow between them had turned to sludge, and in some places it was hard to tell where the houses ended and the muddy ground began.

'Is this the place you were thinking of, Cap'n?' murmured Krill. 'It don't look prosperous to me!'

Petrel thought she saw movement, but when she jerked around, there was just a scrap of filthy curtain trembling over a glassless window. 'Where's all the people?' she whispered.

'Watchin' us,' said Mister Smoke, from her right shoulder.

'Scared,' said Missus Slink, from her left.

They're not the only ones, thought Petrel. *Blizzards, I wish I was back on the ship!*

'Come,' said the captain, and they waded through the mud to what seemed like the middle of the village.

Krill looked relaxed, except for the muscles in his neck, which were as taut as stay wires. Fin eyed the mean little cottages with a mixture of fascination and disgust.

They saw no one.

'Don't reckon they want to talk to us,' whispered Petrel. 'We might as well go—' Her whisper turned to a yelp as a rock flew out of nowhere and hit her on the leg.

Her instinct, honed by years of survival, told her to run for her life. But Fin grabbed her hand, and the captain stepped forward and cried, 'We do not mean you any harm!'

A whisper came from one of the cottages. 'Go away!' A man, from the sound of it, not wanting to be heard by his fellow villagers.

'We wish to help you,' cried the captain. 'We will teach you how to build a water pump so you do not have to carry—'

Another rock splashed into the mud by his foot. 'Scat, the lot of yez!'

Somewhere a baby started to wail, and was instantly silenced. The air was sour with fear.

Petrel swallowed. More than anything else, she wanted to be back on the ship. 'Let's go,' she whispered.

But the captain did not move. He raised his voice again. 'We are also searching for a Song—'

'Scat!' hissed the man a third time.

At which Fin suddenly lost his temper. 'Is that all you can say?' he shouted. 'You ignorant peasant!'

'Shhh!' said Krill.

But Fin wouldn't be silenced. 'We came here to help you, and you will not even—'

A woman's voice interrupted him. 'Our beloved leaders, the Devouts, are on their way.' Unlike the man, she spoke loudly and carefully, as if she had tested each word beforehand to see how it would sound. 'They will be here shortly after midday. They are always interested in travellers; you must wait and speak to them.'

That stopped Fin in his tracks. 'Let's go!' urged Petrel again. And this time the captain listened to her.

'D'you reckon they'll tell the Devouts about us?' she asked, when they at last reached the headland. She felt horribly exposed standing there in the open, with the hostile land at her back.

'Course they will,' said Krill. 'Didn't you hear what the woman said? She was warning us, which was right kind of her. Especially after the way a *certain person* spoke to 'em.'

Fin reddened. 'I— I did not mean to shout. But they *are* ignorant. That is the truth.'

'They're scared,' said Krill severely, 'and with good reason, from the sound of it. And if they're ignorant

24

as well, who made 'em that way, hmm? The Devouts, that's who. Seems to me you're in no position to go around shouting insults at folk, lad.'

Fin was a proud boy, and Petrel knew that apologies did not come easily to him. But he swallowed and said, 'You are right. I am— sorry.'

Krill glared at him for a moment longer, then softened. 'Ah, you're not doing too badly, considering where you came from.'

'It is not long till noon,' said the captain. 'By the time the Devouts arrive we will be gone.' He looked over his shoulder in the direction of the village. 'But I wish the people had liked us more. How are we to help them if they will not talk to us? How are we to find the Song?'

'Look at it this way, Cap'n,' said Krill. 'We mightn't have got any further with the song or the water pumps, but those poor folk told us more by their silence than they could've done with a thousand words. We've got a huge task ahead of us.'

That stopped the conversation dead, and they waited for the *Maw* in silence, staring out over the water. Petrel kicked at a rock, wishing Skua would hurry up and take her back to the ship, where she belonged.

Noon came and went.

'D'you think he's forgotten us?' asked Petrel after a while. She shaded her eyes with her hand. 'Can you see any sign of him, Mister Smoke? Look, over there, is the water moving?'

'That's the tide, shipmate,' said the rat. 'It's on the turn.'

Petrel made herself wait another few minutes, then said, 'He should be here by now. We'd best remind him.' She took the telegraph device from her bag. 'How does this thing work, Cap'n?'

'It is quite simple,' said the captain, sounding pleased that she had asked. 'I took a spark gap transmitter and changed the—'

'Sorry, Cap'n, I'm sure that's really interesting, but it's not what I meant. How do I *use* it?'

'Oh,' said the captain. 'It is like banging on the pipes. You tap the key, and it sends that same tapping to the device on the bridge.'

'Dolph'll be on duty by now,' said Krill. 'Ask her what's happening.'

But before Petrel could begin, the telegraph key began to move by itself, clicking out a message in general ship code.

At first Petrel thought it must be a joke. She looked at Krill and he was obviously thinking the same thing. But then his smile died. Because Third Officer Dolph would never joke about something as serious as—

26

'Mutiny!' whispered Petrel. The word tasted so foul in her mouth that she could hardly continue. But Fin didn't understand general ship code, not when it was rattled out fast, so she had to translate the whole message, stumbling over the dreadful meaning of it.

'Albie's locked the First and Second Officers in their cabins and taken over the ship!'

'*What?*' said Fin.

'He told everyone that – that Skua came to fetch us – but we were dead – murdered on the rocks and – and the cap'n smashed to smithereens!'

'But that is not true!' said the captain. 'I am not smashed. Why would he say it if it is not true?'

The tapping continued. Petrel felt sick. 'Albie's saying we should never have left the ice in the first place, and – and he's demanding that the *Oyster* goes south again!'

Krill roared like a wounded sea lion. But the captain said, 'Why would he *do* that? It is not logical.'

Petrel thought of Albie's uncharacteristic helpfulness, and Skua's smirk. She thought of all she knew about the Chief Engineer, from a lifetime of hiding from him. 'Reckon he prefers the way things *used* to be on the *Oyster*, Cap'n,' she whispered. 'With the payback and the treachery, and everyone being scared of him. Since you woke up, he's had to take orders, and he's

27

not an order-taking sort of man.' She stared blindly at the telegraph. 'I *knew* he wasn't to be trusted. I did! I should've seen this coming!'

Small paws patted her shoulder. 'So should we all,' said Missus Slink. 'But we didn't—'

'Hush, there is more!' said Fin, as the telegraph began to click again. 'What is it saying?'

Petrel listened. The thought of the *Oyster* sailing south without them filled her with such horror that it was hard to concentrate. But the next bit of news was not quite so bad. 'Dolph and Squid and a few others have – have barricaded themselves – on the bridge. They've got a bit of food and water – which means – which means Albie *can't* go south! Not yet anyway – cos they control the steering—'

The tapping stopped abruptly. Petrel shook the device, but there was no further sound from it. Quickly she sent a return message, begging Dolph not to go south without them – *please* not to leave without them! But there was no reply.

'Cap'n,' she said, thrusting the device into his hands, 'it ain't working! I think your spark thing's broken!'

The captain inspected the device, then shook his head. 'There is nothing wrong with it. The fault must lie at the other end, on the *Oyster*. A loose wire, that is all it would take.'

'So did Dolph get my message?' asked Petrel.

'Probably not,' replied the captain.

Petrel stared at her companions, and they stared back. Krill looked as if he was going to explode. Fin's face was deathly white. Even the captain seemed dumbfounded.

'Then we're stranded,' whispered Petrel. And suddenly the countryside around her looked more hostile than ever. 'We're stranded, and the Devouts are coming.'

A DUTY TO
STAY ALIVE

At that very moment, two hundred miles north-east of Petrel and her friends, Sharkey was shouting orders. 'Up aerial!' There was no time for a message turtle. 'Send a comm to *Rampart*!'

Cuttle leaped for the aerial crank, and Gilly tapped away at the comm key. *Attention* Rampart! *Hungry Ghosts overhead! Attention* Rampart! *Hungry Ghosts overhead!*

'Tell 'em they've been spotted,' cried Sharkey. 'Tell 'em to get underway before the Ghosts eat 'em!'

Yr position discovered, tapped Gilly. *Get underway!*

Sharkey cursed the clearness of the sea hereabouts, which had allowed the Ghosts to spot the big submersible from their strange bubbles. And then he cursed the big submersible, because there was no answer to Gilly's message, which meant *Rampart* was below aerial depth. And comms didn't pass through water.

'Try again,' he snapped, and as Gilly tapped out the futile message, he pressed his eye to the periscope.

All Sunker children knew the tale of the Hungry Ghosts off by heart. They'd heard it from Granfer Trout, who was the oldest of all the old salts on *Rampart*, and had no duties at all except to eat, sleep and tell stories.

Three hundred years before, a horde of Ghosts had escaped from the darkness of Hell and invaded the Up Above. These ghosts had bellies as big as mountains! They were always hungry, and their favourite food was machines. They ate automobiles, trains and omnibuses; steamships, rockets and flying machines. And when that didn't satisfy them, they gobbled down the people who *invented* the machines, and the people who used them.

Anyone who tried to stop the Hungry Ghosts was killed and eaten. Nowhere in the Up Above was safe. And so, Presser Surgeon Lin Lin and her husband, First Adm'ral Cray, built a fleet of giant submersibles and took to the Undersea, along with family, friends, and a hundred waterproof boxes of surgeon papers.

Things were fearfully hard for that first generation. They weren't used to being crammed into such small spaces, sharing bunks and bumping into their neighbours whenever they turned around. But they gritted their teeth and stayed. And it was only at night, with the fleet running on the surface, renewing air and batteries, that they gave in to their homesickness and stood on the outer decks straining their eyes to see the land from which they were exiled.

Sharkey couldn't imagine feeling homesick for terra. The Undersea was the only world he'd ever known. Like all the Sunkers, he ate mussels, oysters, seaweed and fish, cooked and raw. His clothes were made from sea silk, and any metal he needed was mined from the ocean floor and smelted in one of the onboard workshops.

Life was still dangerous, of course, and smelly, and either too hot or too cold, depending on the season. The water from the distillers always tasted of oil, the air was usually a little stale, and over the centuries, most of the submersibles had been destroyed by storms or rust or accidents, until only huge *Rampart* and tiny *Claw* were left.

But no one complained. It was what they were used to, and besides, it was a hundred times safer than the Up Above. In all those years, the Sunkers had seen the Hungry Ghosts' skimmers from afar any number of times. But the Ghosts had never seen the Sunkers.

Until now.

The skimmers were furling their sails, revealing immense structures on their decks. Sharkey had a bad feeling about those structures – which worsened when he saw rocks being loaded onto them, and figures hauling at a winch, turning it tighter and tighter.

'Looks like some sort of catapult,' he muttered.

'Still no answer,' said Gilly. 'What now, sir?'

Sharkey's mind was awhirl. Would the rocks damage *Rampart*? Maybe not! They'd lose some of their force when they hit the water, so maybe they'd bounce off the hull, leaving nothing but a few dents.

But then the first catapult fired its load – and a moment later the children heard a muffled *whoomp*, like an undersea avalanche. *Claw* shuddered. A gout of water spurted upward.

Sharkey groaned. 'They've got explosives!'

The second catapult fired. And the third. Then the first again! *Whoomp. Whoomp. Whoomp.* Explosives tumbled into the water all around *Rampart*.

'Sir?' said Poddy. 'We're going to help 'em, aren't we?'

Sharkey hesitated. He was horrified by what was happening, but he was also pretty sure that *Rampart* was doomed – and he wasn't about to risk his own precious skin for a lost cause. 'Nay,' he said.

The three middies stared at him. He knew what they were thinking. *But it's Ma and Fa they're attacking, and Granfer Trout and Ripple and Adm'ral Deeps and Presser Surgeon Blue—*

'It's not going to help anyone if we get eaten as well,' he said. 'If *Rampart* goes down, we'll be the last of the Sunkers. We'll be the only ones who know where the boxes are, and what's in 'em. We've got a duty to stay alive.'

It sounded good, which didn't surprise him. His mind was always calculating, even in an emergency. Always thinking about what things *sounded* like, and how to survive, and how to fool people so that he came out the other end looking like a hero.

The three middies nodded. Poddy's eyes were brimming, but Sharkey knew she wouldn't cry. Sunkers hardly ever cried. They just followed orders and made the best of things.

He put his good eye to the periscope again. '*Rampart* must be trying to get away,' he said, keeping his voice flat and sensible. 'But the Ghosts are pointing to her – the skimmers have caught up—'

He stopped as a roil of water, like the breath of a dying whale, broke the surface. The skimmers rocked from side to side. The Ghosts rushed to re-aim their catapults.

'*Rampart*'s surfacing!'

And now at last the comm began to work. First came Adm'ral Deeps's call sign. Then the quick, desperate message.

Rampart *holed and taking on water. Abandoning ship. Position fifty-one degrees twenty-five minutes north, four degrees twenty-two minutes west. Save yourselves. Go! That's an order!*

None of middies moved.

Sharkey snapped at them. 'You heard the adm'ral! All ahead two-thirds! Ten degrees down angle!'

At that, Cuttle, Poddy and Gilly rushed to their posts. 'All ahead two-thirds, aye sir!'

'Ten degrees down angle, aye sir!'

As *Claw's* bow sank, Sharkey took one last look through the periscope. He thought he saw one of the giant bubbles break from its moorings and blow towards *Claw* . . . and then the sea washed over the glass, and the Up Above, with all its hatred and destruction, was gone.

'Make your depth sixty feet.' Sharkey stood over the helm, snapping out orders and watching the depth gauge. No one spoke except to acknowledge his instructions, but the air in the little submersible was thick with grief.

There'll be no survivors, thought Sharkey. *The Ghosts'll get 'em, every one. Which makes us the last of the Sunkers.*

'Steady on sixty feet, sir!' said Gilly.

Sharkey nodded. 'Adjust trim. Heading east-sou'-east.'

He sounded completely calm. But if he was good at hiding his feelings from his crew, he couldn't hide them from himself. His parents had died two years ago, killed in the accident that sank *Retribution*, but his aunties and uncles and cousins were still on *Rampart* and he couldn't imagine a world without them.

He thought of what it must have cost Adm'ral Deeps to abandon the giant submersible and let it sink to the bottom. He thought of the Hungry Ghosts, who had eaten so much and were still not satisfied—

To port, something tumbled down through the water.

Sharkey's first thought was that they were under attack, but then he saw the billowing cloth and the thrashing legs. Someone had escaped from the Ghosts!

'Hard port rudder!' he shouted.

Claw turned quickly, though not quickly enough for Sharkey. Those frantic legs touched the seabed and tried to push off, but the cloth had snagged on something and wouldn't come free.

Sharkey threw himself into the retrieval seat and grabbed the lever. 'All stop!'

He pulled the lever back quickly, and the mechanical claw shot out towards the frantic figure, knocking the box out of the side airlock and probably losing it forever. But there was no time for regret. No time for caution, either, or for worrying about bruised flesh or broken bones.

'Stay still!' he hissed, but the figure struggled harder.

Bubbles swirled around the little claw, and so did sand. It was almost impossible for Sharkey to see what he was doing. The talons closed around something. He hoped it was the figure; he wouldn't get a second chance at this.

Behind him, Poddy opened and shut valves, compensating for the weight of the little claw and whatever it held. Sharkey pushed the lever forward and the figure was hauled back into *Claw*'s side airlock.

'Seal outer hatch!' he snapped. 'Blow water! Unseal inner hatch!'

He scrambled for the side airlock, which was aft of the chart table. He flung the inner hatch open and dragged the limp, sodden figure into the control room.

It was a girl, her eyes closed, her hair in pale strings around her face. She coughed, and a stream of salt water gurgled out of her mouth.

Sharkey backed away from her in horror, his ruined eye aching behind its patch. In that moment of confusion, he'd thought he was saving one of his cousins. But the girl who coughed and puked on the deck was a complete stranger.

He had rescued a Hungry Ghost and brought her onto *Claw*.

★★★

When the telegraph device started chattering out a new message, Petrel almost jumped out of her skin with relief. 'It's Dolph!'

But it wasn't.

'That's not ship code,' rumbled Krill. He'd been pacing up and down, his face thunderous, ever since the message from the *Oyster* came through. Now he stopped and glared at the device. 'Nor is it Cook code.'

'It's not any sort of code,' said Petrel, her shoulders slumping.

The telegraph fell silent. But a few minutes later it tapped again.

'I believe it *is* a code,' said the captain. 'And I have nearly enough information to calculate—' He listened. 'Yes, there are numbers. Fifty-one degrees twenty-five minutes north, four degrees twenty-two minutes west.'

'That's a chart readin', shipmates,' said Mister Smoke. 'Someone out there's sendin' their position to someone else.'

The members of the stranded company stared at each other. 'But that is impossible,' said Fin. 'They would need another telegraph device, would they not? And such things are unknown outside the *Oyster*.'

'*Someone* must know about 'em.' Krill ran his fingers through his beard. 'Cap'n, where's fifty-one thingummy? It's not close enough to do us any good, I know that.'

38

'It is two hundred and seven miles, sixty-five yards and two feet north-east of here,' replied the captain. 'Which puts it forty-three miles off the coast in the Nornuckle Sea. Near the Banks of Kell, which are famous for their fishing.'

'A fishing boat would not have a telegraph device,' said Fin, firmly. '*No one* would have a telegraph device. The Devouts would have found it and destroyed it years ago. You do not understand how clever they are, how persistent. They even found the *Oyster* in the end!'

Krill started pacing again. 'But they didn't destroy us, so maybe they're not as clever as you think, lad. Or maybe there's a ship out there that's even better at hiding than we were. But like I said, it won't do us any good, not two hundred miles and more away.'

'Two hundred and seven miles is not far, not for Mister Smoke and Missus Slink,' said the captain. 'They could run that distance in—'

'No!' said Petrel. And then they were all looking at *her*, and she couldn't say what she was thinking – that Mister Smoke and Missus Slink had been a part of her life for as long as she could remember; that without the *Oyster*'s deck under her feet she already felt as if she'd lost a big chunk of herself, and now here was the cap'n trying to slice off *another* chunk and send it north!

So all she said was, 'I don't think we should split up like that. Sorry, Cap'n, but it doesn't sound like a good idea to me.'

'All the same, he is right,' said Fin. 'We must get back to the *Oyster* before Albie goes south and leaves us behind. Which means we need a boat.'

'Course we do,' said Petrel. 'But there must be one closer than two hundred miles!'

'I thought there'd be boats all along this coast,' said Krill, 'but I ain't seen a single one.'

'The Devouts have probably confiscated them for their own use,' said Fin.

Krill peered at the captain from under his heavy brows. 'How long would it take the rats to get to this other ship?'

'I cannot give you an exact time,' said the captain. 'If they keep to the coast, they will have to pass very close to the Citadel, which will slow them down. And then they will somehow have to get from the shore to the ship. My best estimate is twenty-six hours, or perhaps a little more. That is, if the ship does not move from its current position. How long will Squid and Dolph hold out against Albie, if they do not hear from us?'

'As long as they can,' said Krill gruffly. 'That daughter of mine won't believe me dead until she sees my bones laid out in a row, and even then she'd probably tell me to get up and stop lazing around.'

'Then Smoke and Slink should go now,' the captain said.

'No!' Petrel couldn't believe that they were going to do it. She tried to think of sensible reasons to keep the two rats with them. 'What if they can't get from the shore to the ship? What if the weather's bad? What if the crew's hostile or mad or – or just plain nasty, like Albie?'

Mister Smoke winked up at her. 'Don't you worry about us, shipmate. We'll find a way.'

'But what do *we* do in the meantime?' That was Fin. 'We cannot stay here, not with the Devouts on their way.'

'We will go up the coast too,' said the captain, 'but at a slower rate. We will look for villagers who *want* to learn about water pumps and mechanical ploughs. We will search for the Song. And when Mister Smoke and Missus Slink find the boat—'

'*If* they find it,' said Petrel quickly, 'which I don't see how they can.'

'—they can send us a telegraph to get our new position.'

Fin winced. 'We will be travelling towards the Citadel. There will be spies and informers everywhere.'

'Then we will have to be wary,' said the captain. 'Mister Smoke, Missus Slink, are you ready?'

It was going to happen, and there was nothing Petrel could do to stop it. She wanted to pick up the two rats and hold them so tightly that they couldn't go anywhere, but she knew she mustn't.

Her hand touched each grey head, as light as a snowflake. 'You'll come back, won't you?' she whispered.

'Aye, shipmate,' said Mister Smoke. 'We'll come back.'

'Don't worry about us, girl,' said Missus Slink.

And with that, the two of them turned tail and dashed off. Petrel watched them go, wondering if she would ever see them again.

THE HUNGRY GHOST

The four Sunker children stood well away from the Hungry Ghost, studying her warily. They half expected her to leap to her feet and attack them, but once she'd finished puking she just lay curled up on the deck, with her eyes closed and her fists clamped under her chin.

Which was a nuisance.

Claw was basically a metal tube, no more than twenty-five paces from one end to the other, and every inch of her was packed with instruments, valves, pipes and pumps. Her control room, in the bow, was really just a stool set in front of an array of dials and switches. Her engine room, in the stern, was hot and cramped, and so was her little workshop. Her batteries, with a single bunk perched on top of them, butted up against the dive wheels, which in turn nudged the tiny galley and the chart table. And in the middle of it all, so that everyone had to breathe in as they edged past, was the periscope station and the ladder that led up to the conning tower.

Even without a Ghost on board, there was hardly room to move.

'Maybe the salt water hurt her,' whispered Gilly. 'Maybe she's dying.'

'Ghosts can't die,' said Sharkey.

He wasn't sure if that was true, but Gilly nodded seriously and said, 'She might sort of melt, though, sir. If we leave her alone. She might disappear.'

Sharkey hoped his cousin was right. He had no idea what to do with the Ghost. Granfer Trout had been wrong about 'bellies as big as mountains'. Apart from her white hair and pinky-brown skin, the girl looked almost human, and Sharkey had to keep reminding himself that she wasn't.

I should shove her back out the airlock, he thought. But he didn't want to touch her again. Didn't *dare* touch her, if he was being truthful with himself. No matter what she looked like, she was a Ghost, and Ghosts were dangerous.

So in the end, he left her where she was, with Gilly standing guard.

Early next morning, they returned to the scene of *Rampart*'s sinking. Sharkey didn't want to go, but he gave the order all the same. If it'd been *Claw* down there on the seabed instead of *Rampart*, Adm'ral Deeps would've gone back to check. It'd look bad if Sharkey did anything else.

They surfaced forty-five minutes before sunclimb, with the periscope showing a dark, overcast sky and no sign of skimmers or giant bubbles. Sharkey ordered the diesels started, to recharge the batteries and air. Then he edged past the Ghost.

Right up to that moment, he hadn't been sure about leaving the middies alone while he went to check on *Rampart*. But apart from flinching when the diesels roared to life, the Ghost still hadn't moved. *Maybe she IS dying,* thought Sharkey. *Or maybe she's just too sick to hurt us. Wish Presser Surgeon Blue was here; I bet he'd know.*

He beckoned Cuttle and Poddy. 'Watch her carefully,' he said, over the clatter of the diesels.

'Aye, sir!'

'If she moves, call Gilly – she'll be up on deck, keeping watch.'

The two middies saluted and took up guard positions.

With a weight-belt and a waterproof lantern slung over his arm, Sharkey climbed the ladder inside the conning tower. Then he unsealed the two hatches and stepped out onto the small flat deck, just two feet above the waterline. Gilly followed him.

The sea was calm and the horizon was a dark line. Sharkey screwed up his good eye and said, 'You've got the conn while I'm gone.'

Gilly saluted. 'I've got the conn, aye sir!'

'Keep an eye on Poddy and Cuttle. Make sure the Ghost doesn't try anything. And watch out for skimmers and bubbles.'

'Aye, sir.'

Sharkey took off his sea-silk pants and jerkin and hung them over one of the stay wires. He undid his eye patch and tucked it into the pocket of his pants. Then, with his back to his cousin, he strapped on the weight-belt with the waterproof lantern attached, slipped out of his smallclothes and jumped over the side.

The water was so cold it made his teeth hurt, but he'd been swimming in temperatures like this since before he could walk, and thought nothing of it. He hung on to a porthole, taking in lungfuls of air and letting them out again. Then he took a deep breath – and dived into the darkness.

His strong legs drove him down and down and down. Fish darted across his path. Strings of kelp brushed against his hands. When his ears felt as if they were going to burst, he held his nose and blew, to even the pressure.

On that first dive, he found nothing except the rough seabed. On the second, he thought he saw something to the east – something grey and silent – but when he brought the lantern closer it turned out to be an outcrop of rock.

He went up again, for another breath. He felt sick and angry, and the rumble of the diesels seemed to drag on him like an anchor chain.

It took him another ten minutes to find *Rampart*. By then the horizon was growing light, and Sharkey was so cold he could barely think. *One more try,* he told himself. And he drew the air into his aching lungs and dived.

Rampart was lying on her side, some way west of where Sharkey had been looking for her. Even in the semi-darkness, he could see the battering she'd taken. There was an enormous jagged hole just behind the conning tower, and another two further for'ard. The water must have rushed in like a king tide. It was a wonder Adm'ral Deeps had managed to get a message sent. It was a wonder anyone had got out.

If they *had* got out.

Sharkey picked up a rock and banged on the bow hatch, in case someone was still alive in one of the watertight compartments. There was no answer. He banged again on the stern hatch, trying to remain hopeful. But he couldn't ignore what he knew in his heart. The holes in the hull were too big. The watertight compartments weren't watertight, not any more. If there was anyone left on *Rampart*, they were dead.

He dropped the rock and swam for the surface. His fingers and toes were numb, but he didn't *feel* cold, not any more. He'd lost his fear of the dying Ghost girl, too. There was a ball of rage inside him, and he wanted to grab hold of the girl and shake her until she rattled.

It wasn't until he had dragged himself back onto the deck of *Claw*, with the diesel engines thumping away under his bare feet, that he realised Gilly was no longer there.

Sharkey hated it when crew weren't where they were supposed to be. Life on the submersibles was dangerous enough as it was. There were so many things that could go wrong – a stuck valve, a hot bearing, a loose connection. There was no room for half-measures, no room for inattention. For the Sunkers, it was all or nothing. Watertight or holed. Alive or dead.

Which meant that Gilly wouldn't have left her post unless there was some sort of emergency.

The Ghost! thought Sharkey.

And with murder in his heart, he threw on his smallclothes and leapt for the conning tower.

RAIN

She was not a fighter, but she did her best. As the three savage children pummelled her from all sides, she put her arms over her head and pressed forward. She thought she had nearly made it, but then, without warning, one of the children kicked her behind the knees. Her legs crumpled and she tumbled to the floor.

'That'll teach you!' cried the child, sitting on top of her so she couldn't move. 'Stinking Ghost!'

Rain said nothing. She had retreated into her own world and was doing what she always did when things turned bad. Singing under her breath.

Her name was Rain,
And like rain
She fell from the sky . . .

She heard a thud of footsteps, and the fourth savage,

the boy with black hair, came hurtling bare-chested
down the ladder from outside.

'What happened?' he snapped. 'Gilly, report!'

The older of the two girls – the one who had kicked
Rain – leapt to her feet. She had very short brown hair
that looked as if it had been hacked off with a knife,
and she wore trousers instead of an overskirt.

'The Ghost tried to eat the depth gauge, sir! We
barely stopped her in time.'

The savages had an odd way of talking. They slurred
some of their letters, chopped off others and used
strange words, so that at first Rain had thought they
were speaking a completely different language. But
now, after a day or so of listening, she was used to it.

Depth gauge, she thought, and she automatically
started to weave it into a song. She did it silently, in case
the savages disapproved of singing, the way Brother
Thrawn did.

I tried to break the depth gauge
To save my brother's life—

Rain liked singing, though she was not very good
at it. She was not very good at anything, according to
her Uncle Poosk.

'Nevertheless, Brother Thrawn wants to try you in
one of the new hot air balloons,' he had said. 'I did
my best to persuade him otherwise, but he would not

budge. Since returning from the failed demon-hunting expedition, he will not tolerate weakness of any kind, and if you make a mess of it, he might well punish your brother. So please try to get it right.'

Of course Rain *had* made a mess of it, which was why she was here now, trapped in this terrifying underwater ship with bruises rising on her legs and arms. All around her, iron wheels stuck out of the walls, along with a hundred other things she did not have names for. Somewhere not far away, *machines* rumbled out their frightful tune.

She was afraid, of course. She was afraid of most things, including hot air balloons and throwers and the infernal devices called 'bombs'. Such things had not been seen in West Norn for hundreds of years – hardly anyone even suspected they still existed. But after he came back from the southern ice, Brother Thrawn had ordered them dug out of buried storehouses, and had set teams of men to test and repair them.

For the last few weeks, everyone in the Citadel had been repeating his words with a mixture of awe and excitement. 'The demon is coming and we must protect ourselves. We will use the devil's tools to fight the devil.'

The balloons and the bombs were frightening enough. But the machines at the far end of the underwater ship were far worse. They hadn't stolen Rain's soul, not yet, but it was only a matter of time. She imagined them stalking stiff-legged towards her, like savage dogs—

She shuddered. *What will happen to Bran, when I am no longer there to protect him?*

'It was our fault, sir,' said the boy sitting on Rain's ankles. He looked a bit like the girl, though his face was narrower and he seemed younger. 'We weren't watching her close enough. Sorry.'

The boy they called 'sir' nodded. Then, without a word, he found a rope and bound Rain's feet together.

The other two children stood up cautiously, but Rain made no move to escape. After all, where could she go? She was trapped and helpless, and her captors were both stronger and fiercer than she was.

The bare-chested boy trussed her arms behind her back, then pulled her into a sitting position and tied her to the leg of a table. Like the other savage children, he was streaked with oil, but beneath the dirt his skin was as white as a winter grub.

'What are we going to do with her, sir?' asked Gilly.

'Sir' did not answer. Instead, he leaned closer to Rain and tapped his face. 'See this?' he hissed.

Rain looked directly at him for the first time – and gulped. His eye socket was puckered and hollow, and the skin around it was a web of scar tissue.

'I fought a Massy shark,' whispered the boy, baring his teeth in a vicious grin. 'A big one. Bigger than you could imagine.'

Rain had no idea what a Massy shark was. She tried to slide away from the boy, but the rope held her tight.

'And you know who won?' he asked, still grinning. 'Me. Shark got my eye, but I got its guts. That's why they call me Sharkey. So when we're safely away from here, you're going to tell me everything I want to know. And don't try holding anything back, cos if you do I'll slice you open like I sliced that shark. And then I'll chuck your dead body overboard. You understand me?'

Rain nodded jerkily. The machines growled, as if they could smell her fear.

'Good,' said Sharkey.

Then he stood up and said to the other children, '*Rampart*'s busted wide open. There's no one left on board, not alive, anyway.'

Rain peeped at their faces, expecting tears and other signs of grief, but saw nothing.

'It's close to sunclimb,' continued Sharkey. 'Poddy, get my clothes. Cuttle, you've got the conn. Take her down.'

'Take her down, aye sir!' shouted Cuttle, as Poddy, a small round-faced girl, scrambled up the ladder. 'Prepare to dive!'

For a moment, Rain thought they were going to leave Poddy to drown. But the little girl was back down the ladder with Sharkey's clothes quicker than Rain would have thought possible.

And then they were all shouting incomprehensible phrases like, 'Pressure in the green!' and 'Five degrees down bubble!' and 'Switch to batteries!' They closed some things and opened others, they turned the huge wheels, they ran back and forth, ducking their heads and edging around the table, and shouted some more.

Or at least, the three younger children did. Sharkey tied a black patch over his empty eye socket, then stood with his legs braced and a superior look on his face, watching the activity around him.

As the iron ship sank beneath the water, Rain stole a glance at the patch and gulped again. She was not a brave person. She was shy and timid, and the only way she had ever been able to make sense of the world was by singing at it. She even thought in songs much of the time, as if they were a code that only she could understand.

Now she sang under her breath:

I will tell him everything

I know.
I will tell him names and days
And places—

She stopped, knowing that there was one thing she must *not* tell him, must not tell anyone. Ever. Something she did her best not to even *think* about.

Because she *might* get away from these savages, though she could not imagine how. And her little brother *might* survive without her.

But if anyone learned the truth, and traced it back to Rain, Bran's life would be worth less than a scrap of kindling. And so would hers.

★★★

Sharkey didn't really lose his eye in a fight with a Massy shark. He didn't lose it in a fight with anything. It was just a dreadful accident.

There were always accidents on the submersibles, but no one expected Sharkey to get caught by one. He was born on a fortunate tide. Not only that, but he came into the world with a head of straight black hair, just like the old engravings of Lin Lin. His ma and fa were so pleased that they named him straight off, rather than waiting a few months in case he didn't survive. They gave him a good strong name, too, instead of calling him Winkle or Sprat, or one of the other baby names that got changed to something better as children grew older.

No way was Sharkey changing *his* name. There wasn't a better name to be had, except perhaps for Adm'ral Deeps.

His straight black hair fell out, the way it usually did with babies. But to his parents' delight, it grew back even straighter and blacker.

'He's Lin Lin's boy, that's for sure,' said everyone who saw him. 'He's got great things ahead of him. Expect he'll make adm'ral one day.'

And as Sharkey grew older, he thought the same. Why wouldn't he? He was clever, keen-eyed and lucky. He had everything on his side – until the dreadful day, when he was eight years old, that ruined everything.

It was an accident, nearly everyone agreed on that. *Retribution*, where they lived, was old and tired, and there were always gaskets bursting and pipes breaking. Crew usually managed to skittle out of the way in time, but every now and again someone got hurt.

The steam from that particular burst gasket cost Sharkey his right eye and most of the skin around it. He could still remember the agony of it, and how Ma held his hand while Presser Surgeon Blue applied cold water to the burns.

That was the end of 'Expect he'll make adm'ral one day'. Crew stopped mentioning the fortunate tide, and how much he looked like Lin Lin. Instead, Sharkey was reminded over and over again how lucky he was that he'd lost one eye, instead of two.

He didn't feel lucky. He didn't want to spend the rest of his life huddled in a greasy corner of *Retribution*, doing someone else's bidding. He didn't want crew looking away so they wouldn't have to see his ruined eye, even after his ma had sewn a patch to cover it. He didn't want to be at the bottom of things.

But that's where he had been, and that's where he'd seemed likely to stay – until the night of his tenth birthday, a year and three months after the accident. When the miracle happened.

This is how he'd told it, breathless, on his return to *Retribution*. He was out swimming, when a turtle spoke to him. Yes, a turtle, a flatback, as pretty as moonlight! It swam right up close, and he was thinking of turtle soup. But before he could kill it, it put its horny head close to his, and said, 'Do not go west, Great Grandson, not this week.'

Then it swam away into the deep blue, leaving Sharkey half-drowned with shock.

He was still spluttering when Fa dragged him over to *Rampart*, to talk to Adm'ral Deeps. 'Adm'ral, you've got to hear this!' said Sharkey's fa. 'It's—' He shook his head, speechless.

Sharkey told the story again. And again, as the Sunkers gathered around him, firing questions.

'It *spoke*? The turtle *spoke* to you?'

'You *sure* it was a turtle?'

'How far down were you? Might've been raptures, if you were deep enough.'

'Not far down at all,' said Sharkey, standing up for himself. 'Maybe half-periscope, that's all. It wasn't raptures, I'm sure of it. And it *was* a turtle.'

'Turtles don't speak,' said Adm'ral Deeps, and everyone nodded. That was a fact, on a day when facts seemed few and far between.

'*What* did it call the boy?' asked one of the old salties from the back of the crowd.

'Great Grandson,' replied someone else. 'It called him Great Grandson!'

Everyone grew very quiet then, staring at Sharkey as if they'd never seen him before. He stood as straight and tall as he could, trying not to shiver, trying not to flinch when Adm'ral Deeps turned her cool eyes on him.

'And why would a flatback turtle name *you* Great Grandson, Sharkey?' she asked.

It was his ma who answered. 'Because it wasn't a turtle at all, Adm'ral. It was the spirit of Lin Lin!'

'That's right,' said Sharkey, drawing his ten-year-old bones even taller. 'It was the spirit of Great Granmer Lin Lin!'

And with that, his life changed forever.

Of course Lin Lin wasn't really Sharkey's great granmer; she had died too long ago for that, and people had lost count of the generations in between. But everyone called her Great Granmer, because it was respectful, and respect was important to the Sunkers.

They respected Sharkey, once they heard his tale. And their respect grew when, a month later, both Great Granmer Lin Lin *and* Great Granfer Cray spoke to him. This time they appeared in the form of dolphins, and warned Sharkey not to go north, which was where the fleet had been heading.

Everyone took the warnings seriously. In three hundred years, the Hungry Ghosts had never found them, but that could change at any moment. So instead of going north, they went east and south, and saw no sign of their enemies. None of the submersibles broke down either, and everyone knew it was because of Sharkey and Lin Lin.

It wasn't long before they started mentioning that fortunate tide again. Even Adm'ral Deeps smiled at Sharkey, and she wasn't a woman who gave her smiles easily.

Sharkey loved the attention, loved being so important. He was allowed to take *Claw* out whenever he wanted to, and he got the best food and the fewest hard duties. And whenever he came back from a swim, someone was sure to ask, 'Any word from Lin Lin or Adm'ral Cray?'

Sometimes there was and sometimes there wasn't. And right now, with *Rampart* lying broken on the ocean floor, and the rest of the Sunker community dead, Sharkey's honoured ancestors weren't talking.

Which was no great surprise to Sharkey, who had made the whole thing up.

THE LAST OF
THE SUNKERS

Meanwhile, on the besieged bridge of the *Oyster*,
Third Officer Dolph was testing the barricades, making
sure Albie and his mutineers couldn't break through.

Behind her, a dozen voices went over the same old
arguments.

'Maybe Skua's telling the truth. Why would he lie
about such a thing?'

'Because his da told him to, why else?'

'But what if they *are* dead? Where does that leave
us? We can't hold out against Albie forever, not with
the whole ship behind him—'

Squid's sensible voice broke in. 'The whole ship's
not behind him!' she said. 'Glory be, haven't you been
listening to the pipe messages? The Engineers are
behind him right enough, but—'

'Engineers always do what Albie tells 'em.'

'Exactly,' said Squid. 'But it sounds as if a goodly number of Cooks don't want any part of it – didn't you catch that pipe message about barricades in Dufftown? As for the senior Officers, there's no way *they're* behind him. But they can't do much while they're locked up.'

'Still, there's an awful lot of folk listening to Albie.'

'And who can blame 'em?' said Squid sharply. 'Here we are in hostile waters, and the first thing that happens is the shore party gets murdered – at least, that's what Albie's telling everyone. And you know how shipfolk feel about the cap'n; he's like a talisman, and losing him just about strips the heart out of 'em. Then there's Krill and Petrel and Fin, and each one of 'em leaves a gap. If First Officer Hump could've taken charge it mightn't've been so bad, or Second Officer Weddell. But Albie's no fool. He's got 'em both under lock and key, along with anyone else the crew might listen to. Most folk don't *want* to follow him, it's just that he hasn't left 'em much alternative.'

'What about Dolph—'

'Dolph might be Third Officer, but she's young and untried, and when things turn bad shipfolk want someone with a bit of experience in charge. And right now that means Albie. He's got it all worked out. Mind you, he's not infallible. If the shore party turned up alive, this mutiny'd be over in a heartbeat.'

'If Orca was still with us,' said Minke, 'Albie wouldn't dare pull a trick like this.'

It's true, Dolph thought miserably, as she went back to jamming lengths of driftwood into place. *If Mam was alive, she would've stopped this before it began. Which means I should've stopped it. I might be young, but I'm Third Officer, and it was my job to keep the ship safe till the cap'n got back.*

She rested her head against the driftwood, wondering what to do next. The folk behind her were expecting a decision, she knew that. Some of them wanted to negotiate with Albie. Others wanted to hold out as long as possible.

She turned around and caught Squid's eye. When the older girl strode over to join her, Dolph whispered, 'D'you think Skua's lying? Really?'

'I do,' said Squid.

'We haven't had a reply to that message I sent.'

'Could be something's gone wrong with the tele-graph device.'

'Albie?'

'Not necessarily,' said Squid. 'Might just be bad luck. It got bumped around a fair bit when we were rushing to build the barricades. Maybe something's come loose. I've had a look, but it's got all sorts of strange innards and I don't know what I'm supposed to be looking for.' She folded her arms. 'But message or no message, this is how I see it. I can imagine the cap'n being caught unawares – he's too trusting for his own good. And Fin isn't that canny either, not when it comes to survival. But Da?' She laughed. 'It'd take more than a few Devouts to beat him. Same for Petrel. And the two of them combined are a powerful force.'

Dolph nodded slowly. 'So – what d'you think we should do?'

'That's up to you,' said Squid. 'You're Third. You're in charge.'

The younger girl flushed. Up till now, she'd liked being Third Officer. She'd been learning navigation mostly, and taking her turn at the wheel. And every now and then, when she thought she could get away with it, she'd practised bossing people around.

But this was different. This was the future of the ship.

'Right,' she said. Then 'Right!' louder this time, so that the arguments stopped and everyone turned to stare at her.

'Um— Squid thinks her da and Petrel are still alive, at least,' said Dolph. 'So do I. And we don't abandon our shipmates, do we?'

Dead silence. A few sideways glances.

Dolph summoned up memories of her mam; tried to get that Orca ice into her voice. '*Do we?*'

To her surprise, it worked. Minke said, 'No, you're right, girl. We don't.'

'So,' said Dolph, clasping her hands behind her back where no one could see them shaking, 'we're going to keep sending telegraph messages, um – at the beginning of each watch, just in case they can hear us. And we're *not* giving in to Albie, no matter what he says. We're going to hold out as long as we can.'

She paused, expecting argument, and got none. 'Squid, you're in charge of food and water.'

'There's not much of either,' said Squid.

'Then we're on short rations,' said Dolph. 'It won't be the first time. Minke, you're in charge of pipe messages. Tell the ship that Skua's lying. Tell 'em over and over again, and hope they start to believe us. And – and if anyone has any useful ideas, like how we can take the ship back from Albie, I'm willing to listen. But *no more arguing*. We're all in this together.'

She glared at them, Orca-style, then dismissed them with a nod, hoping she could reach the nearest seat before her legs gave way and ruined everything.

I'm doing my best, Mam, she thought, as she lowered herself carefully into the pilot's chair. *I'm doing my best. I just hope it's good enough.*

★★★

As soon as *Claw* was running smoothly, with Gilly at the helm, Sharkey squatted in front of the Ghost girl again. His anger had not cooled, and it overrode any remaining fears.

'Have you got a name, Ghost?' he demanded.

The girl licked her lips. 'My name is Rain.'

'What?' said Sharkey.

'My name is Rain.'

Sharkey turned to Poddy. 'What's she saying? Can you understand her?'

'I think she said her name's Rain, sir,' said Poddy. 'She's got a funny way of talking. Maybe Ghosts've got another lingo, and she's only just starting to learn human.'

Sharkey turned back to the girl. Speaking loudly, to make sure she understood, he said, 'Three hundred years and your lot never found us. Why now?'

'Because of B-Brother Thrawn.' Her voice was so quiet he could hardly hear it.

'Louder,' he said. 'Slower.'

'Because of B-Brother Thrawn. The leader of the Devouts. He has— He has recently come back from the far south. Where the demons live.'

This time Sharkey managed to catch most of it, but it still didn't make much sense. Devouts? Demons? He scowled, and the Ghost girl flinched away from him and said, 'He was— He was hurt, the demon hurt his body. But his mind – his mind is as clear and sharp as ever—'

'The truth!' snarled Sharkey.

'The truth,' gasped the girl. 'The truth is that we – we were not looking for you at all, we were watching for the demon ship! That is why B-Brother Thrawn sent out the balloons and the infernal d-devices. When we saw the big underwater ship, no one knew what it was.' Her voice faded. 'But we were told to kill it.'

Sharkey sat back on his heels and stared at her. She was too foreign, too strange, and he couldn't be sure he was reading her right. She looked terrified, but that was probably just a Ghost trick. She looked as if she was lying about something, but that might be wrong too. For all he knew, she could be laughing at him!

His anger flared up, hotter than ever, and he almost gave the order, right there and then, to chuck her out of the airlock.

But even as he opened his mouth, his clever mind was working away, telling him that it might be *useful* to have a captive Ghost, and that he shouldn't be in too much of a hurry to get rid of her.

Cuttle cleared his throat. 'Sir, me and Poddy've been thinking. Maybe some of those on *Rampart did* survive.'

Poddy nodded. 'And we could rescue 'em!'

'Nay,' said Sharkey, standing up. 'They didn't have a chance. I told you, they're all gone. We're the last of the Sunkers.'

He thought that was the end of it, but Cuttle, who wasn't usually so contrary, said, 'But what about the ones who abandoned ship, sir?'

'They drowned,' Sharkey said bluntly. 'Or else the Ghosts ate 'em.'

The Ghost girl made a squeak of protest, and said, 'You mean the D-Devouts? They do not eat people! They have probably taken them to the camp.'

'What camp?' demanded Poddy.

'The re-education camp. Near the Citadel.'

Camp. Citadel. None of it meant anything to Sharkey. 'Be quiet,' he said. 'Don't talk to my crew. Don't try to trick 'em.'

'I am not—' began Rain, but Sharkey shot her one of his blackest looks, and she fell silent.

Claw was heading east, towards the Greater Seddley Current. Sharkey set the course with as much outward confidence as he could muster, then kept the middies busy cooking, cleaning pumps and lines, and scrubbing away at bits of rust. At night they surfaced to fish, swim, recharge the batteries and renew their air. They slept in shifts, partly due to lack of room, and partly to keep an eye on the Ghost.

Sharkey spent most of his time in the tiny workshop aft of the diesel engines, hammering out spare parts. It was heavy work, which he usually avoided, but now he hoped it'd stop him thinking too much.

We're the last of the Sunkers.

It was a world that had existed for three hundred years, a world of knowledge, secrets and responsibility. And now the whole thing rested on Sharkey's shoulders. He felt as if he'd fallen into one of the deep ocean trenches, and the pressure of the water above was crushing him. He could hardly breathe from the weight of it.

The last of the Sunkers!

He would never have admitted it to the middies, but he was scared witless. Apart from everything else, he was used to having Adm'ral Deeps checking his decisions and saving him from mistakes. He was used to taking all the credit and none of the blame, and coming out the other side all shiny and heroic.

He wished desperately that the adm'ral was with them now. She'd know what to do. She'd take this weight off his shoulders.

He wished too that the ancestors would speak to him. *Really* speak to him this time. Give him a sign, a hint. Anything.

And on the third night, they did. Or so it seemed …

★★★

It was past sunfall, and they'd seen no skimmers or giant bubbles since the attack. But Sharkey wasn't taking any risks.

'Up periscope,' he said, and Gilly heaved the periscope into place, and snapped its handles open.

The Ghost girl watched silently, as she watched everything. Sharkey had been surprised to discover that she ate real food, instead of just chewing on machines and people. He hated wasting fish on her, and still wondered if it'd be best to simply push her out the airlock.

'All clear, sir,' said Gilly, after turning in a circle twice, once quick and once slow. 'It's raining.'

'Take her up,' said Sharkey.

But before anyone could respond, something banged against the periscope.

Gilly squawked. Sharkey's heart leapt into his mouth. He was about to shout, 'Flood the quick dive tank!' when Gilly cried, 'Can't be Ghosts, sir! There's no one out there. Must be something floating.'

Poddy, who hadn't been sleeping well since the attack on *Rampart*, whispered, 'Might be a corpse.'

Cuttle's mouth tightened. Gilly lowered the periscope a little and said, 'Nay. It's too small.'

They surfaced cautiously, ready to dive at the slightest sign of danger. But when Sharkey climbed the ladder and opened the double hatch, there was nothing there except grey clouds and rain, and the sea water still pouring off the hull.

A cloud of spray hit him in the face, blinding him for a second or two. He wiped his eye and stepped out onto the deck, bracing himself against the swell. 'All clear!' he called.

The object bobbing off *Claw*'s bow looked like an odd-shaped bottle, though Sharkey couldn't be sure. He shouted down the hatch, 'Bring a net, Poddy!'

'Aye, sir!'

They hauled the strange bottle on board, handling it gingerly as if it might blow up in their faces. It had something inside it. A scrap of paper maybe.

As Sharkey examined it, Poddy gasped. 'Dolphins, sir! Look!'

There were two of them, poking their smooth noses above the water as if they had come for a visit. In the rain, Poddy's face shone. 'Is it *them*, sir?' she whispered. 'Is it Lin Lin and Adm'ral Cray? Are they going to say something?'

Sharkey scowled. 'It's not them. Come on, I want to see if there's anything on this paper.'

They went below, where the yellow lamps ran off batteries, day and night. 'It's a message,' cried Poddy, as she swung down the ladder. 'From Lin Lin!'

'It's *not* from Lin Lin,' snapped Sharkey. He dried his face and hands with a rag, propped himself against the berth that straddled the batteries, and unfolded the scrap of paper.

Like all the Sunkers, he had learned to read as a middy. But the spiky scrawl in front of him was nothing like the square, sensible writing of real people.

He turned the paper this way and that, frowning. He didn't want to admit that he couldn't read it, so he said, 'Must be in Ghost lingo' and thrust it under the nose of the Ghost girl. 'What's it say? And don't lie.'

Rain scanned the paper and blinked. 'It is from—' She looked up. 'It is from Brother Thrawn.'

'Him?' said Gilly. 'The one who ordered the attack on *Rampart*? What's he want, a bang on the head? I'll give it to him!'

'He wants—' Rain squinted at the paper '—to make an exchange. For me!'

'What sort of exchange?' demanded Sharkey.

'If you give me back, he will give you one of *Rampart*'s crew.'

Cuttle said, 'But they're all dead, sir. He *can't* give 'em back, can he?'

'Maybe he's going to give us a corpse,' said Gilly, glowering. 'Maybe he thinks it's funny.'

But Poddy's face was bright with hope. 'They're alive, sir! They *are!*'

'Nay,' said Sharkey fiercely. 'It's a trap. Ghosts are trying to lure us Up Above so they can eat us too. Don't be fooled, Poddy.'

Rain cleared her throat. 'The Devouts are not ghosts. And they do not eat people.'

Sharkey wasn't listening to her. 'How'd they find us? That's the question. One little bottle in such a big ocean?'

'Maybe there are dozens of bottles, sir,' said Gilly. 'All with the same message. All chucked into the water at different spots. And the current brought one of 'em this way.'

'Mm.' Sharkey nodded cautiously.

'And maybe,' said Poddy, her face still glowing, 'some of the crew *did* survive. Maybe the Ghosts didn't eat 'em all. They might be waiting for us to rescue 'em, sir!'

Sharkey didn't want his crew thinking about rescues. Such things were for real heroes, not fake ones. He ignored Poddy and said to Rain, 'What makes you so special? Why does Brother Thrawn want you back?'

The girl reddened. 'I— I do not know. M-maybe he is doing a favour for my uncle.'

'Who's your uncle? Someone important?'

Rain shook her head vigorously. 'He is Brother Thrawn's nurse, that is all. He does the things Brother Thrawn cannot do for himself any more. He is not the least bit important, but – but he took us in four months ago, when Mama died. My little brother and I. We would have starved but for Uncle Poosk.'

'Uncle *Poosk*?' Gilly snorted at the name, but Sharkey watched the Ghost girl, trying to separate lies from truth.

'What's your brother's name?' asked Poddy.

For the first time, Rain's face lit up with a genuine smile. 'Bran. He is six. He is the sweetest boy—'

Sharkey pushed himself away from the bunk, saying, 'This isn't getting us anywhere. I don't care about *Uncle Poosk* and sweet little *Bran*—'

The girl's smile disappeared.

'—I just want to know if this is a trap or not.'

'I don't think it's a trap, sir,' said Poddy. 'I think it's a sign. I've been asking for one for days. We all have.' She beamed up at the ancestor shrine. 'Thank you, Lin Lin! Thank you, Great Granfer Cray!'

'What about the Hungry Ghosts?' asked Cuttle. 'How could we make a swap without getting eaten?'

Poddy ignored him. 'I bet those two dolphins pushed the bottle towards us!'

'What about the Hungry Ghosts?' asked Cuttle again.

'It *might* be a sign—' began Gilly.

'What about the Hungry *Ghosts*?' This time Cuttle was so loud that they had to take notice.

Everyone fell silent, even Poddy. All their lives they'd known that going Up Above after sunclimb was almost certain death. The Hungry Ghosts would find them and eat them. It was madness to even think about it.

But Poddy wasn't about to give up. 'If the ancestors want us to do it, sir, there must be a way.'

Sharkey felt like laughing, though there was nothing funny about the situation. Of course it was a trap! He couldn't believe he was even considering it.

But then he started wondering who they might get in exchange for Rain. A middy? An auntie or uncle?

Or Adm'ral Deeps?

Once the idea was there in his mind, it wouldn't go away. Adm'ral Deeps, who'd know what to do next. Who'd take this great weight of responsibility off his shoulders.

He glanced at Rain. Was that a flicker of hope in her eyes? Or was it scorn? Did she think he was afraid? Did she think he wouldn't dare go Up Above, not even to get Adm'ral Deeps back?

I asked for a sign, he thought, *and I got one. Maybe Poddy's right. Maybe there IS a way.*

Gilly said, 'When's the handover? And where?'

'The day before the next full moon,' said Rain, reading the scrap of paper. 'Early morning, due west of where the Devouts attacked your big ship. Behind the beach, at the grand monument.'

Whatever a mon-u-ment is, thought Sharkey. He felt as if he was about to step off the edge of an abyss, into water deeper than he'd ever known. 'Four days away,' he muttered.

'We could just go and look, sir,' said Poddy. 'Watch from periscope depth, see if they come.'

Sharkey took a breath – and nodded. 'Gilly, find the right chart.'

'Aye, sir!'

And with that, the decision was made.

WE SHOULD NEVER HAVE LEFT THE ICE

Mister Smoke and Missus Slink had been gone for far too long.

Something's happened to 'em, thought Petrel, as she and her friends stumbled along a rough coastal track. *According to the cap'n's calculations, they should've reached that ship by now. They should've sent a message, but they haven't. They ain't coming back, I'm sure of it! I'm never going to see 'em again.*

Her only consolation was the messages from the *Oyster*, which came every four hours, and were disjointed and scrappy.

'. . . *stil. . . here,*' said each message. '*St . . . . . . hold . . . out. Wher . . . ar . . . you?*'

'There must be a loose connection at their end,' said the captain. 'That is why they are not getting our replies. I wish they would fix it.'

'So do I, Cap'n,' said Krill grimly. 'But at least they're alive, and they've still got the bridge. Albie hasn't won yet.'

All the same, he was dreadfully worried, and so was Petrel. Between one message and the next, she imagined Albie storming the barricades, Squid and Dolph dead and the *Oyster* turning south.

As bad as the situation was, hunger made it worse. The dried fish was long gone, and this particular bit of coast seemed to offer nothing but stunted trees, low thorny bushes and rocks.

Last night, Petrel had dreamed she was eating a toothyfish, so sweet and juicy that she could still taste it when she woke up. The withered roots called 'taters', which Fin had found halfway through the morning, were a poor substitute.

What's more, the captain insisted on going into every village they passed. The others did their best to dissuade him, but on this one matter he would not be budged. 'We are here to change the world,' he said.

The trouble was, they *weren't* changing the world. They weren't even changing a tiny part of the coast of West Norn. No one in the villages would talk to them, no matter how politely they offered information about water pumps, mechanical ploughs and windmills. Fin had been sure that folk would be grateful for simple machines that made their lives easier, but it seemed he was wrong. The villagers of West Norn were too frightened of the Devouts to be grateful for anything.

It bothered Petrel to see them so cowed and voiceless. It reminded her of the way *she* used to be, which she didn't want to think about, and she found herself getting angry with the villagers, and blaming them for their own misery – which made her feel even worse.

The only one not dispirited by their failure was the captain. He simply grew more determined to find the Singer and the Song which, he said, would make all the difference.

And now they were walking again. The snow had melted, the day was damp and miserable, and everyone except the captain was snappish. To take her mind off her worries, Petrel trotted up close behind Fin, and said, 'What does your mam look like? What colour's her hair?'

Without turning, Fin said, 'You have asked me that a dozen times since we left the ice.'

'And I'm asking again.'

'I cannot remember her hair.'

'What about her eyes?'

There was an edge to Fin's voice now. 'I cannot remember her eyes, either.'

Petrel knew she should give up. Instead she walked closer, so she was almost treading on his heels. 'How about her name?'

Fin stopped dead and said through gritted teeth, 'I was three years old, Petrel. Her name, as far as I was concerned, was Mama. Now can you tell me how, in the whole of West Norn, I am going to find a woman called *Mama*?'

He didn't wait for her reply. As he walked away, Petrel thought she heard him mutter, 'Besides, she is probably dead.'

There was no answer to that. But Petrel might have kept digging anyway, if the captain hadn't suddenly stopped and picked something up from the path.

'It is a bird!' he said. 'A pigeon, look.' And he opened his hands to show them.

The pigeon was smaller than the gulls and albatrosses of the icy south, and its feathers were blue-grey, with dark stripes across the wings and tail. Its eyes were closed and it lay panting in the captain's grasp.

He ran his clever fingers over its wings. 'Nothing is broken,' he said. 'Perhaps it was chased by a hawk, and is exhausted. If I take care of it, it should recover.'

He made a cooing sound, and the bird opened its orange eyes and blinked at him.

'It belongs to the Devouts,' said Fin. 'See?' He gently extended the pigeon's leg, which had a scroll of waxed paper tied to it. 'They use them as messenger birds.'

'What's it say?' asked Krill.

Fin unravelled the bit of paper. *'Demon and companions sighted in coastal village, District 2. Believed to be heading north.'*

'Just as well *that* didn't get through!' said Petrel. She stroked the bird's feathers. 'I'm sorry for you, pigeon, being attacked and all. But it's a good thing you didn't make it.'

Fin shook his head. '*This* bird did not make it, but the Devouts always send more than one. Which means they know we are here. They will be hunting—'

He broke off, his eyes darting back the way they had come. Petrel froze. So did Krill. The captain was as still as a bollard, his hands cradling the bird.

A slow, rhythmic thud reached their ears.

'Horses!' mouthed Fin. 'Coming up behind us!'

For a moment, Petrel felt as if she was back on the *Oyster*, and the Officer bratlings coming after her with the tar bucket.

Except she knew every single hidey-hole on the old icebreaker, and could conceal herself easily. Not like here.

She caught her breath. *There must be somewhere to hide!* She stared frantically at the unfamiliar landscape, and saw a clump of vines and fallen trees. She pointed. *There!* The others hurried off the track after her, moving as quietly as they could through the low scrub.

The sound of horses grew louder. One of them snorted. A man called out, 'Are you sure they were heading this way? If you are wasting our time, you will be sorry.'

When she heard that, Petrel just about fell over with fright. *That last village! I* told *the cap'n we should go round it!*

She urged her friends on, scrambling around bushes and over rocks, until she and Fin and the captain were tucked up inside the clump of vines, with the pigeon lying on the ground beside them. Krill was nearly there too, he just had to climb over those last few wet rocks.

Except he was going too fast, and his foot slipped. One of the rocks tipped under him. His weight skewed in the wrong direction – and he fell sideways, his starboard leg suddenly useless, his hands grabbing at the ground so he wouldn't make too much noise as he fell.

There was no time to lose. Fin, Petrel and the captain grabbed hold of Krill and dragged him into the shelter of the vines. He didn't make a sound, not even a whimper, but his face was contorted with pain and the sweat poured off him in torrents.

And then the horses were passing by, no more than fifteen paces away, and all Petrel and her friends could do was crouch behind the thin curtain of vines and hope they would not be discovered.

The horses were long-nosed creatures with hoofs as big as portholes. The two men riding them wore brown robes and wide-brimmed hats to keep the rain off, and had shiny, satisfied faces, as if they'd recently eaten a large meal. Across their backs, they carried axes, and tied to each of their saddles was a wicker cage containing several pigeons.

A third man walked in front of the horses. *He* didn't look satisfied. His cheeks were so hollow that it hurt Petrel to look at him.

'I am sure they went in this direction, gracious sirs,' said the thin man in an anxious voice. 'There is a reward for sighting them, is there not? *I* sighted them, I did. Four of them! What is the reward, gracious sirs?'

'The reward is for *us* sighting them, you fool,' said the plumper of the two riders.

The second rider said, 'How long ago did you see them?'

'No use asking him that,' said the first man. 'The peasants are not capable of measuring time.'

The villager, his face unreadable, said, 'Not long at all, gracious sir. The clouds have barely moved in the sky since they left our village.'

'Really?' The second rider shaded his eyes. 'They cannot be far ahead of us then. Come, let us hurry!' And they disappeared up the track.

Petrel waited for several minutes, to be sure they'd gone, then she crept out from under the vines. Behind her, she could hear the captain murmuring questions. 'Do you have pain *here*, Krill, around the medial malleolus? What about *here*, around the lateral? No? My medical knowledge is not as good as my maps or my telegraphy, but I do not think your ankle is broken.'

'We're stuck now, ain't we?' Petrel said to Fin when he followed her out. 'Krill's ankle might not be broken, but it's sprained at the very least. He won't be able to walk on it, not for a week or so.'

Fin nodded. 'And we cannot carry him. Not even the captain is that strong.'

Neither of them suggested going on without the big man. He was crew, and they couldn't leave crew behind.

'We will have to stay here,' continued Fin, 'and wait for Mister Smoke and Missus Slink.'

'Which might not be so bad,' said Petrel, doing her best to sound cheerful.

But it *was* bad, and she knew it.

She thought back to the time, all those weeks ago, when they had decided to leave the ice and head north. She had had everything she wanted then. Good friends. Good food. The reassuring decks of the *Oyster* under her feet.

And now nearly all of it was gone.

She felt a tear spring to her eye, and wiped it away. But she couldn't wipe away the thought that came with it. It sat there inside her like a tater, wrinkled and sour.

Albie was right. We should never have left the ice in the first place.

★★★

By the time *Claw* reached the coast, Rain had been singing under her breath for days, and the world still did not make any sense.

Un-cle Poosk wants me back
Because blood is thicker than water
Un-cle Poosk wants me back
Because blood is thicker than tea—

She had tried to believe it, and could not. Uncle Poosk might have saved her from starvation, but beyond that he did not care what happened to Rain. Girls could not become Devouts.

No, it was her brother he wanted – Bran, who was young enough to be an Initiate, young enough to be moulded into the right way of thinking.

She tried again.

Bro-ther Thrawn wants me back

Because—

Cuttle was at the periscope, watching the coast road. To her own surprise, Rain was getting used to life on the underwater ship. By listening carefully, she had learned the names of things, and had even grown accustomed to the sound of the machines.

What was more, she was beginning to like Cuttle, who was quieter than the others and more cautious. She liked Poddy, too. The two younger children did not pinch or bully her the way Initiates would have done, or whip her to show who was in charge. Since the fight, when she had tried to break the depth gauge, they had mostly treated her like a strange sort of animal that had to have its ankles tied to the chart table for its own good.

Rain was still making up her mind about Gilly. But she did *not* like Sharkey, not one bit. She did not like the way he ordered everyone around, and the way the other children looked at him as if he could do no wrong.

Right now he was pacing up and down, though he could only take three steps before he had to turn around and go the other way, and with two of those steps he had to duck his head. Occasionally he paused, jerked his chin at Cuttle and said, 'Well?'

'Two Ghosts on foot, sir,' said Cuttle, without taking his eyes from the periscope. 'Heading sou'-west.'

'That's all?'

'Aye, sir. That's all.'

Rain went back to her singing.

Bro-ther Thrawn wants me back

Because—

'Sir,' cried Cuttle, 'come and look at this! There's a thing with wheels, and Ghosts marching beside it, heading nor'-east—'

Sharkey bent over the eyepiece. He watched whatever it was for a few minutes, then straightened up and glowered at Rain. 'A beast,' he said. 'Pulling a box on wheels.'

'A horse?' said Rain, who had come to realise that the Sunkers knew almost nothing about life on land. 'A horse and cart?'

Without a word of thanks, Sharkey went back to the periscope, turning the little knob that made things look bigger and closer. 'Three Ghosts walking. And there's a couple more in the – the cart. Least, I think they're Ghosts.'

'Must be, sir,' said Cuttle. 'Can't be Sunkers. They'd've been gobbled up already.'

'Aye ...' said Sharkey. For once, he did not sound sure of himself.

'The Devouts do not eat people,' said Rain. As usual, they ignored her.

'Wake Gilly,' said Sharkey. 'She's got the best eyesight in the fleet.'

Cuttle's sister was curled up on the bunk above the batteries, where the Sunkers took it in turns to sleep. Cuttle shook her gently. 'Gilly.'

The girl was awake in an instant, running her fingers through her short hair and rubbing her eyes. 'What?'

Sharkey made way for her. 'Have a look, Gill. Who's that in the cart? Can you see?'

Gilly yawned, rubbed her eyes again, and took the periscope handles. 'Where, sir?' Then she stiffened. 'It's the adm'ral!'

'That's what I thought,' said Sharkey, as grim as Rain had ever seen him. 'But it can't be.'

'I know it can't,' said Gilly, her voice muffled by the eyepiece. 'They should've eaten her. But it is, sir! It's the adm'ral and she's alive!'

At the helm, Poddy swung around, her face shining. 'Does that mean Ma and Fa might be alive too?'

'They might be—' began Gilly.

'Nay,' said Sharkey. 'It doesn't mean anything.' He snapped out a series of orders, his shoulders stiff. 'Cuttle, take us down to eighty-five feet. Heading one three four. Make your speed nine knots. Gilly, get the collapsible skiff ready.'

'Aye sir!' they cried – and Rain put her hands over her ears so as not to hear the orders repeated three or four times.

But when Cuttle came to check something on the chart above her head, she whispered to him, 'Where are we going?'

'North,' said Cuttle, 'to tomorrow's handover. Doesn't look like a trap, but we're going early just in case.'

Rain nodded, as if she was pleased. And she was! She needed to see Bran again, needed to make sure he was all right. That was more important than anything.

And so, even though she liked Poddy and Cuttle, she did not say a word about the exchange. Not out loud, anyway.

But under her breath she sang one of the oldest songs she knew. One that Mama had taught her, after making Rain promise that she would never sing it where she might be overheard.

Would you walk into the jaws of a tiger?
Would you pat a hungry bear on the snout?
Would you trust a rabid dog
Or walk a rotten log
Or believe the words of a Devout?

TERRA

Sharkey's elbows felt too big for his body, and his body felt too big for the collapsible skiff. He didn't want to go ashore, not at all. The mere thought of it set his teeth on edge, and he wished he could send Gilly in his place, on the grounds that a captain shouldn't leave his ship. But Adm'ral Deeps would never make an excuse like that. No hero would, and the middies knew it. Sharkey was trapped.

He didn't show his fear, not to the middies left behind on *Claw*, and certainly not to Rain, sitting wordless in the bow of the skiff with her arms wrapped around herself and the whites of her eyes showing in the moonlight.

Gilly's voice drifted across the water. 'Fair tides and clear water, sir! The ancestors go with you!'

Sharkey raised a deliberately casual hand in acknow-ledgement, made sure that the telling-scope still hung at his waist, and dug the paddle deeper. The skiff shot towards the shore.

I'm going to set foot on terra! The first Sunker for three hundred years!

The beach he had chosen for landing was a rocky one, two miles north of the rendezvous point. He manoeuvred the skiff between the rocks, with no sound except the *dip dip dip* of the paddle and the hiss of water. Rain hugged herself tighter.

To Sharkey, the rocks still seemed like part of the sea, so it took no great effort to jump out of the skiff onto a flattish one. He dragged the Ghost girl out too, then hauled the skiff from the water and draped it with kelp to hide it. The night was clear and cold, and the moon looked too close.

The scramble over the rocks wasn't so bad either, mainly because he was trying not to slip and fall, and had no time for thinking about anything else.

But then they reached the place where rocks gave way to soil. And Sharkey found himself stopped dead, with his breath hitched in his throat and three words rattling around his brain.

I'm. On. Terra!

It was almost too much for him. He felt dizzy. He felt as if the world had suddenly started speaking a different lingo and he didn't understand a word of it.

Where were the fish? Where was the seaweed, and the salt water? Where were the dive planes and depth gauges, and the double hulls that had protected him all his life?

Even the air smelled wrong. And the ground beneath his feet was too solid and the night was too big – and – and the only thing that stopped Sharkey dropping to his knees and crawling back to the skiff as fast as he could, was Rain. *She* seemed pleased to be on terra, and Sharkey hated her for it, hated the way she stood so steady while his own legs shook!

'Are you all right?' she asked.

'Of course I am,' snapped Sharkey, and he grabbed her wrists and whipped a rope around them, as if he thought she might try to run away. But really he felt as if he was drowning, and she was the only thing that could save him.

Two miles was no distance at all in a submersible, but on foot – on *terra* – it seemed a long, long way. Every step took Sharkey further from *Claw*, and his Sunker soul howled in protest.

What's more, he saw danger everywhere. When a small grey creature with long ears peered at him from under a bush, he tightened his grip on the rope and muttered, 'That thing over there.'

'What thing?'

Sharkey pointed. Rain screwed up her face. 'You mean the rabbit?'

'It's – watching us.'

The corner of Rain's mouth twitched. Sharkey said fiercely, 'Don't you laugh at me! In the Undersea, the smallest creatures are often the deadliest.'

'I was not laughing. I was smiling, because I did not think you were afraid of anything.'

'I'm not,' said Sharkey.

'I am afraid of everything,' Rain said matter-of-factly. 'I always have been. Sometimes even getting up in the morning scares me. Mama used to say I would grow out of it, but I have not.'

Sharkey couldn't believe that anyone would confess to such a thing. For a moment his own fears receded and he almost saw Rain as a real person, instead of a Hungry Ghost.

'What about the giant bubble?' he asked. 'You went up in that.'

'The balloon? I thought I was going to die of fright.'

'But—'

'Sometimes you have to do things, even when you are scared,' said Rain.

Which made sense, though Sharkey would never have said so, not out loud.

The grand mon-u-ment, when they reached it, turned out to be nothing but a gigantic pile of rocks.

'This is where the Great Cleansing started,' said Rain. 'There used to be a building here, full of soul-stealing machines, but the Devouts pulled it down.'

Sharkey wasn't listening. He was peering down the road to where it disappeared in the darkness. *Hungry Ghosts are on their way,* he thought. And he wondered if he would ever see *Claw* again.

★★★

By the time the winter sun came sidling up from the east, Sharkey's belly was clenched so tight he could hardly breathe.

He and Rain were tucked up in a thicket some distance away from the mon-u-ment. In the dark, all those close-growing trees had felt reassuring, but now they seemed like feeble protection. Sharkey wanted to burrow. He wanted to dig a deep hole and crawl into it, so the Hungry Ghosts couldn't find him. Or maybe – as the sun touched the horizon – maybe he should just run out into the open, and get it over as quickly as possible.

'Are you all right?' asked Rain again.

Sharkey didn't bother answering. The sun was just above the horizon, and his good eye was streaming from the unaccustomed brightness. He heard a clinking sound, followed by a rumble. And around a bend in the road, in ragged formation, came the Hungry Ghosts.

'Don't you shout,' Sharkey hissed to Rain. 'Don't you give us away, or else!' Then he wiped the tears from his eye, and raised the telling-scope.

The first thing he saw was the horse and cart. The second was the tall familiar figure who sat in the middle of the cart, with her arms tied at her sides.

Something unwound in Sharkey's chest. *Adm'ral Deeps. It's really her. We're really going to get her back!*

Beside him Rain twisted her fingers. Sharkey shifted the telling-scope.

A Ghost rode in the cart next to the adm'ral and another three walked beside it, wearing long brown robes that flicked out in front with the tramping of their feet. Sharkey looked for a trap and couldn't see one. The Ghosts had knives strapped around their waists, but apart from that they didn't look particularly dangerous. Their bellies weren't as big as mountains and they weren't gobbling up everything they passed. In fact, they looked as ordinary as Rain.

Sharkey wondered how they were going to do the swap. He didn't want to step out from the safety of the thicket, not for anything. But he might have to.

The formation stopped next to the mon-u-ment, and the rumbling sounds died away. One of the Ghosts helped Adm'ral Deeps down from the cart. In the circle of the telling-scope, her face was hard and closed, and there was a red mark across her cheek, as if she'd been struck. A second Ghost picked up a rock and put it on the mon-u-ment. Then they all settled down to wait.

Sharkey crawled forward, wondering if this was the last thing he'd ever do. Rain followed him. The branches thinned in front of them. The rays of the sun touched Sharkey's white skin.

He braced himself.

Somewhere behind him, a small rough voice whispered, 'Don't do it, shipmate. It's a trap.'

IF I LIVE

For the briefest of moments, Sharkey thought that the trees themselves had spoken. But Rain's wide eyes told him that trees, like seaweed and coral, weren't supposed to talk.

'Who's there?' he whispered, trying to see past the twigs and branches.

'A friend, shipmate,' replied the voice, 'with a friendly warning. There's men hidin' over yonder. Got 'ere a couple of hours before you. You show yourself, you'll get an arrow in the guts. I'd creep away if I was you, quiet as a shrimp.'

'*Quick* as a shrimp,' said a second voice, more precise than the first.

'No,' whispered Rain, grabbing Sharkey's arm. 'You have to swap me! You said you would swap me!'

Sharkey glared at her. 'Don't you make a sound!'

he hissed. 'Or I'll – I'll kill you. Just like I killed that Massy shark!'

He pulled her deeper into the thicket, searching for the source of the two voices. He thought he saw a patch of fur, as small and grey as a rabbit.

Can't have been rabbits that warned me, though. I don't reckon rabbits can talk, any more than turtles can.

But if it wasn't rabbits, who was it? Why had they warned him? And most important of all, were they telling the truth?

He lifted the telling-scope and peered back at the group around the mon-u-ment. His mind raced. Surely, if the Ghosts had set a trap, Adm'ral Deeps would've given him a sign of some sort? All she had to do was shake her head, or—

Unless there was a reason why she couldn't, a reason why she stood so tight and stiff, as if she didn't want to be part of what was happening.

Sharkey shifted the telling-scope to the cart, trying to see past its wooden sides. Why hadn't the fourth Ghost climbed down? Why was he still sitting there, with his knife in his hand and his eyes fixed on something at his feet?

Some*thing* or some*one*?

A shiver ran down Sharkey's spine. 'There's someone else hidden in that cart,' he whispered. 'Another

Sunker, I bet, held at knifepoint so the adm'ral won't shout a warning.'

He shifted the telling-scope again, and scanned the bushes along the side of the road. He knew what he was looking for now, and it wasn't long before he saw it. A twitch of leaves. The curve of a shoulder, half-hidden by a branch.

The mysterious voices were right. It was a trap.

It crossed his mind then that Rain might be part of it; that this might've been what she had wanted from the very start. To make her way onto *Claw*, and bring him here where he could be killed.

But they weren't going to kill Sharkey, not if he could help it! He was as sorry as he could be for Adm'ral Deeps, stuck in the Up Above. But he wasn't going to risk his life to save her.

He grabbed Rain's arm, tight as a lobster claw. 'You're going to get me back to the skiff,' he hissed in her ear, 'and no nasty tricks. You hear me?'

The girl looked at him sadly. 'Will you not let me go?'

Sharkey shook his head, impatient. He wasn't sure if he could find the skiff without her. And if things got bad, at least he'd have his own hostage.

'No tricks!' he said again.

They crept back the way they had come. The going was too slow for Sharkey's liking – he wanted to be back home right now, with the Undersea closing around him and the familiar stink of *Claw* calming his nerves. But he couldn't go faster. Tree branches threatened to snap in his face or poke out his good eye, and he had to push them aside with one hand, while hanging on to Rain with the other.

And then they came to bare ground. They must have crossed it earlier, but Sharkey hadn't noticed, not in the dark.

He noticed it now. No cover, not for a hundred yards or so. Just earth and rock. And back down the road, the Ghosts waiting for him.

If we run, he thought, *they'll see us.*

Which meant they should crawl, and hope not to be spotted. But the thought of crawling across that wide open space, with no kelp beds to hide in, gave Sharkey the horrors.

'We're going to run,' he said. 'Straight across to that next lot of trees.'

'*Please* let me go,' said Rain. 'I will not tell them anything about *Claw.* I promise I will not.'

'Now!' said Sharkey. And he dashed out into the open, dragging the girl by her arm.

The light of the sun hit him like a hammer. It was so bright that Sharkey's good eye started watering again, and he could hardly see the ground in front of him. On his port side, he thought he glimpsed a flurry of grey fur.

They were no more than halfway across the bare ground when Sharkey heard a shout. 'There! Brother Thrawn was right, there are more of them! Shoot! *Shoot!*'

And arrows began to fall about their ears.

Rain yelled with fright. Sharkey forgot about the rabbit, forgot about everything except the arrows. He wasn't used to running, but he was strong and lean from swimming long distances, and his body did what he asked of it. He let go of the girl's arm and dodged this way and that like a school of fish, all the while heading for the cover of the trees, and fearing that he wasn't going to make it.

Something whacked into his starboard shoulder. He cried out, and stumbled. To his surprise, Rain grabbed his hand and pulled him upright.

'Nearly there!' she panted. 'Come on!'

It seemed to Sharkey that they ran and ran, and the arrows fell and the trees came no closer. His shoulder was starting to hurt now, and he wanted to cry out again, but didn't have the wind for it.

And then, to his relief, the trees were right there in front of him, and he was slipping between them.

The arrows stopped, and so did Sharkey and Rain. But only for a moment. Rain shook her head as if to clear it. 'They could have *killed* me, shooting like that! They did not care!'

Sharkey put his hand to his shoulder and felt something poking through it. His clothes were sticky with blood.

Speared like a tunnyfish, he thought. *I never knew it'd hurt so much.*

He didn't feel like running any more. But Rain looked back again and said, 'They are coming after us!'

They set off between the trees, and this time it was Rain who held Sharkey's arm, instead of the other way round. Sharkey didn't think he could've made it by himself. His shoulder felt as if it had been rammed up against a hot engine. He wanted to groan, but he jammed his mouth shut and gnawed his lip instead.

Every step hurt. But Rain wouldn't let him slow down. She kept looking over her shoulder, and once or twice she squeaked with fright. Sharkey stumbled along, half running, half walking. He had lost all sense of direction, and for all he knew, the Ghost girl was taking him in circles. There was no sign of the rabbit.

When they came to the rocks, Rain pulled him out into the open, shouting in his ear, 'Keep going! We are nearly there!'

Sharkey didn't believe a word of it. *I'm going to get eaten,* he thought dizzily. *I'll never see* Claw *again. I'll never be adm'ral.*

Behind them, someone shouted, 'There they are!'

Sharkey gathered what little strength he had left and stumbled over the rocks, hanging on to Rain for dear life. Arrows hissed past them, sharp as knives.

If I live, I'll never spear another tunnyfish, thought Sharkey.

He was so close to the Undersea now that he could almost taste it. It helped drag him forward, when his shoulder was trying to stop him in his tracks. The rabbit was back, though now there seemed to be two of them. Or maybe it was just a couple of mud crabs, scuttling away from the intruders.

Sharkey didn't care. He left a spatter of blood on every rock he passed, and he didn't care about that either. The strength was draining out of him and all that mattered was getting back to *Claw.*

'Where's the boat?' cried Rain.

'Boat?' Sharkey raised his numb head, wondering what she was talking about.

'The one you hid!'

She means the skiff, thought Sharkey, and he rubbed his eye and tried to remember what he'd done with it.

'Over there,' he mumbled, pointing with his chin. 'I think.'

Rain dragged him towards a heap of kelp, and there was the skiff. Sharkey stood, swaying from side to side, while the girl pushed it into the water. Then he climbed in and picked up the paddle, wondering how on earth he was going to get them back to *Claw*.

He dug the paddle into the water and almost blacked out with the pain. 'Can't – do it!' he gasped. Except he was a Sunker, and Sunkers never gave up, not till they breathed their last. So he dug the paddle in again—

Rain scooted forward and knelt in front of him. She put her hands around his, and when the paddle went back into the water, she pushed at it with all her strength, so that Sharkey just had to guide it.

It still hurt. He couldn't hold the groans back now, no matter how hard he tried. But at least they were moving.

Rain was singing in a halting, breathless voice,

'*Run run – run,*

Do not stumble – or fall,

The race – is not done

Till you hear – the call . . .'

Her shoulders were up around her ears, and her eyes had that telltale whiteness about them. But her hands kept pushing at the paddle, one side then the other.

Sharkey heard a *thunk* as an arrow hit the seat behind him.

Rain squeaked, 'Where is *Claw*?'

'Don't know.' Sharkey was so full of pain that he couldn't see anything except a red blur, but he waved his hand vaguely. 'Periscope depth. They'll be watching for us.'

'Well, they had better hurry up,' cried Rain, as half a dozen arrows hissed past her. 'Or they will be too late.'

Sharkey thought he saw a swirling in the water, twenty yards or so to port. *Fish,* he thought. *A big one, going down.*

But it wasn't a fish, and it wasn't going down, it was coming up. The water churned and swirled as a grey conning tower poked out of the depths. The skiff rocked from side to side. The top of the conning tower flew open and Gilly stuck her head out.

'There!' cried Rain, and she tried to make Sharkey paddle towards the tower, but his arms wouldn't do a thing and they spun in circles, round and round, while the arrows came closer and closer.

Sharkey thought Gilly threw something, and maybe Rain caught hold of it. Whatever it was, they started to move, even though his arms were hanging by his sides.

And then Cuttle was lying on the deck clinging to the bow of the skiff while Rain and Gilly grabbed hold of Sharkey, and Gilly said, 'Come on, sir!'

He staggered along the slippery deck, with the arrows still falling and Gilly shouting over her shoulder, 'Leave it, Cuttle!'

Then somehow they were all scrambling down the ladder, with Rain in front of him and Gilly yelling, 'Fasten the hatches! Open main vents! Dive! Dive!' and Sharkey hoping it wasn't *him* who was supposed to get the hatches or the vents, cos right now he wasn't even sure where they were.

His foot slipped on a rung. Air roared out of the ballast tanks. *Claw* began to sink.

Somewhere nearby, Gilly shouted wordlessly, and Sharkey heard a *clunk* as the hatches were locked. The portholes darkened. He stood at the bottom of the ladder, swaying.

Then the last bit of strength drained out of him and the lights were going . . . going . . . gone.

IT'S THEM!

For all her misery, Petrel hadn't forgotten how to make a good hidey-hole. This might not be the *Oyster*, but the idea was the same.

Make sure you've got at least two exits. Make the inside comfy and the outside ragged, as if no one's been there for months. Leave some peepholes so you can see danger on its way. Cover up your tracks when you come and go.

And so, while the captain bandaged Krill's sprained ankle with strips of bark, and the pigeon watched in exhausted silence, Petrel and Fin set to work lining the space under the vines with sticks and plaited reeds, and packing mud between them to stop the rain coming in. They made sure it didn't look any different from the outside, then they went back over their first hurried pathway, brushing away footprints.

Only when that was done did they go hunting for something to eat.

The first day, they found a few scraps of more-or-less chewable seaweed. The second day they came back with a handful of tiny nuts, which were better than the seaweed, but not much.

By the fourth day, Petrel's hunger was raging so fiercely that all her other worries faded into insignificance. She knew that Krill must feel even worse, because he was so big and needed so much more to keep him going.

'Fish,' she whispered, as she and Fin crept through the scrub, watching out for danger. 'That's what I want.'

'We cannot light a fire,' said Fin. 'Someone would see it, or smell it.'

'Doesn't matter, I'll eat 'em raw.' Petrel licked her lips. 'Three of 'em. Raw and juicy. Then I'll take a dozen back to Krill.'

'But we do not have a line,' said Fin. 'We do not have hooks.'

'I *know* that, I'm not stupid.'

'We will be lucky to find more taters.'

'I know that too!'

'Then why do you pretend?' Fin's voice was harsh. 'Why do you talk about finding things that we have no hope of finding? It just makes it worse.'

Petrel stared at him. 'Is this about your mam?'

'No.'

'It is! Don't you want to look for her? I'm sure she's—'

'Stop it, Petrel! Please!' And his face was so unhappy that Petrel fell silent.

Despite their lack of fishing lines, they headed down to the shore, where they managed to find some limpets. They wiggled a few out of their shells and ate them, then collected the rest for Krill.

They returned to the shelter a roundabout way, so as not to make a trail. As they came closer, they saw the captain waiting for them, his face streaked with mud. The pigeon, who had recovered her strength but showed no desire to leave, perched on his arm.

'The Devouts rode past again,' said the captain.

'*What?*' said Petrel.

'When?' asked Fin.

'They came from the north, fourteen minutes and twenty-six seconds ago. One of their horses is going lame. They should not be riding it. It is not *right* to ride a lame horse.'

From inside the shelter, Krill said, 'Is that the bratlings back at last? Petrel, you've got to leave me here and keep going.'

'Not without you,' said Fin, crawling into the hidey-hole.

Petrel followed him. 'Here, Krill, we brought you some limpets. What's this about the Devouts? I thought they were gone.'

Hungry as he was, the big man brushed the food aside. 'They were searching all over. Sheer luck they didn't find me and the cap'n. You've gotta go before that luck runs ou—'

He was interrupted by the chatter of the telegraph device. And this time, the message was not from the *Oyster*.

Have boarded small underwater vessel Claw. *Need your position. Signed, Slink.*

It was the most beautiful sound Petrel had ever heard. She put her hand over her mouth, hardly able to contain her relief, and when she took it away, she was smiling for the first time in days.

She poked her head out of the shelter. 'Cap'n! Mister Smoke and Missus Slink have found an underwater vessel and they're coming to get us! What's our position?'

'But we have not found the Song or the Singer yet,' said the captain, crawling in to join them. The pigeon fluttered after him. 'We cannot go.'

Petrel sat back on her heels. The captain was smarter than all the rest of the *Oyster*'s crew put together, but once he settled on an idea, it was hard to shift him.

And the search for the Song and the Singer seemed to have gripped him like nothing else.

It's that programming stuff, she thought. *Feels as if someone's reaching out from the long-ago and moving us around to suit themselves. Which is all very clever, but what if it doesn't suit* us?

Aloud, she said, 'Song's not going to do anyone much good, Cap'n, if Albie overruns the bridge and takes the *Oyster* back south without us.' Inspiration struck her. 'And – and besides, maybe the Singer is on this underwater vessel!'

The captain nodded. 'That is logical. Very well, our position is fifty degrees thirty minutes north, seven degrees twelve minutes west.' He stroked the pigeon's feathers. 'But according to my charts, the water on this coast is dangerously shallow. A large vessel will not be able to get anywhere near us.'

'It's all right, it's small,' said Petrel. 'Missus Slink said so.'

She tapped out the coordinates in general ship code and waited, breathless, for a reply. It came quicker than she expected.

Estimate time of travel twenty-one hours forty-four minutes.

'We'll have to help you down to the water, Krill,' she said.

'I'm better than I was,' said Krill. 'I'll get there.'

Petrel beamed at him. 'And then we'll be heading back to the ship, and everything'll be all right. Folk won't want to follow Albie once they know how he lied to 'em. And Squid and Dolph'll be safe and we'll—'

'Shhh!' Fin grabbed her arm.

'What?'

Very quietly, Fin said, 'The Devouts have returned. I think they heard us.'

Petrel shot up so fast that she almost fell over. 'Where?'

Fin pointed. And there were the same two men, sitting very still on their horses, and staring in the direction of the shelter.

'Blizzards!' whispered Petrel. 'We've got to get out of here! Krill—'

The Head Cook picked up a rock and hefted it in his hand. 'You three go. Creep out the back way. I'll keep 'em busy for as long as I can.'

'No,' whispered Petrel, coming to a rapid decision. 'Fin and I'll draw 'em off. Cap'n, will you stay here with Krill?'

The captain looked as if he was about to argue. Petrel said quickly, 'You can't run as fast as Fin and me. It's logical, right?'

The captain nodded. 'It is logical.' Then he looked out one of the peepholes and said, 'They are coming this way.'

Petrel grabbed the telegraph device, worried that it might start clattering again and give away the position of the hidey-hole. 'Fin, let's go,' she whispered. And the two of them crawled out the back exit.

The horses were snorting like whales, and stamping their hooves. The children crept away from the shelter, still hidden by the bushes and rocks.

Can't jump up too soon, thought Petrel, *or they'll figure out where we came from. Can't go too late or they'll find Krill and the cap'n. A bit further . . . A bit further . . . Now!*

With a yelp, she leapt to her feet, as if she'd been tucked up in the bushes and had only just noticed the Devouts. Fin was a heartbeat behind her, crying, 'It is them! Run!'

And run they did.

★★★

When Sharkey woke up at last, he was lying on the berth above the batteries with a rabbit stitching his shoulder.

Despite the sharp pain of the needle, he thought he must still be asleep. He thought it was a dream and that any minute now he'd see Adm'ral Deeps flying past in a cart, with an arrow in her hand. Because that's the sort of thing that happened in dreams.

But instead of the adm'ral, what he saw was Poddy, leaning over him with an expression that was half-worried, half-jumping out of her skin with excitement.

'Sir, you're awake!' she cried. She turned her head. 'Gilly, Cuttle, he's awake!'

The needle bit into Sharkey's shoulder and he winced, and turned his head to peer at the rabbit. Its ears weren't as big as he remembered, and its tail was long and grey instead of short and white. It was poking the needle in and out of his flesh, right where the arrow had come through, and muttering to itself. Around its neck was a tattered green ribbon.

Sharkey winced again, and croaked, 'R-rabbit.'

'It is a rat,' said Rain, from his other side, in disapproving tones. 'It sneaked onto *Claw* with us. Or rather, *they* did.'

'That's right, shipmate,' said a rough little voice. 'There's two of us.' And a long grey nose, with whiskers sprouting from it, poked over Sharkey's good shoulder.

He was glad of the distraction. He dragged his eyes away from the needle and said, 'You – warned me. Back there. You – warned me about the trap. Why?'

Poddy leaned over him again and whispered, her eyes as bright as the sun, 'Cos it's them, sir! It's *them*!'

Sharkey had no idea what she was talking about, and his shoulder was hurting too much for him to work it out. With a groan, he closed his eye and went back to sleep.

★★★

When he woke the second time, there was an argument going on above his head.

'Rats cannot talk,' said Rain. 'I have never heard of such a thing.'

'That's cos you're from the Up Above,' retorted Poddy, 'and there's plenty you haven't heard of. I bet you think turtles can't talk either, or dolphins. But they talk to Sharkey.'

His nose was running. He sniffed, and both girls leaned over him. 'Where are we?' he croaked.

'Heading sou'-sou'-west, sir,' said Poddy, 'as ordered.'

'Wha—?' Sharkey rubbed his eye, wondering if he'd misheard her. He hadn't given any orders, had he? 'W-What's the time?'

Cuttle, who was at the helm, looked over his shoulder. 'Seventy-five minutes till sunclimb, sir. You slept right through.'

'You should've woken me,' said Sharkey.

'You lost a lot of blood,' said Rain. 'The rats advised us—' She hesitated, as if she still didn't want to admit that rats could talk.

Poddy broke in. 'They said we should let you sleep as long as you wanted, sir.'

Sharkey rubbed his eye again. The rumble of diesels cut through his muddled thoughts, and he struggled up onto one elbow, grimacing with pain. 'We're running on the surface?'

'Aye, sir,' said Cuttle.

'Who's on watch?' Sharkey felt a surge of panic, remembering what had happened to *Rampart*. 'We *are* keeping a watch?'

'Course we are, sir,' said Poddy. 'Don't worry, every-thing's good. Gilly's up above. And *he's* got the conn.'

'Who's *he*? And why are we going sou'-sou'-west? Did I give you the direction?'

'Nay,' said Poddy. 'It was *him*.'

Sharkey felt as if he was going around in circles. '*Who?*'

Poddy beamed. 'Great Granfer, of course.'

'Great Gran— What are you talking about, Pod?'

Poddy edged back a little so Sharkey could see the two rats. 'It's *them*, sir,' she said proudly. 'They've come to help us. It's Lin Lin and Adm'ral Cray!'

LIN LIN AND
ADM'RAL CRAY

I'm going mad, thought Sharkey. *The sun must've scorched my brain.*

He stared at the rat. 'Adm'ral Cray,' he said flatly.

The rat looked back at him, its fur scruffy, its silver eyes expressionless. 'That's what they call me, shipmate.'

'And Lin Lin,' said Sharkey.

The second rat, the one with the green ribbon, bobbed its head. 'At your service.'

I need air, thought Sharkey. *I need—*

He grabbed hold of the periscope casing with one hand, dragged himself upright and hung on until his head stopped swimming. Then he said, 'I have the conn. Poddy, stop both motors.'

Poddy didn't move. 'But sir, the adm'ral said—'

'I don't care what the adm'ral said. I'm in charge of this boat.'

'Aye ... sir,' said Poddy, as if there was some doubt about it. 'But we have to keep going.'

'They've got friends who're stranded, sir,' said Cuttle. 'We have to get there as quick as we can.'

Sharkey couldn't believe it. They were arguing with him! The middies were *arguing* with him!

He set his teeth in a snarl. 'Who's your cap'n, Poddy?'

'You are, sir. But Adm'ral Cray said—'

'Stop. Both. Motors.'

Rain looked pleased. Poddy looked as if someone had smacked her, but she trotted back to the big switches without further argument. *Claw* slowed. The rats watched and listened, their heads swivelling back and forth like little grey rudders.

Sharkey didn't care what any of them thought. *He* was in charge, no one else. The submersible wasn't going anywhere without his orders, and he hadn't yet decided what those orders would be.

I need air.

Climbing up the conning tower was a challenge with only one good arm. He managed it without groaning, but by the time he stepped out onto the open deck, he was shaking with pain.

Gilly sprang to her feet when she saw him and said, 'Sir, you shouldn't be up here. Go and rest. We're all right, we've got the adm'ral and Lin Lin to—'

'Shut up,' said Sharkey. 'Just – shut up. And go below.'

'But I'm on watch, sir.'

'Don't argue! I'll take the watch. Go below.'

And then it was just him, sitting there with the stars above and the dark waves rising and falling around him, and his mind trying to tear itself in two.

Adm'ral Cray? Lin Lin? Really?

He shook his head. *Nay.*

But what if—?

Nay, I don't believe it.

The middies did, though, which he was going to have to change, quick smart.

They argued with me! Cuttle and Poddy ARGUED with me! They've never done that before.

Uncertainty hit him again. What if the rats really *were* Lin Lin and Adm'ral Cr—

NAY!

He wasn't thinking clearly, that was the problem. He hadn't been thinking clearly since *Rampart* went down. That had torn something out of him, and now, whatever he did seemed to make things worse.

What was it the Ghosts had shouted when they saw him? *Brother Thrawn was right, there are more of them!* Which meant they hadn't known for sure that there was another submersible. Not until Sharkey had turned up and proved it.

I shouldn't have gone, he thought. *I've put* Claw *at risk. I've put ALL of us at risk.*

He wasn't used to being in the wrong, and it made him angry. With himself, with the middies, with the pain in his shoulder, which was getting worse instead of better. With the rats.

Mustn't forget I'm on watch.

He glanced around the horizon, knowing he'd see nothing. The skimmers were never about this early. Suntime was when the Ghosts went hunting, and by then *Claw*'d be deep in the Undersea. And Sharkey'd be laying down the law to his crew.

I'm in charge. No one else, no matter who they claim to be.

He heard a quick scuff of feet climbing the conning tower, and turned his back. He didn't want to talk to anyone, not yet. Not with this fizz of anger and confusion in his belly.

'Sir?' It was Poddy, right behind him.

'Go away, Pod.'

'Sir, we thought you'd be pleased.'

Sharkey stared at the eastern horizon. 'Go away.'

'But sir, they're the *ancestors*.'

'Don't be a fool, Poddy.'

'They *are*. I knew it as soon I saw them. And – and sir, if Adm'ral Deeps is alive then maybe Ma and Fa are too, and we can rescue all of 'em and get *Rampart* watertight again, and everything'll be back the way it used to be!'

Sharkey's shoulder felt as if the arrow was still in there, jabbing away at him until he wanted to scream. And now here was Poddy jabbing away too.

'Can't we do what they say, sir? Can't we go and find their friends, who are in trouble? And then we could ask 'em for help.'

He wanted to stop her and didn't know how. Not without admitting that the whole talking-to-the-ancestors business was a lie. And if he told her that, the middies would never listen to him again.

There was a bitter taste in his mouth. It had been there, he realised, ever since he saw Adm'ral Deeps through the telling-scope. Because Poddy was right – if the adm'ral was alive then maybe everyone else was too. Maybe they were sitting in the Ghosts' camp, expecting Sharkey to rescue them.

Because he was a hero.

It was as if Poddy could read his thoughts. 'They'll be waiting for us, sir. Ma and Fa and all the others. They know we'll come for 'em. And we will, won't we? 'Specially now we've got the ancestors.'

It was too much for Sharkey. His guilt flared white-hot and he whirled around, so quick and nasty-faced that Poddy flinched backwards. 'If it *was* the ancestors,' he snarled, 'you wouldn't hear 'em talk, cos you're just an ordinary little middy and why would they want to talk to a middy, eh? They talk to *me*, cos I'm favoured, I'm going to be adm'ral one day—'

It was like listening to someone else. He tried to stop, and couldn't. The bitterness spilled out like poison, and Poddy copped every bit of it.

'—I'll be adm'ral one day and you'll *still* be nothing, so shut up, you don't know what you're talking about. Lin Lin and Adm'ral Cray don't care what happens to us, which means your ma and fa are lost and so's Adm'ral Deeps and the babies and the salties and everyone else, and you might as well get used to it.'

Then he turned his back again, and sat trembling with anger and indignation.

He heard a gulp behind him, but didn't turn around. *I'm just telling her the truth,* he thought. *I'm doing her a favour.*

Another gulp, quickly covered up. Then Poddy said, in a small voice, 'If we're not going anywhere just yet, may I – may I go for a swim, sir?'

Sharkey heaved a put-upon sigh. 'I suppose so.'

'Thank you, sir.' And with that, she wriggled out of her jerkin and trousers and slid over the side, into a sea that was as grey as the pre-dawn sky.

Sharkey knew he should call her back, but he was stuck in place, the poison in his blood turned to glue.

It had to be said, he told himself. *She's got to stop believing that we're going to get the others back. It's a stupid waste of time. We should be getting on with our lives.*

He wished it was *him* who'd gone for a swim instead of Poddy. Not that he could swim with his shoulder like this. Not that he could do anything. He was useless. One eye and one arm.

The bitterness filled him again and he sat there feeling sorry for himself and wondering if Poddy'd get back before the sun roared up over the horizon. If she didn't, they'd have to stay Up Above and risk getting eaten by the Hungry Ghosts.

Except – Adm'ral Deeps hadn't got eaten. And Rain wasn't at all dangerous. In fact, she'd saved Sharkey's life. So was it true or wasn't it, what the Sunkers had always believed?

As Sharkey sat there, trying to make sense of it, the sky grew lighter and the nor'-westerly wind picked up. It wasn't long before he began to worry. Poddy should've been back by now. Everyone knew how far you could swim before sunclimb, and everyone was careful.

'Where are you, Pod?' he muttered, not looking up. 'What are you playing at? You get back here, quick smart.'

Half of him thought she was probably no more than a few yards away, treading water. Playing a trick to get back at him for the things he'd said. But the other half knew that he shouldn't have let her go. It was risky swimming alone when your feelings were hurt.

'Poddy?' he called, over his shoulder. 'You there?'

No answer. Sharkey climbed to his feet and turned around, feeling angry all over again for the worry she was causing him. He squinted at the edges of the boat to see if she was hiding. Then he raised his eye towards the west – and saw four skimmers, bearing down on *Claw*, with the first no more than half a sea mile away.

Sharkey's heart almost stopped beating. Skimmers before sunclimb? He'd never heard of such a thing. But there they were!

He leapt for the conning tower, with the word 'Dive!' on his lips. Then he remembered Poddy. They *couldn't* dive, not while she was still out there.

'Poddy!' he shouted, scanning the water for that small dark head. '*Poddy!*'

Gilly came scrambling up from below. 'What's the matter, sir?'

'Skimmers!' cried Sharkey. 'And Poddy's out there somewhere and I *can't see her!*'

Gilly dived down the hatch again and came back with the telling-scope in her hand, and Rain and the rats at her heels. Sharkey grabbed the telling-scope and jammed it to his good eye, but it didn't tell him a thing. He swept it north and south, east and west, right up to the approaching skimmers and back again, but he couldn't find Poddy anywhere. All he saw was grey light and grey water, and the white sails closing in.

'Where *are* you, Poddy?' he muttered.

The rats stood on their hind legs, peering at the waves. 'She ain't got much chance if she's still out there, shipmate,' said the fake Adm'ral Cray.

'She *might* be all right,' said Gilly uncertainly.

Sharkey shouted again, at the top of his lungs, '*Pooooddyyyyy!*'

And then he saw her. In the growing light, halfway between *Claw* and the skimmers. Swimming for her life.

'Gilly, Cuttle!' yelled Sharkey. 'Due west, full speed!'

Gilly dashed below. Sharkey danced from foot to foot, afraid to take his eye off that bobbing head. He felt as if the telling-scope was a rope between them, and if he took it away from his eye, Poddy'd be lost.

'Hurry!' he cried.

'They need a hand down there, shipmate?' asked the fake adm'ral.

'Aye!' said Sharkey.

The rats dashed below again, and a moment later the submersible was underway. Sharkey groaned under his breath, knowing they weren't going to get there in time. *Claw* wasn't made for going fast in the Up Above. She plunged through the waves like a wounded porpoise, up and down, up and down, with Rain clinging to the stay lines. Salt water spattered Sharkey's face, and he was soaked within seconds. His wounded shoulder throbbed, but he hardly noticed.

Poddy looked so tiny, even through the telling-scope. And the skimmers were so big.

'They're nearly on her,' whispered Sharkey. He groaned aloud as one of the skimmers yawed to the side, its sails dropping. 'They've seen her. No! *Poddyyyyyy!*'

It was no use screaming. It was no use doing anything except watching, right up to the very last moment. Rain ran to the hatch and shouted something, and the motors slowed. Sharkey just watched, his heart almost bursting out of his chest, as his little cousin changed direction, still swimming strongly, still trying to get away from the Ghosts who had spotted her.

There was a bustling along the side of the skimmer, brown robes running hither and thither. Sharkey cursed them, cursed their parents and their grandparents and every single one of their ancestors – if they even *had* ancestors – right back to the dawn of time.

But it did no good. A sail billowed. The skimmer came around again. A dozen hands threw a net out over the water—

—and hauled it back in, with Poddy inside, kicking and fighting every inch of the way.

In a daze, Sharkey lowered the telling-scope. 'They've got her,' he said. He felt numb. 'They'll be after us next.'

He let Rain go through the hatch first, then he squeezed inside, shut both sets of clamps and half fell down the ladder.

'Emerg—' his voice broke. He swallowed and tried again. 'Emergency – deep.'

A muscle in Cuttle's cheek clenched, but all he said was, 'Emergency deep. Aye, sir.'

The familiar sequence took over. Out of the corner of Sharkey's eye, he saw Gilly at the motors and the rats turning the big brass wheels.

The little submersible dived.

Without Poddy.

WITHOUT
PODDY

They dived without Poddy.

I should be pleased, thought Rain. *One of them has been caught. I should be celebrating.*

But she was not. She had grown fond of *Claw*'s youngest crew member. And besides, ever since the Devouts had sprung their trap, and almost killed *her* in the process, she had realised that her original plan was not going to work.

In her first dreadful days on the submersible, she had managed to convince herself that if she could only smash its instruments and make the Sunkers surrender, the Devouts would be so pleased with her that they would let her little brother go.

But as the trap was sprung and the arrows fell around her, she had realised that the Devouts didn't care about her one way or the other. If she captured the Sunkers for them, they would be pleased, but they wouldn't release Bran. No, if she wanted to save him, she would have to be more devious.

That was why she had dragged Sharkey to safety. That was why she was sitting on the bunk now, watching him and waiting for the right time to say her piece.

She was not the only one watching him. He had taken *Claw* right down to the deep seabed, where the Devout ships could not find them. He had ordered the motors cut. Then he had slumped on the seat next to Cuttle with his head in his hands.

Now everyone was waiting for him to speak. Even the rats were quiet, though they glanced at each other frequently.

At last Sharkey raised his head and said in a bleak, terrible voice, 'Poddy's been caught.'

Rain knew guilt when she saw it, and Sharkey was weighed down by it. *Something happened up on that deck,* she thought. *Something that made Poddy swim too far.*

But no one was asking, and Sharkey was not telling. Instead, he looked at Rain with his single eye. 'You said the Ghosts don't really eat people. That the Sunkers'd be taken to a camp.'

This was what Rain had been waiting for. 'Yes. The re-education camp.'

Cuttle blinked. 'Education? Well, that doesn't sound so bad, sir, does it? Poddy's good at her letters.'

'That's not the sort of education she's talkin' about, shipmate,' said the rat who called himself Adm'ral Cray.

'You stay out of this,' said Sharkey. 'It's nothing to do with you.'

Gilly said, 'But it is, sir! They're our ancest—'

'Stop *arguing* with me!'

A strained silence fell over the little group. Rain listened to the sound of water pressing against the hull, and wondered what would happen if it pressed too hard.

Sharkey rubbed the patch that covered his ruined eye. 'Tell me about the camp,' he said.

'Manners, boy,' said the rat with the green ribbon.

Sharkey ignored her.

'It is not really re-education,' said Rain. 'It is hard work. Breaking rocks and building roads.'

Cuttle began, 'Poddy doesn't mind hard w—'

But Sharkey held up his hand. 'Go on.'

Rain gnawed her lip, as if she did not want to answer. Then she said, 'I have not been inside the camp. But my brother is an Initiate, and they are supposed to help watch the prisoners. Bran is only little, and he is a kind-hearted boy. Broth— Brother Thrawn set him to watch the prisoners in the quarry while they broke rocks, and told him that if someone stopped work, even for a moment, he must tell one of the guards. There was an old woman – Bran said she looked sick and hungry. So did the other prisoners, but she looked *really* sick. And she stopped work, and – and Bran told the guard, because he thought the old woman might be allowed to lie down for a while. Only—'

Sharkey seemed to be having trouble breathing. 'Only – what?'

'Whippings,' said the rat with the green ribbon. 'Whippings and beatings and all sorts of nastiness, that's what *we* saw.'

'That's right, shipmate,' said the rat adm'ral. 'Before we met up with you, we passed by the Citadel. Took a peek at the quarry while we was there. And I can tell you that the Devouts don't like folk who stop work. They don't like anythin' much, as far as we could tell. Don't reckon their prisoners last long. Couple of months at the most.'

Gilly flinched. Cuttle stared at his hands.

'I asked Bro— Brother Thrawn if Bran could stay away from the quarry,' said Rain. 'I thought he might be able to just – just study or something.' She sighed. 'I should have known better. Broth— Brother Thrawn likes making people do things they do not want to do. He knew I was scared of the balloon – that is why he sent me up in it. And he knew Bran hated the whippings, so he made him watch them.'

There were lies in there, which Rain did her best to make believable. But what she said next was completely honest. 'I— I am afraid that Bran will get used to it. He is only little, and he wants to be a good Initiate, so he is doing his best not to mind so much. He is doing his best to despise the prisoners, like the Devouts do.'

She stopped herself then, though she wanted to keep going, wanted to tell them the *real* truth. The *whole* truth. But she must not. There was too much at stake.

Sharkey sat very still, staring at the deck. The only movement came from his shoulders, which jerked several times, as if he was struggling with something inside himself.

Cuttle opened his mouth and shut it again. Gilly watched Sharkey, her own shoulders twitching in unison with his.

When Sharkey looked up at last, there was a light in his eye that Rain had never seen before. 'We have to get her back,' he whispered.

Cuttle sat up very straight. 'How, sir?'

'Don't ask questions,' said Sharkey. 'I'll work it out.'

'What if she's— What if she's been eaten already, sir?'

'The Ghosts didn't eat Adm'ral Deeps,' said Sharkey.

Gilly leaned towards him. 'Maybe the Ghosts haven't eaten any of 'em. Ma and Fa, and Barnacle. And Blubber and Sprat—'

Sharkey laughed, though there was no humour in it. 'If they're alive, we'll get 'em all back,' he said recklessly. 'Why not? The whole lot of 'em.'

'How will you do it?' asked rat Lin Lin.

'None of your business,' said Sharkey.

'It might be our business, boy. You might need our help.'

Sharkey shook his head. 'You heard Rain. She knows about the camp.'

'But can she slip into it and out again without being seen?' asked the rat. 'Can she carry messages? Can she crawl under floors and over rafters and through pipes?'

The reckless gleam in Sharkey's eye turned to uncertainty, and then to cunning. He stood up, so that he towered over the rat.

'All right, *Great Granmer*,' he said. 'Let's make a bargain.'

★★★

'Can you see them?' whispered Fin.

'Hang on.' Petrel wriggled forward and peered through the bracken. 'Nope. They're gone.' She yawned. 'Just as well too. Don't reckon I can run any more, not without something to eat. And a bit of sleep.'

The two children had spent the afternoon and most of the night luring the horsemen away from Krill and the silver captain. They'd run, they'd crawled, they'd hidden. They'd scrambled over sharp rocks and through dense thickets, where the horses couldn't go. They would almost certainly have been caught in more open country. As it was, the growing lameness of one of the horses and the tangled nature of the bushland had worked to the children's advantage.

Now Petrel was so tired and hungry that she could hardly spit. But she was satisfied, too, as if she had regained a bit of herself that was lost.

'There's no one knows how to run and hide as well as me,' she said to Fin.

He nodded agreement. 'But they will not give up, you know. They will send a pigeon for reinforcements.'

'We'll be back on the *Oyster* by then,' said Petrel, 'eating Krill's best fish stew.' She grinned, imagining the deck under her feet. 'With grilled fish for pudding and a nice bowl of fish soup to finish off. Albie'll be in chains and everything'll be right again.'

The thought of it made her want to dance. Despite her tiredness, she picked up the telegraph device and jumped to her feet. 'We'd best get going. We've come a long way.'

They didn't bother retracing the devious back-and-forth path that had brought them there – that would have taken the rest of the day. Instead, Petrel used the sun to guide them in an almost-straight line, with Fin watching out for danger.

They were well underway when the telegraph device began to chatter out another message in general ship code.

Petrel gasped. 'Oh!'

'What is it?' asked Fin.

'*Claw*'s been delayed.'

'When will they—'

Petrel held up her hand, still listening. '*Claw*'s cap'n wants a bargain.' Her voice rose in protest. 'What? Blizzards, no! He says he'll only pick us up if we agree to help rescue his people from the Devouts.'

'We could try. After we get back to the *Oyster*.'

'No,' said Petrel. '*Before* he takes us to the *Oyster*.'

She and Fin looked at each other in dismay.

'What'll I tell 'em?' she whispered. 'I thought we'd be back where we belong by first watch, or sooner. And Squid and Dolph and everyone else who's trapped on the bridge'd be safe. But now— Who knows how long this'll take?'

'But we have no other way of returning to the ship,' said Fin. 'Which means—'

'Which means we ain't got a choice.' And, feeling as lost and desolate as she ever had, Petrel began to tap out a reply.

★★★

'They agree,' said the rat, taking her paw off the comm key. 'They'll help get your friends back, and so will the adm'ral and I. And then you'll take us to our ship.'

'So where are they?' asked Sharkey, who didn't like all these messages going back and forth in a code he didn't understand.

The rat gave him the coordinates, and he stiffened. 'But that's—'

'That's what, shipmate?' asked the fake adm'ral, who was perched on top of the echo sounder.

'That's the Sealy Coast,' said Sharkey, and the air around him seemed to grow colder. 'Part of the Great Puddle.'

Rain looked from one face to another, her forehead creased. 'What is the Great Puddle?'

'It's a big stretch of shallow water,' said Gilly. 'Too shallow for submersibles, except for a couple of channels, and they're too narrow. Sunkers never go anywhere near the Great Puddle.'

The rat adm'ral, up on his perch, went very still. 'You're not backin' out of our agreement already, are you, shipmates?'

Cuttle and Gilly began to speak over the top of each other.

'We can't go into the Great Puddle—'

'You *know* we can't, Adm'ral, not even for Poddy—'

'It's an old rule, never go into the Great Puddle—'

'It's too dangerous—'

'It's too *shallow*!'

The rat adm'ral took no notice of them. He was watching Sharkey.

'They're right,' said Sharkey. 'It'd be madness.'

He realised, as he said it, that this was his way out. He'd made that stupid announcement – *We'll get 'em all back* – in the heat of the moment, and was already regretting it. Now he could throw his hands in the air and say, 'Well, we tried. But we can't go into the Great Puddle.'

Except that wouldn't save Poddy, would it?

He thought of the re-education camp, with its whippings and beatings. Thought of cheerful little Poddy getting sick and hungry, thought of her *dying*, all because of a bit of shallow water.

All because of *him*.

The recklessness took hold again. 'The Puddle might be too shallow for *Rampart*,' he said. 'That doesn't mean *Claw* can't make it. Cuttle, find me a chart of the Sealy Coast.'

When the chart came, he stared at it, making quick calculations in his head. 'We'll need the tide with us. High water'll be just after eighteen hundred hours down that way. We'd better allow for delays—'

He spun around. 'Send another message to your friends,' he said to rat Lin Lin. 'Tell 'em – we've got no chance of getting there tonight. Tell 'em we'll pick 'em up tomorrow night. Seventeen hundred hours – that's an hour after sunfall. Tell 'em to be ready, we won't be able to contact 'em again, not till we're nearly there. If we have to go into the Great Puddle, we'll use one of the channels, and run as deep and silent as we can. No periscope. No aerial. Nothing. Not till we have to.'

He swung back to Gilly. 'What's the charge on the batteries?'

'Full charge, sir.'

'Air?'

'Air's clean, sir.'

'Good,' said Sharkey, though he didn't *feel* good. His belly was hollow, as if he hadn't eaten properly for days, and he could hardly believe he was doing this.

'Sir,' whispered Cuttle. 'Are you sure? The Great *Puddle*?'

'Course I'm sure,' said Sharkey. 'Don't worry, Cuttle. The batteries are charged, the air's topped up and we've got the ancestors on our side.' He bared his teeth at the rats. 'What could possibly go wrong?'

THE GREAT PUDDLE

As the sun rose the next morning, Petrel, Fin, Krill and
the captain were tucked up in a rock cave, several feet
above the high-tide mark. There was snow on the ground,
and the pigeon's feathers were fluffed out with the cold.

'I don't like this,' said Krill for the hundredth time.
'We should be going straight back to the *Oyster*, not
wasting our time on someone else's business. It's ten
days since we left the ship, d'you realise that?'

'And we still have not found any trace of the Song,'
said the captain. 'Or the Singer.'

'Cap'n, with all due respect, it's getting harder
and harder for me to worry about a song when my
daughter's trapped on the bridge, along with Dolph
and who knows who else! Maybe today's the day Albie
overruns 'em, and what are we doing? Going off to
rescue a bunch of strangers!'

'Who might know the Song,' said the captain in his sweet, determined voice. He put his hand on the ground and the pigeon clambered onto it. 'I do not think she wants to go back to the Devouts. I am going to call her Scroll.'

With a sigh, Krill turned his frustration on Petrel and Fin. 'You should never have agreed to such a bargain, bratlings.'

'We didn't have a choice,' said Petrel. 'I don't like it any more than you do, Krill, but we ain't seen another ship all this time, and you know it.'

'She is right,' said Fin. 'This is our only chance of getting back to the *Oyster*.'

'Hmph,' the Head Cook rumbled deep in his throat. 'I wish we'd never come north. Our troubles started when we left the ice.' And he subsided into gloom.

Petrel gazed out at the water, thinking, *He's right. I don't care about changing the world, not any more. It's too big and too nasty. I want to go back to the ice.*

She felt a brief flicker of guilt over Fin's mam. *He believes she's dead,* she reminded herself. *And maybe she is. No point staying in this horrible place for a dead woman.*

And for the rest of the morning she comforted herself with dreams of heading south, back to the ice, and of penguins and bergs and the sweet flesh of toothyfish.

It was past noon, and the snow had melted away at last, when Scroll suddenly grew restless, bobbing up and down on the captain's wrist, as if something was wrong.

Petrel shaded her eyes and stared at the horizon. 'What's that, Cap'n? Looks like the sun coming up, only nowhere near as big and bright.'

The captain was already on his feet. 'It is a hot air balloon with a basket underneath. And there is another one. Look, they are tethered to sailing ships!' He turned to Fin. 'You did not tell us that the Devouts used hot air balloons.'

Fin's face was ashen. 'But they do not! At least – they did not when *I* was with them. I have never seen such things before!'

'Those two men must have sent a pigeon for them,' said the captain. 'We will have to conceal the front of the cave or the people in the baskets will see us.'

'It's not just us they'll see,' growled Krill, pushing himself up onto his elbows. 'That water's a mite too clear for my liking. Petrel, send a message to Missus Slink, quick smart. Tell her about those balloon things, and the Devout ships. *Claw* mustn't come in, not yet. Not in daylight.'

Petrel tapped out a warning on the telegraph device. But although she waited and waited, there was no reply.

'They said they would be travelling underwater,' said the captain. 'They will not receive our message until they surface.'

'Then we'd best keep sending it,' said Krill, 'and hope like blazes they get it in time.'

★★★

By the time *Claw* came to the edge of the Great Puddle, the ocean floor was shelving upwards and there were reefs everywhere. Sharkey kept his eye on the dark green water outside the porthole, and didn't share his thoughts with anyone.

At the helm, Gilly said, 'Sir, we're coming up to the channel entrance.'

'How long?' asked Sharkey.

'Ten minutes, sir.'

'What's our depth?'

'Eighty-five feet, sir. And we've got forty feet of water under the keel.'

'Steady as she goes.'

'Aye, sir.'

Sharkey glanced at the chronometer and raised his voice so that everyone could hear him. 'We'll make the entrance to the channel at 13.20 hours. All stations!'

The two rats scurried to the dive-plane wheels. Cuttle stood by the motors, feet braced on the metal decking. Rain sat on the berth above the batteries, her eyes closed, her mouth moving silently.

At exactly 13.20 hours, Sharkey said, 'Helm, make your heading due west. Two degrees up bubble. Dead slow ahead.'

The voices came back to him in rapid fire.

'Due west, aye sir,' cried Gilly.

'Dead slow ahead, aye sir,' shouted Cuttle from the motors.

The rats stood on their hind legs and hauled at the dive-plane wheels. As *Claw* swung around, her bow rose and her running lights fell on the entrance to the channel.

It was like a gorge cut out of rock, and even narrower than Sharkey had expected. But other than trying to make it all the way across the Great Puddle in shallow water, and probably grounding themselves in the attempt, he could see no other way of getting close to the shore.

'Make your depth seventy-six feet,' he said.

'Seventy-six feet, aye sir.'

And when they reached seventy-six feet: 'Ease your bubble.'

'Ease bubble, aye sir.'

As *Claw* nosed forward between the rock walls, Rain began to sing, very quietly. The words whispered across the little cabin and curled around Sharkey's head.

> *'Hobgoblins tiptoe through the night*
> *And imp and ghost and evil wight—'*

Sharkey had no idea what a hobgoblin was, but he knew all about tiptoeing. That's what they were doing now, tiptoeing into dangerous waters.

> *'They do their best to give us fright,'* sang Rain,
> *'And fill us with dismay.'*

Outside the porthole, the sides of the channel were so close that seaweed and sponges wavered as they passed. The running lights touched clamshells and rocks and schools of fish. Sharkey saw a crab frantically kicking up sand to conceal itself, and bag-trout dashing into the weeds, as shy as oysters.

> *'But will we cower, will we hide?*
> *Will we lock ourselves inside?'*

As they approached the coast, the channel grew shallower, though nowhere near as shallow as the waters on either side of it. The skin on the back of Sharkey's neck tightened every time he gave the order to go up a few feet. He didn't *want* to go up. He wanted to hurry back to deep water and dive, down down down, so far that the Ghosts'd never find them.

He knew that Cuttle and Gilly wouldn't say a word against him, if that's what he decided. They'd just nod and keep on believing that he was a hero.

'*Or will we hold ourselves with pride*
And chase those ghouls away?'

Sharkey gritted his teeth and said, 'Up five.'

'Up five, aye sir.'

At 15.40 hours, Sharkey took another look at the chart. If they kept following the channel they'd end up too far north of the rendezvous. Which meant they had to leave its relative safety and go up into the *really* shallow water. The tide was on the rise and sunfall wasn't far away, but still he didn't like it one bit.

Maybe we should wait till after sunfall. Except that'd make us late, and if anything slowed us down we'd miss the tide.

He realised he was chewing his thumbnail, and quickly glanced around to make sure no one had noticed. Rain was still singing. Gilly was tapping the gyroscope, while Cuttle oiled the drive shaft. The rats were watching Sharkey with eyes that were too knowing for comfort.

He flushed and said, louder than he'd intended, 'Take her up to twenty-five feet.'

The rats turned the dive-plane wheels, and *Claw* began to rise.

'Fifty-five feet,' sang Gilly. 'Fifty feet. Forty-five. Forty. Thirty-five. Thirty.'

Outside the porthole the water went from deep green to pale blue. The sides of the channel gave way to a sandy bottom.

'Twenty-five—'

'Zero bubble,' cried Sharkey. 'Keep your trim.'

The upward movement stopped. And there they were, easing into the sandy reaches of the Great Puddle, as quiet as a flounder, with no more than ten feet of water under them. And unknown dangers above.

★★★

The Devouts' ships sailed up and down the coast all afternoon, with the balloons drifting high above them. Petrel and her friends crouched in the cave, hardly daring to move. The captain held Scroll in the palm of his hands, stroking her gently and occasionally whispering in her ear.

Late in the day, the wind turned. Now it blew offshore, and no matter how close to land the ships sailed, the balloons pulled out to sea.

It might have been funny if it wasn't for the *Claw* on its way, and the water in the bay so clear and shallow that there was nowhere to hide.

'Go away, stupid Devouts,' whispered Petrel. 'Give up. Go *away*!'

Krill glowered at her. 'How long since you sent that message, bratling? Send it again, and keep sending it.'

She did. She tapped out warning after warning on the telegraph, her fingers slipping in their haste.

But then Fin groaned. 'Listen!'

'Someone is shouting,' said the captain. 'I think it is the people in the baskets. They have seen something!'

And as Petrel watched in horror, the sailing ships turned away from the shore and headed out across the bay. Out across the clear shallow water, where there was nowhere to hide.

NOWHERE
TO HIDE

Sharkey had said that he wouldn't use periscope or aerial until he had to. But now the moment had come. If there was danger ahead, he needed to know about it.

The casings rattled as he cranked them upwards. Water gurgled past the hull. A shadow passed over the water.

Sharkey put his eye to the periscope and turned in a circle. It was one of those times when he wished he had two good eyes. He felt as if there was something creeping up on his blind side, something nasty that he needed to spot before it surprised him—

There was a clatter of sound from the comm behind him. 'A message!' cried rat Lin Lin. '*Danger! Balloons! Devouts!*'

At the same time, Sharkey roared at the top of his voice, 'Hard astern!'

Cuttle threw himself at the switches, and *Claw* shuddered into reverse. The words *Flood the quick dive tank!* were burning on Sharkey's tongue, but he couldn't let them go, not yet, not until they were over the channel again.

He felt as if someone had glued him to the periscope. There were two skimmers coming straight at him, their sails growing bigger by the second. Behind him, Cuttle was coaxing the propeller to greater and greater speeds. The rats were poised beside the dive wheels, ready to throw themselves into action.

'What's happening, Sharkey?' cried Gilly, all formality forgotten.

'They're gaining on us. How far to the channel?'

'Nearly there.'

The propeller rattled louder than Sharkey had ever heard it. 'C'mon, *Claw*,' he shouted to the little submersible. 'Come *on*!'

He was afraid they wouldn't make it, but at last they were over the channel. He whipped the periscope back into its housing and shouted, 'Half-ahead! Flood quick dive tank, twenty degrees down angle!'

The rats threw themselves at the wheels, and Gilly's hands took them down to safety. Except they *weren't* safe, not yet, and they all knew it. The Ghosts wouldn't give up so easily.

As *Claw* rumbled past seaweed and rock faces, Sharkey gnawed his thumbnail, no longer caring who saw him. 'Not deep enough,' he whispered, through gritted teeth. 'Not fast enough.'

But they were already going too fast for such a narrow channel. Any faster and they'd run into one of the rock walls, and then nothing would save them.

Sharkey thought he saw another of those dreadful shadows pass overhead. The hairs on the back of his neck stood up. He could almost *feel* the skimmers gaining on them ...

And then it happened, the thing he'd been dreading ever since *Rampart* was attacked. Something clanged against the hull right above his head, so hard and loud that his ears rang. He yelped with the surprise of it, and so did Rain.

Gilly swore, 'Blood of the ancestors!'

Another clang — and the thing that had hit them exploded.

Claw bucked under their feet, and slewed sideways. Gilly fought the helm, trying to get control. Rain fell off the berth. The rats clung to the dive wheels, their little paws skidding on the deck.

As the reverberations died away, Rain picked herself up and began to sing. '*H-H-H-Hobgoblins tiptoe through the n-n-night—*'

Sharkey wished he could sing with her. He'd never been so afraid, not even in the Up Above. But future adm'rals didn't sing. They didn't yelp either, and he would've taken that dreadful sound back if he could've. He clenched his teeth, and gripped the overhead locker so tightly that his hands cramped.

Dodge? he thought. *But there's nowhere to dodge to, not until we get back to open water.*

Clangggg! Something else hit them. Sharkey waited for the explosion, but it didn't come. *Maybe they don't always work,* he thought. *All the same—*

'Cut running lights and switch to instruments,' he said, trying to stop his voice cracking.

The lights went off, and the water outside turned dark green. 'We need to get deeper,' he said. 'What's under us, Gilly?'

'Only five feet, Sharkey.'

Which meant they were already running so close to the seabed that they risked tearing the submersible open from bow to stern. They couldn't *go* any deeper. They couldn't go faster either. Not with the lights off. Not with those rock walls looming on both sides.

'*And imp and g-g-ghost and evil w-w-wight—*' sang Rain.

Up to this point, the two rats had said nothing. But now Sharkey felt small claws scrabble from the chart table up onto his shoulder.

A rough voice in his ear said, 'We ain't gunna lose 'em like this, shipmate. Water's too clear. Reckon it's time for a bit of clever thinkin'.'

'What's Great Granfer saying, Sharkey?' shouted Cuttle.

A third impact, somewhere near the stern. *Clanggggg!* This one *did* explode – *whoomp!* And despite Gilly's desperate grip on the helm, *Claw* slewed sideways again.

'We've lost steering,' cried Gilly.

'Hard astern!' shouted Sharkey.

Cuttle threw the motors into reverse. The submersible slowed, but not quickly enough.

Sharkey shouted again. 'Grab hold!'

Small claws dug into his shoulder. Cuttle grabbed the nearest pipe, while Gilly still clung to the helm. Rain hung on to the berth, and rat Lin Lin hung on to Rain.

With an ugly crunch, *Claw* rammed the channel wall.

Sharkey's bad shoulder hit the locker. The inside lanterns flickered. The bow bulkhead, right next to the porthole, crumpled inward.

We've been breached, thought Sharkey. *There'll be water pouring in any second!*

But *Claw*, for all her great age, was a strong little vessel. Gradually, as the expected surge of water didn't come, Sharkey realised that although they were battered, they weren't yet holed. The pressure hull had survived the collision.

All the same, we're done for, he thought. *We can't go anywhere, not without steering. All the Ghosts have to do is sit up there and drop their explosives one by one until our hull gives way altogether.*

He couldn't bear it. The thought of the little submersible lying broken on the seabed, like *Rampart*, made his throat hurt. The thought of Cuttle and Gilly dead or captured—

'Didn't you hear me, shipmate?' said a rough voice, and with a jolt Sharkey realised that the rat was still there on his shoulder.

'What?' he said.

'Clever thinkin', shipmate,' said the rat. 'That's what we need now.'

Sharkey shook his head wordlessly. There wasn't a scrap of cleverness left in him. If he'd been a real hero he might've been able to get them out of there. But he wasn't real. He was as fake as rat Lin Lin and rat Cray.

Behind him, Rain was trembling violently. Even Gilly and Cuttle were shaking, which was something Sharkey had never thought he'd see.

'Can you sing a bit more, Rain?' asked Cuttle. 'Sharkey'll c-come up with something, I know he will, but—'

Rain raised her voice. '*But d-do we cower, d-do we hide?*'

Gilly and Cuttle sang along with her. '*Do we l-lock ourselves inside?*'

But the rat adm'ral dug his claws deeper into Sharkey's shoulder, saying, 'Clever, shipmate. That's what we want. Clever.'

'*Or do we hold ourselves with p-pride,*
And chase those g-ghouls away?'

Sharkey felt sick. For all Cuttle's faith in him, he knew he was helpless. And Rain's song was wrong. Sometimes hiding was the only sensible thing to do. He'd hide *Claw* like a shot if he could.

He thought of the crabs that stirred up the sand as the little submersible passed. And the others that dropped a leg if they had to, if it gave them a chance of getting away.

Wish WE could drop a leg, thought Sharkey. *Make the Ghosts think they'd killed us already—*

The impossible idea and the next explosion hit at exactly the same moment. *Clannnnggggg! Whoooooomp!* Poor old *Claw* shuddered like a jellyfish, and Sharkey's mind shuddered with it. He gripped the locker, feeling stunned and frightened and hopeful, all at once. Was it impossible? *Was* it?

There was only one way to find out.

He dragged himself upright. 'Cuttle,' he snapped. 'Drain some oil off the diesel engines into a bucket. And find some bits of – of *stuff* that'll float to the surface. The berth – yes, the berth. Smash it. And take anything else you can think of. Anything we don't need. Rain, you help him. You too, Lin Lin. The more the better.'

The boy, the girl and the rat hurried to do his bidding.

'Gilly, give me power to the little claw,' said Sharkey.

As Gilly threw the switch, Sharkey slid into the retrieval seat and grabbed the lever. On his shoulder, rat Cray was silent.

There was sand beneath them, for which Sharkey blessed his ancestors. *Lots* of sand. As soon as he dug the little claw into it, it swirled against the porthole. Behind him, Rain was banging away at the berth with a hammer.

'More,' he mumbled to himself, and dug the claw into the seabed again and again, until there was sand everywhere, hanging in the water like a shroud.

Sharkey turned to the rat on his shoulder and said, through gritted teeth, 'They won't be able to see us now.'

'Mebbe not, shipmate,' said the rat. 'But sand won't stop bombs.'

As if to prove his words, there was another *clannngggg* and the *whooomp!* that they had come to dread. A terrible grinding sound told Sharkey that part of the outer hull had gone.

'Quick, Cuttle!' he shouted, scanning the bulkhead for leaks. Nothing yet, but it was only a matter of time.

Cuttle dashed for'ard with a bucket half-full of oil. Rain and rat Lin Lin trailed behind him, dragging the remains of the berth, a pile of clothes, the blades of a broken propeller, two plates and an ancient saucepan.

'Cuttle, give me the oil and take the little claw,' snapped Sharkey, jumping up from his seat. 'Keep stirring that sand up. Rain, come with me.'

He climbed the ladder to the double hatch, ignoring the pain in his shoulder. Rain handed the bits of bunk up to him, and the propeller blades and everything else. Sharkey dumped it all above the inside hatch, and rested the bucket in among the clothes.

'More sand,' he cried to Cuttle.

He sealed the inside hatch and climbed down. Then, with everyone watching him expectantly, he waited.

His heart hammered against his ribs. His belly was hollow. If this didn't work they were gone. *Everything* was gone.

Cllllaaaannngggg! Whooooooomp!

Claw rocked sickeningly. Sharkey's ears rang.

'Last bit of sand,' he shouted. Then, 'Gilly, blow the top hatch.'

There was a *whoosh* above their heads, as oil, clothes, plates, saucepan, propeller, the remains of the bunk and a good chunk of their precious air were forced out of the hatch and up to the surface.

'Now quiet!' hissed Sharkey, holding up a warning hand. 'Not a sound!'

It wasn't hard to picture what was happening Up Above. The air would get there first, boiling up in a great bubble. Then the bits of bunk and the propeller and the clothes. And finally the oil, spreading across the surface of the water in a tell-tale slick.

To any Sunker, it'd look like a fatally damaged submersible. If it was Sharkey up there, he'd be expecting bodies any moment. And when they didn't come, he'd assume they were trapped below. Dying. Or already dead.

There was a fierce hope in Gilly's eyes, and in Cuttle's too. But no one said anything.

Clannngggg on *Claw*'s bow.

There was no explosion, which meant it must've been another dud. But still the sound pierced Sharkey's heart. The impossible idea hadn't worked. The one thing he had been able to think of, and it hadn't—

Now it was rat Lin Lin who held up a paw. 'Wait,' she whispered. 'That might just be a test. Or a fare-thee-well.'

So they waited. With every moment that passed, Sharkey was expecting the next explosion, the one that would rip the damaged hull right open and kill them all.

But it didn't come.

And it didn't come.

And it didn't—

He glanced at the chronometer. How long had they been sitting there in silence. Half an hour? More? Night must be falling in the Up Above. Surely if the Ghosts were going to keep bombarding them it would have happened by now?

Except, if it was him up there, he'd hang around for a while, watching. Listening. Even when he thought his prey was dead. Make sure it wasn't a trick.

'Shhhh!' he whispered, putting his finger to his lips. Then he cupped his hand over his ear to make sure everyone knew what he meant. Sound travelled easily through water. They mustn't do anything that would tell the listeners above that they were still alive.

★★★

Rain had no idea how long they sat there, as still as clods of earth. Her fingers hurt from clasping them so tightly. But at last Sharkey yawned and said, in a more-or-less normal voice, 'What's the charge on the batteries, Gilly?'

'Low,' said Gilly, peering at her instruments. She copied his yawn. 'Air's getting bad too, sir.'

Rain stretched her legs cautiously. Her throat felt raw, as if she had been shouting.

'It'll be dark Up Above,' said Sharkey. 'Moon won't've risen yet. I say we go up and take a look. What do you reckon?'

In all the days that Rain had been on the submersible, she had never heard its captain ask anyone else's opinion. Cuttle looked surprised, and so did Gilly, but they nodded agreement.

The rat who called herself Lin Lin pointed her nose at Rain and said, 'You know more about the Devouts than anyone here, girl. What do *you* think?'

A dozen possibilities ran through Rain's head, but the only one that would help Bran was the truth. 'I think they will be gone,' she said. 'They would not know you could trick them like that. I am sure they think they have killed us all.'

Including me.

Sharkey nodded and declared, 'We'll take her up then.'

'Without steering?' asked Rain.

'Don't need steering to go up and down,' said Sharkey with surprising cheerfulness. 'It's just handy if you want to go anywhere else.'

★★★

To Sharkey's relief, the periscope was still working. He did a quick check to make sure that the Ghosts had indeed gone, and nodded to Gilly.

Claw surfaced with what sounded like a shout of relief, though really it was just louder-than-usual gurgles and thumps. Sharkey scrambled up the ladder and forced open the hatches, and fresh air whistled into the cabin like a blessing.

It wasn't enough. He jumped out onto the deck, with the others close behind him.

Even in the dark he could tell how battered *Claw* was. Gone was the sleek outline that made the little submersible so agile underwater. Gone were the stay lines, and the telegraph aerial. The deck plates were sprung and twisted, and part of the outer hull looked as if it had peeled away.

But for a while at least it hardly mattered. The sky was bright with stars and the air was so clean and beautiful that Sharkey felt like weeping.

I'm alive, he thought. *They didn't get us. We're ALL alive.*

Gilly leaned against the conning tower, taking deep breaths. 'Only good thing about the Up Above,' she said. 'They've got decent air.'

'And stars,' said Rain. She pointed to a cluster of bright points low in the sky. 'That is Hope over there.'

'Nay, that's the Lobster,' said Cuttle. 'You can navigate by him.'

'That's no lobster,' said the rat adm'ral, waving a small paw. 'That's Solomon's Eye.'

'No, it is *not*,' said Rain. 'Mama knew all about the stars. That is Hope and the ones just past it are Truth Abandoned.'

'Hope? Truth Abandoned?' said Gilly. 'What sorts of names are those? The truthy ones are the Lobster's Tail, which make up the beginning of the Great Reef. See, there's the rest of it, sprawled to the north.'

'You're both wrong,' said rat Lin Lin. 'What you're calling the Reef—'

Sharkey grinned at Rain. He knew he'd have to start being captain again soon. It was a fair way to shore, but he thought he could swim it, even with his bad shoulder. He'd take a line with him, one end tied to *Claw*, in case the rats' friends couldn't swim. He'd find them and bring them back. Fix the steering and patch the worst of the damage. Check for leaks. Get out of here before sunclimb.

But for now—

For now he just stood there, smiling into the darkness. And breathing. *There are no words for this,* he thought.

And for the next few minutes he gave himself up to letting the world spin in whatever direction it wanted, and not even trying to control it.

'WHO'S YOUR CAPTAIN?'

Petrel was crying. She hadn't cried many times in her short, hard life, but now the tears streamed down her cheeks and she couldn't stop them.

'Coooo,' said Scroll. 'Cooooo.'

None of them had moved since that awful moment when cheering and celebration had broken out on the sailing ships. Even the captain, a mechanical boy made of silver and wire, seemed stricken. Their best chance of getting back to the *Oyster* was gone. Folk who might have been allies were gone. Worst of all, Mister Smoke and Missus Slink were gone.

Petrel felt as if all the blood had drained from her body, leaving nothing but a shadow. Except shadows didn't grieve, not like this.

'They m-mightn't be dead,' she said, though she knew they were.

No one answered her. They just sat, staring at their hands and feeling sick.

Out in the bay, something splashed. 'Fish,' said Krill sadly. 'We should try and rig some sort of net.'

Still no one moved.

The fish jumped again, closer.

And closer.

A pulse hammered in Petrel's throat. She stood up, her face wet, her hand pressed over her mouth.

A boy walked out of the water.

★★★

There were three of them, stumbling over the rocks towards Sharkey. Behind them limped a fourth, a huge man from the look of him, though it was too dark for details.

Sharkey stopped, with the sea swirling around his ankles and that odd feeling of contentment lingering in his veins. 'Are you—'

'*Claw*?' asked one of the dark figures. A girl.

'Aye,' said Sharkey.

The girl took another step towards him, her voice fierce with hope. 'Mister Smoke and Missus Slink – are they all right?'

'Who?'

'The rats!'

'Oh. Aye,' said Sharkey. He was already walking up over the rocks with the line in his hand, but he said over his shoulder, 'Aye, they're alive and well.'

The girl laughed, a ragged, hiccupy sound. 'Alive and well, Fin!' she said to one of her companions. 'Alive and well!'

Sharkey found a good solid rock and knotted the line around it. The other end ran out across the water, all the way to *Claw*. 'Can you swim?' he asked, when he'd rejoined the four dark figures.

'No,' said Fin.

'Not likely,' said the girl.

'*None* of you?'

'None of us,' said the girl. 'Unless— Cap'n?'

Instantly, Sharkey's feeling of contentment vanished. Another captain? Another *captain*, coming onto his boat? He bristled at the outline of the big man. 'You're in charge of this crew?'

'No, I am,' said the fourth figure, a child no bigger than Poddy, with a hood concealing his face and some sort of bird on his arm.

Sharkey snorted under his breath. 'Well, don't expect to be captain of anything while you're on *Claw*. You'll do what you're told on my boat. You all will, or you're not coming aboard.'

There was a moment of silence, then the girl said, 'We're good at doing what we're told, ain't we, Krill?'

'Hmph,' said the big man, which might have meant anything. 'About this bargain, lad—'

'Don't try to back out of it,' said Sharkey quickly. 'We're heading north as soon as we can. We get my people out first, *then* I'll take you to your ship.'

That silenced them again. Sharkey nodded towards the line. 'Use that to drag yourselves out to the boat. But take your outer clothes off first, or there'll be nothing dry for you to change into.'

The girl hesitated. 'You waterproof, Cap'n?'

'I believe so,' said the small figure, 'though I have never tested it.' He turned to Sharkey. 'Do you know any songs?'

Sharkey didn't bother answering. *They're mad,* he thought. *Can't see how they'll be any help getting Poddy and the others back. But there's no one else.*

The strangers took off their outer clothes and put them in a pile next to him, along with a bag. Sharkey thought there was something odd about the little captain's face, though it was too dark to see properly.

I'll get a good look at him soon, he thought, as the strangers slid into the water one by one, clinging to the line for dear life. The bird fluttered over their heads.

Sharkey took a smaller line from around his waist and tied the clothes in a ball, with the bag in the middle. When he heard a distant 'Hoy!' from Gilly, he set about loosening the line that he had fastened around the rock.

It took much longer than he'd expected. The knot had jammed, probably because of the big man's weight, and although he dug at it until his fingers were bruised, it wouldn't budge.

Rope was too valuable to lose, so Sharkey didn't want to cut it. But there were urgent repairs to be done, and he had already wasted too much time. So in the end, he took out his knife and sliced through the knot.

He swam back out on his side, holding the clothes above the water with one hand. By the time he saw the battered bulk of the submersible, half a dozen yards away, his shoulder felt as if it was on fire.

But he wasn't going to show any sort of weakness, not with another captain on board. He passed the bundle up to Gilly, and hauled himself onto the deck, gritting his teeth against the pain.

'Are you all right, Sharkey?' whispered Gilly, as he dried himself and put his clothes on. 'You were gone so long! I was just getting ready to come after you.'

Sharkey grunted. He was in no mood to be fussed over.

168

'Did you see the bird?' continued Gilly. 'And the little cap'n? He asked me about songs – isn't that odd? Did you see that man Krill? He could hardly fit through the hatch. How're we going to feed someone that big?'

'We're not,' muttered Sharkey. 'He can find his own food, they all can. The bargain's for rescuing our people in exchange for taking 'em to their ship. No one said anything about feeding 'em.'

'But that wouldn't be fair, and besides—'

'Are you arguing with me?'

'Nay, but Krill's alr—'

'Who's your cap'n?' Sharkey glowered at her.

'But he's—'

'*Who's* your cap'n, Gilly?'

He thought she pulled a face, but it was too dark to see, which was just as well for her.

'You are,' she mumbled.

'Sir.'

'You are. Sir.'

'Glad to hear it.'

Gilly didn't answer, but Sharkey knew he'd made his point.

The rats started this, he thought, as he pulled on his eye patch and made his way down the ladder. *The middies never argued with me before the rats came. And it'll be worse now with so many strangers on board. I'll have to stamp on it before it gets out of hand.*

He stepped off the ladder, already issuing instructions. 'Gilly's bringing your clothes down. Get 'em on and stow yourselves out of the way. And don't touch anything. Cuttle, bring me the big wrench, then you and Gilly start work on the hull. I'm going to see what's wrong with the steer—'

His voice dried in his throat. Cuttle was standing by the chart table with the little captain . . . whose face was made of *silver*.

Cuttle looked up at Sharkey and beamed. 'He's only small, but he knows all about navigation, sir. He says our chart's wrong in a few places, so we've been changing it. And then he's going to help us fix the hull in exchange for us telling him all the songs we know. And Fin and Rain and Petrel are making plans to get everyone out—'

'And Krill is cooking supper,' added Rain. 'Though he said he has never had to do it in his long underwear before.'

Which was when Sharkey realised he'd been smelling fried fish ever since he came on board.

'I tried to tell you, sir,' said Gilly from somewhere above him. 'But you wouldn't listen.'

★★★

Sharkey had been hoping that the steering wouldn't be too difficult to fix. A problem with the linkages, maybe. But when he slid back over the side of the little submersible, into the cold water, he found that the rudder shaft was bent and could not be straightened.

Two-handed, replacing it would've been a hard job. One-handed and furious, it was wretched. But Sharkey wouldn't give up. He ducked below the surface to heave and tug and wrench at the stubborn metal, came up for a breath then ducked down again, his teeth chattering, his shoulder aching.

Somewhere above him, the little silver captain was working alongside Gilly and Cuttle, hammering deck plates into place, patching the outer hull and checking the ballast tanks. Last time Sharkey had looked, Krill and Petrel were helping them, and so were the rats. Sharkey didn't like all these strangers touching his boat, but he didn't have much choice, not if he wanted *Claw* back in working order before sunclimb.

By the time the new shaft was in place, he was exhausted, and so cold that he could no longer feel his fingers or toes. The sound of muffled hammering had stopped a quarter of an hour ago.

He dragged himself up onto the deck, where Gilly was waiting for him. 'Well?' he croaked.

'It's not bad, sir,' said Gilly. 'That odd little cap'n of theirs knows what he's about. I reckon we're watertight, but we won't know for sure till we try it out.'

With a great effort, Sharkey nodded. Then he pulled his clothes on and staggered below, shivering so badly that he could hardly speak.

'Breakfast, bratling?' asked Krill, looming out of the tiny galley and banging his head on a pipe. He rubbed his skull ruefully, as if the same thing had happened several times before, and said, 'Rain and Fin caught a dozen pickle-heads while we were working. Never tried 'em myself, but Cuttle says they're tasty. Reckon you could do with a feed.'

Sharkey ignored him. 'You've got the conn,' he croaked to Gilly, who'd come down the ladder behind him. 'Take her down to periscope depth and watch the pressure. If it stays steady, head down the channel to deep water. Then set a course for ten miles or so south of the Citadel. And since *he* knows so much about everything—' he jerked his head at the child with the silver face '—let him find us a nice safe bay where we can go ashore without being seen.'

Then he turned his back on everyone, curled up under the chart table and was asleep before the dive siren sounded.

★★★

Petrel's belly was full of pickle-heads, she had a rat on each knee, and her back rested against good, honest metal. It was the closest she'd come to being happy for days. Even *Claw*'s crew seemed familiar, in a way that the Devouts and the starving villagers had not.

But deep inside, that lost feeling lingered. *I won't be right till I'm back on the* Oyster, she thought. *I wish I was there now.*

Beside her, Krill was trying unsuccessfully to make himself smaller so he didn't take up so much of the tiny cabin. Cuttle and the captain shared a stool, with Scroll on the captain's arm. Gilly had the helm, and Fin and Rain were leaning against the dive wheels, talking quietly to each other.

Their hair's almost the same colour, thought Petrel. *I wonder if she knows his mam. I wonder if that's what they're talking about.*

Claw had reached deep water twenty minutes ago, and the hiss of it on the double hull was like a lullaby.

'Must be time for a story,' boomed Krill.

'Or a Song,' said the silver boy in a quiet voice. 'We must not give up on our purpose.'

Petrel didn't say anything, but she wished the captain *would* give up. It seemed to her that he was pulling one way, determined to find his song, and she and Fin and Krill were pulling the other, trying to get back to the

Oyster. And until they all pulled the same way, nothing good would happen.

She wriggled sideways until she was leaning against Krill's comforting bulk. She knew that the Head Cook missed the old icebreaker as much as she did. What's more, he must be half-mad with worry about Squid. But somehow he was still himself. He wasn't lost, not like Petrel.

'Stories? Songs?' Cuttle looked uncertainly at the sleeping Sharkey. 'I'm not sure—'

'It's either that or dancing,' said Krill, 'and I don't reckon anyone except me'd survive the latter, not in a space like this.'

Rain laughed, and Krill winked at her. 'You volunteering to go first, bratling?'

'Me?' squeaked Rain. 'No!'

Fin leaned forward. 'Rain says the Devouts returned from the ice a month ago. And Brother Thrawn is still alive, I did not kill him after all! It was he who ordered the use of the balloons, and the throwers and bombs. That is right, is it not, Rain?'

The girl's laughter stopped abruptly. 'Um—Yes.'

'If I had not seen them with my own eyes,' continued Fin, 'I would not have believed it. Brother Thrawn was always strictly against such things, even though they are not quite machines.'

'He— He was changed by his injury,' said Rain. 'But—'

'That's not the sort of story I meant,' said Krill, interrupting. 'I want something with a happy ending. How about you, Mister Smoke? You got a story for us?'

'Why do you call him Mister Smoke?' asked Cuttle. 'He's the adm'ral.'

Krill raised his bushy eyebrows. 'You been promoted, Mister Smoke?'

The rat ignored him. 'When you've lived as long as I 'ave, shipmate,' he said to Cuttle, 'you accumulate names like barnacles on a ship's bottom. But they don't mean much. It's what's inside that counts.'

Then, before anyone could ask another question, he leapt down from Petrel's knee, straightened his whiskers, struck a dramatic pose and cried, 'I'll tell you a story, shipmates. A story about a place so cold that it can freeze the blood in your veins. So cold that your breath turns to ice as it comes out your mouth. I'll tell you the story of the *Oyster* . . .'

But Petrel was no longer listening. All she could hear were five words, ringing like a ship's bell in her ears. Like a message banged on the pipes, so loud that she couldn't ignore it.

It's what's inside that counts.

Ever since the shore party had walked towards that first village, Petrel had felt lost – as if the only time she could be happy, the only time she could be *herself*, was on the *Oyster*.

But now she wondered if that was right.

For the first time in weeks she took herself back to that life-changing moment on the icebreaker's bridge, immediately after the battle with the Devouts, when she had finally had enough of being Nothing Girl. She remembered the heat inside her. The noise that wouldn't be silenced. The words that had burst out of her.

I'm not nothing. Never was, never will be. I'm Petrel. Quill's daughter. Seal's daughter too!

Surely those words still counted. Surely it was all still there inside her. The heat, the noise – and the *Oyster*, if she could only find it.

She closed her eyes and imagined herself walking those familiar passageways. Imagined it so hard and fierce that before long she could almost see the rivets and bolts and patches of rust, and feel the clank of the engines beneath her feet.

It's all there, she thought. *It's inside me. I'm not nothing. Never was, never will be, no matter WHERE I am.*

It didn't entirely fix things, but it made her feel more solid, as if she could think about what was coming with a clear head and a clear heart.

And so, as Mister Smoke's story wound around her, she set herself to working out how she could get a message to Squid and Dolph.

***

Sharkey lay under the chart table with his eye closed, pretending he was still asleep. He didn't believe half of what he heard. All that stuff about solid ocean and freezing blood was as false as his own stories.

They're just trying to impress the middies, he told himself.

He heard Cuttle laugh, and winced. None of his crew had laughed like that since *Rampart* was lost. It should've made him happy to hear it, but it didn't. It made him feel left out, and at odds with everyone.

He tried to summon the fury that had got him through the rudder change. *I should get up,* he thought. *Remind 'em who's cap'n of this boat.*

Except then the laughter would stop.

So in the end he didn't move. He just lay there, feeling useless, and wondering who he was if he wasn't the most important person on board.

I AM NOT LIKE THE HUNGRY GHOSTS!

When Rain was little, her mama used to sing a song about persistence. Rain thought she had forgotten the words years ago, but now a bit of the chorus came back to her.

. . . and wa-ter

Can wear away a stone.

Petrel was the water. She had been arguing with Sharkey ever since he got up, turning things this way and that, trying to convince him to send someone back to the *Oyster*.

'So when we get to this bay,' she said, 'the one the cap'n's picked out, Gilly and Cuttle ain't going ashore with us, right?'

Since Poddy had been captured, Sharkey had started changing for the better. Unfortunately, having these new people on board seemed to have changed him back again. He heaved one of those long-suffering sighs that made it sound as if he was the only person in the world with any sense, and said, 'I *told* you. They're going to sit out to sea, where they won't be caught.' He nodded at the box in Petrel's hands. 'And bring *Claw* back in when we send 'em a comm.'

Rain breathed in the stink of the little submersible, wondering if she was brave enough for what was coming.

I have to be, she thought, and she glanced sideways at Petrel. Mister Smoke's story last night had ended with a description of the Devouts' bloodthirsty attack on the *Oyster*, and how it was mostly Petrel who had foiled it.

I have to be as brave as she is, thought Rain.

'They're gunna sit out there doing nothing?' asked the girl she admired.

'There's still repair work to do,' replied Sharkey.

Petrel screwed up her face, as if she was thinking. 'Tell you what, Cap'n Sharkey, how about one of us stays with 'em?'

Sharkey began to speak, but Petrel cut him off. 'You see, we've worked out a good solid plan for rescuing your friends, and I reckon it'll do the trick, especially if we can get the masks right, and if Mister Smoke can smuggle 'em into the re-education camp. But no one's said anything about what we do with all these Sunkers *after* we rescue 'em.'

'We can—'

'Now I'm sure you've thought about it long and hard, and you've prob'ly got something clever up your sleeve that you ain't told us about yet—'

Sharkey reddened.

He has nothing up his sleeve, thought Rain. *He has not thought any further than getting Poddy away from the whippings. But Petrel is right. He cannot take anyone else onto* Claw. *Even now there is hardly room to breathe.*

She squeezed closer to the chart table, pretending to study one of the maps. Cuttle was at the helm, and Fin and Krill were crammed up next to the batteries. Behind them, the silver boy was asking Gilly about Sunker songs. But each time she sang a line or two, he shook his head and said, 'No, that is not it. Try another one, if you please.'

'Rain's the one you should talk to,' said Gilly. 'She knows lots of songs.'

Petrel's voice rose above all the others. '—what you *really* need is a ship. A big one that'll take all your people and get 'em away nice and quick. And once that's done, you can think about getting *Rampart* afloat again.'

'We don't need—'

'And the good thing is, we've *got* a ship – or at least we will have, once we get it back from Albie. And all Cuttle and Gilly'd have to do is take a couple of us to where it's anchored. They could take Krill and the cap'n maybe—'

This time it was Sharkey who broke in. 'I need Krill.'

'His ankle—'

'His ankle's nearly better.'

'Perhaps you could sprain it again,' Fin murmured to Krill. 'It would be worth it, if it would get us back to the *Oyster.*'

Rain did not know quite what to make of Fin. The demon-hunting expedition had left the Citadel before she and Bran had come to live there, so all she knew of the boy was the stories she had overheard. At first, he had been famous for his courage, for being the Initiate who would risk his life on the ice. Then, when the battered expedition had returned, he became known as the worst of all possible traitors.

Rain wished he would not quiz her about what was happening in the Citadel – she was afraid he might stumble upon the truth.

'I need your cap'n too,' said Sharkey, ignoring everyone but Petrel. 'I need *all* of you. That was the bargain, and you agreed to it.'

'How about a rat? One little rat? That wouldn't make much difference to you, but it'd help us a *lot*. Missus Slink could run up the *Oyster*'s anchor chain, creep onto the bridge and tell Dolph and Squid that we're alive. She could fix the telegraph, too, so we could talk to 'em—'

'Nay!' said Sharkey, very loudly, as if that was the last word on the matter.

Petrel looked hard at him, and he reddened again. Neither of them said anything for more than a minute.

Someone tapped Rain's arm, and she turned, startled. It was the silver boy. 'According to Gilly, you know many songs,' he said. 'Will you sing them to me?'

Rain knew she should be afraid of him. After all, this was the demon the Devouts feared and hated. But she had seen how easy Petrel and Fin were with him, and besides, there was something about him that reminded her of Bran. 'What sort of songs?' she asked.

'Every sort. I will not know what I am looking for until I hear it.'

Behind them, Petrel was speaking again, her voice no more than a murmur. 'I know you're top high brass of this vessel, Cap'n Sharkey, and everyone does what you tell 'em. And I know that's the Sunker way. But we do things differently on the *Oyster*. We try to bend a bit if we can, to help our friends.'

Rain peeped over her shoulder, to see how Sharkey would respond.

But Petrel was still talking. 'Course you don't *have* to bend. Cos you're right, we *did* agree to the bargain. But I gotta tell you that you're reminding me more and more of Fin's stories about the Devouts. They're the ones you call Hungry Ghosts. *They* don't bend either.'

And with that, she walked away, though she couldn't go far, not on *Claw*.

Sharkey's face went from red to white. He raised his hand, as if to summon her back, then lowered it again.

As brave as Petrel, AND as clever, thought Rain. Then she turned to the silver boy and said, 'Yes, I will sing to you.'

★★★

Sharkey raised the hammer and brought it down with a whack on the sheet of tin. *I am nothing like the Hungry Ghosts.*

He raised it again. Brought it down harder. *I'm NOTHING like the Ghosts. She doesn't know what she's talking about. None of 'em do. I shouldn't take any notice.*

But still Petrel's quiet words clung to him like a suckerfish.

He tightened his grip on the hammer. Beside him, at the bench of the minuscule workshop, the silver child was tapping at a second sheet, persuading it into the right shape for the masks Petrel had suggested. The pigeon, which seemed to follow him everywhere, was perched on the lathe, its head turning back and forth with every swing of the hammer.

At the far end of the bench, Rain was singing.

'Would you walk into the jaws of a tiger?

Would you pat a hungry bear on the snout—'

The silver child interrupted her, just as he had done with the last twenty songs. 'That is not it. Another one, please.'

Sharkey gritted his teeth. 'I am nothing.' *Whack.* 'Like.' *Whack.* 'The Hungry Ghosts!' *Whack.*

He didn't realise he'd spoken aloud until the silver child looked up and said, 'Of course you are not. You love machines and the Devouts hate them. You are pale from lack of sunlight, whereas their skin has a little colour, like Rain's.'

The pigeon cooed agreement.

'It's more than that!' said Sharkey.

The silver child regarded him thoughtfully. 'They are not kind to their horses, but I have not seen you with a horse, so I cannot make a comparison.' And he went back to his task, shaping the tin masks and placing them in the sealskin bag that held the comm, while Rain sang to him.

Sharkey was speechless. He told himself that he should be angry, but somehow the anger would not come. Instead, his mind wavered. Petrel was one of the most annoying people he'd ever known, and yet there was something about her—

'*I went wandering,*' sang Rain,

'*Over the hills so bright—*'

'No,' said the captain. 'Another one, please.'

Sharkey put down his hammer and said abruptly, 'The rat with the green ribbon. Lin Lin, Missus Slink, whatever she calls herself. Could she ride one of our turtles? The mechanical ones? You've seen 'em, haven't you?'

'What is their range?' asked the silver child.

'Several hundred miles if the sea's calm. But their direction-finders won't work over that distance.'

'She could steer by the stars.'

'Right,' said Sharkey. And he went out to issue new orders.

★★★

The following night, *Claw* sidled into a deepwater bay, nine and a half miles sou'-west of the Citadel.

The weather was clear, the moon was rising, and Missus Slink was long gone, riding her mechanical turtle across the waves towards the last known position of the *Oyster*.

One by one, everyone except Gilly and Cuttle climbed the ladder to the deck, and jumped across the gap onto a disused stone pier. Then, as the little submersible slid away, with orders to stand well out to sea until summoned, they set their course nor'-nor'-east.

This is the third time I've been on terra, thought Sharkey. *There's nothing to be afraid of . . . except for the Hungry Ghosts.*

'They are not ghosts,' murmured Fin in his ear.

'What?' Sharkey turned to stare at the other boy.

'You keep muttering about ghosts, and that is wrong. They are the Devouts. They are as human as you and me. You need to know that if you wish to fight them.'

Sharkey was about to laugh out loud at the notion, when he realised that Fin was right. After all, there was no denying that Rain was human, though Sharkey wasn't sure when he had started to see her that way. And the men who had brought Adm'ral Deeps to the rendezvous had looked human enough. Which meant that all the old stories were wrong.

'How do you know about 'em?' he asked Fin.

'I used to be one of them.'

Sharkey had half realised it, from the conversations and stories he'd overheard. But hearing it said so plainly was a different thing altogether. 'No—'

'They sent me south to destroy the *Oyster* and its captain. But I met Petrel – and I changed.' A smile transformed Fin's rather serious face. 'She has that effect on people.'

That was too much for Sharkey. 'Not on me, she doesn't,' he said. And he sped up until he was right at the front of the little group, like a proper captain, with no one and nothing to distract him except his own thoughts.

They had been walking for a bit more than two hours when the silver child stopped. The road they'd been following was potholed and rutted, with ditches on either side. Now, enormous piles of stone loomed out of the darkness like silent messengers from three hundred years ago.

'That was the university,' said the silver child. 'That is where the man who made me, Serran Coe, had his laboratory.'

Sharkey tried to picture it, and couldn't. Krill growled, 'The world's changed since you saw it last, Cap'n, and not for the better.'

There was no sign of Hungry Ghosts in the ruined university, but a little way past it was a clump of houses – at least that's what Rain told Sharkey they were. He couldn't imagine living inside such poor-looking things. They just sat motionless on the side of the road, tiny boxes of mud and straw with square portholes.

'And not a fish to be seen,' he whispered to Rain as they crept past. 'What a miserable life!'

Rain's eyes crinkled at the corners. They walked together for another hour, occasionally whispering to each other about the things they saw, which helped Sharkey forget his fears.

'What happened to your songs?' he asked at one point. 'The ones you were singing for the little captain? Did he find what he was looking for?'

'No,' said Rain. 'I sang everything I could remember, but—' She stopped, jerking to a halt. 'There,' she breathed. 'Can you see it?'

'See what?' Sharkey peered into the darkness, his heart thumping like a badly tuned engine. Ahead of him, pretty much due north, the land rose up in a sort of seamount.

'It is the Citadel,' said Fin, coming up behind them. Like Sharkey, he sounded as if he'd rather be somewhere else.

Petrel joined them, shifting the bag that held the comm and the masks from one hand to the other. 'That whole hill?'

'Nah,' said Mister Smoke, teetering on her shoulder. 'Citadel's just the bit at the top. The rest of it's a rubbishy sort of town called Tower of Strength. Used to be a nice little city—'

'Three hundred years ago it was called Gouty Head,' said the silver child.

'That's right,' said the rat. 'But it looks like the Devouts tore down anythin' that'd been built with machines, and remade it. It's all rammed earth and misery these days, 'cept for the Citadel, which is made of hand-cut marble and self-righteousness.'

'The Citadel is where B-Brother Thrawn lives,' whispered Rain.

There was no crinkle at the corner of her eyes now, and the way she said 'B-Brother Thrawn', each time with that fearful hesitation, was starting to worry Sharkey. It reminded him of the time a Massy shark had swum right up to one of *Claw*'s portholes and looked in.

It'd been bigger than the submersible, with monstrous jaws and an eye like stone, and Gilly and Cuttle had had nightmares for weeks afterwards. Sharkey too, though he'd never admitted it.

Brother Thrawn sounded a bit like that Massy shark. Cruel by nature. Too big to fight. Made you want to crawl under a rock until he went away.

But he's human, according to Fin, Sharkey told himself. *And if he's human, he can be fooled.*

'Come on,' muttered Krill. 'Let's get to the quarry and find somewhere to hide for the day.'

The hill grew bigger as they approached it, until at last it squatted above them like a toadfish waiting for its prey. Moonlight touched the town's earthen walls, and Sharkey shuddered and looked away. Scroll cooed softly into the darkness.

'There is the Devouts' dovecot,' whispered Fin, pointing to a shape set well back from the road. 'The goats are next to it, and horses next to the goats – that is, if they have not changed things.'

Sharkey turned to Rain, trusting she wouldn't mock him for his ignorance. 'Goats?'

'Um— a bit like horses, only smaller. And trickier.' Rain smiled anxiously. 'Bran likes them.'

'Where's the re-education camp?'

'It is further up the road. About a mile beyond the quarry.'

They passed the mouth of the quarry and climbed its northern edge, with Mister Smoke issuing directions. 'Straight ahead, shipmates. Now turn the wheel to starboard – no, you've overcorrected. Port half a degree and up the rise. That's it, hold that bearing.'

The ground was rough, and covered in dense prickly bushes that came up to Sharkey's chin and made it hard going, despite the moonlight. He put one foot in front of the other, wondering if he was about to tumble off the edge or get grabbed by something he couldn't see.

'Starboard twelve degrees,' said Mister Smoke. 'Past that outcrop. Now swing the wheel half a turn – and drop anchor.'

Sharkey found himself in a narrow clearing with trees and bushes on one side and the rim of the quarry on the other. He sank to his knees, with Rain beside him. Behind them, Krill sat down with a hiss of relief.

The silver child said, 'Is your ankle hurting? Would you like me to bind it again?'

'No, Cap'n, it'll be all right,' said Krill. 'I just need to sit for a bit.'

Above their heads, Scroll flew in a wide circle, then settled onto a tree branch and tucked her head under her wing. Petrel put the sealskin bag down, slid forward to the edge of the cliff and peered over. After a while she crept back and said, 'Fin, what are those big posts for, in the middle of the quarry?'

'They are whipping posts,' said Fin quietly.

'*Whipping* posts?'

'For prisoners who stop work without permission.'

Krill, Petrel and Sharkey stared at him. Rain said, 'I told you.'

The silver child shook his head. 'They should not whip people. It is not right.'

'Of course it is not,' said Fin. 'But—' He hunched his shoulders, as if there were things he didn't want to remember. 'But when you are in the middle of it, you somehow persuade yourself that it *is* right. That it is the best thing to do.'

'That is why they take children so young,' said Rain. 'So they can twist their thinking.'

Petrel sighed. 'What time do they come to work?'

'An hour after sunrise,' said Fin.

'Well, I'm gunna sleep till then,' said Petrel. 'Mister Smoke, will you wake me up when it's time?'

'I will, shipmate. I'll stand guard, too, though I doubt if anyone but us'll set their course in this direction.'

Like Petrel, Sharkey was used to sleeping when and where he could. But tonight he was too restless. He lay there in the darkness, thinking about friendship, the sort that Petrel and Fin had. *He* had never had a friendship like that. He'd been respected and obeyed, but that was all based on a lie. Petrel and Fin wouldn't lie to each other, he was sure of it.

He wondered if he was changing, like Fin had said. He wondered if he and Rain were friends.

Maybe . . .

Beside him, Rain was singing quietly.

'*How tall the tree*
The first to fall,
How wise to flee—'

She was interrupted by a flurry of movement from the silver child. 'You did not sing me *that* song,' he said, his eyes fixed on Rain's face.

'I only just remembered it,' said Rain. 'It is from a circus that came to our village when I was seven. I have not sung it for years.'

'A circus?'

'There was a girl called Grim who could fold herself into a tiny box and slow down her heart until we all thought she was dead, and a blind boy who could hear the world breathing, and fortune-telling ducks, and that song, which the girl sang at the end.'

'Will you sing it again?' asked the silver child. 'Mister Smoke, come and listen.'

The rat joined them, and Rain began to sing in a sweet, true voice.

'*How tall the tree*
The first to fall,
How wise to flee,
The worst of all.
But hear the song

The singer gives,
The trunk is gone,
The root still lives.'

By the time she finished, Petrel, Fin and Krill were there too, crouched in front of her with expressions of astonishment on their faces.

'Is that *it*?' asked Krill.

'It is,' said the silver child.

Krill shook his head. 'What are the chances you'd stumble on the Song and the Singer, Cap'n, just like that?'

'Rain is *a* singer,' said the silver child, 'not *the* Singer. She is not the one I am looking for.'

'Many people know that song,' said Rain, 'not just me. They sing it secretly, where the Devouts will not hear them – or at least they used to. There was another verse, about the sun and the moon, but I cannot remember it.'

'I have never heard it,' said Fin. 'What does it mean?'

'It is about hope,' replied Rain. 'Terrible things happen, but underneath there is still hope.'

Petrel's eyebrows pinched together. 'I s'pose I should be glad. But to be honest, Cap'n, it's a bit of a let-down. All that fuss for a song about hope? I thought it was gunna be something big and important. A song with teeth. Something we could use against the Devouts.'

'The Song is not about hope,' said the silver child. 'It is about something else, but I do not know what, not yet. It is like a code, and I need more information before I can solve it. I must find the Singer.'

Krill nodded slowly. 'Fair enough, Cap'n. But first we've gotta free the Sunkers and get the *Oyster* back from Albie. What d'you say to that?'

'I agree,' said the silver child. 'If the Sunkers are free and the *Oyster* is ours, we will have more resources to search for the Singer.'

'Good,' said Krill. He turned to the children. 'It's only a couple of hours till dawn, bratlings, but I suggest we all try and get some sleep.'

Sharkey lay down again, with his head on his arm. Rain sang the song quietly once more, then she lay down too, with her back to Sharkey.

I like her, he thought. *She's braver than she thinks.*

And he closed his eyes and didn't move until Mister Smoke tapped him on the shoulder, whispering, 'Rise and shine, shipmate. Keep your head low and your voice quiet. They're on their way, comin' down the road from the camp.'

HOPE . . . AND DESPAIR

Dolph hadn't had so much as a sip of water for two days. None of them had. And that was a serious problem.

When the food ran out, five days ago, Squid had crossed her arms and said, 'We're all used to going hungry. An empty belly won't hurt us, not for a while.'

But water was a different matter. Even in the leanest winters down south, when shipfolk had died by the dozens, there'd been plenty of water.

To make it worse, for the last few days there'd been a constant rattling in the ship's pipes – not proper messages, just nonsense to stop them communicating with the rest of the crew. Dolph *thought* that a few of the Cooks were still holding out, and maybe one other lot of Officers, but she couldn't be sure.

And now Skua had taken to mocking them from the other side of the barricade. 'Water, sweet water,' he shouted, every few hours. 'All you can drink! What, you don't want any? Then I'll have to drink it all myself.' He made loud glugging sounds. 'Ooooh, that is *so* good.'

Dolph and Squid stood firm. But for Minke and her friends, Skua's mockery was the last straw. Hard-faced and dry-tongued, they advanced on the two young women.

'Move aside,' said Minke, over the rattling of the pipes. 'We're taking the barricade down.'

'No,' said Dolph, though it hurt her throat to speak.

'Krill's not coming back,' said Minke. 'He's dead.'

'I don't believe it,' said Squid.

'The barricade stays,' said Dolph, with as much authority as she could muster.

'You can't keep us here,' said Minke.

Dolph shrugged. 'If you want to go, then go. But Squid and I ain't joining Albie, not for anything.'

At that, Minke and her friends backed off, whispering among themselves. But then they came forward again, their faces harder than ever.

'You two can stay here and die,' said Minke, 'but we're going. Let us through.'

Dolph and Squid looked at each other – and nodded.

They had to take part of the barricade down to let the others out. They worked quickly and silently, hoping that Albie and Skua were off somewhere else, bullying folk, and wouldn't take this moment to launch an attack.

They had just removed one of the largest bits of driftwood, which had been braced hard up against the base of the bulkhead, when Dolph thought she heard a scraping sound, like something being dragged.

She held up her hand. 'Wait.' And despite everything, there was still enough of Orca in her to make Minke hesitate.

Next to Dolph's foot, right where the driftwood had been jammed in place, a screw turned. A patch of bulkhead was lifted out of the way by small paws. Dolph thought she saw the flash of a tiny screwdriver, then that disappeared and Missus Slink came into sight, with a sealskin harness around her chest and a large water flask dragging behind her.

If Albie had attacked at that moment, no one would have been capable of stopping him. They couldn't move. They couldn't speak. They just stood there, open-mouthed and staring.

'And about time, too,' said Missus Slink, stepping crossly out of the harness. 'I've been banging out messages to you for hours, but couldn't make myself heard over that stupid rattling.' She peered up at their stunned faces, then pointed to the water flask. 'Well? I thought you were thirsty.'

★★★

Sharkey almost didn't recognise the Sunkers. They stumbled into the quarry like sleepwalkers, a hundred or so of them, their faces as grey as the rags they wore. The babies were crying. The middies and the old salts looked as if they didn't have a hope in the world.

'What's the *matter* with 'em?' whispered Sharkey.

'Don't reckon they're getting enough to eat, poor things,' replied Petrel. 'They look worse than shipfolk after a long, hard winter.'

'Nay.' Sharkey shook his head. 'Sunkers don't despair just cos they're hungry. Sunkers are as tough as sharkskin, as strong as iron. They never give up—'

Fin interrupted him. 'They will have been told about the attack on *Claw*. The guards like to gloat over such things. They probably believe that you and Cuttle and Gilly are dead.'

Sharkey must have made a noise of some sort, because Rain touched his shoulder. 'Do not worry. We will get them out.'

But that wasn't enough for Sharkey. He stared down into the quarry with a sick feeling in his belly. It was a mixture of anger and helplessness, and when he spotted Poddy, looking as grey and beaten as the rest of the Sunkers, it grew even worse.

He hated feeling helpless. He wanted to *do* something, like – like stand up, right there and then, and shout, 'I'm here, Pod! I'm alive, and so're Gilly and Cuttle! And *Claw*'s just a couple of hours away, a bit battered but still watertight. Don't despair! *Don't despair!*'

He didn't do it, of course. There was a score of Ghosts below, most of them with cudgels. *Not Ghosts. Devouts,* he reminded himself. *Humans.*

There were beasts down there too, as big as turtles – nay, bigger. More like small dolphins, only with four legs and wicked teeth.

'Dogs,' whispered Rain, beside him. 'Vicious dogs.'

Sharkey lay on the rim of the quarry, watching the dogs and the Devouts, seeing where they walked and what they did and who they took notice of. After a few minutes, he whispered, 'Mister Smoke, you see Poddy down there? Could you sneak close to her and tell her we're all alive still, and no serious damage to *Claw*?'

'I'm not sure that's wise, lad,' said Krill.

Sharkey suspected that the big man was right. But he still had that desperate need to *do* something, so he ignored his misgivings and said to the rat, 'Tell Poddy we're here to get 'em out.'

'Aye, shipmate,' said Mister Smoke, and he dashed away.

In the sky above the Citadel, an enormous flock of pigeons wheeled and turned in silence. But down in the quarry, the noise was rising. The stronger prisoners used saws and chisels to cut blocks out of the quarry wall. The middies and the weaker adults gathered smaller bits of stone and hammered them to chips. Before long everyone was so covered in rock dust that Sharkey struggled to recognise them.

Still, he managed to pick out Poddy's parents, and Cuttle's and Gilly's, and all his aunts and uncles and cousins. With a flood of relief, he realised that almost everyone had survived. The feeling of helplessness lessened.

Can't wait to see Gilly's face, he told himself, *and Cuttle's too, when they find out their ma and fa are alive.*

He heard a gasp from Rain. 'There is Bran! Over there!'

Rain's brother stood beside one of the Gho—, beside one of the Devouts, wearing brown robes that were too big for him. His shoulders were hunched and his feet scuffed the dirt. As Sharkey watched, the Devout leaned over and said something, and Bran immediately stood up straight and stiff, as if he was trying to be something he wasn't.

'Where's Mister Smoke?' whispered Petrel. 'Cap'n, can you see him?'

'He is approaching a girl,' said the silver child. He indicated a spot not far from Bran. 'Is that Poddy?'

'Aye,' said Sharkey grimly.

His cousin was pounding stones to chips, her head bowed, her spine a curve of grief. Her arm rose and fell as if it weighed a ton.

Sharkey saw the exact moment when she spotted the rat. For a split second, her hammer hesitated in midair – then it fell, exactly as it had done so many times before. Her head was still bowed. The curve of her spine looked as heartbroken as ever.

But now, beneath that heartbreak there was something else.

Hope.

She shuffled to one side, and bent her head, as if she was trying to come at the stones from a different angle. Or as if she was listening to a small, rough voice, and hearing the truth about what had happened to *Claw*.

And then the hammer was lying idle in her hands, and *she* was talking, very quickly and quietly.

Sharkey could see her lips moving, and the urgency of it, and the way her eyes flickered from side to side, watching the guards, checking to see that *they* weren't watching *her*.

Sharkey held his breath. There was something happening over the other side of the quarry. One of the Sunkers had blood running down his arm. A Devout was standing over him, ordering him back to work.

'That is not right,' said the silver child, half rising to his feet. 'He is injured. He needs medical treatment—'

'Shh, Cap'n!' said Krill, pulling him down again.

The other guards were scanning the prisoners, in case they took this as an excuse to stop work. No one seemed to have spotted Poddy – no one except Bran, who ducked his head and stared at the ground. Beside Sharkey, Rain was singing under her breath, her eyes fixed on her little brother.

At last Poddy raised her hammer and went back to bashing at the stone. At the same time, she whispered something to the person next to her, who passed it on to the next person and the next and the next.

It was like the turning of a tide, subtle but strong. Folk still stumbled from one rock to the other. Their shoulders still sagged. Their faces still *seemed* hopeless and defeated.

But Sharkey knew better. The Sunkers had woken up.

Poddy, at the centre of it, was pounding away with her hammer as if the crumbling rock was Brother Thrawn's head. She must have thought she'd got away with that brief stoppage. No one had shouted at her. No one had dragged her to the whipping posts.

All the same, the sick feeling in Sharkey's guts grew suddenly worse. *It was a mistake,* he thought, *sending Mister Smoke down into the quarry. I should've listened to Krill.*

He was right. The guard next to Bran grabbed the boy's shoulder and said something.

Bran shook his head. *No. No!*

But the guard was nodding. *Yes!* And pointing at Poddy. He *had* seen her stop work; he must've been watching out of the corner of his eye, waiting for Bran to report her.

Except Bran *hadn't* reported her. Now both he and Poddy were in trouble, and it was Sharkey's fault.

'No,' he whispered.

'No,' breathed Rain, her eyes fixed on her little brother.

'Steady,' growled Krill. 'Remember the plan.'

The guard hustled Bran over to where Poddy was smashing rocks. When she saw them, her hammer faltered and her shoulders hunched, as if she was trying to hide. The guard shouted at her. His voice was carried off by the wind and the hammering, but his meaning was clear. He hauled Poddy to her feet and began to drag the two children towards the whipping posts.

Behind him, every single prisoner laid down their hammer and chisel.

The sudden silence was like a blow. Sharkey's ears rang with it. And they rang again when the guards began yelling and lashing out with their cudgels.

Still no one picked up their tools. They stood, ragged and stubborn, their faces as hard as the rock behind them, their eyes fixed on Poddy and the guard who held her.

Sharkey felt a moment of intense pride. But then the guard shouted again. And this time his voice carried right up to the lip of the quarry.

'She is to be punished for stopping work. Fifteen lashes of the whip. The boy will be punished for not reporting her. He has been warned before. Five lashes of the whip.'

'No,' said Rain, and a sob caught in her throat. 'That is too cruel!'

The guard continued. 'And if you lot do not get back to work, the punishment will be doubled. For both of them.'

For a long moment, no one moved. Then, down in the quarry, Adm'ral Deeps stepped forward, her voice strong. 'She's too young for fifteen lashes. I'll take her punishment. I'll take it for both of 'em.'

It just about tore the breath out of Sharkey's lungs, to hear those words. Shook him from head to toe. Made him realise for the first time ever what being an adm'ral was about. It *wasn't* just the respect and the admiration. It wasn't just the power, either. Adm'ral Deeps was looking after her people. She was stepping in to save them.

Except it wasn't going to work. The guard sneered at her. 'You can be whipped *as well*, if that is your fancy,' he cried, and his fellow guards laughed. 'Or you can have this for free.'

And he raised his cudgel and knocked her down.

Sharkey was on his feet in an instant. He wasn't the only one. Rain scrambled up too, saying, 'We must stop them!'

Petrel and Fin pulled them down again. 'We *can't*, not till tonight! That's the plan, remember?'

'We cannot wait till tonight,' cried Rain. 'We must do something *now*, before they are hurt!'

'She is right,' said the silver captain. 'They should not be whipped.'

'Shh!' said Krill. 'Keep your voices down!'

It was then that Mister Smoke returned, trotting towards them with his ragged coat covered in rock dust. 'Poddy says there's a secret tunnel, shipmates—'

'She's going to be whipped,' said Sharkey. 'They saw her stop work. I shouldn't have sent you.'

'—up the road at the camp where they sleep. The prisoners've dug it as far as the shoreline—'

'Didn't you *hear* me?' said Sharkey.

'—but they can't use it, cos the guards are out there all night and every night with their dogs. They need a diversion, something that'll give 'em time to—'

'A diversion,' cried Rain. 'That is what we want *now*!'

Sharkey wanted to save Rain's little brother almost as much as he wanted to save Poddy. But for all his anger and guilt, his clever mind would not stop working. 'No, we'd be caught in an instant. And that wouldn't do anyone any good.'

'But we have to do *something*!'

'*Shhhhh!*' warned Krill.

Too late. One of the guards raised his head and stared up at the cliff top. Then he began to shout.

There was no time for discussion. Mister Smoke dived into the undergrowth, and Petrel threw the bag of masks after him. Krill leapt to his feet with amazing agility for such a big man. Sharkey grabbed Rain's hand, and they ran for their lives.

It wasn't until they were a hundred yards away that he realised the others weren't with them.

CAPTURED

Krill started out strongly. But the ground between the trees was pitted with rabbit holes, and by the time they'd gone twenty yards his ankle had given way again. Petrel and Fin grabbed his elbows and tried to haul him along, but that just made things worse.

'Leave me!' he gasped, leaning against the base of an enormous rocky outcrop. 'Save the cap'n! They'll smash him if they catch him.'

Petrel could hear the Devouts crashing up the hill towards them. A dog barked, and ten more answered it. Scroll fluttered above the captain's head in agitation.

'They will smash you, too,' said the captain. 'I will not leave you here, Krill, it would not be right. A captain does not desert his crew.'

The Head Cook hissed through his teeth. 'You *must* go. You're the one who matters, not me. Get out of here!'

'I will not,' said the captain.

The dogs were howling now – a deep, hungry sound that made Petrel's skin tighten. She wanted to keep running – every fibre in her body urged her to escape while she still could. But the captain was right. They couldn't leave Krill behind.

She swallowed. 'Looks like we're staying. Can you fight, Krill?'

'Reckon so, bratling, as long as it doesn't involve walking.'

'Fin?' said Petrel.

Fin looked as if he wanted to run as much as she did. But he nodded at Petrel and they began snatching up good solid branches that they could use as weapons.

'This way!' shouted a man from in among the bushes. 'They have not got far!'

Petrel, Fin and Krill backed into a semicircle around the rock face, with the captain behind them. They were only just in time. Four men burst out of the bushes with dogs straining at their leashes. Two of them saw Sharkey and Rain disappearing into the distance, and kept running. The other two stopped and shouted over their shoulders, 'We have them!'

The dogs drew their lips back from their teeth and snarled. Petrel shivered. Beside her, Fin gripped his branch with white knuckles.

'We've fought worse than this,' said Krill in a quiet rumble. His face was grey with pain, but his eyes were determined and the bones in his beard rattled ferociously.

'Aye,' whispered Petrel, though her legs trembled, and she couldn't imagine fighting anyone. Fin's shoulder nudged hers, and she nudged him back. Scroll's wings churned the air above the captain's head.

'Here we go,' said Krill. 'Here come the rest of 'em.'

Men and dogs milled out of the bushes, shouting and barking so loudly that Petrel could hardly hear herself think. She held her branch in both hands, copying Krill, and braced her legs as if she was on the deck of the *Oyster* with a storm coming.

She thought the men would rush them. That's what she'd have done, with so many against so few. Instead, they stopped some distance away and held their dogs back. The shouting was replaced by a low murmur.

'They are still afraid of him,' whispered Fin. 'Listen!'

'Demon,' murmured the men.

'Demon!'

'*Demon!*'

Petrel drew in her breath and shouted across the gap, 'He'll kill you if you come any closer!'

'I will not,' said the captain in her ear. 'I cannot.'

'Shh!' whispered Petrel. 'It's what they think that counts.'

Fin took a half-step forward. 'It is true,' he cried. 'I have seen it myself. You will be dead before you can blink.'

The Devouts glowered at him. One of them, his beaky nose shining with suspicion, turned to his fellows and said, 'Who is that boy? I have seen him before.'

Someone else said, 'Is he not the Initiate who went south with us? The one who attacked Brother Thrawn? Is he not *the traitor*?'

For a few seconds, the words seemed to hang in the early-morning air like icicles. Then the Devouts erupted with hatred. 'Traitor!' they screamed. 'Consorter with demons! You will pay for your crimes. You *and* your mother!'

Petrel felt Fin go rigid beside her. His mouth opened and shut, but nothing came out.

Krill's steady rumble broke the spell. 'It's words, lad, that's all. They're trying to divide us. It's all part of the fight, just as much as the cudgels and the dogs. Don't let 'em see that they've got to you.'

'They have not,' Fin said quickly. 'They have not got to me.' And he raised his voice again. 'The demon will boil the blood in your veins, men and dogs. You will all die.'

To Petrel's surprise, the captain stepped forward then. 'If your blood boils, you will certainly die,' he said, in a high, clear voice. 'But first I think you will swell up, and leak through the skin. You might even burst from the pressure.'

He sounded horribly convincing. Petrel watched the men whisper to each other, heads nodding and shaking in argument. One of them pointed down the hill, and three men ran back the way they had come.

The man with the sharp nose turned to the small, defiant group and shouted, 'You are lying, demon. If you were going to kill us, you would have done so already.'

All the same, he and his fellows seemed in no hurry to advance. The dogs strained at their leashes, and the men held them back.

The captain whispered in Petrel's ear. 'I did *not* lie. I did not say that *I* would make those things happen.'

The Devouts had clearly taken it that way, however. Petrel felt a flicker of hope. This was a nasty trap, but she'd spent her whole life escaping from nasty traps. Maybe she and her friends could escape from this one.

What we need is a back door, she thought. *Except we ain't got one, not here, not unless we could climb up on top of this outcrop. But if WE could do it, so could . . .*

The realisation hit her as hard as any cudgel. Those three men who had been sent away!

She swung around, shouting a warning, 'Cap'n, watch out above!'

But she was too late. The three men were already up there, with an enormous rock in their hands. As the words left Petrel's mouth, the rock fell, plummeting through the air like a thunderbolt.

The captain looked up . . . and the rock hit him.

He took three ungainly steps, then fell to the ground with half his beautiful face crushed. At the same time, the Devouts rushed in.

The next few minutes were among the most dreadful Petrel had ever known. Dogs and men flew at her, and she did her best to hold them off, ducking away from cudgels and teeth, then leaping back in with her branch flailing.

Beside her, Krill roared with fury and lashed out at anyone who came within reach. Two men fell under his fearsome blows, and then another. A dog yelped with pain. Another dog threw itself at Krill's legs, and he scooped it up and tossed it away.

On Petrel's other side, Fin was straddling the captain's body, and smashing his branch in a wide arc that no one could get past. Scroll pecked wildly at dogs and men. And all the time, the captain lay still and silent, and Petrel's heart was breaking.

In the end, it was a question of numbers. There were so many Devouts that even Krill's great strength couldn't hold them off for long. It took seven men and three dogs to bring him down, but bring him down they did. One moment he was fighting, the next he too lay silent on the ground, with blood trickling from his scalp.

With Krill gone, Petrel and Fin didn't have a hope. They fought on, trying to protect the captain's body, but it wasn't long before their weapons were knocked from their hands, and they were thrown to the ground.

Scroll gave a mournful *coo* and flew away.

Petrel knew what was going to happen next, and had no idea how to stop it. She could see the men's feet shuffling past as they gathered around the captain, hefting their cudgels and murmuring to each other.

'Do you think it is still dangerous? Might it wake up and boil our blood?'

'I do not know.'

'We must make sure it is truly dead.'

'Yes. We will crush it completely. Tear it apart.'

For all Petrel knew, the captain *was* truly dead. She had no idea how he worked, or whether he could be mended after that crushing blow to the face. *She* couldn't do it, that was for sure, and neither could Fin or Krill. But maybe Mister Smoke and Missus Slink could fix him – if they could only get him back to the *Oyster*.

There's still a chance, she told herself fiercely. *We might still get out of this. I might be able to save my friends.*

But if the Devouts tore the captain apart, if they crushed him completely, there'd be nothing left to save.

She tried to wriggle away from the man who held her. He snarled, as vicious as the dogs, and twisted her arm until she yelped. Behind her, the other Devouts were raising their cudgels—

'Wait!' shrieked Petrel. 'Wait or we'll all die!'

She saw the cudgels hesitate, and ploughed on, not knowing what she was going to say until the words were out of her mouth. 'If you smash the rest of him, a – a *gas*'ll come out.'

She hoped they knew what a gas was. But maybe they didn't. After all, they had turned their back on every sort of knowledge except superstition. 'A *poisonous* gas,' she shouted.

'A miasma,' said Fin in a muffled voice.

'Aye, a miasma, that's right. A nasty one. It'll kill every-one here and – and then it'll spread, and kill everyone in the Citadel. Including Brother Thrawn.'

Her words were greeted by a deathly silence. The men who had been looming over the captain took a step backwards.

Someone said, 'She is lying.'

Someone else said, 'Perhaps. We must seek Brother Thrawn's advice.'

'What shall we do with them in the meantime?'

'Tie them to the whipping posts. Then, when we kill them, we can make a show of it. Let the peasants see what happens to those who defy us.'

And with no further ado, the Devouts picked up Petrel, Fin and the captain and carried them down the hill towards the quarry.

Krill they dragged.

★★★

Sharkey and Rain reached the bottom of the hill without being stopped. Sharkey wasn't sure where they were going – he just wanted somewhere to hide for the rest of the day, somewhere safe and familiar, where he could think about what to do next.

'The sea,' he said. 'Set course for the sea, quick.'

And so they headed towards the coast, with Rain leading the way. It was easier in daylight than it had been in darkness, but Sharkey didn't like it any better. *Wish I had good solid metal around me,* he thought as his bare feet squelched through the mud. *Instead of all this – this earth.*

Tower of Strength and the Citadel were behind them now, but there were people everywhere, poor, hungry-looking creatures carrying bundles of sticks, or leading scrawny animals. The two children ducked from cover to cover, until at last they left the fields and the trees behind and stood on a rise with a little crescent beach below them, and no sign of Devouts or anyone else.

And there was the sea, sighing and swelling like an old friend.

Sharkey couldn't take his eyes off it. He wanted to dive in, right there and then. He wanted to swim and swim, until the Devouts and Brother Thrawn and the whipping posts were far behind him.

But that wouldn't help Poddy.

He turned to Rain and said, 'We need a good hiding pl—'

'*There they are!*'

The shout, from the trees behind them, was like a blow to the belly. Sharkey grabbed Rain's hand again and tried to drag her towards the beach, crying, 'Run!'

But instead of running, Rain dug in her heels. And when Sharkey let go of her hand, she grabbed his arm. Then, to his horror, she turned towards the approaching Devouts and shouted, 'I have him! Come quickly! Do not let him get away!'

Sharkey was so shocked that for a moment he couldn't move. He just stood there, staring at Rain. She shouted again, 'Come quickly!'

That was enough for Sharkey. With a cry of disgust he tore himself loose and ran. His legs pumped. His arms swung to keep his balance. His bare feet leapt over clods of earth and rocks and anything else that got in his way.

Behind him, the men egged each other on with great shouts. Sharkey couldn't hear the dogs. *They* ran in silence, and so did he, heaving the salty air in and out of his lungs, thinking of Poddy, and how he *had* to remain free, had to save her.

When he came to the beach, he tore across the sand and into the water with gouts of spray splashing up around him. As soon as it was deep enough, he began to swim.

He'd taken no more than three strokes when the dogs were upon him, a writhing mass of coarse hair and sharp teeth and paws. They bit him and pushed him under and tried to drag him back towards the shore.

But Sharkey was a Sunker, and Sunkers fought to the very end, even when they'd been betrayed. He squirmed and wriggled and punched until he was free of the teeth and the scrabbling paws. His head shot to the surface and he took a quick breath and dived under again. He couldn't see a thing, but he knew where open water lay, he could feel it in his bones, and he dragged himself towards it, with his heart and soul bent on escape.

He thought he'd made it. He gave one last kick and thought he was free. But then a hand grabbed hold of his leg. Another hand seized his foot and hauled it upwards. Sharkey's head hit the sand and bounced off. He took a mouthful of water – and was dragged to the surface, spluttering and choking.

Before he could catch his breath, the men had his hands tied behind his back, and he was trussed up like a crab ready for the pot.

BROTHER
THRAWN

The Devouts dragged Sharkey along the beach, jerking the rope this way and that, and laughing when he fell to his knees on the sand. He tried to catch Rain's eye, but she wouldn't look at him.

Instead, she said, 'He is the last of the underwater savages. I am glad you caught him. Thank you for saving me.'

One of the men, whose brown robe was hitched up over his trousers so he could run, looked down at her. 'Brother Thrawn thought you were dead.'

Rain shuddered. 'At times I *wished* I was dead.'

'Well, you are safe now and Brother Thrawn will be wanting to see you as soon as possible. He will want to see the savage too, no doubt.' The man tipped his head towards Sharkey. 'Is he really the last of them?'

'Yes,' said Rain. 'There are a couple of small children somewhere, but they will die soon enough without anyone to look after them.'

Sharkey stared at her in disbelief. *I thought we were friends. How could I've been so stupid?*

The man jerked at the rope, and Sharkey stumbled up over the rise and into the trees, with the dogs nipping at his heels. He kept his head down, trying to act as if he was beaten. But all the while, he was thinking.

If I can get away, where can I run to? Can I use the tunnel to get Poddy and the others out? And what if I can't get away?

He was scared of what was coming, but he was angry too. Angry at Rain, angry at Brother Thrawn, angry at every single person in the Up Above. What had the Sunkers ever done to them? Nothing, that's what. Sunkers just wanted to be left alone, to live their lives the way they'd done for three hundred years.

But the Devouts wouldn't let them.

By the time they came to Tower of Strength, Sharkey was fuming. Which was just as well, because otherwise his courage might have failed him. There was the Citadel high above him, more toadlike than ever, and he was being dragged up the busy road towards it, with the Devouts discussing his fate.

'What do you think Brother Thrawn will do to him?'

'Hang him. That is what I would do. Hang the lot of them.'

Four men on horses overtook them. Another three strode down the hill with purposeful faces. The Devouts hauled Sharkey out of the way, still talking.

'Break his bones.'

'Drown him.'

They both laughed at that, and Rain said, 'It would serve him right to drown. If he loves water so much, give it to him.'

'You *are* a fierce one,' said the man with the hitched-up robes, in admiring tones. 'I always thought you were meek as a mouse.'

'I have had to fight for my life,' said Rain, 'and it has changed me. No more meekness.'

Sharkey saw her throat move, as if she was singing under her breath. *A treachery song,* he thought, and he looked away.

The road that ran up through Tower of Strength was made of tiny stone chips, like the ones Poddy had been pounding in the quarry. It was a neat road, despite the comings and goings of men and horses. But all around it was squalor.

For as long as Sharkey could remember, *Claw* and *Rampart* had stunk of sweat, engine oil and fish.

Occasionally, if the recyclers broke down, the reek of sewage was added to the mix for a day or so.

But this was different. The houses on either side of the road were crumbling, their walls propped up with sticks and stones, their roofs half caved in. There was no glass in their portholes, just flaps of filthy cloth, and the stink of hopelessness that rose from them made Sharkey recoil.

Pale-haired children played in some of the doorways, their faces gaunt with hunger, their limbs so thin that they looked as if they might snap. Others just sat in their mothers' laps, as if they didn't have the energy to move. But as the horsemen trotted past, holding their robes over their noses, the women and children scuttled back inside.

Like fish, thought Sharkey, *hiding from a predator.*

At first it was a relief to come to the top of the hill and leave the houses behind. The smell lessened, the road flattened out, and there was even a bush or two growing beside it. But then Sharkey saw the Citadel.

From below, he had thought it looked like a squatting toad, but now he could see that there was another part to it, a tall pointed thing that rose above it, white and hard. In fact, the whole thing was white and hard, like a bird skeleton lying on its back with its beak in the air.

Dead, he thought. *It looks dead.*

'Feast your eyes, savage,' said one of the Devouts. 'That is the spire of our Citadel, and the centre of the civilised world. People can see it from a hundred miles away on a clear day. You poor ignorant savages never had anything so fine.'

We had better things than dead-bird houses, thought Sharkey. *We had* Rampart. *We had* Resilience *and* Rogue *and* Rumbustious. *And* Claw*, which is still out there somewhere. Least, I hope it is.*

The road took them to a high stone wall with a well-guarded wooden gate, and the gate took them to a world of neatness and order. Sharkey had never seen so many straight lines. Even the pebbles seemed to line up one behind the other, as if they were too scared to do anything else.

There were Devouts everywhere, in the same brown robes as Sharkey's captors. They were all men – there was not a woman among them, which to Sharkey was as strange as the straight lines. He stared around and realised that there were no middies either, or babies, which probably accounted for the neatness.

It's mean, he thought suddenly. *It's mean and hollow, and it's got nothing to do with real life.*

The new Devouts had an air of excitement about them, and one of them, a big man with scratches on his face, stopped and said, 'Have you heard? We captured the demon and its helpers.'

'*And* the boy traitor,' said a second man, 'the one who injured Brother Thrawn so grievously. What a thumping we gave *him*.'

'Tomorrow morning they will be put to death, all four of them. It will be quite a spectacle.'

Sharkey's anger slid away like dirty water, and he was almost knocked down by a wave of horror. Because of him and his rescue expedition, the others had been caught, every one of them. And now they were going to die.

The man with the scratched face peered at him. 'Is this another of the demon's cohort?'

'No, he is one of the underwater lot,' said the hitched-robe man. 'The last, thankfully.'

The other men spat on the ground, and as Sharkey was dragged away, one of them said, 'They are as hard to get rid of as cockroaches.'

Up close, the Citadel looked bigger and more corpse-like than ever. Everything about it was white and bleak, and the only sounds were footsteps and the muttering of passers-by. Sharkey felt as if he was dead already, and lost in some terrible afterworld where the Hungry Ghosts would torment him for the rest of time.

'Punishment cells,' asked one of his captors, 'or Brother Thrawn? What do you think?'

'Brother Thrawn, definitely.'

'Poosk will be there, of course.'

They both snorted, as if Poosk was someone they enjoyed despising. 'Pathetic little man,' said one of them. 'I do not know how Brother Thrawn puts up with him.'

'He is well-named. Poosk. Flea. Parasite.'

'Have you heard him going on and on about what an honour it is to serve our leader?'

'Well, he is right. It *is* an honour to serve. As a member of the Circle, or a hunter of demons, or a warrior. But as a *nursemaid*?'

They snorted again. Then they became very serious, and hustled Sharkey and Rain through a hatch— *Nay*. Sharkey made himself concentrate. Made himself find the right word. They went through a *door* – and into the Citadel itself.

And now at last he saw the workings of the empire that had eaten the world. The wide passages were packed with men, all of them bustling back and forth with scrolls in their hands, and important expressions on their faces.

Every now and then, a couple of them would stop and talk to each other in low voices, before hurrying about their business.

As Sharkey was dragged past, he overheard snatches of conversation.

'—have *five* fields? They only reported three. Find out the truth, and then—'

'—news from the Northern Zone suggests that—'

'—someone trying to teach the peasants to read in District Four. I have ordered a purge, and I think we should also—'

There was no crowing over the new prisoners here, and no one so much as glanced at Sharkey and his captors. They were too busy, and the crowded passages seemed to go on forever. But at last Sharkey was shoved into a long line of men that was creeping, bit by bit, through a doorway.

It took them nearly half an hour to shuffle from the end of the line to the door. Plenty of time to think about the tunnel. Plenty of time to think about Petrel and her friends, and to wonder if they were expecting him to come to their rescue.

I can't, he thought. *I'll be lucky to save myself. And if by some miracle I manage that, the next thing'll be Poddy. And then Adm'ral Deeps and the rest of the Sunkers. That's why I'm here.*

He felt as if he was standing in front of Petrel, trying to excuse himself, and not doing a very good job of it. The despair threatened to grab him again, and he fought it with all his Sunker strength.

I'm sorry, he said to the imaginary Petrel, *but I can't afford to worry about anyone else. I hope you escape, I really do. But I can't help you.*

It was an ugly thing to say, especially after they'd come here to help *him.* But he knew it was sensible. *No distractions,* he said to himself. And with that resolution, he turned his mind away from the other four captives and focused on what was in front of him.

As soon as he passed through the doorway, Sharkey knew where he was. *This is the control room,* he thought. *This is centre of everything.*

It was ten times as big as the whole of *Claw.* The ceiling was carved in intricate patterns and the walls were draped with silver-grey cloth that looked even finer than sea silk. Spaced out along the base of the walls were cavities, and in each cavity was an enormous fire, so that, despite the stone underfoot, the room was as warm as a summer's night.

At the far end was a wheeled chair with a man sitting in it.

And that, thought Sharkey, *is the high adm'ral. Brother Thrawn.*

The man in the wheeled chair was thin and angry-looking, with lines on his face that might've been carved with a knife. There was a coldness to him, and a heat as well, and his eyes were so full of hatred that

Sharkey took an involuntary step backwards, and Rain went very still, as if she didn't want to be noticed.

Ahead of them, the long line of men made their reports.

'Brother Thrawn, the grain harvest from Sub-District Seven, Village Number Four, was only half of last year's harvest. The peasants claim they are starving, and have asked for their tithe to be halved as well.'

'Brother Thrawn, I am pleased to report that the factional rebellion in the Northern Zone has been quashed, and the ringleaders hanged. This *does* leave us with a temporary problem of leadership—'

'Brother Thrawn, three of our informers in District Nine have died in the last six months. Their deaths appear to be accidental—'

The horrible thing about it, thought Sharkey, was that it was all so ordinary. The Devouts spoke in dry, level voices, as if they were talking about marks on paper rather than people's lives, and, after a pause, Brother Thrawn answered in an equally dry voice.

'The tithe will not be halved. They are not starving, but lazy.'

'Send Brother Trounce to assume leadership of the Northern Zone. He will come down hard—'

'Of course the deaths are not accidental. Hang twenty peasants from each village.'

Sharkey and his captors moved forward step by step. Rain's face was so stiff that she might have been made of coral. The line in front of them grew shorter—

And suddenly Sharkey realised that it wasn't Brother Thrawn speaking, after all. It was his nursemaid. Brother Poosk.

Rain's uncle was such a nondescript little man that Sharkey hadn't even noticed him. Like the other Devouts, he wore brown robes, but his were made of rougher cloth, and although they were neat, they were also old and threadbare.

Whenever someone asked Brother Thrawn a question, Poosk would bend a respectful ear to his leader, listen to the answer, and pass it on in that arid voice. Between questions he held a cup to Brother Thrawn's lips, then wiped them gently with a cloth.

When it was Sharkey's turn, the hitched-robe man shoved him forward and said, 'Brother Thrawn, I am pleased to report that we have caught the last of the underwater savages. He was with the demon, but ran off separately. I do not know how he escaped the attack of three days ago.'

The figure in the wheeled chair mumbled something. Poosk bent closer. 'What is that you say, dear leader? They are crowding you?'

The two men holding Sharkey quickly shuffled back a few steps. Sharkey glanced at Rain. Her eyes were fixed on Brother Thrawn. Her throat moved.

Brother Thrawn said something else, though Sharkey couldn't pick out the words, not from where he was. He wondered what was wrong with the man, and whether he could be healed.

I bet Presser Surgeon Blue could fix him, he thought. *And Thrawn'll never know, because I'll never tell him.*

Poosk raised his voice and passed Brother Thrawn's message on. 'The day's audience is finished. Our dear leader is tired. You may leave the prisoner here, roped to a chair, so he cannot escape.'

The dozens of men who had been waiting in line behind Sharkey left without a murmur, their sandalled feet slapping on the marble floor. But the hitched-robe man said, 'The prisoner is slippery, Brother, and violent. Perhaps we should stay.'

Poosk drew himself up to his not-very-impressive height. 'Are you doubting our leader's wisdom?'

'No,' said the man. 'I just thought—'

Poosk held up a hand for silence. Then he bent his head closer to Brother Thrawn's lips. 'It is not your place – to think,' he relayed. 'Tie him up and leave us. The girl can stay too.'

At that, Poosk looked up with a surprised expression, as if he'd been so busy passing on Brother Thrawn's instructions that he'd hardly noticed who else was in the room. 'Niece,' he said, 'is that *you*? Are you alive after all?'

'She helped catch the boy,' said the hitched-robe man. 'He was trying to drag her away and she grabbed hold of him. She is a hero, she is.'

'Oh,' said Poosk, 'I am so relieved, so proud—'

There was a sound from Brother Thrawn and Poosk broke off, his plump cheeks flushed. 'Yes, of course,' he said. 'My apologies, Brother.'

Through most of this, Sharkey was looking for ways out. Looking for things he could use. He hadn't found anything yet, but his gaze kept coming back to Brother Thrawn's frozen figure. To the hatred that radiated from him, so powerful that Sharkey could almost touch it.

No wonder everyone jumps to obey him. He might be stuck in that chair, but he's got enough nastiness in him for a dozen Massy sharks.

Brother Poosk, on the other hand, was like one of the tiny fish that cleaned the teeth of those sharks, ducking in and out of their dreadful jaws day and night. The little fish were necessary, but no one liked them or took any notice of them. Not even the Massy sharks.

If I could get loose, thought Sharkey, *I could shove Poosk out of the way as easy as a baby. He'd probably cry as soon as*

I touched him. But not Thrawn. He's the one to watch, even though he can't move. I bet he's got a few tricks up his sleeve.

Unfortunately, getting loose was about to become even harder. Sharkey's captors tied him to a heavy chair, then placed it a couple of yards away from their leader.

Before he left, the hitched-robe man whispered, 'You keep a polite tongue in your head, savage, when you speak to Brother Thrawn. Or else.' Then he and his friend left the room, closing the door quietly behind them.

And that's when Sharkey discovered where the *real* danger lay.

UNCLE POOSK

It was subtle at first. Brother Poosk still bent to listen
to his leader. Still mopped the helpless man's face and
bobbed and ducked around him, attending to this
and that.

'Brother Thrawn wants to know,' he said, as the
door closed, 'how you escaped from the underwater
machine. He was sure his men had destroyed it.'

Sharkey didn't answer. Something had changed, and
he was trying to work out what it was.

He looked at Rain, but she was staring at the floor. He
looked at Brother Thrawn, at the mad glint in his eyes, at
the rage and the viciousness and the nastiness. From this
close, Sharkey could see that it was directed at—

—at Brother Poosk.

Sharkey blinked. Hang on, that wasn't right. What
had Poosk done except run around being helpful,

and pass on messages? Look at him, even now he was moving Brother Thrawn's left arm so it didn't rub against the edge of the chair, then trotting around to the other side—

In the end, it was the spring in Poosk's step that gave him away. Everyone else probably thought it was eagerness to serve. But to Sharkey, with his history of deception, it looked like something else.

A subtle glee.

Sharkey's eyes widened involuntarily. Everyone seemed to think of Brother Poosk as nothing more than an irritating servant. They despised him. They laughed behind his back.

But what if *he* was the one laughing? What if *he* was in charge?

Sharkey looked again, and listened, and knew he was right. It wasn't *instructions* coming out of Brother Thrawn's mouth. It was meaningless mumbles. *He* hadn't condemned sixty villagers to hanging. It was Poosk!

Which meant it was Poosk who had sent Sharkey's captors out of the room. It was probably Poosk who had caused *Rampart* to be bombarded, and *Claw* too. The handover trap, the catapults, the balloons – they were all Brother Poosk.

And Rain knew it.

Sharkey didn't look at the girl. He didn't look at Poosk, either. He kept his face blank, and his eyes fixed on Brother Thrawn, as if he still believed the masquerade. Because if Rain's uncle was clever enough to snatch this sort of power, to keep this sort of secret, then he was far more dangerous than he appeared to be. And if Sharkey wanted to save his own skin, and Poddy's too, he'd better keep quiet about it.

'Well?' said Brother Poosk in his humble I'm-just-passing-on-the-question voice. 'You must not keep Brother Thrawn waiting, savage. How did you escape?'

Sharkey had no intention of answering any questions. But it made no difference. Rain answered for him.

With lowered eyes, she told her uncle how Sharkey had tricked their pursuers. She told him about the oil and the broken-up berth and the expelled air. She even told him about the little claw, and how it had been used to stir the sand.

The only thing she didn't mention was the part *she* had played. In *her* story, she'd been a helpless prisoner the whole time, unable to do anything except watch in terror.

If Sharkey hadn't hated her so much, he would've admired her. This was a side of Rain he'd never seen before. But he should've guessed it was there. After all, just about everything she'd ever said to him had been a lie.

At the end of Rain's story, Poosk put his ear to Brother Thrawn's mouth, and nodded several times. Then he said, in a surprised voice. 'Really? You want *me* to question the savage boy? I am not at all sure, dear leader – I do not have your intellect—'

He really was astonishingly clever, thought Sharkey. His words, his voice, the look on his face – it was so convincing.

And all the time, Brother Thrawn's eyes burned with hatred.

'Very well,' said Brother Poosk. 'I will do my best.' He turned his nondescript expression to Sharkey. 'What is your name, boy?'

Rain murmured, 'It is Sharkey.'

'A savage name for a savage boy,' said Poosk. 'Dear me, how I hate to think of my niece in his company.' Those mild eyes inspected Rain. 'I hope none of the savagery rubbed off on her. Her little brother would be so upset.'

'No, Uncle,' said Rain, staring at her hands. 'It did not rub off.'

'Good,' said Brother Poosk. 'Now—' he turned back to Sharkey '—Brother Thrawn would like to know what you and the demon were doing above

237

the quarry. You might as well tell him. If you do not, my niece will. Family is so important, is it not, Sharkey? Hmm?'

He stepped closer, his head tilted to one side. 'Where is *your* family, by the way? Were they in the quarry? Did you see them cutting rocks, I wonder? It looks like hard work, I know, but really it builds character, and no one can argue with that, can they? Mind you, Admiral Deeps does not need any character-building. Such a *fine* leader. It must have been hard to lose her, dear me, yes. And harder still to carry on without her. Such a responsibility . . .'

Sharkey wasn't sure how it happened, but there was something about that quiet voice that sidled past his defences. He found himself nodding. After all, Adm'ral Deeps *was* a fine leader. And it *had* been hard to lose her. Where was the harm in admitting such a thing?

But once he had agreed with that, it was difficult to stop. And when Brother Poosk said kindly, 'I suppose you came to the quarry with some thought of rescuing your fellows, did you not?' Sharkey croaked, 'Aye.'

'Of course you did,' cried Poosk. 'Any loyal person would have done the same. But loyalty is not enough, is it? It takes courage to walk into the lion's den.'

Sharkey didn't know what a lion's den was, but he agreed with the rest of it. 'Aye,' he said again.

'I expect you had a plan,' said Poosk. He looked over his shoulder to where Brother Thrawn seethed in his chair. 'A brave, clever boy like this would have had a plan, dear leader.'

Sharkey saw the trap and knew without a doubt that he mustn't say another word, no matter how harmless it seemed. But there was that quiet voice again, sneaking into the cracks, crawling into the spaces between who Sharkey was and who he wanted to be.

'Or perhaps there was no plan when you got here,' murmured Poosk. 'But then something came to you. Some little weakness you saw? Something you could exploit? Why, all those people are relying on you, Sharkey. Waiting for you to save them. And you are not going to let them down. That is not the sort of boy you are, I can see it in your face. The determination. The courage. The cleverness—'

It's true, thought Sharkey. *I'm NOT going to let them down. I'm going to get out of here, and then—*

'Then what?' asked Poosk.

To his horror, Sharkey realised he'd spoken his thoughts aloud. 'And then— And then—' he stuttered.

'There *is* a plan, is there not?' asked Poosk. 'Or perhaps just the beginnings of one? A loose end that we have not caught? A hole in the careful fabric that Brother Thrawn has woven? I wonder what it is, hmm?'

Sharkey clamped his lips together, determined not to give anything away. But the nondescript little man kept talking at him, and talking and talking, and before long, he found himself nodding again.

He felt like a fish on the end of a line, being dragged along with a hook in its mouth, and no way of saving itself. He was sure he'd eventually let something slip. Something important. Or else Rain would do it. She'd told her uncle pretty much everything else. It was only a matter of time before she remembered Poddy's message about the tunnel.

I have to stop this, thought Sharkey. *I have to stop it in its tracks. Now!*

Except he could think of only one way to stop that mild voice, and he didn't want to do it. He opened his mouth – and shut it again. *Say it,* he told himself. But he couldn't. His whole life had been about self-preservation, and the habit was too strong to break.

But then Rain said, 'Uncle—' and Sharkey was *sure* she was going to say something about the tunnel. In desperation, he thought, *What would Petrel do?*

The answer was obvious. Sharkey dragged in a ragged breath and, before he could change his mind, said, 'And then I'm going to kill you.'

He saw the shock in Rain's eyes as he stammered, 'I— I didn't realise at first. I thought Brother Thrawn was running things. But it's not. It's you. So it's you I have to kill. Then everything will fall apart and my people'll be able to escape.'

Brother Poosk folded his hands on his chest and twiddled his thumbs. All pretence was gone now, and his hard little eyes bored into Sharkey's. 'My my,' he said. 'What a clever little savage it is. Or did *you* tell him, Rain?'

The girl's face grew white with horror. 'No, Uncle! I said nothing, I promise. He is just – clever.'

'I see. And do you admire this clever boy, niece? Have you developed a *fondness* for him?'

'No, Uncle.'

'Good, good. Because we cannot keep him, can we? Not when he goes around saying this sort of thing.' He smiled. 'What do you suggest we do with him?'

Rain ducked her head and whispered. 'I am sure you will think of something, Uncle.'

'I am sure I will,' said Poosk. 'Now let me see—'

He bustled across the room, mumbling to himself. Sharkey wondered if the little man was going to kill him now or later. He hoped it was later. He hoped that Poosk wouldn't question Rain any further, wouldn't find out about the tunnel. If it remained a secret, the Sunkers might eventually find their own way of distracting the guards and the dogs. They might escape without Sharkey's help.

They'd better be able to, he thought. *I haven't been much use so far. I haven't saved Poddy. I haven't saved anyone, not even myself.*

But he hadn't betrayed anyone either, and that was something to cling to.

He took a deep breath, wishing he could say good-bye to Poddy. *I'm scared,* he thought.

Behind him, Poosk said, 'Ah, here we are. A nice bit of silk left over from Brother Thrawn's undershirt. Just the thing.'

And before Sharkey knew it, a piece of cloth had been thrust into his mouth, and another piece tied tight around it.

'Now, how is he going to die, I wonder?' Poosk scratched his chin and turned to Brother Thrawn. 'Dear leader, I await your advice.'

Thrawn glared. But Poosk nodded vigorously, as if his leader had replied, and said, 'An excellent idea. Killed while attempting to escape! What could be more appropriate? The boy gets one pathetic chance at freedom and dies in the attempt.'

He swung around. 'What do you think, niece? You helped capture him, after all. You should have a say in his exit. Killed while escaping, yes?'

'Yes, Uncle,' whispered Rain.

Sharkey thought he heard a quiet *hmmm*, and Poosk's eyes narrowed. 'You are not *singing*, are you?'

'N-no, Uncle.'

'You know Brother Thrawn cannot abide singing.'

'Yes, Uncle.'

'Now, where were we? Ah, the escape attempt—'

'Uncle,' whispered Rain.

Sharkey's heart jolted. Had his sacrifice been for nothing? Had Rain remembered the tunnel at last?

But if she had, she wasn't saying so. 'Uncle. I was wondering about Br— about my brother.'

'What about him? He is to be whipped tomorrow morning, after the demon and its fellows are executed.'

'Yes, I-I know. But since I helped capture the savage boy—' Rain didn't so much as look at Sharkey, '—I thought maybe Brother Thrawn might let my brother off. Just this once.'

Poosk sniffed. 'A dangerous precedent. What do you think, Brother Thrawn? Are we feeling merciful? Are we feeling kind?'

A low growl escaped from Thrawn's lips. Poosk smiled delightedly. 'We are? Well then, Rain, your request is granted. Consider yourself and your brother exceptionally lucky.'

'I do, Uncle. And thank you.'

'Well, don't just stand there simpering, girl. Go and tell those guards to come back. Brother Thrawn wants a word with them.'

As Rain hurried to the door, Sharkey braced himself. Behind the gag, his breath came in short, painful gasps. *Now? Will they kill me now?*

But when the guards shuffled back into the room, Poosk merely said, 'Brother Thrawn wants the savage thrown into the punishment hole. And you are to release the young Initiate while you are there. Our dear leader has forgiven him, because of the heroism of his sister.'

Sharkey trembled with relief. But as the men untied him from the chair and marched him out of the room, he knew that the relief would not last. Sooner or later they would come for him. And then they would kill him.

THE
PUNISHMENT
HOLE

Something was haunting the *Oyster*.

It started as a whisper, seeping out of the bulkheads whenever the rattling in the pipes died down for a moment or two. '*Albie's lying . . . Albie's lying . . .*'

From Braid to Grease Alley it went, and back again, with the same words over and over.

'*Albie's lying . . .*'

It was more effective than any pipe message, and more puzzling. No one could tell where it came from or who it was. Some folk, listening carefully, swore that the voice belonged to First Officer Orca, which was a frightening thing considering how long Orca had been dead.

Others said it was Dolph, Orca's daughter. But that was impossible, because Dolph and a few others were still barricaded on the bridge and refusing to come out.

Soon, the same conversation was springing up all over the ship.

'So if it's not Orca and it's not Dolph, who is it?'

'Must be a haunt.'

'Or maybe it's the ship itself, growing a voice!'

No one speculated on the message itself – at least not out loud, not where one of Albie's cronies might hear them. But they all wondered what the whisper would say next. And before long, they had an answer.

'*Albie's lying,*' said the whisper. '*The cap'n's alive, and so's Krill.*'

That set the crew a-buzzing! They'd heard more or less the same thing from the bridge, before Albie's folk had started the constant rattling in the pipes. But this wasn't just Dolph or Squid banging out a message. This was a haunt – or the ship itself! And while it was true that folk wanted strong leadership, they didn't like being lied to, not one bit. In every corner of the *Oyster*, they started asking the questions that should have been asked two weeks ago.

An infuriated Albie tried to find the source of the whispers, but was no more successful than anyone else. So he summoned most of his mutineers down to Grease Alley for new orders.

It was his first and only mistake, but it was enough. In Braid, a large group of young Officers took advantage of the situation to demand that First Officer Hump and Second Officer Weddell be released, along with the other ranking prisoners. And when the few remaining mutineers refused, the Officers overpowered them and threw them down the Commons ladderway with their jackets tied over their heads.

In Dufftown, the Cooks who had blockaded themselves in the galley gathered round the burners with hope in their eyes for the first time in days. And before ten minutes had passed, they'd rolled up their sleeves and agreed that if Krill truly was alive, they were going to do something about it.

Even in Grease Alley, which was the centre of Albie's power, folk began to question whether they wanted him running the *whole* ship, which is what would happen if they headed south without the captain or Krill.

'He's the best possible Chief Engineer,' they whispered, looking over their shoulders to make sure they couldn't be overheard. 'But he's a bit too quick with his fists to make a good cap'n.'

By this time, Albie and his mutineers were cracking heads as enthusiastically as they'd done in the old days. But they were too late. The whispers had done their damage.

And there was more to come. In the secret tunnels that ran throughout the ship, previously known only to

Mister Smoke, Missus Slink and Petrel, Third Officer
Dolph wiped the rust from her face, took a swig of
water from a lidded cup and started whispering again.

'*Alive . . . they're alive . . . Petrel and Fin too . . . they're
all alive, north of here . . .*'

★★★

The punishment hole was set in the middle of a
courtyard, with a solid wooden cover on top of it, and
an iron grating beneath the cover. The guards raised
the grating and pushed Sharkey down a set of narrow
stone steps. The smell that rose to meet him was old
and terrible.

'Hey, Initiate!' shouted one of the guards from the
top of the steps. 'Get up here. Thanks to your sister,
you have escaped punishment.'

There was a scuffling sound from one corner, and
Bran appeared, blinking in the light. His robes were
crumpled and filthy; his face was streaked with tears.

'Hurry up,' said the man. 'And do not get into
trouble again. I doubt Brother Thrawn will be so
merciful a second time.'

Bran scrambled up the steps. The grating clanged
shut and the wooden cover was drawn over it. Total
darkness descended.

Sharkey stood at the bottom of the steps, listening. He was used to confined spaces and darkness, and although the punishment hole was obviously meant to frighten him, it didn't. Or at least, it didn't make him any more afraid than he already was.

He heard the slow trickle of water, and a skittering sound that made him think of small animals. And something else. A movement. A breath.

Poddy.

He couldn't speak because of the gag, and his hands were still tied behind his back. But he managed to grunt.

'Sharkey, is that you?' came a whisper.

He grunted again, and next thing he knew a familiar hand was pulling the gag away from his mouth. He drew the foul air into his lungs, and whispered, 'Poddy! You all right?'

'Aye, mostly.'

'Can you untie my hands?'

It took Poddy a while to get the knots undone, but Sharkey stood patiently while she fumbled at them. Except for the stink, he could almost imagine they were in *Claw*, with the lights off and Cuttle napping under the chart table.

Sunkers weren't much given to shows of emotion, but when the ropes fell from Sharkey's wrists at last, he threw his arms around Poddy, and they hugged each other fiercely. Then they felt their way along the wall, running their hands over damp stones, until they came to a corner. The skittering sound grew louder.

'Careful,' said Poddy. 'Don't tread on the rats.'

'Rats?' said Sharkey. 'Not Mister Smo—' He paused, realising that his cousin wouldn't know who he was talking about. 'I mean, not Adm'ral Cray?'

'Nay, these ones don't talk. Bran was scared of 'em at first, but he got used to 'em. Sharkey, what's happening? Where's *Claw*? They told us you were dead, and we believed 'em until I talked to Adm'ral Cray.'

Sharkey let out a breath, and began to tell Poddy everything that had happened since she'd been captured. He left out nothing except his own death sentence.

When he finished, Poddy hissed through her teeth. 'I never thought Rain'd do something so nasty.'

'I reckon she did it to save Bran from a whipping,' said Sharkey.

'Still, she shouldn't have. This is all her fault.'

The old Sharkey would have agreed with her, so he'd come out of it looking nice and shiny. The new one said, 'Nay, Poddy. I mucked things up. I should've thought more carefully before I sent Mister – Adm'ral Cray with that message.'

The foul air moved as Poddy shook her head. 'It gave us hope, knowing you were out there. And we need a bit of hope. Specially me, right now. With this—' For the first time, her voice wobbled. 'This whipping on its way.'

'You don't want to be whipped, Pod? I can hardly believe it!'

The wobble turned to a snort of reluctant laughter.

'We'd best work out how we're going to escape, then,' continued Sharkey. 'I suppose you've tried that grate.'

'It's bolted from above. Bran and I both tried it. He didn't want to, not at first. He thought he deserved to be down here. But I talked to him and after a bit he changed his mind.'

'What about the walls?'

'They're solid all round. There's a waste hole in the floor, right in the middle, but it's too small to climb through.'

'Hmm,' said Sharkey, trying to sound as if he had a few ideas. But the only ideas he had were bad ones, about what was coming. *Killed while escaping.* He couldn't tell Poddy about it – if she knew the guards were going to kill him, she'd try to stop them. And then she'd be killed too.

What would Petrel do?

'Tell you what,' he said. 'Those guards're gunna come back for me at some stage. Don't know when, but old Thrawn wants to – to ask me some more questions, because he didn't have time earlier. So when they come for me, I'm gunna kick up a fuss, and you're gunna make a run for it.'

'Not without you.'

'Aye, without me. Cos you see—' Sharkey was thinking on his feet, twisting things around, the way he had done so often in the past. But it wasn't to make himself look good, not this time. 'Cos you see, it's – it's easier for me to escape if I know you're away already. If I have to think about you, that'll hold me back.'

Silence from Poddy. Then slowly she said, 'I suppose that makes sense.'

'Course it does, Pod. And once you're out of here, head south—'

As best he could, he described the bay where Cuttle and Gilly were waiting with *Claw*. With any luck, Missus Slink would've reached the *Oyster* and fixed the telegraph, in which case the ship might be there too. With a bit more luck, Petrel, Fin, Krill and the silver child would've escaped, and maybe even the rest of the Sunkers. And they'd all head south and meet up. All except Sharkey.

'You'll join us, won't you?' asked Poddy. 'Soon as you can get away?'

'Course I will. Keep your eyes open and you'll see me skipping along behind you, glad to be getting back to the Undersea.' He yawned. 'I'm a bit short of sleep, Pod. It's still daylight out there, and I don't reckon they'll come for me till tonight some time.'

And when they do, he thought, *I'll kick up such a fuss that Poddy'll be out of here and away before they even notice she's gone. And once that's done—*

But he didn't want to think about what was going to happen after that. He wanted to think about *Claw*, and the Undersea, and maybe a couple of dolphins swimming past the porthole.

And freedom.

★★★

The Devouts weren't taking any chances with their dangerous new prisoners. Once they'd marched the Sunkers back to the re-education camp, they trussed Petrel, Fin, Krill and the captain to the whipping posts in the middle of the quarry, and surrounded them with armed guards.

Petrel had tried to count the guards several times, but there were too many. A group of them was hammering away at something behind her, but the rest were watching her and her friends. If she so much as twitched, scores of eyes focused on her, glaring and suspicious, as if she was an army of warriors rather than one small, dusty girl.

It might have been funny if it wasn't so terrible.

Krill had regained consciousness some time ago, and glared back at the guards with such ferocity that Petrel half expected to see smoke rising from them. Fin had retreated to somewhere deep inside himself, and the captain – the poor broken captain – slumped in his ropes as if he would never move again.

He found his Song, thought Petrel, *but it didn't do him any good.* And again she thought of that mysterious someone reaching out from the past and moving things around to suit themselves. *Bet they didn't expect things to end up like this.*

She knew that Sharkey had been captured and that Rain had betrayed him. The guards had taken great pleasure in telling them so. She knew, too, that she and Krill and Fin were to be hanged tomorrow morning, right here in the quarry, and that the captain was to be burned on the hottest possible fire, to destroy the poison miasma.

She licked her parched lips and tried to think, but hunger, thirst, and the fear of what was coming made it almost impossible.

Got to get us out of here.

As darkness fell, the Devouts fetched dozens of flaming torches and set them in a ring around the whipping posts, so that the prisoners were lit almost as brightly as day. There were shadows, of course, which danced and moved with the movement of the flames, and the hammering continued behind Petrel's back. But the rest of the guards still watched so keenly that she couldn't even blink the quarry dust out of her eyes without attracting their attention.

Got to make 'em look away, she thought. *Got to make 'em think I'm so useless there's no reason to watch me any more.*

She knew how to do it. Up until a few months ago, it had been her only weapon against the crew that had rejected her. She hadn't dared do it since then because she'd been afraid of losing everything she'd gained.

But now there was nothing left to lose.

Slowly – infinitesimally slowly – she let her head droop. She thought of defeat and misery and loss. She hunched her shoulders and made her eyes blank and stupid.

It shouldn't have worked. After all, some of the guards had heard her talk, and seen her fight. They knew she wasn't stupid.

But as Petrel's face grew dull, the men nearest to her began to shuffle their feet as if they'd lost interest in her, as if Krill, Fin and the captain were the real threat, and Petrel was just someone who'd been swept up in the excitement. They'd still hang her, of course, but there was no reason to watch her so closely.

It wasn't long before Krill caught on to what Petrel was doing, and turned his ferocious gaze upon her. 'This is your fault, witless girl,' he hissed, just loud enough for the guards to hear. 'If you had half a brain we'd never have been caught. We should've known better than to let you tag along.'

His words shouldn't have hurt – after all, he was pretending, just like Petrel. But they did hurt a little, and so did the sniggering from the guards. For a moment Petrel felt dreadfully alone—

She glanced sideways at Fin and saw his eye close in a barely perceptible wink. *He HASN'T retreated inside himself,* she realised. *He's pretending too!*

That gave her courage. She wasn't alone. She was with her friends, her fierce, clever friends.

She made her face stupider than ever. She didn't have a plan. She didn't even have much hope, not if she was being honest with herself. But she couldn't just stand there and wait for the end.

And so, as the shadows from the torches flickered, and the guards turned their attention to Fin, Krill and the captain, Petrel began to work on the ropes that tied her wrists.

'ARE WE FRIENDS, YOU AND ME?'

When Poddy woke Sharkey, with a hand over his mouth, he knew the moment had come. He nodded to show he was properly awake, and sat up, his heart beating as fast and rackety as *Claw*'s pistons.

At first he could hear nothing except the scurrying of rats. But then there came a sound from above them, a scraping noise, as if someone was trying to drag the wooden cover off the grating, and not quite managing it.

Sharkey braced himself, ready to start shouting and hitting out at anyone who tried to grab him. *I'll give 'em a black eye or two,* he promised himself. *I'll give 'em something to remember me by.*

There was a *thunk*, and fresh air wafted down to them from where the wooden cover had shifted a little. Another *thunk*. Sharkey had expected to see daylight, but the darkness of the punishment hole hardly changed.

He gripped Poddy's hand, his nails biting into her palm. 'It's night-time,' he whispered. 'I didn't mean to sleep so long. You be ready to run.'

She nodded.

Bit by bit the wooden cover was dragged away from the grating. Sharkey couldn't work out why it was taking so long. The men who had brought him here had picked it up with no trouble at all. Had Poosk sent a weakling to kill him? Or were they just teasing him, drawing out the moment so he'd suffer more?

He tried to make himself relax, but he was wound too tight and couldn't let any of it go.

It seemed like forever before the cover was removed. Sharkey heard the bolt being dragged back, then someone leaned over the grating and whispered, 'Poddy!'

Before Sharkey could stop her, Pod replied, 'Bran?'

'I cannot lift this by myself,' said Bran. 'Can you and Sharkey help me?'

Poddy was already on her feet, but Sharkey pulled her back. 'No,' he whispered.

'But Sharkey, it's Bran. He's come to free us!'

'It's a trap,' said Sharkey, knowing that *this* was the escape attempt, *this* was where he would be killed. 'Bran might think he's helping us. But he's not alone up there.'

'I can't hear anyone else.'

'Doesn't matter,' said Sharkey. 'They're there somewhere.'

He knew he had to move. If he wanted to give Poddy a chance of getting away safely, he had to climb out of the hole. Had to distract whoever was waiting to kill him. Trouble was, he wasn't sure he could do it. Life had never seemed more precious.

'*Poddy!*' whispered Bran again.

'I'm coming,' said Sharkey, raising his voice so the boy could hear him. 'I'll help you.' To Poddy he whispered, 'Stay where you are until you hear shouting. Then run for your life.'

'But Sharkey—'

He could've snapped out an order, and she would've obeyed him. But he was sick of orders. And besides, he didn't want her last memory of him to be a bad one. So instead he said, 'Are we friends, you and me, Pod?'

'Friends?' She sounded startled, as if she'd never even considered such a thing. But then she said, 'Aye, Sharkey!'

'Then out of friendship, I'm asking you to do this.' He nodded towards the grate. 'It's a trap, and I know how to deal with it. So I want you stay here till the shouting starts. Then run. Understand?'

He could feel her staring at him in the darkness. But in the end she whispered, 'All right. But you be careful.'

He squeezed her hand one last time, then crept towards the stone stairs.

Going up them nearly broke his nerve. With every step, he expected to see Bran shoved to one side by half a dozen men. He wondered how his death would come. A knife? An arrow? A crack over the head with one of those cudgels?

Don't think about it, he told himself. *Think about giving Poddy a chance. Think about causing as much trouble as I can before they get me.*

He reached the top of the stairs without anything bad happening, and crouched there, looking up at Bran through the bars of the grate. He couldn't see the boy's face, but he could hear his breath coming quick and shallow, as if he was frightened half to death.

Me too, thought Sharkey.

Aloud, he said, 'Have you got the bolt pulled right back?'

'Y-yes,' said Bran.

Once unbolted, the grating wasn't hard to lift, not for someone of Sharkey's size and strength. He lowered it carefully to the ground.

'Where is Poddy?' whispered Bran. His breath was a cloud on the night air, and the pebbles at his feet were white with frost.

'She's coming in a minute,' said Sharkey, and he made himself straighten up. 'Thanks for helping us. You'd better run along now, back to your bed. Don't want you to get into trouble.'

Bran nodded. But before he went, he whispered, 'Nearly everyone is at the quarry. Rain said there will be a diversion just before dawn.' Then he turned and ran into the darkness.

Sharkey stood there, waiting for death to arrive. Bran's words lingered in his ears, but they made no sense. Every inch of his skin prickled with tension. He wished he was iron-clad and double-hulled. He wished there were two hundred feet of good clean seawater between him and the Devouts.

Beside him, someone whispered, 'What'd he say?'

Sharkey almost jumped out of his skin. 'I told you to stay below!'

'I *did* stay below. And now I'm here. What'd he *say*?' asked Poddy.

But Sharkey couldn't answer, he was so afraid for her. 'Get out of here, Pod,' he whispered. 'Right now. Run!'

He pushed her, but she stood her ground. 'We're friends, that's what you said. I'll run when you run.'

Sharkey could've screamed with frustration. 'Just go!'

'Not without you.'

Which meant that Sharkey had to grab her hand and drag her across the cobblestones towards the wall, all the time expecting someone to leap out and grab them – and how would he save Poddy then?

But no one leapt at them. The night remained quiet – and Sharkey didn't trust it, not one bit.

It's one of Poosk's games, he thought. *He wants us to think we've escaped. That's when he'll take us.*

To Poddy he whispered, 'Same rules as before, Pod. If I start shouting, you run.'

There was no point even trying the well-guarded gate. The two children crept along the base of the wall, keeping to the deep shadows and running their hands over the stone.

'Here,' breathed Sharkey.

The cracks he had found were tiny, but they were enough for Poddy, who dug in her fingers and toes and scrambled right to the top, quick and silent, as if she was scaling a tier of bunks in the belly of old *Rampart*. Sharkey scanned the shadows one more time, then followed her, his fingers clutching at the crevices, his bad shoulder hurting all the way up and all the way down the other side.

With the wall behind them, they crept onto the road that wound down the hill. The moon was up, which meant it must be past midnight. But it was still too low to give much light, and they made their way by instinct as much as anything. They slipped and skidded on patches of ice, and a couple of times they almost ran head first into one of those stinking hovels, but they caught themselves just in time.

Sharkey's skin prickled worse than ever, but they saw no one. And – as far as Sharkey could tell – no one saw them.

They were at the bottom of the road before he remembered Bran's words. *Nearly everyone is at the quarry. Rain said there will be a diversion just before dawn.*

Sharkey didn't want to think about Rain, who had been her uncle's tool all along. But maybe she was telling the truth this time. Maybe nearly everyone *was* at the quarry. Maybe he was supposed to wait until just before dawn, for the diversion, then try to get the Sunkers out through the tunnel. Maybe *that* was the trap.

It didn't make sense. But then, nothing the Devouts did made sense, not to Sharkey. And Rain was a Devout, whatever she said.

He peered south and saw a glow, like the beginnings of sunclimb, in the direction of the quarry. Petrel and Fin were down there somewhere, waiting for their deaths, and so were Krill and the silver child.

I can't help 'em, he reminded himself. *I've got to get the Sunkers out. No distractions!*

'Pod,' he whispered. 'The camp where you sleep, it's just up the road from here, right?'

'Aye, no more than a mile.'

'And the guards bring you to the quarry an hour or so after sunclimb?'

'That's right. The rest of the time they're patrolling outside – there's always a dozen or more of 'em. With dogs. They go all the way down to the shore and back.'

'Can you see 'em from inside the camp?'

'Nay. But sometimes we hear 'em. And we've been told they're always out there. *Always.* A few of the older middies wanted to try the tunnel anyway, but the adm'ral wouldn't let 'em. She says we'll never get the chance to dig another one, if this one's discovered. And the dogs've got noses so keen, they'd smell us as soon as we came out the other end. We've been trying to come up with a way of getting rid of 'em, and of *knowing* we've got rid of 'em.'

'Well, tonight might be the night, Pod. Can you take us to this camp, nice and quiet?'

'What about the dogs?'

'We'll stay downwind, just in case.'

'Aye, Sharkey!'

They set off again, with the wind in their faces. Poddy guided Sharkey off the road and across ploughed fields that were capped with white, like storm waves.

Their bare feet made no sound, and they didn't speak until they reached the camp.

It was as dark as the rest of the countryside, except for a single fire. In its glow, Sharkey saw walls higher than those around the Citadel, and a gate that was bolted so firmly that it looked as if it would stand forever.

'Can't climb *those* walls,' whispered Poddy. 'We tried, but there's not a crack in 'em.'

As the children crouched in the darkness, two men walked into the light of the fire. They stopped and talked briefly, then went in opposite directions.

'What are we going to do?' whispered Poddy.

'Wait. Let's see how many of 'em there are.'

They waited for at least half an hour, clenching their teeth against the cold. In that time, the same men came back again, greeted each other in the light of the fire, and kept walking. The moon was a bulge of silver, halfway up the sky.

'There's only the two of 'em,' whispered Poddy. 'And *no dogs*!'

'Aye. They must all be at the quarry. Adm'ral Deeps could bring everyone out now, and the Devouts'd be none the wiser.'

'But she won't *know*, Sharkey! She's got no way of telling!'

Sharkey chewed his thumbnail. *Rain thinks I'm going to wait till just before dawn. All the more reason to do it now!*

'Where does this tunnel come out?' he asked.

'Near the shore. In a bunch of trees. I reckon I could find it.'

'Let's go and see.'

They crept away from the camp as silently as they had come, and headed for the shore. It was no more than three hundred yards away at that point, and Sharkey could hardly wait to get there, to smell the salt water and the seaweed, to hear the murmur of the waves.

Still, he didn't take any risks, and neither did Poddy. For the last hundred yards, they crawled on their bellies through the frosty grass, stopping frequently to listen for the sound of footsteps or voices. But they heard nothing.

It took them another forty minutes or so to find the end of the tunnel, which was so well hidden that they crept past it a dozen times without seeing it. But at last Sharkey pulled a pile of brambles to one side, and there it was.

Poddy's eyes gleamed with excitement. 'Are we going in?'

'I am,' said Sharkey. 'You're going to wait here.'

'Nay, Sharkey. You won't be able to find your way around. It's not just Sunkers in the camp, there's other prisoners too. And Adm'ral Deeps reckons a couple of 'em aren't really prisoners – they're there to keep an eye on us and tell the guards what we're up to. You wouldn't believe the tricks we had to pull to stop 'em finding out about the tunnel.'

Sharkey didn't want to send Poddy back into danger, not now she was free. But he didn't want to blunder around the camp and mess everything up, either.

Besides, dawn was still some way off. If Poddy went into the camp, *he* could sneak back to the top of the quarry and search for the portable comm device. With that, they could signal *Claw*.

'All right,' he said. 'But you be extra careful, Pod!'

'Aye, Sharkey!' And she wriggled headfirst into the tunnel.

Sharkey pulled the brambles across the entrance. Then, with a quick glance at the stars to make sure he was going in the right direction, he set off back towards the quarry.

★★★

When the message came through, Dolph was down in Grease Alley. She had an iron rod in her left hand and a knife in her right, and Chief Engineer Albie was trying to kill her.

'Haaa!' roared Albie, and his wrench swung through the air with deadly accuracy.

But Dolph ducked under the blow, the way her mam had taught her, and jabbed the iron rod towards Albie's ribs. With her other hand, she sliced at his bare arm and drew blood.

The Chief Engineer didn't even flinch. He swung hard and low at Dolph's knees, and she leapt out of the way just in time, her heart racing. In the background she could hear the rest of the fighting, like a muffled roar, as the core of the mutineers battled to keep the crew away from the engines.

'Give – up – Albie,' she panted.

His lips parted in a vicious grin. '*You* – give – up, Orca's girl.'

'Never.' And Dolph's knife darted in and out again, so quick that Albie couldn't guard against it.

More blood, though not enough to slow the Chief Engineer down. Dolph bounced on her toes, trying to look as if she still had all the energy in the world. But she was tiring, and she knew it.

Albie's next swing clipped her right arm, so that she nearly dropped the knife. She didn't make a sound, but Albie laughed and swung again. Dolph stepped backwards – and found herself wedged into a corner next to the digester.

The stink of the ship's waste. The greasy floor. Nowhere to jump. For the first time, she realised that she might be about to lose this fight. Albie's grin spread as he realised the same thing.

Mam, thought Dolph. *Help me!* And she surged out of the corner, using her knife to drive Albie back.

He grunted with surprise— And all around them, the pipes began to rattle out a message from First Officer Hump on the bridge.

Shore party due to be executed in morning, said the pipes, in general ship code. *They need us NOW!*

It was impossible not to be distracted by it. Dolph's first thought was that Missus Slink must have fixed the telegraph. Her second thought was that Albie was still taking in the message, and that she could kill him right now, if she wanted to. It was probably the best thing to do – otherwise he'd always be a problem. Her mam, Orca, would have killed him without hesitation. And Dolph was as loyal as she could be to Orca's memory.

But at the same time, she was trying to do things differently. And so, instead of using her knife, she raised the iron rod and whacked Albie across the skull. And as he fell to the deck, unconscious, she leapt over his body, shouting, 'Put him in the Dufftown brig. And get those engines going. We're heading north, full speed!'

WE KNEW YOU'D COME FOR US

Sharkey crept up the north side of the quarry, as quickly and silently as he could. The moon was high now, and he could almost see where he was going, which was just as well. Prickly bushes jabbed at him from all sides. Stones and pebbles turned under his feet. Below him, in the heart of the quarry, a hundred small fires burned, and the sound of hammering filled the night air.

No distractions, Sharkey told himself. *I can't help 'em, so it's a waste of time even thinking about it.*

He heard something moving up ahead, and froze. It was a dragging sound, a rustling of grass and twigs, and for a moment he wished Rain was there with him – *she'd* know what it was.

But then he remembered. Rain was the enemy. *If she was here, she'd just betray me again.*

He waited. The dragging sound stopped. Somewhere near Sharkey's foot, a small rough voice said, 'Come to 'elp, 'ave you, shipmate?'

Sharkey almost fell off the edge of the quarry, he was so startled. 'Mister Smoke,' he whispered. 'What are you doing here?'

'Been sendin' a message to the *Oyster*. Givin' 'em our position. Lettin' 'em know what's happenin' down yonder.' He twitched his long nose towards the quarry.

Sharkey swallowed. 'What's happening?'

'Ain't you looked?'

'Not yet.'

The rat beckoned him. Sharkey didn't want to go, but he found himself dropping to his hands and knees and crawling to the edge.

What he saw was like a scene from a nightmare. A hundred or more crude torches were arranged in a circle, so they lit up the quarry like sunclimb. No one was chipping at the rocks, however. There were no prisoners at all, just the Devouts and their dogs, standing beside the torches, with anticipation rising from them as hot and hungry as a diesel engine.

No. Wait. There *were* prisoners. In the middle of the circle, like the eye of a storm, the whipping posts held four sagging figures. Petrel. Fin. Krill. The silver child.

The hammering stopped, then started again. With an effort, Sharkey dragged his eyes away from the four figures to where a score or so of Devouts were building a platform, with three posts on it.

Sharkey's guts tried to tie themselves in a knot. 'What's that for?' he whispered.

'That's a gibbet, shipmate. They're gunna hang Petrel, Fin and Krill at dawn. And over yonder you'll see a bonfire. That's for the cap'n. They're gunna burn what can be burned, and melt the rest.'

Sharkey stared at him. 'Will the *Oyster* get here in time? To save 'em?'

'Not a chance, shipmate.'

I can't help 'em, thought Sharkey. *I've got to rescue my people. No distractions.*

Except if their positions were reversed, if it was Sharkey down there in the quarry, he couldn't imagine Petrel walking away. She'd be up here plotting, and so would Krill and Fin. And the little silver captain would be wanting to help, and Rain would—

No. Don't think about Rain.

'I could come back,' whispered Sharkey, his eyes fixed on the gibbet. 'I've got to get the Sunkers out and send 'em down the coast, but then I could come back. I don't know what I can—'

'I knew you wouldn't let us down, shipmate,' said the rat. ''Ere, do you want this?' And he dragged the

272

sack out of the bushes and dumped it in front of Sharkey.

'The comm,' said Sharkey. 'Adm'ral Deeps'll need it to signal *Claw*.' He opened the sack, and his fingers brushed against tin.

The masks.

The original plan, thought up by Petrel and added to by everyone else, had involved Mister Smoke smuggling the masks into the re-education camp, along with enough wood and rags to make several flaming torches, and a note to explain how terrified the Devouts were of the 'demon'.

Because of the tunnel, the masks were no longer needed. But it struck Sharkey that maybe he could use them for a different purpose ...

'I'll take the whole thing,' he said, tying the mouth of the sack shut and slinging it over his shoulder. 'I don't know if I can help, but I'll do my best. What about you, Mister Smoke?'

'Don't worry about me, shipmate. I got me own plans. Gotta find Scroll, for a start. I'm 'opin' she can 'elp me with somethin'.'

'Well then,' said Sharkey. 'Fair tides and clear water.'

'Same to you, shipmate.' Mister Smoke turned away.

Sharkey whispered, 'Wait!'

'Aye? What is it?'

'You're not—You're not really the adm'ral, are you? You're not really one of the ancestors?'

He heard a whisper of sound, like rat laughter. 'What do you think, shipmate?' said Mister Smoke. And, with a twitch of his nose, he was gone.

★★★

Rain was curled up on her bed in the little closet, waiting for the night to pass. Now that she was back, it was hard to believe that the last two weeks with the Sunker children had happened. Everything was exactly as it had been before. She had managed to talk to Bran, after he was released from the punishment hole, but apart from that all her time had been spent acting as her uncle's unpaid servant.

After supper he had locked her in her room and would not let her out until an hour or so before dawn. Her job then would be to feed Brother Thrawn spoonfuls of gruel, while Uncle Poosk tucked into a breakfast of eggs, black pudding, crab cakes, roast goose and pastries – all of it meant for his 'dear leader'.

Once breakfast was finished, the day's audience would begin, with Devouts from all over the world bringing their reports and questions. At least, that was the normal order of things. Today would be different, because of the executions.

Rain turned her face to her wooden pillow, trying not to think about anything except Bran. She had managed to save him from a whipping, but she was not sure that she could save him from turning into a proper Devout. Not unless she got him away from here.

'*And that is why,*' she sang under her breath,

'*I WILL do this.*

No matter how

Afraid I am—'

A sharp rap on her door made her flinch. She heard the key turn in the lock, and dressed quickly, throwing on skirt and vest and pulling on her boots. Then she crept out the door.

Uncle Poosk was already seated at the dining table, his face pink with pleasure at the sight of the crab cakes. 'Executions give me an appetite,' he said to Rain. 'Hurry up and feed our dear leader, and we will be on our way.'

Brother Thrawn was sitting in his wheeled chair in the next room, dressed in clean robes. His mad eyes stared at Rain as she draped a rug over his knees. 'Gurr—' he mumbled. 'Gurr-lll.'

Rain froze. Was that a word? A *proper* word? She licked her lips. 'Did— Did you say *girl*, Brother?' she whispered.

There it was, the slightest nod, and sweat breaking out on the man's gaunt forehead as if the movement had taken nearly all his strength.

'Are you— Are you getting better?'

Another infinitesimal nod.

Rain stood there, gaping. What did this mean? Should she tell her uncle? Did it change things?

No.

'Brother Thrawn,' she whispered. 'Do you want to get your revenge on Uncle Poosk? Do you want your people to know the truth about what he is doing?'

She could see the answer in Thrawn's eyes. It was like a shout, and she almost fell backwards with the force of it.

But she sang a quick silent song for courage, then said, 'I will help you. But you will have to help me, too. Can you pretend, just for the next little while, that you are *not* getting better?'

A third nod.

'Good. This is what we are going to do,' said Rain.

She bent closer, and whispered hurriedly in his ear. Then she grabbed the back of the chair and wheeled it into the dining room, where Uncle Poosk was stuffing himself as if he could not get enough of the rich food – which was probably true.

Like Rain's mama, Poosk had grown up in poverty and had struggled all his life to climb out of it. He was not the sort of man who would ever rise to wealth and power on his own. But in the weeks since the disastrous expedition had returned from the icy south, he had done it through Brother Thrawn.

'Greetings, revered leader,' he murmured as Rain pushed the chair to the other end of the table. 'What a day we have ahead of us, beginning with an execution at dawn. You must be there, of course. How would we manage without your wise presence?'

His words were humble, but the sarcastic tone gave him away. He never bothered pretending when it was just Rain and Brother Thrawn in the room with him. Brother Thrawn couldn't betray him, and Rain wouldn't. Not when he could so easily hurt Bran.

She fed Brother Thrawn as quickly as she could, which was not very quickly at all. He hated the gruel, and she hated spooning it into him. But at last, with a quarter of the bowl still full, he clenched his teeth and refused to eat any more.

Rain picked up the bowl and stood there, as if she wasn't sure what to do next.

'What is the matter?' asked her uncle, looking up from his plate with a crumb of pastry clinging to his lip. 'Have you forgotten your duties?'

'No, Uncle.'

'Then put the bowl next to mine, here.' He rapped the table with his knuckles. 'I have nearly finished.'

'Yes, Uncle.' Rain walked towards him, singing under her breath, *'But will we cower, will we hide . . .'*

And then, somehow, in the middle of her song, she tripped, and the bowl flew out of her hand and spilled gruel all over her uncle's clean robe.

'Oh! I am sorry!' she gasped, backing away with her hand over her mouth.

Apologies were never enough for Uncle Poosk. He leapt to his feet with a cry of anger, and slapped her across the face. 'Useless girl! Now I will have to change.'

'I am sorry,' whispered Rain again. She dared not touch her stinging cheek. 'Can I help? Tell me what to do and I will do it.'

She ran ahead of him, opening the door of his room and hovering there anxiously.

'Bah!' said her uncle, elbowing her to one side. 'Make sure Thrawn's hands are clean. I do not want to waste another minute.'

And he slammed the door in her face.

With trembling fingers, Rain turned the key in the lock. Uncle Poosk was too busy cursing to hear it, but she knew she didn't have long. She ran back to the table, grabbed Brother Thrawn's chair and, without a word, wheeled it towards the audience chamber.

They were not quite there when the door handle rattled behind them. Rain flinched.

'What is this?' cried her uncle. 'What have you done, stupid girl? Let me out at once!'

Quickly Rain pushed Brother Thrawn through the empty audience chamber, and shut the heavy doors behind them. Her uncle's cries grew muffled.

The Initiates' dormitory was four long corridors away, just past the door that led to the underground storerooms. To Rain, every step seemed like an eternity. Her hands were clammy and cold, and she was having trouble breathing. She kept expecting Uncle Poosk to break free from his prison and come after her.

But then she saw Bran, waiting outside the dormitory as she had instructed. She hugged him with all her strength. 'Are you ready?' she whispered.

The little boy nodded.

Rain dredged her memory for the bravest song she knew. To her surprise, it was one of her own.

'*I tried to break the depth gauge*
To save my brother's life—'

She nodded to herself. She had been terrified then, just as she was now. But she would do what had to be done.

With her heart beating wildly, she went over the words she had prepared for the guards at the gate. *Brother Thrawn is going to oversee the execution of the demon and its followers. Let us through.*

Then she and her little brother pushed the leader of the world out the door of the Citadel.

★★★

By the time Sharkey made it back to the mouth of the tunnel with the sack over his shoulder, Adm'ral Deeps was already crawling out.

She was filthy and bruised, but when she saw Sharkey she pulled herself up to her full height and gripped his arm. 'Well done,' she murmured. '*Very* well done. We had no idea the guard dogs were gone! Without you, we'd never have tried the tunnel tonight.'

'It was Poddy, Adm'ral, as much as me,' said Sharkey.

Deeps laughed under her breath. 'Modest as usual, eh? Here, give me a hand.'

More people were coming out of the tunnel by then, some of them so weak they had to be dragged along. There were two of them, then three, then a dozen. Sharkey and Adm'ral Deeps stood on either side of the entrance, helping the Sunkers to their feet and propping them up until they were steady.

Out came Sharkey's uncles and aunts and cousins, and Cuttle's ma, and Gilly's fa and all the other people he had been so relieved to see in the quarry. Only now it was even better, because they were right there in front of him, and he could grip their hands and clasp their shoulders without even trying to wipe away his tears.

Nearly everyone who emerged whispered, 'We knew you'd come for us, Sharkey.'

'It wasn't just me,' he said, over and over again. 'There's others, and they're in trouble.' But no one seemed to hear that last bit, no matter how often he said it.

At last the whole of *Rampart*'s crew was gathered under the trees, a filthy, ragged, whispering crowd, as familiar and dear to Sharkey as his own two hands. With a quick signal, Adm'ral Deeps called the senior salties to her side and said, 'We're heading sou'-west, keeping well away from the road. No stragglers. Stickle, Pike, Scale, you three bring up the rear. Sharkey and I'll lead the way. Come!'

Sharkey started to obey her. It was automatic, and besides, he *wanted* to go with her, he really did. After all the confusion and fear of the last fortnight, he was back with his people. What's more, he was a hero, a *real* one this time. Everyone loved him. He could go with them, and no one would know he'd deserted Petrel and her friends just when they needed him most.

No one except him and Mister Smoke.

Before he could change his mind, he stopped and took the comm device out of the bag. 'Adm'ral, you can use this to signal Gilly on *Claw*. She'll only be able to take four or five, and the rest of the crew'll have to hide. Did Poddy tell you about the *Oyster*?'

'She did,' said the Adm'ral, accepting the comm. 'Will they pick us up?'

'I reckon so, though not straight away. Some of their people are in trouble. Ship's coming to the rescue, but they're too far away to help. Which is why I have to go back.'

'Go back?' Deeps stared at him, the bruises on her face as dark as ink. 'Nay, Sharkey, you're coming with us.'

'But I want—'

'It's not what you *want*, Sharkey, it's what you *must do*.' The Adm'ral's voice hardened. 'I thought you understood that. Your duty is to your people. And if we have to manage without the *Oyster*, we will.'

'But I—'

'Nay, I'll have no argument. What if you get caught again? We can't take such a risk. Who else among us can hear the ancestors?'

Sharkey stared at her, his heart sinking. 'But—'

'Poddy told us about the talking rats, but I don't believe they're Lin Lin and Adm'ral Cray, any more than you do. You're the only one the ancestors have ever spoken to. And right now, we need their wisdom more than ever. Which means we need *you*.'

Her hand gripped Sharkey's wrist. He tried to pull away, but even half-starved she was stronger than he was, and he found himself being hauled through the trees, towards the waterline.

He knew that Adm'ral Deeps was right, in one way. The Sunkers *did* need him. Not to talk to the ancestors, but to guide them across strange country and make sure they found the bay where *Claw* was waiting.

Trouble was, Petrel and her friends needed him more.

He didn't have to ask himself what she would do, not this time. He knew what was right. And he knew the exact words that would make Adm'ral Deeps let him go. But he didn't think he could get them out. Because once they were said, there'd be no more 'hero'. There'd be no more back-patting and 'Well done' and 'We knew you'd come for us'.

In fact, he'd be lucky if any of the Sunkers ever spoke to him again. Especially Adm'ral Deeps.

He dug in his heels. The Adm'ral jolted to a stop, saying, 'What *is* the matter?'

'It was—' The words stuck like a fishbone in Sharkey's throat.

All around him, Sunkers were heading to the waterline as quickly and quietly as they could. Anyone too weak to hobble was carried. Presser Surgeon Blue was limping from one small group to another. And there was Poddy, trotting towards Sharkey, her face bright with joy. Which made it even harder.

But not as hard as walking away, with the gibbet and the bonfire behind him.

'It was a lie,' he said.

'What?' Adm'ral Deeps was losing patience with him, hero or not. 'What are you talking about?'

Sharkey took a jagged breath. Then he looked straight at the adm'ral and said, 'The ancestors never spoke to me. *Never.* I lied. I'm sorry.'

The joy in Poddy's face went out like a light. At the same time, the Adm'ral's fingers loosened with shock.

'I'm sorry!' said Sharkey again, more to Poddy than to anyone else. And he pulled his hand free and ran back the way he had come.

★★★

One hand, thought Petrel. *All this time, and I've only got one hand free.*

But one hand was better than none. And no one had noticed, not yet, which meant she could start work on the other hand. Her head still bowed. Her face still dull with stupidity. And in her heart, the desperate need to save her friends.

She'd hoped the Devouts might grow careless, standing guard all night, but they showed no sign of it. If anything, they watched Krill, Fin and the captain more closely than ever. The only one they ignored was Petrel.

Her left hand was easier to untie than her right. Carefully, she flexed her wrists, keeping the rope around them and watching the guards out of the corner of her eye. Something was happening. What was it? The hammering behind her had stopped and the Devouts were milling around purposefully.

They went for Krill first, a mob of them with cudgels at the ready. They untied the ropes that held him to the whipping post, then dragged him bodily past Petrel, with the Head Cook struggling all the way. But his hands were bound and his ankle was useless, and all he could do was bruise a few of them, and get worse bruises in return.

Petrel turned her head as he passed, and saw the platform behind her. With its ropes. And its nooses. And Krill being dragged towards it.

Her heart almost tore itself from her body in fright. They were going to hang him. They weren't going to wait for dawn, they were going to do it now. What's more, another group of Devouts was advancing on Fin and the captain. And on *her*. Her hands might be free, but that wasn't nearly enough. It was time for the executions, and she couldn't do a thing to stop them.

EXECUTION

Sharkey ran south along the road, feeling as if he had a fever. His face burned at the thought of what he had just done. His chest ached. He knew there was a good chance he'd never see *Claw* again. And if he did, it certainly wouldn't be as captain.

Maybe the Oyster*'ll take me,* he thought bleakly. *I could work in the engine room and pretend I'm still in the Undersea.*

He tightened his grip on the sack, and looked up at the stars. By the position of the Lobster, it was less than an hour till dawn, which meant he had to be extra careful. Rain's trap was about to be sprung, and he was determined not to get caught in it.

He'd just passed the road that led up to the Citadel when he heard something coming down the hill towards him. A cart maybe, its wheels rattling on the icy pebbles. Sharkey slid into the ditch and crouched there in the mud and the weeds, trying to quieten his breathing.

The rattling sound came closer. And there in the moonlight was Brother Thrawn, hunched in his wheeled chair, with Rain and Bran pushing him towards the quarry.

If Sharkey could've killed them with a look, he would've done it, and danced around their dead bodies. He shrank down as they passed, his face inches above the freezing mud, his eye half-closed so as not to catch the moonlight. A frog croaked nearby. The rattle of the wheeled chair grew louder and louder, then it passed him and continued down the road.

Sharkey didn't move. Poosk'd be along any second, keeping an eye on Brother Thrawn. There'd be guards too, ready to spring the trap.

Which I'm not going to fall into.

He waited, with the cold seeping through his clothes. But there were no more footsteps. Brother Poosk and the guards did not come.

Sharkey's pulse hammered in his ears. Where were they? Had they gone to the re-education camp instead of the quarry? Was that part of the trap?

No. Poosk wouldn't let Brother Thrawn go anywhere without him! It'd be too easy for things to go wrong, for the whole pretend nursemaid thing to fall apart. So if he's not here, where is he?

Sharkey inched his way out of the ditch, staring after the chair. This didn't make any sense. What was Rain doing? She had betrayed him, so she *must* be against him. She *must* be working with Poosk. But if that was the case, where *was* Poosk? Where were the guar—

The realisation hit him like a flood tide. If Poosk wasn't here, maybe he didn't know what was happening. Maybe it *wasn't* a trap after all!

And suddenly Sharkey saw the sense in Rain's betrayal.

Those two guards and their dogs would've caught him in the end – he knew that now. For all his determination, he'd been lost from the moment they came out of the trees. He hadn't understood it at the time. But Rain had.

And she'd understood, too, that she was more useful free than as a prisoner. Free, she could send Bran to let Sharkey and Poddy out of the punishment hole. Free, she could set up a diversion.

Sharkey felt as if the weight of oceans had lifted off his shoulders. She hadn't betrayed him after all! She'd just been clever.

He almost laughed out loud at the beauty of it. She'd fooled him as effectively as he'd ever fooled the Sunkers. What's more, she'd fooled Poosk.

He raced after the wheeled chair, leaving a trail of mud behind him. *Hope I'm right,* he thought. *Hope this isn't the stupidest thing I ever did.*

And he hissed, 'Rain!'

She stopped dead, but didn't turn around. Sharkey thought he heard a whisper of song, trembling on the night air. He tried again. 'Rain! It's me, Sharkey!'

Rain spun around, her hand to her mouth. Her little brother leaned against her, his face concealed by his hood.

'Sharkey,' whispered Rain. 'You got away.'

'Aye, and Poddy too, and all the rest of the Sunkers—'

There was a grunt of protest from the man in the wheeled chair, and a barely formed word. 'Nnno-o.'

Rain bent over him and said, 'If you want, I can always give you back to Brother Poosk. I do not mind.'

At which Brother Thrawn fell silent.

'Are you taking him to the quarry?' asked Sharkey. 'Is he your diversion?'

'Yes.'

'It's a good start, but I don't think it'll be enough.'

'I know,' said Rain. 'But it was all I could think of.'

'Mister Smoke's around somewhere – he's got plans too, though he didn't say what. And I've got these.' Sharkey tapped the sack. 'You start things off, and I'll come in when they're already shaken up a bit.'

He was trying to sound confident, and it must have worked because Rain beamed at him and said, 'We are going to save them!'

'Aye,' said Sharkey, 'course we are. Bran, do you know much about goats?'

The little boy pushed his hood out of his eyes and nodded.

'He is good with animals,' said Rain.

'Then he'd best come with me,' said Sharkey. 'Because all I know is fish, and I suspect goats are a bit different.'

***

The noose around Petrel's neck was coarse and scratchy. The stool she balanced on had a wobbly leg. One of the Devouts stood ready to kick it out from under her.

Where are you, Mister Smoke? she thought. *I wish you'd come!*

But even if Mister Smoke *did* come, it could only be to say goodbye. Because Fin had a stool beneath *his* feet and a noose around *his* neck too. So did Krill. And on the other side of the quarry, three men waited for the signal to plunge their flaming torches into the wood stacked around the silver captain.

Petrel's hands were loose inside their ropes, but what good was that? Even if she could grab the noose as she fell, the Devouts would be upon her in an instant. She'd still die. It'd just take a bit longer.

This is the end, she thought. *I wish Krill and Fin weren't so far away. I wish I could hug 'em. I wish I could talk to the cap'n one last time, tell him I'm sorry we never found his Singer.*

She wondered what the Devouts were waiting for. Someone important, maybe? Whoever it was, she hoped they never came! She hoped—

A movement near the quarry entrance caught her attention. The ranks of Devouts were parting to let someone through. Someone important.

A chill of horror ran down Petrel's back. The waiting was over.

★★★

The doves in their cote fluttered restlessly as the two boys crept past. Next door to them, the goats were quiet. Sharkey followed Bran into the pen and closed the gate behind them. Under his feet, the ground was chopped, and frosted with ice.

'Du–usk!' called Bran softly. 'Mee-eek!'

Sharkey heard a crying sound, like a baby wanting its ma, and a patter of hooves. Next moment, he found

himself surrounded by a dozen or more hairy bodies, all
butting up against him and trying to nibble his fingers,
as excitable as a bunch of middies and twice as smelly.

He stood very still and tall, trying to keep his hands
away from the curious mouths. But Bran rubbed the
goats' heads and scratched their ears and chatted to
them as if they were old friends.

'What are we going to do with them?' he asked.

Sharkey undid the neck of the sack and showed
Bran the contents. 'I want to tie these to 'em, and send
'em running into the quarry.'

'Where the Brothers are?' Bran's eyes were enormous.

'Aye. Can we do that?'

The little boy thought for a minute, scratching his
lip with his finger, then said, 'If I take a bucket of grain
they will follow me up the road, and then I could
throw the bucket – except I cannot throw very far.'

'I can,' said Sharkey.

And they set to work.

★★★

The last person Petrel expected to see was Rain. But
there she was, her face white in the torchlight, pushing
a stooped figure in a wheeled chair. A murmuring rose
all across the quarry, and the Devouts edged forward.

Petrel turned her head carefully to look at Fin and Krill, and they looked back at her with desperate eyes. Rain might have pretended to be their friend on *Claw*, but she had shown her true colours when she betrayed Sharkey. She wasn't here to help them. She was here to watch them die.

The wheeled chair stopped halfway between the platform and the unlit bonfire. Rain bent over the stooped figure, listened – and moved the chair back ten yards towards the quarry entrance, as if to get a better view.

The Devouts made way for her, nudging each other into position with their elbows. The three men on the platform, waiting to kick away the stools, straightened up expectantly. The guards with the flaming torches moved closer to the silver captain.

Petrel heard a flurry of wings overhead, and the torches guttered, then sprang high again. She stared at the figure in the wheeled chair. It was Brother Thrawn. She'd only seen him once, but the harsh lines of his face had stuck in her mind.

The man nearest the chair held up his hand for silence. Rain said something to him, and he repeated her words. 'Before the executions are carried out, our dear leader wishes to make an announcement,' he bellowed.

His voice reached every corner of the quarry, and bounced off the rough stone in a wave of echoes. *Announcement . . . announcement . . . announcement . . .*

'He has important news that he particularly wishes to convey to us. In person.' *Person . . . person . . .*

'He cannot speak above a whisper, but—'

Rain gestured an invitation. The man with the loud voice puffed out his chest with importance. 'But *I* will listen and pass on his words.'

And he bent over Brother Thrawn.

For half a minute or more, nothing happened. The man shifted uncomfortably, waiting for his leader to say something.

Petrel thought she heard a grunting sound. And suddenly, she felt a spark of hope. She wasn't sure why. Nothing had changed – or had it? She flexed her fingers, trying to get the blood flowing.

'What was that, Brother?' asked the man.

Another grunt, like someone trying – and failing – to speak. The man straightened up, his face red. He whispered to Rain, and she whispered back.

'*What?*' cried the man, his eyes bulging. 'I do not believe it!'

Somehow, quiet Rain found her voice. 'It is true!' *True . . . true . . . true . . .* 'He cannot talk.' *Talk . . . talk . . .*

Disbelief rippled from one side of the quarry to the other. Voices rose in protest.

'Of course he can talk, he has been giving us orders.'

'You are not listening carefully enough.'

'Where is Brother Poosk? The man is a fool, but at least he knows how to listen.'

One voice could be heard above them all – the man who had first spoken. 'His condition has grown suddenly worse, yes? Is *that* what he wanted to tell us?'

Petrel had to make herself breathe. The hope that they might not be going to die after all was almost as painful as the despair.

'No,' said Rain. 'He has *not* suddenly grown worse.' Then she cleared her throat and began to sing, softly at first, then more strongly.

'He has been like this
Since he came back from the south.
He cannot say a word.
Brother Poosk has taken you all
For fools.'

The Devouts stared at each other. 'Fools?' they said. 'No, I do not believe it!'

Within seconds, both Rain and the man with the loud voice were pushed aside by a dozen brothers, who pressed as close as they could to Thrawn's chair, begging him to speak.

But all Brother Thrawn did was grunt.

The men stepped back, staring at each other in horror. 'The girl was right,' said one of them in a low voice. Then he raised his head and shouted it. 'The girl was right! He cannot speak! Poosk has taken us for *fools!*'

Fools ... fools ... FOOLS ... The word echoed around the quarry, bouncing off stone and growing in volume as the Devouts repeated it in outraged voices.

'*Fools? Us?*'

Those disciplined ranks disappeared as if they had never existed. Torches waved this way and that. Some of them fell to the ground and were extinguished by the mud. The three men on the platform jumped down and joined their fellows, surging towards Brother Thrawn in a shouting throng.

Petrel eased her wrists out of the ropes and hopped off the stool. No one tried to stop her. They were too wrapped up in their own anger, bellowing at Rain, who cowered behind the wheeled chair. 'Where is he?' they screamed. 'Where is Poosk? *Where is he?*'

Petrel slipped the noose from Fin's neck and untied his ropes with quick fingers. 'You do Krill,' she whispered. 'I'll do the cap'n.'

The ropes that pinioned the captain's arms and legs were too tight, and she couldn't untie them, not with time so short. But the rope that tied him to the stake was looser. Petrel dug at it with her broken nails until it came free, then looked around for Fin to help her carry the captain. But Fin was beckoning *her*—

Which was when Petrel remembered Krill's ankle.

The blood roared in her ears. *We can't carry both of 'em. But we can't leave one of 'em behind, either.*

She began to drag the captain towards the platform, thinking that maybe Krill could carry him, while she and Fin supported the Head Cook.

Somewhere in the shouting crowd, the man with the loud voice bellowed, 'Quiet! *Quiet!* We will find Poosk and bring him to justice. But we cannot all go.'

Petrel froze.

'Some of us must stay here and guard the prisoners.'

NO!

But the brown-robed men at the back of the crowd were already remembering their duty, and turning around . . .

In the sudden shocked silence, as the Devouts saw that the platform was empty and their prisoners loose, Petrel thought she heard three things.

Wings overhead.

A baby crying.

A grunt of effort, as if someone had thrown something with all their strength.

The next minute, that *something* came hurtling over the heads of the Devouts. It was a wooden bucket, and it hit the empty platform with a *thud*. A man shouted. A dog barked. Another man, closer to the quarry mouth, screamed. Echoes bounced off the rock walls, and heads turned in every direction, trying to work out what was happening.

More screams. Then someone cried, 'Demons! *Demons!* A *horde* of them!' And the Devouts scattered in every direction.

But not all of them were panicking, not yet. Two men ran grim-faced towards Petrel and the captain. Four more closed in on Fin and Krill. Petrel lowered the captain to the ground and stood over him with clenched fists, determined to defend him to the last. She heard the wings again, but dared not look up.

The first man knocked her aside with a single blow. The second one raised his cudgel to smash the captain—

'*No!*' shrieked Petrel, scrambling to her feet and throwing herself at him. But he was more than twice her size and he shrugged her off as if she hardly existed, then raised his cudgel again. Ten yards away, Fin and Krill were taking a battering.

Petrel looked around frantically. She couldn't believe this was the end. There must be a weapon or – or *something*—

And then she saw it. She threw herself at the man a second time, with such ferocity that she spoiled his aim. The cudgel smashed into the ground, an inch from the captain's head. The man cursed, and began to lift it once more.

But before he could strike, Petrel pointed to a spot behind him and screamed, '*Demons!*'

Fin's head jerked up, his cheek dark with blood. He saw what Petrel had seen. '*Demons!*' he shouted.

And '*DEMONS!*' bellowed Krill. '*COMING THIS WAY!*'

For men whose whole lives had been built on superstition and fear, it was impossible to ignore. All six of the Devouts glanced over their shoulders – and then *they* were screaming too, everything else forgotten as a horde of hairy demons raced towards them. Or rather, a flock of goats with shiny tin masks tied between their horns – masks that, in the torchlight, looked exactly like the captain's silver face.

The six men fled without a backwards glance. A single captured demon, half-dead and trussed up, was one thing. But a *horde* of the creatures, free to wreak their terrible revenge, was another.

Petrel was breathing hard, as if she'd just run the length of the *Oyster* and back. She bent down and grabbed the captain under his arms.

A familiar voice said, 'Stand aside, shipmate!'

'Mister Smoke!' cried Petrel, and there was the rat, grinning up at her, with his fur filthy and a feather tucked behind his ear.

'You 'elp Krill,' said Mister Smoke. 'We'll take the cap'n.'

He whistled. And suddenly Petrel heard the wings again, directly overhead, and found herself in the midst of hundreds of pigeons.

But before they could land, the goats dashed past a second time, and now there was a pack of dogs nipping at their heels. The pigeons took to the skies. Goats and dogs raced around the platform and back the way they had come.

Somewhere a boy's voice cried above the uproar, 'Haiiii! Haiiii! *Run!*'

Mister Smoke whistled again, and again the birds came down. This time, their claws fastened onto the ropes that bound the captain's arms and legs. A third whistle, and they began to beat their wings so hard that Petrel was driven backwards by the rush of air. For a moment the captain did not move. The wings beat harder. The birds strained. Petrel thought she saw Scroll in the middle of them.

The captain lifted off the ground.

'Outta the way!' cried Mister Smoke, and as the captain rose into the sky, the rat leapt onto his chest and clung there.

'Where are you taking him?' shouted Petrel.

'To find the Singer,' replied Mister Smoke.

'But he's broken!'

Mister Smoke didn't answer. Petrel heard his rough voice one last time. 'Full speed ahead, shipmates!'

And the pigeons wheeled as one, and disappeared into the darkness.

★★★

Sharkey was hoarse from shouting. Every time the goats tried to run out of the quarry, he and Bran sent them back. 'Haiiii! Haiiii! *Run!*'

One or two of the masks had fallen off, but most of them stayed where Sharkey had tied them, reflecting the firelight, so that the goats not only looked like hairy demons, but like hairy demons with flaming eyes.

All through the quarry, brown-robed men tumbled over each other, trying to escape. Some of them managed to climb a little way up the steep walls, only to slide down again in a flurry of panic. Their frantic cries added to the chaos, and the goats, already unnerved by the fires and the nipping dogs, jibbed and jumped in all directions.

But Sharkey knew it couldn't last. He grabbed Bran and dragged him towards the gibbet. On the way, they met Rain, shaky, but singing at the top of her voice.

'*Hobgoblins tiptoe through the night*
And imp and ghost and evil wight—'

'Quick!' cried Sharkey. And the three of them ran towards the platform.

Petrel was staring up at the sky with a strange look on her face. Fin had his shoulder under Krill's arm, trying to help the big man hobble along. There was no sign of the silver child.

'Where is he?' asked Sharkey, looking around. 'Where's your cap'n?'

'He's gone,' said Petrel. For a moment she sounded lost, but then her face cleared and she snapped back to practicalities. 'And we'd best be gone too. Rain, you coming with us?'

Rain nodded. 'Yes, please. And Bran.'

'Come on, then.' Petrel tucked herself under Krill's other arm, and grimaced as she took some of his weight. Sharkey snatched up a discarded cudgel. Bran flapped along in his too-big robes, Rain still sang – though quietly now – and they hustled towards the road.

Sharkey kept expecting someone to stop them. But the demon goats were still cutting a swathe from one side of the quarry to another, and the torches were guttering and the dogs were howling, and not one of those superstitious men could gather his wits for long enough to stop the prisoners escaping. In the middle of the chaos, Brother Thrawn sat in his chair, seething.

The children and Krill reached the road without being challenged, and headed sou'-west as fast as they could go, which wasn't nearly fast enough for Sharkey. He looked over his shoulder and said, 'Someone'll stop being scared soon, and start thinking. And then they'll be after us. Krill can't run, which means we need somewhere to hide.'

'What about a horse?' asked Petrel. 'If we stick Krill on its back, and maybe Bran too, we *could* run.'

Sharkey nodded. 'Bran, d'you know where the horses are kept?'

The little boy pointed past the dovecot and the goat pen, and they hurried off the road, dragging Krill over a stile and across a ploughed field.

Behind them, a dog yelped. Sharkey thought he heard someone shout, 'Poosk!'

He hoped the Devouts would be so furious with the man who had fooled them that they wouldn't bother with their escaped prisoners. But he knew it was unlikely. *Some* of them might go after Poosk. But any moment now, the rest would be on the heels of the escapees.

'Rain,' he said. 'Can you and Bran run ahead and bring back a horse? Fast as you can?'

Rain and her little brother set off running into the darkness. The others followed, with Petrel and Fin stumbling across the furrows, and Krill wincing with pain every time he put his bad foot on the ground.

Bran and Rain didn't come back.

'Horse must've taken – one look at Krill and – refused to budge,' panted Petrel.

But there was worry in her voice, and worry in Krill's too when he rumbled, 'None of your – cheek – bratling. Any horse'd be – honoured – to carry me.'

'Perhaps they are – lost,' said Fin. 'Though I—' He broke off abruptly. Ahead of them, looming up against the background of stars, were three enormous round shapes.

'Balloons,' whispered Sharkey.

'They must be tethered – behind the stables,' said Fin. 'Perhaps Rain and Bran – have been caught.'

'Then we'll have to – uncatch 'em,' said Petrel. 'Sharkey, will you swap – for a bit?'

Sharkey gave her the cudgel and took her place under Krill's arm. They set off again.

When they reached the stables, Krill leaned against the wooden wall, breathing heavily, while Fin slipped inside. He came back with the news that there was no sign of Rain or Bran. 'Let us try around the back,' he whispered.

'Wait! Listen!' Petrel held up a hand.

Sharkey pinned back his ears, wondering what—
Then he heard it too. A shout from the road behind
them.

'They're after us,' he whispered. 'No time for horses.
We'll have to take a balloon.'

It was a mad suggestion, but the others nodded
grimly, knowing what would happen to them if they
were caught a second time. Petrel, Sharkey and Fin
crept around the back of the stable, with Krill hopping
after them, hanging on to the wall for balance.

Sharkey wondered what they'd find. Bran and Rain
tied up and helpless? An armed guard blocking the
way to the balloons?

The first person he saw was Rain. She wasn't tied
up. In fact, she had a knife in her hand and was hacking
at the rope that tethered one of the balloons to the
ground. Even as Sharkey watched, the balloon jerked,
bobbed – and soared up into the night sky with its
basket dangling empty beneath it.

Petrel gasped. 'What's she *doing*?'

The word *betrayal* tried to slip into Sharkey's mind,
but he wouldn't let it. He saw a second figure lying
unconscious on the ground. A guard, maybe. And a
third, standing next to one of the remaining balloons—

'It's Poosk,' he breathed. 'He's got Bran.'

The little boy was a limp bundle of robes in his uncle's arms. At his throat was another knife, glinting in the moonlight.

'Hurry up, girl,' snarled Poosk. 'Loose the other one. I will not have them coming after me.'

Rain started sawing at the next rope. Poosk glanced towards the Citadel – and that's when Sharkey saw a stream of torches, pouring down the hill towards them.

He nudged Petrel and pointed. There were Devouts behind them – running across the fields – and more Devouts chasing Brother Poosk. They had to get out of here *now*. But the knife at Bran's throat didn't waver, and Sharkey couldn't think of a single way past it, not without causing the little boy's death.

The second balloon disappeared upwards with a rushing sound, like a flock of gulls. The children edged forward, with Sharkey and Fin supporting Krill, and Petrel gripping the cudgel. Rain's eyes gleamed for a fraction of a second, as if she'd seen them.

Poosk hadn't seen them, not yet. He hadn't noticed the men running across the fields either. All his attention was on the river of torches flowing down the hill. And on the sole remaining balloon.

'Get into the basket, girl,' he snapped. 'Get ready to release the rope. And don't think to take off without me. If you do, your brother will die.'

Rain sidled towards the balloon, her head hanging. Sharkey's breath burned in his lungs. *Do something*, he told himself, and he slid out from under Krill's arm.

Behind him, there was a chorus of shouts as the men running across the field saw the torches coming down the hill. 'This way!' they shouted. 'This way!'

Poosk spun around, startled. At that crucial moment, as the knife in his hand wavered, Rain dashed forward and kicked her uncle in the shins. At the same time, Bran bit his fingers, and Petrel flew across the last few yards and whacked at him with the cudgel.

With a cry of rage, Poosk dropped the little boy and turned on Petrel. His knife slashed the air in front of her. She skipped out of range, shouting, 'Bran, get in the basket!'

'No!' growled Poosk, and he tried to seize Bran again, but Sharkey leapt onto his back and clung there, knocking him off balance.

'Bran, go!' cried Sharkey.

Rain grabbed hold of her brother and threw him into the basket. Poosk tried to stab Sharkey in the arm, but Petrel dashed in a second time, swinging the cudgel, and the knife went flying off into the darkness.

Poosk was desperate now, Sharkey could feel it. It was like trying to ride a Massy shark, but he dug in his heels and hung on, determined to keep the man away from the balloon.

A dozen Devouts with burning torches rounded the corner of the stables, shouting, 'There he is! And the prisoners too! Stop them!'

Rain clambered up the side of the basket and tumbled in. Krill hauled himself over the edge, and Petrel and Fin followed him. The torches were no more than twenty yards away.

'Sharkey!' screamed Petrel. 'Come *on*!'

But now Sharkey was the one who couldn't get free. Poosk held him with one hand and pummelled him with the other, blow after blow, until he was dizzy. In desperation, Sharkey threw his arm over Poosk's eyes. Poosk staggered five blind steps – and tripped over the unconscious guard. As he fell, Sharkey sprang away from him and ran for the basket.

He had his hands on the rim when Brother Poosk, staggering to his feet, grabbed him from behind.

Sharkey saw Fin's blood-streaked face staring at him in horror. He saw the burning torches and the brown robes closing in fast. He saw—

'SHARKEY!' bellowed Krill. And a giant fist shot out of the basket and hit Brother Poosk square on the chin. Poosk's head snapped back, and he fell to the ground.

Sharkey scrambled into the basket quicker than he had ever moved in his life. 'Go!' he gasped.

Rain seized hold of a lever and pulled it down. A rope flew out of its socket. The basket jerked. The leading Devouts threw themselves forward, their faces distorted with effort, their hands grabbing—

And the balloon soared upwards out of their reach.

THE BALLOON

So the sun rose and they were still alive. Petrel leaned over the edge of the basket and watched the grey sea pass slowly beneath them. Behind her, Rain fed the fire pot with scraps of wood, and Bran perched on Krill's knee, talking about goats. His brown robes had been stuffed unceremoniously in a corner of the wicker basket, and he was wrapped in the Head Cook's jacket. Everyone else wore the mittens and scarves that Rain had dug out of that same corner.

'Where are we going?' asked Fin, who was standing beside Petrel.

'I don't know.' She looked over her shoulder. 'Rain, can you steer this thing?'

Rain shook her head. 'It goes where the wind goes, unless it is tethered to a ship.'

'In that case,' said Petrel, 'we're going sou'-east.'

'Nothing sou'-east of here except ocean,' said Sharkey. His lip was swollen and he'd be covered in bruises tomorrow. But for now he looked happy.

Petrel gazed out over the water. 'I hope the cap'n's safe,' she said. 'I hope Mister Smoke can mend him, and that they can find the Singer and—' She broke off, shading her eyes with her hand. 'What's that?'

'What?' said Fin.

'Where?' said Sharkey, coming to stand next to them.

Petrel pointed to a dent in the smooth line of the horizon. She wasn't even sure there was anything there. It was just a smudge, slowly growing bigger . . .

'It's the *Oyster*!' she cried.

Krill dropped Bran like a hot fish fillet and hauled himself upright. 'Where?'

'*There!*'

'Looks like a gull to me,' scoffed the Head Cook. But his face was wreathed in smiles, and he gripped the side of the basket as if he could make it go faster.

'Our courses won't cross,' warned Sharkey. 'They'll go west of us unless they turn.'

'No,' said Petrel. 'They'll see us.'

'They will think we are the Devouts,' said Fin.

Petrel stared at him, horrified. 'Then we'll have to show 'em we're *not*,' she said. And she began to wave and shout, though the ship was much too far away to hear her.

'Dolph!' she screamed. 'Missus Slink! It's *us*!' She turned to her companions. 'Help me.'

They waved until their arms were almost falling out of their sockets and their voices were hoarse from shouting. But the ship continued on its course. Petrel could hardly bear it. After everything that had happened, to see the *Oyster* sailing straight past, not knowing who they were.

Beside her, Sharkey said tentatively, 'Would they pick us up if we were in trouble?'

'What do you mean?' asked Petrel.

'I—' He flushed. 'You said I was like the Devouts—'

'Not any more,' said Petrel quickly. 'I don't think that now.'

Sharkey nodded. 'But you said that your people bend, to help their friends. Might they also bend to help their enemies, if those enemies were in trouble?'

'What are you thinking, lad?' asked Krill.

Sharkey said, 'I thought we might go down. Land in the water.'

'But we cannot swim,' said Fin. 'You are the only one—'

'The basket will float,' said Rain. 'Even if it turns over we can cling to it. But if the *Oyster* does not pick us up, we will be lost.'

'Aye,' said Sharkey. 'That's the idea.'

Krill's knuckles were white. 'If Albie's in charge, he'll go straight past. Probably laugh in our faces.'

'He *can't* be in charge,' said Petrel. 'If he was, the ship'd be heading south, fast as it could go. It must be Dolph or Hump, or Weddell maybe.' She gulped air. 'I say we do it. It's either that, or keep flying till we run out of firewood.'

No one liked *that* idea. Bran stuck his thumb in his mouth, his eyes enormous. Rain picked up the lid of the fire pot. 'We will have to cut the ropes,' she said, 'at just the right moment. Otherwise the balloon will collapse on top of us.'

Everyone nodded. She covered the fire pot.

Without the heat of the fire to keep it aloft, the balloon began to descend. Sharkey and Fin sawed at the ropes, cutting them just far enough – but not too far – so they could be finished off at the last minute. The basket swayed. Petrel kept her eyes fixed on the *Oyster*, willing it to turn, *begging* it to turn.

'Grab hold!' cried Sharkey.

They hit the water in a long bumpy skid, sending spray everywhere and throwing Petrel hard against Fin. The two children clung to each other as the balloon began to settle over their heads. Just in time, Rain whipped the lid off the fire pot and Sharkey hacked the final strands of rope apart, and the balloon rose up again, up and up into the sky—

Leaving the basket bobbing in the water.

They were all wet and bruised, but that didn't matter, not now. All that concerned them was the *Oyster*, a couple of miles away and showing no sign of turning.

No one spoke. Petrel's whole being was focused on the ship, on the wind turbines and the cranes, and the familiar superstructure of the bridge.

Please turn, she begged silently. *Dolph? Pleeeease turn!*

She closed her eyes and imagined she was a gull, and could fly across the waves and beat her wings against the bridge windows. She imagined—

'*SHE'S TURNING!*' roared Krill in a voice that almost sank the basket.

Petrel's eyes snapped open. And there was the bow of the *Oyster*, slowly coming around as the ship changed course towards them.

She didn't realise she was crying until she looked at the others. Tears poured down every face – even Sharkey's. They wept, and waved to the ship, and wept some more.

But as the *Oyster* came closer, Petrel wiped her eyes and said, 'Soon as we're safe, we'd better pick up the Sunkers. Don't want to leave 'em there for the Devouts to catch again. And then we'll have to see if we can get *Rampart* afloat.'

Sharkey smiled at her. 'And retrieve the boxes.'

'What boxes?' asked Petrel.

'Just – Sunker stuff.'

'Your folk'll be pleased to see *you*, lad,' said Krill.

'Nay,' said Sharkey, his smile vanishing. 'I don't think so. I don't think they'll want me back.'

'Don't see why not,' said Petrel. 'Specially when you got 'em out of the camp and all. But if they don't want you, you can stay with us, along with Rain and Bran. And then—'

And then we turn south, she thought. *That's what I want, isn't it? We could go back to our old course, as far from the Devouts as possible. And with any luck, one day we'll spot a flock of pigeons, and there'll be the cap'n, as good as new. And Mister Smoke riding on his shoulder.*

The ship was so close now she could see folk standing at the rail. She waved frantically, and heard someone say, 'Is that *Petrel*? And *Krill*?'

'Aye, it's us!' screamed Petrel. 'And Fin too!'

There was a whoop of joy, and the next minute the rail was crammed with shipfolk, elbowing each other and shouting at the tops of their voices.

'It's Petrel! Look!'

'Where's the cap'n? I can't see him. Can you see him?'

'Here, give way, I was here first.'

'Who's the boy with the patch?'

'Where's the *cap'n?*'

'Hey, Krill, cooking's improved since you left. Ha ha ha.'

Two voices rode over all the others.

'Da! *Da!*' That was Squid, almost falling over the rail in her excitement.

'Petrel!' And that was Dolph, jumping up and down on the spot like a bratling.

Krill's grin was so wide that his beard looked as if it was about to split in half. Fin was laughing. Petrel felt like crying again, but she laughed instead.

Sharkey wasn't laughing, and neither were Rain and Bran. They huddled in the back of the basket, glad to be rescued, but taking no part in the celebrations.

Petrel thought of Bran when she had first seen him, in the quarry. She thought of the whipping posts and the starving Sunkers, and the villagers she had seen, so thin and frightened that it hurt to look at them.

They're Nothing folk, she realised, *just like I used to be. Only there's a whole country full of 'em!*

And then she thought, *We can't just sail away and forget about 'em. That wouldn't be right.*

She took a long, slow breath and said, 'We've gotta stop the Devouts.'

Everyone in the basket turned and stared at her. 'I thought I wanted to go back to the ice,' she said, 'but I don't. Not yet, anyway. I want to bring back machines, so folk don't have to wear 'emselves out carrying water and suchlike.'

'And *feed* 'em,' said Krill. 'I've never seen so many hungry folk in my life.'

Fin was smiling. 'And find my mama, so the Devouts cannot harm her. And the captain. And Mister Smoke.'

'Aye,' said Petrel. 'And find the Singer too, like the cap'n wanted. And stop the whippings, and – and—' Her voice trailed off. There was so much to do and she had no idea where to start.

They were right up against the ship now, so close they could feel the throbbing of the great engines. Four ropes slithered down, each with a strong hook on the end. Petrel and Sharkey jammed the hooks under the rim of the basket, then waved.

Rain started singing, quietly at first, then louder. Petrel joined in, and Bran and Fin and Krill. And last of all, Sharkey, so that, as the basket rose slowly up the great vessel's side, they were all singing at the tops of their voices.

'*But will we cower, will we hide?*
Will we lock ourselves inside?

Or will we hold ourselves with pride
And chase those ghouls away?'

And it seemed to Petrel that, just as they reached the rail and fell into all those welcoming arms, a freak wind snatched their voices up and carried the song across the water towards land.

Where it fell upon a thousand starving villages like a promise.

ACKNOWLEDGEMENTS

This book was inspired by a visit to the captured World War II German submarine that sits in the basement of the Museum of Science and Industry, Chicago. As soon as I set foot on that battered old sub, I knew I had to write about life underwater. Trouble was, I knew nothing about it. The two men who helped me most were Lieutenant Commander David Jones, RANR, who advised me on steering and navigation, and Commander Ian Dunbabin, RANR, who read the whole manuscript and talked me through various situations onboard submarines. Both men gave generously of their time and expertise, and if the world of the Sunkers is a convincing one, it is largely due to them. Any mistakes that remain are mine.

As usual, my Australian publishers Allen & Unwin were brilliant to work with. I'd particularly like to

ACKNOWLEDGEMENTS

thank the editorial team of Kate Whitfield, Eva Mills and Susannah Chambers, who pushed me to make *Sunker's Deep* a much better book than it would otherwise have been. Also at A&U, thanks must go to Lara Wallace and her replacement Clare Keighery, to Jyy-Wei Ip, Julia Imogen, Liz Bray, Angela Namoi and all the other people who have worked so hard to get the Hidden series out into the world.

It's always exciting to see my characters come to life visually, and Arden Beckwith has captured them perfectly with this cover, while Design by Committee have made it even stronger.

Last but not least, thanks to the excellent Peter Matheson, and to my wonderful agent Margaret Connolly.

ABOUT THE AUTHOR

Lian Tanner is a children's author and playwright. She has worked as a teacher in Australia and Papua New Guinea, a tourist bus driver, a freelance journalist, a juggler, a community arts worker, an editor and a professional actor. It took her a while to realise that all of these jobs were really just preparation for being a writer. Nowadays she lives by the beach in southern Tasmania, with a large fluffy tomcat called Harry-le-beau, and three chooks, Dolly, Clara and Floss.

THE HIDDEN SERIES: BOOK ONE

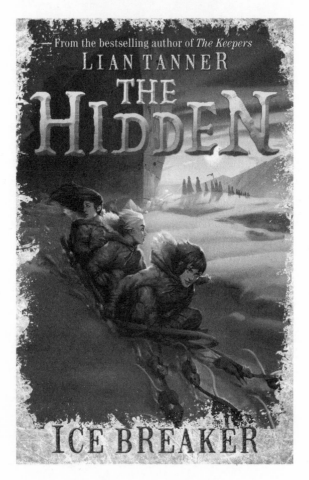

From the author of the wonderful Keepers series comes a
vividly exciting fantasy-adventure.

THE HIDDEN SERIES: BOOK THREE

The thrilling conclusion to the Hidden series

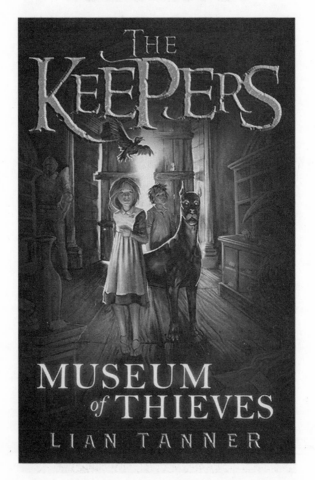

In the city of Jewel, impatience is a sin and boldness is a
crime. Goldie Roth is both impatient *and* bold. When she
escapes the clutches of the Blessed Guardians to find haven at
the Museum of Dunt, an unforgettable adventure begins.

THE KEEPERS SERIES: BOOK TWO

When Toadspit's sister Bonnie is abducted by a mysterious criminal called Harrow, Goldie must leave home in a bold attempt to rescue her friends.

THE KEEPERS SERIES: BOOK THREE

The final heart-stopping adventure in the Keepers series.
When all is nearly lost, Goldie must walk the secret and
perilous Beast Road.

Author's Note

The world of Chrestomanci is not the same as this one. It is a world parallel to ours, where magic is as normal as mathematics, and things are generally more old-fashioned. In Chrestomanci's world, Italy is still divided into numbers of small States, each with its Duke and capital city. In our world, Italy became one united country long ago.

Though the two worlds are not connected in any way, this story somehow got through. But it came with some gaps, and I had to get help filling them. Clare Davis, Gaynor Harvey, Elizabeth Carter and Graham Belsten discovered for me what happened in the magicians' single combat. And my husband, J.A. Burrow, with some advice from Basil Cottle, actually found the true words of the *Angel of Caprona*. I would like to thank them all very much indeed.

For John

CHAPTER ONE

*S*pells are the hardest thing in the world to get right. This was one of the first things the Montana children learnt. Anyone can hang up a charm, but when it comes to making that charm, whether it is written or spoken or sung, everything has to be just right, or the most impossible things happen.

An example of this is young Angelica Petrocchi, who turned her father bright green by singing a wrong note. It was the talk of all Caprona – indeed of all Italy – for weeks.

The best spells still come from Caprona, in spite of the recent troubles, from the Casa Montana or the Casa Petrocchi. If you are using words that really work, to improve reception on your radio or to grow tomatoes, then the chances are that someone in your family has been on a holiday to Caprona and brought the spell back. The Old Bridge in Caprona is lined with little stone booths, where long coloured envelopes, scrips and scrolls hang from strings like bunting.

You can get spells there from every spell-house in Italy. Each spell is labelled as to its use and stamped with the sign of the house which made it. If you want to find out who made your spell, look among your family papers. If you find a long cherry-coloured scrip stamped with a black leopard, then it came from the Casa Petrocchi. If you find a leaf-green envelope bearing a winged horse, then the House of Montana made it. The spells of both houses are so good that ignorant people think that even the envelopes can work magic. This, of course, is nonsense. For, as Paolo and Tonino Montana were told over and over again, a spell is the right words delivered in the right way.

The great houses of Petrocchi and Montana go back to the first founding of the State of Caprona, seven hundred years or more ago. And they are bitter rivals. They are not even on speaking terms. If a Petrocchi and a Montana meet in one of Caprona's narrow golden-stone streets, they turn their eyes aside and edge past as if they were both walking past a pig-sty. Their children are sent to different schools and warned never, ever to exchange a word with a child from the other house.

Sometimes, however, parties of young men and women of the Montanas and the Petrocchis happen to meet when they are strolling on the wide street called the Corso in the evenings. When that happens, other citizens take shelter at once. If they fight with fists and stones, that is bad enough, but if they fight with spells, it can be appalling.

An example of this is when the dashing Rinaldo Montana caused the sky to rain cowpats on the Corso for three days. It created great distress among the tourists.

"A Petrocchi insulted me," Rinaldo explained, with his most flashing smile. "And I happened to have a new spell in my pocket."

The Petrocchis unkindly claimed that Rinaldo had misquoted his spell in the heat of the battle. Everyone knew that all Rinaldo's spells were love-charms.

The grown-ups of both houses never explained to the children just what had made the Montanas and the Petrocchis hate one another so. That was a task traditionally left to the older brothers, sisters and cousins. Paolo and Tonino were told the story repeatedly, by their sisters Rosa, Corinna and Lucia, by their cousins Luigi, Carlo, Domenico and Anna, and again by their second-cousins Piero, Luca, Giovanni, Paula, Teresa, Bella, Angelo and Francesco. They told it themselves to six smaller cousins as they grew up. The Montanas were a large family.

Two hundred years ago, the story went, old Ricardo Petrocchi took it into his head that the Duke of Caprona was ordering more spells from the Montanas than from the Petrocchis, and he wrote old Francesco Montana a very insulting letter about it. Old Francesco was so angry that he promptly invited all the Petrocchis to a feast. He had, he said, a new dish he wanted them to try. Then he rolled Ricardo Petrocchi's letter up into long spills and cast one of his strongest spells over it. And it turned into spaghetti. The Petrocchis ate it greedily and were all taken ill, particularly old Ricardo – for nothing disagrees with a person so much as having to eat his own words. He never forgave Francesco Montana, and the two families had been enemies ever since.

"And that," said Lucia, who told the story oftenest, being only a year older than Paolo, "was the origin of spaghetti."

It was Lucia who whispered to them all the terrible heathen customs the Petrocchis had: how they never went to Mass or confessed; how they never had baths or changed their clothes; how none of them ever got married but just – in an even lower whisper – had babies like kittens; how they were apt to drown their unwanted babies, again like kittens, and had even been known to eat unwanted uncles and aunts; and how they were so dirty that you could smell the Casa Petrocchi and hear the flies buzzing right down the Via Sant' Angelo.

There were many other things besides, some of them far worse than these, for Lucia had a vivid imagination. Paolo and Tonino believed every one, and they hated the Petrocchis heartily, though it was years before either of them set eyes on a Petrocchi. When they were both quite small, they did sneak off one morning, down the Via Sant' Angelo almost as far as the New Bridge, to look at the Casa Petrocchi. But there was no smell and no flies buzzing to guide them, and their sister Rosa found them before they found it. Rosa, who was eight years older than Paolo and quite grown-up even then, laughed when they explained their difficulty, and good-naturedly took them to the Casa Petrocchi. It was in the Via Cantello, not the Via Sant' Angelo at all.

Paolo and Tonino were most disappointed in it. It was just like the Casa Montana. It was large, like the Casa Montana, and built of the same golden stone of Caprona, and probably just as old. The great front gate was old knotty wood, just like their own, and there was even the same golden figure of the Angel on the wall above the gate. Rosa told them that both Angels were in memory of the Angel who had come to the first Duke of Caprona bringing a scroll of music from Heaven – but the boys knew that. When Paolo pointed out that the Casa Petrocchi did not seem to smell much, Rosa bit her lip and said gravely that there were not many windows in the outside walls, and they were all shut.

"I expect everything happens round the yard inside, just like it does in our Casa," she said. "Probably all the smelling goes on in there."

They agreed that it probably did, and wanted to wait to see a Petrocchi come out. But Rosa said she thought that would be most unwise, and pulled them away. The boys looked over their shoulders as she dragged them off and saw that the Casa Petrocchi had four golden-stone towers, one at each corner, where the Casa Montana only had one, over the gate.

"It's because the Petrocchis are show-offs," Rosa said, dragging. "Come on."

Since the towers were each roofed with a little hat of red pantiles, just like their own roofs or the roofs of all the houses in Caprona, Paolo and Tonino did not think they were particularly grand, but they did not like to argue with Rosa. Feeling very let down, they let her drag them back to the Casa Montana and pull them through their own large knotty gate into the bustling yard beyond. There Rosa left them and ran up the steps to the gallery, shouting, "Lucia! Lucia, where are you? I want to *talk* to you!"

Doors and windows opened into the yard all round, and the gallery, with its wooden railings and pantiled roof, ran round three sides of the yard and led to the rooms on the top floor. Uncles, aunts, cousins large and small, and cats were busy everywhere, laughing, cooking, discussing spells, washing, sunning themselves or playing. Paolo gave a sigh of contentment and picked up the nearest cat.

"I don't think the Casa Petrocchi *can* be anything like this inside."

Before Tonino could agree, they were swooped on lovingly by Aunt Maria, who was fatter than Aunt Gina, but not as fat as Aunt Anna. "Where have you been, my loves? I've been ready for your lessons for half an hour or more!"

Everyone in the Casa Montana worked very hard. Paolo and Tonino were already being taught the first rules for making spells. When Aunt Maria was busy, they were taught by their father, Antonio. Antonio was the eldest son of Old Niccolo, and would be head of the Casa Montana when Old Niccolo died. Paolo thought this weighed on his father. Antonio was a thin, worried person who laughed less often than the other Montanas. He was different. One of the differences was that, instead of letting Old Niccolo carefully choose a wife for him from a spell-house in Italy, Antonio had gone on a visit to England and come back married to Elizabeth. Elizabeth taught the boys music.

"If I'd been teaching that Angelica Petrocchi," she was fond of saying, "she'd never have turned anything green."

Old Niccolo said Elizabeth was the best musician in Caprona. And that, Lucia told the boys, was why Antonio got away with marrying her. But Rosa told them to take no notice. Rosa was proud of being half English.

Paolo and Tonino were probably prouder to be Montanas. It was a grand thing to know you were born into a family that was known world-wide as the greatest spell-house in Europe – if you did not count the Petrocchis. There were times when Paolo could hardly wait to grow up and be like his cousin, dashing Rinaldo. Everything came easily to Rinaldo. Girls fell in love with him, spells dripped from his pen. He had composed seven new charms before he left school. And these days, as Old Niccolo said, making a new spell was not easy. There were so many already. Paolo admired Rinaldo desperately. He told Tonino that Rinaldo was a true Montana.

Tonino agreed, because he was more than a year younger

13

than Paolo and valued Paolo's opinions, but it always seemed to him that it was Paolo who was the true Montana. Paolo was as quick as Rinaldo. He could learn without trying spells which took Tonino days to acquire. Tonino was slow. He could only remember things if he went over them again and again. It seemed to him that Paolo had been born with an instinct for magic which he just did not have himself.

Tonino was sometimes quite depressed about his slowness. Nobody else minded in the least. All his sisters, even the studious Corinna, spent hours helping him. Elizabeth assured him he never sang out of tune. His father scolded him for working too hard, and Paolo assured him that he would be streets ahead of the other children when he went to school. Paolo had just started school. He was as quick at ordinary lessons as he was at spells.

But when Tonino started school, he was just as slow there as he was at home. School bewildered him. He did not understand what the teachers wanted him to do. By the first Saturday he was so miserable that he had to slip away from the Casa and wander round Caprona in tears. He was missing for hours.

"I can't help being quicker than he is!" Paolo said, almost in tears too.

Aunt Maria rushed at Paolo and hugged him. "Now, now, don't you start too! You're as clever as my Rinaldo, and we're all proud of you."

"Lucia, go and look for Tonino," said Elizabeth. "Paolo,

you mustn't worry so. Tonino's soaking up spells without knowing he is. I did the same when I came here. Should I tell Tonino?" she asked Antonio. Antonio had hurried in from the gallery. In the Casa Montana, if anyone was in distress, it always fetched the rest of the family.

Antonio rubbed his forehead. "Perhaps. Let's go and ask Old Niccolo. Come on, Paolo."

Paolo followed his thin, brisk father through the patterns of sunlight in the gallery and into the blue coolness of the Scriptorium. Here his other two sisters, Rinaldo and five other cousins, and two of his uncles, were all standing at tall desks copying spells out of big leather-bound books. Each book had a brass lock on it so that the family secrets could not be stolen. Antonio and Paolo tiptoed through. Rinaldo smiled at them without pausing in his copying. Where other pens scratched and paused, Rinaldo's raced.

In the room beyond the Scriptorium, Uncle Lorenzo and Cousin Domenico were stamping winged horses on leaf-green envelopes. Uncle Lorenzo looked keenly at their faces as they passed and decided that the trouble was not too much for Old Niccolo alone. He winked at Paolo and threatened to stamp a winged horse on him.

Old Niccolo was in the warm mildewy library beyond, consulting over a book on a stand with Aunt Francesca. She was Old Niccolo's sister, and therefore really a great-aunt. She was a barrel of a lady, twice as fat as Aunt Anna and even more passionate than Aunt Gina. She was saying passionately, "But the spells of the Casa Montana always have a certain elegance. This is graceless! This is—"

Both round old faces turned towards Antonio and Paolo. Old Niccolo's face, and his eyes in it, were round and wondering as the latest baby's. Aunt Francesca's face was too small for her huge body, and her eyes were small and shrewd. "I was just coming," said Old Niccolo. "I thought it was Tonino in trouble, but you bring me Paolo."

"Paolo's not in trouble," said Aunt Francesca.

Old Niccolo's round eyes blinked at Paolo. "Paolo," he said, "what your brother feels is not your fault."

"No," said Paolo. "I think it's school really."

"We thought that perhaps Elizabeth could explain to Tonino that he can't avoid learning spells in this Casa," Antonio suggested.

"But Tonino has ambition!" cried Aunt Francesca.

"I don't think he does," said Paolo.

"No, but he is unhappy," said his grandfather. "And we must think how best to comfort him. I know." His baby face beamed. "Benvenuto."

Though Old Niccolo did not say this loudly, someone in the gallery immediately shouted, "Old Niccolo wants Benvenuto!" There was running and calling down in the yard. Somebody beat on a water butt with a stick. "Benvenuto! Where's that cat got to? Benvenuto!"

Naturally, Benvenuto took his time coming. He was boss cat at the Casa Montana. It was five minutes before Paolo

16

heard his firm pads trotting along the tiles of the gallery roof. This was followed by a heavy thump as Benvenuto made the difficult leap down, across the gallery railing on to the floor of the gallery. Shortly, he appeared on the library windowsill.

"So there you are," said Old Niccolo. "I was just going to get impatient."

Benvenuto at once shot forward a shaggy black hind leg and settled down to wash it, as if that was what he had come there to do.

"Ah no, please," said Old Niccolo. "I need your help."

Benvenuto's wide yellow eyes turned to Old Niccolo. He was not a handsome cat. His head was unusually wide and blunt, with grey gnarled patches on it left over from many, many fights. Those fights had pulled his ears down over his eyes, so that Benvenuto always looked as if he were wearing a ragged brown cap. A hundred bites had left those ears notched like holly leaves. Just over his nose, giving his face a leering, lop-sided look, were three white patches. Those had nothing to do with Benvenuto's position as boss cat in a spell-house. They were the result of his partiality for steak. He had got under Aunt Gina's feet when she was cooking, and Aunt Gina had spilt hot fat on his head. For this reason, Benvenuto and Aunt Gina always pointedly ignored one another.

"Tonino is unhappy," said Old Niccolo.

Benvenuto seemed to feel this worthy of his attention. He withdrew his projecting leg, dropped to the library floor and arrived on top of the bookstand, all in one movement, without seeming to flex a muscle. There he stood, politely waving the one beautiful thing about him – his bushy black tail. The rest of his coat had worn to a ragged brown. Apart from the tail, the only thing which showed Benvenuto had once been a magnificent black Persian was the fluffy fur on his hind legs. And, as every other cat in Caprona knew to its cost, those fluffy breeches concealed muscles like a bulldog's.

Paolo stared at his grandfather talking face to face with Benvenuto. He had always treated Benvenuto with respect himself, of course. It was well known that Benvenuto would not sit on your knee, and scratched you if you tried to pick him up. He knew all cats helped spells on wonderfully. But he had not realised before that cats understood so much. And he was sure Benvenuto was answering Old Niccolo, from the listening sort of pauses his grandfather made. Paolo looked at his father to see if this was true. Antonio was very ill at ease. And Paolo understood from his father's worried face, that it was very important to be able to understand what cats said, and that Antonio never could. I shall have to start learning to understand Benvenuto, Paolo thought, very troubled.

"Which of you would you suggest?" asked Old Niccolo. Benvenuto raised his right front paw and gave it a casual lick. Old Niccolo's face curved into his beaming baby's smile. "Look at that!" he said. "He'll do it himself!"

Benvenuto flicked the tip of his tail sideways. Then he was gone, leaping back to the window so fluidly and quickly that he might have been a paintbrush painting a dark line in the air.

He left Aunt Francesca and Old Niccolo beaming, and Antonio still looking unhappy. "Tonino is taken care of," Old Niccolo announced. "We shall not worry again unless he worries us."

Chapter Two

*T*onino was already feeling soothed by the bustle in the golden streets of Caprona. In the narrower streets, he walked down the crack of sunlight in the middle, with washing flapping overhead, playing that it was sudden death to tread on the shadows. In fact, he died a number of times before he got as far as the Corso. A crowd of tourists pushed him off the sun once. So did two carts and a carriage. And once, a long, gleaming car came slowly growling along, hooting hard to clear the way.

When he was near the Corso, Tonino heard a tourist say in English, "Oh look! Punch and Judy!" Very smug at being able to understand, Tonino dived and pushed and tunnelled until he was at the front of the crowd and able to watch Punch beat Judy to death at the top of his little painted sentry-box. He clapped and cheered, and when someone puffed and panted into the crowd too, and pushed him aside, Tonino was as indignant as the rest. He had quite forgotten he was miserable. "Don't shove!" he shouted.

"Have a heart!" protested the man. "I must see Mr Punch cheat the Hangman."

"Then be quiet!" roared everyone, Tonino included.

"I only said—" began the man. He was a large damp-faced person, with an odd excitable manner.

"Shut up!" shouted everyone.

The man panted and grinned and watched with his mouth open Punch attack the policeman. He might have been the smallest boy there. Tonino looked irritably sideways at him and decided the man was probably an amiable lunatic. He let out such bellows of laughter at the smallest jokes, and he was so oddly dressed. He was wearing a shiny red silk suit with flashing gold buttons and glittering medals. Instead of the usual tie, he had white cloth folded at his neck, held in place by a brooch which winked like a tear-drop. There were glistening buckles on his shoes, and golden rosettes at his knees. What with his sweaty face and his white shiny teeth showing as he laughed, the man glistened all over.

Mr Punch noticed him too. "Oh what a clever fellow!" he crowed, bouncing about on his little wooden shelf. "I see gold buttons. Can it be the Pope?"

"Oh no it isn't!" bellowed Mr Glister, highly delighted.

"Can it be the Duke?" cawed Mr Punch.

"Oh no it isn't!" roared Mr Glister, and everyone else.

"Oh yes it is," crowed Mr Punch.

While everyone was howling "*Oh no it isn't!*" two worried-looking men pushed their way through the people to Mr Glister.

"Your Grace," said one, "the Bishop reached the Cathedral half an hour ago."

"Oh bother!" said Mr Glister. "Why are you lot always bullying me? Can't I just – until this ends? I love Punch and Judy."

The two men looked at him reproachfully.

"Oh – very well," said Mr Glister. "You two pay the showman. Give everyone here something." He turned and went bounding away into the Corso, puffing and panting.

For a moment, Tonino wondered if Mr Glister was actually the Duke of Caprona. But the two men made no attempt to pay the showman, or anyone else. They simply went trotting demurely after Mr Glister, as if they were afraid of losing him. From this, Tonino gathered that Mr Glister was indeed a lunatic – a rich one – and they were humouring him.

"Mean things!" crowed Mr Punch, and set about tricking the Hangman into being hanged instead of him. Tonino watched until Mr Punch bowed and retired in triumph into the little painted villa at the back of his stage. Then he turned away, remembering his unhappiness.

He did not feel like going back to the Casa Montana. He did not feel like doing anything particularly. He wandered on, the way he had been going, until he found himself in the Piazza Nuova, up on the hill at the western end of the city. Here he sat gloomily on the parapet, gazing across the River Voltava at the rich villas and the Ducal Palace, and at the long arches of the New Bridge, and wondering if he was going to spend the rest of his life in a fog of stupidity.

The Piazza Nuova had been made at the same time as the New Bridge, about seventy years ago, to give everyone the grand view of Caprona Tonino was looking at now. It was breathtaking. But the trouble was, everything Tonino looked at had something to do with the Casa Montana.

Take the Ducal Palace, whose golden-stone towers cut clear lines into the clean blue of the sky opposite. Each golden tower swept outwards at the top, so that the soldiers on the battlements, beneath the snapping red and gold flags, could not be reached by anyone climbing up from below. Tonino could see the shields built into the battlements, two a side, one cherry, one leaf-green, showing that the Montanas and the Petrocchis had added a spell to defend each tower. And the great white marble front below was inlaid with other marbles, all colours of the rainbow. And among those colours were cherry-red and leaf-green.

The long golden villas on the hillside below the Palace each had a leaf-green or cherry-red disc on their walls. Some were half hidden by the dark spires of the elegant little trees planted in front of them, but Tonino knew they were there. And the stone and metal arches of the New Bridge, sweeping away from him towards the villas and the Palace, each bore an enamel plaque, green and red alternately. The New Bridge had been sustained by the strongest spells the Casa Montana and the Casa Petrocchi could produce.

At the moment, when the river was just a shingly trickle, they did not seem necessary. But in winter, when the rain fell in the Apennines, the Voltava became a furious torrent. The arches of the New Bridge barely cleared it. The Old Bridge – which Tonino could see by craning out and sideways – was often under water, and the funny little houses along it could not be used. Only Montana and Petrocchi spells deep in its foundations stopped the Old Bridge being swept away.

Tonino had heard Old Niccolo say that the New Bridge spells had taken the entire efforts of the entire Montana family. Old Niccolo had helped make them when he was the same age as Tonino. Tonino could not have done. Miserable, he looked down at the golden walls and red pantiles of Caprona below. He was quite certain that every single one hid at least a leaf-green scrip. And the most Tonino had ever done was help stamp the winged horse on the outside. He was fairly sure that was all he ever would do.

He had a feeling somebody was calling him. Tonino

looked round at the Piazza Nuova. Nobody. Despite the view, the Piazza was too far for the tourists to come. All Tonino could see were the mighty iron griffins which reared up at intervals all round the parapet, reaching iron paws to the sky. More griffins tangled into a fighting heap in the centre of the square to make a fountain. And even here, Tonino could not get away from his family. A little metal plate was set into the stone beneath the huge iron claws of the nearest griffin. It was leaf-green. Tonino found he had burst into tears.

Among his tears, he thought for a moment that one of the more distant griffins had left its stone perch and come trotting round the parapet towards him. It had left its wings behind, or else had them tightly folded. He was told, a little smugly, that cats do not need wings. Benvenuto sat down on the parapet beside him, staring accusingly.

Tonino had always been thoroughly in awe of Benvenuto. He stretched out a hand to him timidly. "Hallo, Benvenuto."

Benvenuto ignored the hand. It was covered with water from Tonino's eyes, he said, and it made a cat wonder why Tonino was being so silly.

"There are our spells everywhere," Tonino explained. "And I'll never be able— Do you think it's because I'm half English?"

Benvenuto was not sure quite what difference that made. All it meant, as far as he could see, was that Paolo had blue eyes like a Siamese and Rosa had white fur—

"Fair hair," said Tonino.

—and Tonino himself had tabby hair, like the pale stripes in a tabby, Benvenuto continued, unperturbed. And those were all cats, weren't they?

"But I'm so stupid—" Tonino began.

Benvenuto interrupted that he had heard Tonino chattering with those kittens yesterday, and he had thought Tonino was a good deal cleverer than they were. And before Tonino went and objected that those were only kittens, wasn't Tonino only a kitten himself?

At this, Tonino laughed and dried his hand on his trousers. When he held the hand out to Benvenuto again, Benvenuto rose up, very high on all four paws, and advanced to it, purring. Tonino ventured to stroke him. Benvenuto walked round and round, arched and purring, like the smallest and friendliest kitten in the Casa. Tonino found himself grinning with pride and pleasure. He could tell from the waving of Benvenuto's brush of a tail, in majestic, angry twitches, that Benvenuto did not altogether like being stroked – which made it all the more of an honour.

That was better, Benvenuto said. He minced up to Tonino's bare legs and installed himself across them, like a brown muscular mat. Tonino went on stroking him. Prickles came out of one end of the mat and treadled painfully at Tonino's thighs. Benvenuto continued to purr. Would Tonino look at it this way, he wondered, that they were both, boy and cat, a part of the most famous Casa in Caprona, which in turn was part of the most special of all the Italian States?

"I know that," said Tonino. "It's because I think it's wonderful too that I— Are we really so special?"

Of course, purred Benvenuto. And if Tonino were to lean out and look across at the Cathedral, he would see why.

Obediently, Tonino leaned and looked. The huge marble bubbles of the Cathedral domes leapt up from among the houses at the end of the Corso. He knew there never was such a building as that. It floated, high and white and gold and green. And on the top of the highest dome the sun flashed on the great golden figure of the Angel, poised there with spread wings, holding in one hand a golden scroll. It seemed to bless all Caprona.

That Angel, Benvenuto informed him, was there as a sign that Caprona would be safe as long as everyone sang the tune of the Angel of Caprona. The Angel had brought that song in a scroll straight from Heaven to the First Duke of Caprona, and its power had banished the White Devil and made Caprona great. The White Devil had been prowling round Caprona ever since, trying to get back into the city, but as long as the Angel's song was sung, it would never succeed.

"I know that," said Tonino. "We sing the *Angel* every day at school." That brought back the main part of his misery. "They keep making me learn the story – and all sorts of things – and I can't, because I know them already, so I can't learn properly."

Benvenuto stopped purring. He quivered, because Tonino's fingers had caught in one of the many lumps of matted fur in his coat. Still quivering, he demanded rather sourly why it hadn't occurred to Tonino to *tell* them at school that he knew these things.

"Sorry!" Tonino hurriedly moved his fingers. "But," he explained, "they keep saying you have to do them this way, or you'll never learn properly."

Well, it was up to Tonino of course, Benvenuto said, still irritable, but there seemed no point in learning things twice. A cat wouldn't stand for it. And it was about time they were getting back to the Casa.

Tonino sighed. "I suppose so. They'll be worried."

He gathered Benvenuto into his arms and stood up.

Benvenuto liked that. He purred. And it had nothing to do with the Montanas being worried. The aunts would be cooking lunch, and Tonino would find it easier than Benvenuto to nick a nice piece of veal.

That made Tonino laugh. As he started down the steps to the New Bridge, he said, "You know, Benvenuto, you'd be a lot more comfortable if you let me get those lumps out of your coat and comb you a bit."

Benvenuto stated that anyone trying to comb him would get raked with every claw he possessed.

"A brush then?"

Benvenuto said he would consider that.

It was here that Lucia encountered them. She had looked for Tonino all over Caprona by then and she was prepared to be extremely angry. But the sight of Benvenuto's evil lop-sided

28

countenance staring at her out of Tonino's arms left her with almost nothing to say. "We'll be late for lunch," she said.

"No we won't," said Tonino. "We'll be in time for you to stand guard while I steal Benvenuto some veal."

"Trust Benvenuto to have it all worked out," said Lucia. "What is this? The start of a profitable relationship?"

You could put it that way, Benvenuto told Tonino. "You could put it that way," Tonino said to Lucia.

At all events, Lucia was sufficiently impressed to engage Aunt Gina in conversation while Tonino got Benvenuto his veal. And everyone was too pleased to see Tonino safely back to mind too much. Corinna and Rosa minded, however, that afternoon, when Corinna lost her scissors and Rosa her hairbrush. Both of them stormed out on to the gallery. Paolo was there, watching Tonino gently and carefully snip the mats out of Benvenuto's coat. The hairbrush lay beside Tonino, full of brown fur.

"And you can really understand everything he says?" Paolo was saying.

"I can understand all the cats," said Tonino. "Don't move, Benvenuto. This one's right on your skin."

It says volumes for Benvenuto's status – and therefore for Tonino's – that neither Rosa nor Corinna dared say a word to him. They turned on Paolo instead. "What do you mean, Paolo, standing there letting him mess that brush up? Why couldn't you make him use the kitchen scissors?"

Paolo did not mind. He was too relieved that he was not

going to have to learn to understand cats himself. He would not have known how to begin.

From that time forward, Benvenuto regarded himself as Tonino's special cat. It made a difference to both of them. Benvenuto, what with constant brushing – for Rosa bought Tonino a special hairbrush for him – and almost as constant supplies filched from under Aunt Gina's nose, soon began to look younger and sleeker. Tonino forgot he had ever been unhappy. He was now a proud and special person. When Old Niccolo needed Benvenuto, he had to ask Tonino first. Benvenuto flatly refused to do anything for anyone without Tonino's permission. Paolo was very amused at how angry Old Niccolo got.

"That cat has just taken advantage of me!" he stormed. "I ask him to do me a kindness and what do I get? Ingratitude!"

In the end, Tonino had to tell Benvenuto that he was to consider himself at Old Niccolo's service while Tonino was at school. Otherwise Benvenuto simply disappeared for the day. But he always, unfailingly, reappeared around half-past three, and sat on the water butt nearest the gate, waiting for Tonino. And as soon as Tonino came through the gate, Benvenuto would jump into his arms.

This was true even at the times when Benvenuto was not available to anyone. That was mostly at full moon, when the lady cats wauled enticingly from the roofs of Caprona.

Tonino went to school on Monday, having considered

Benvenuto's advice. And, when the time came when they gave him a picture of a cat and said the shapes under it went: Ker-a-ter, Tonino gathered up his courage and whispered, "Yes. It's a C and an A and a T. I know how to read."

His teacher, who was new to Caprona, did not know what to make of him, and called the Headmistress. "Oh," she was told. "It's another Montana. I should have warned you. They all know how to read. Most of them know Latin too – they use it a lot in their spells – and some of them know English as well. You'll find they're about average with sums, though."

So Tonino was given a proper book while the other children learnt their letters. It was too easy for him. He finished it in ten minutes and had to be given another. And that was how he discovered about books. To Tonino, reading a book soon became an enchantment above any spell. He could never get enough of it. He ransacked the Casa Montana and the Public Library, and he spent all his pocket money on books. It soon became well known that the best present you could give Tonino was a book – and the best book would be about the unimaginable situation where there were no spells. For Tonino preferred fantasy. In his favourite books, people had wild adventures with no magic to help or hinder them.

Benvenuto thoroughly approved. While Tonino read, he kept still, and a cat could be comfortable sitting on him. Paolo teased Tonino a little about being such a bookworm, but he did not really mind. He knew he could always persuade Tonino to leave his book if he really wanted him.

Antonio was worried. He worried about everything. He was afraid Tonino was not getting enough exercise. But everyone else in the Casa said this was nonsense. They were proud of Tonino. He was as studious as Corinna, they said, and, no doubt, both of them would end up at Caprona University, like Great-Uncle Umberto. The Montanas always had someone at the University. It meant they were not selfishly keeping the Theory of Magic to the family, and it was also very useful to have access to the spells in the University Library.

Despite these hopes for him, Tonino continued to be slow at learning spells and not particularly quick at school. Paolo was twice as quick at both. But as the years went by, both of them accepted it. It did not worry them. What worried them far more was their gradual discovery that things were not altogether well in the Casa Montana, nor in Caprona either.

CHAPTER THREE

✳

*I*t was Benvenuto who first worried Tonino. Despite all the care Tonino gave him, he became steadily thinner and more ragged again. Now Benvenuto was roughly the same age as Tonino. Tonino knew that was old for a cat, and at first he assumed that Benvenuto was just feeling his years. Then he noticed that Old Niccolo had taken to looking almost as worried as Antonio, and that Uncle Umberto called on him from the University almost every day. Each time he did, Old Niccolo or Aunt Francesca would ask for Benvenuto and Benvenuto would come back tired out. So he asked Benvenuto what was wrong.

Benvenuto's reply was that they might let a cat have some peace, even if the Duke was a booby. And he was not going to be pestered by Tonino into the bargain.

Tonino consulted Paolo, and found Paolo worried too. Paolo had been noticing his mother. Her fair hair had lately become several shades paler with all the white in it, and she looked nervous all the time. When Paolo asked Elizabeth what was the matter, she said, "Oh nothing, Paolo – only all this makes it *so* difficult to find a husband for Rosa."

Rosa was now eighteen. The entire Casa was busy discussing a husband for her, and there did, now Paolo noticed, seem much more fuss and anxiety about the matter than there had been over Cousin Claudia, three years before. Montanas had to be careful who they married. It stood to reason. They had to marry someone who had some talent at least for spells or music; and it had to be someone the rest of the family liked; and, above all, it had to be someone with no kind of connection with the Petrocchis. But Cousin Claudia had found and married Arturo without all the discussion and worry that was going on over Rosa. Paolo could only suppose the reason was "all this", whatever Elizabeth had meant by that.

Whatever the reason, argument raged. Anxious Antonio talked of going to England and consulting someone called Chrestomanci about it. "We want a really strong spell-maker for her," he said. To which Elizabeth replied that Rosa was Italian and should marry an Italian. The rest of the family agreed, except that they said the Italian must be from Caprona. So the question was who.

Paolo, Lucia and Tonino had no doubt. They wanted Rosa to marry their cousin Rinaldo. It seemed to them entirely fitting. Rosa was lovely, Rinaldo handsome, and none of the usual objections could possibly be made. There were two snags, however. The first was that Rinaldo showed no interest in Rosa. He was at present desperately in love with a real English girl – her name was Jane Smith, and Rinaldo had some difficulty pronouncing it – and she had come to copy some of the pictures in the Art Gallery down on the Corso. She was a romantic girl. To please her, Rinaldo had taken to wearing black, with a red scarf at his neck, like a bandit. He was said to be considering growing a bandit moustache too. All of which left him with no time for a cousin he had known all his life.

The other snag was Rosa herself. She had never cared for Rinaldo. And she seemed to be the only person in the Casa who was entirely unconcerned about who she would marry. When the argument raged loudest, she would shake the blonde hair on her shoulders and smile. "To listen to you all," she said, "anyone would think I have no say in the matter at all. It's really funny."

All that autumn, the worry in the Casa Montana grew. Paolo and Tonino asked Aunt Maria what it was all about. Aunt Maria at first said that they were too young to understand. Then, since she had moments when she was as passionate as Aunt Gina or even Aunt Francesca, she told them suddenly and fervently that Caprona was going to the dogs.

"Everything's going wrong for us," she said. "Money's short, tourists don't come here, and we get weaker every year. Here are Florence, Pisa and Siena all gathering round like vultures, and each year one of them gets a few more square miles of Caprona. If this goes on we shan't be a State any more. And on top of it all, the harvest failed this year. It's all the fault of those degenerate Petrocchis, I tell you! Their spells don't work any more. We Montanas can't hold Caprona up on our own! And the Petrocchis don't even try! They just keep turning things out in the same old way, and going from bad to worse. You can see they are, or that child wouldn't have been able to turn her father green!"

This was disturbing enough. And it seemed to be plain fact. All the years Paolo and Tonino had been at school, they had grown used to hearing that there had been this concession to Florence; that Pisa had demanded that agreement over fishing rights; or that Siena had raised taxes on imports to Caprona. They had grown too used to it to notice. But now it all seemed ominous. And worse shortly followed. News came that the Old Bridge had been seriously cracked by the winter floods.

This news caused the Casa Montana real dismay. For that bridge should have held. If it gave, it meant that the Montana charms in the foundations had given too. Aunt Francesca ran shrieking into the yard. "Those degenerate Petrocchis! They can't even sustain an old spell now! We've been betrayed!"

Though no one else put it quite that way, Aunt Francesca probably spoke for the whole family.

As if that was not enough, Rinaldo set off that evening to visit his English girl, and was led back to the Casa streaming with blood, supported by his cousins Carlo and Giovanni. Rinaldo, using curse words Paolo and Tonino had never heard before, was understood to say he had met some Petrocchis. He had called them degenerate. And it was Aunt Maria's turn to rush shrieking through the yard, shouting dire things about the Petrocchis. Rinaldo was the apple of Aunt Maria's eye.

Rinaldo had been bandaged and put to bed, when Antonio and Uncle Lorenzo came back from viewing the damage to the Old Bridge. Both looked very serious. Old Guido Petrocchi himself had been there, with the Duke's contractor, Mr Andretti. Some very deep charms had given. It was going to take the whole of both families, working in shifts, at least three weeks to mend them.

"We could have used Rinaldo's help," Antonio said.

Rinaldo swore that he was well enough to get out of bed and help the next day, but Aunt Maria would not hear of it. Nor would the doctor. So the rest of the family was divided into shifts, and work went on day and night. Paolo, Lucia and Corinna went to the bridge straight from school every day. Tonino did not. He was still too slow to be much use. But from what Paolo told him, he did not think he was missing much. Paolo simply could not keep up with the furious pace of the spells. He was put to running errands, like poor Cousin Domenico. Tonino felt very sympathetic towards Domenico. He was the opposite of his dashing brother Rinaldo in every way, and he could not keep up with the pace of things either.

Work had been going on, often in pouring rain, for nearly a week, when the Duke of Caprona summoned Old Niccolo to speak to him.

Old Niccolo stood in the yard and tore what was left of his hair. Tonino laid down his book (it was called *Machines of Death* and quite fascinating) and went to see if he could help.

"Ah, Tonino," said Old Niccolo, looking at him with the face of a grieving baby. "I have gigantic problems. Everyone is needed on the Old Bridge, and that ass Rinaldo is lying in bed, and I have to go before the Duke with *some* of my family. The Petrocchis have been summoned too. We cannot appear less than they are, after all. Oh *why* did Rinaldo choose such a time to shout stupid insults?"

Tonino had no idea what to say, so he said, "Shall I get Benvenuto?"

"No, no," said Old Niccolo, more upset than ever. "The Duchess cannot abide cats. Benvenuto is no use here. I shall have to take those who are no use on the bridge. You shall go, Tonino, and Paolo and Domenico, and I shall take your uncle Umberto to look wise and weighty. Perhaps that way we shan't look so very thin."

This was perhaps not the most flattering of invitations, but Tonino and Paolo were delighted nevertheless. They were delighted even though it rained hard the next day, the drilling white rain of winter. The dawn shift came in from the Old Bridge under shiny umbrellas, damp and disgruntled. Instead of resting, they had to turn to and get the party ready for the Palace.

The Montana family coach was dragged from the coach-house to a spot under the gallery, where it was carefully dusted. It was a great black thing with glass windows and monster black wheels. The Montana winged horse was emblazoned in a green shield on its heavy doors. The rain continued to pour down. Paolo, who hated rain as much as the cats did, was glad the coach was real. The horses were not. They were four white cardboard cut-outs of horses, which were kept leaning against the wall of the coach-house. They were an economical idea of Old Niccolo's father's. As he said, real horses ate and needed exercise and took up space the family could live in. The coachman was another cardboard cut-out – for much the same reasons – but he was kept inside the coach.

The boys were longing to watch the cardboard figures being brought to life, but they were snatched indoors by their mother. Elizabeth's hair was soaking from her shift on the bridge and she was yawning until her jaw creaked, but this did not prevent her doing a very thorough scrubbing, combing and dressing job on Paolo and Tonino. By the time they came down into the yard again, each with his hair scraped wet to his head and wearing uncomfortable broad white collars above their stiff Eton jackets, the spell was done. The spell-streamers had been carefully wound into the harness, and the coachman clothed in a paper coat covered with spells on the inside. Four glossy white horses were stamping as they were backed into their traces. The coachman was sitting on the box adjusting his leaf-green hat.

"Splendid!" said Old Niccolo, bustling out. He looked approvingly from the boys to the coach. "Get in, boys. Get in, Domenico. We have to pick up Umberto from the University."

Tonino said goodbye to Benvenuto and climbed into the coach. It smelt of mould, in spite of the dusting. He was glad his grandfather was so cheerful. In fact everyone seemed to be. The family cheered as the coach rumbled to the gateway, and Old Niccolo smiled and waved back. Perhaps, Tonino thought, something good was going to come from this visit to the Duke, and no one would be so worried after this.

The journey in the coach was splendid. Tonino had never felt so grand before. The coach rumbled and swayed. The hooves of the horses clattered over the cobbles just as if they were real, and people hurried respectfully out of their way. The coachman was as good as spells could make him. Though puddles dimpled along every street, the coach was hardly splashed when they drew up at the University, with loud shouts of "Whoa there!"

Uncle Umberto climbed in, wearing his red and gold Master's gown, as cheerful as Old Niccolo. "Morning,

Tonino," he said to Paolo. "How's your cat? Morning," he said to Domenico. "I hear the Petrocchis beat you up." Domenico, who would have died sooner than insult even a Petrocchi, went redder than Uncle Umberto's gown and swallowed noisily. But Uncle Umberto never could remember which younger Montana was which. He was too learned. He looked at Tonino as if he was wondering who he was, and turned to Old Niccolo.

"The Petrocchis are sure to help," he said. "I had word from Chrestomanci."

"So did I," said Old Niccolo, but he sounded dubious.

The coach rumbled down the rainswept Corso and turned out across the New Bridge, where it rumbled even more loudly. Paolo and Tonino stared out of the rainy windows, too excited to speak. Beyond the swollen river, they clopped uphill, where cypresses bent and lashed in front of rich villas, and then among blurred old walls. Finally they rumbled under a great archway and made a crisp turn round the gigantic forecourt of the Palace.

In front of their own coach, another coach, looking like a toy under the huge marble front of the Palace, was just drawing up by the enormous marble porch. This carriage was black too, with crimson shields on its doors, in which ramped black leopards. They were too late to see the people getting out of it, but they gazed with irritated envy at the coach itself and the horses. The horses were black, beautiful slender creatures with arched necks.

"I think they're *real* horses," Paolo whispered to Tonino.

Tonino had no time to answer, because two footmen and a soldier sprang to open the carriage door and usher them down, and Paolo jumped down first. But after him, Old Niccolo and Uncle Umberto were rather slow getting down. Tonino had time to look out of the further window at the Petrocchi carriage moving away. As it turned, he distinctly saw the small crimson flutter of a spell-streamer under the harness of the nearest black horse.

So there! Tonino thought triumphantly. But he rather thought the Petrocchi coachman was real. He was a pale young man with reddish hair which did not match his cherry-coloured livery, and he had an intent, concentrating look as if it was not easy driving those unreal horses. That look was too human for a cardboard man.

When Tonino finally climbed down on Domenico's nervous heels, he glanced up at their own coachman for comparison. He was efficient and jaunty. He touched a stiff hand to his green hat and stared straight ahead. No, the Petrocchi coachman was real all right, Tonino thought enviously.

Tonino forgot both coachmen as he and Paolo followed the others into the Palace. It was so grand, and so huge. They were taken through vast halls with shiny floors and gilded ceilings, which seemed to go on for miles. On either side of the long walls there were statues, or soldiers, or footmen, adding to the magnificence in rows. They felt so battered by all the grandeur that it was quite a relief when they were shown into a room only about the size of the Casa Montana yard. True, the floor was shiny and the ceiling painted to look like a sky full of wrestling angels, but the walls were hung with quite comfortable red cloth and there was a row of almost plain gilt chairs along each side.

Another party of people was shown into the room at the same time. Domenico took one look at them and turned his eyes instantly on the painted angels of the ceiling. Old Niccolo and Uncle Umberto behaved as if the people were not there at all. Paolo and Tonino tried to do the same, but they found it impossible.

So these were the Petrocchis, they thought, sneaking glances. There were only four of them, to their five. One up to the Montanas. And two of those were children. Clearly the Petrocchis had been as hard-pressed as the Montanas to come before the Duke with a decent party, and they had, in Paolo and Tonino's opinion, made a bad mistake in leaving one of their family outside with the coach.

They were not impressive. Their University representative was a frail old man, far older than Uncle Umberto, who seemed almost lost in his red and gold gown. The most impressive one was the leader of the party, who must be Old Guido himself. But he was not particularly old, like Old Niccolo, and though he wore the same sort of black frock-coat as Old Niccolo and carried the same sort of shiny hat, it looked odd on Old Guido because he had a bright red beard.

His hair was rather long, crinkly and black. And though he stared ahead in a bleak, important way, it was hard to forget that his daughter had once accidentally turned him green.

The two children were both girls. Both had reddish hair. Both had prim, pointed faces. Both wore bright white stockings and severe black dresses and were clearly odious. The main difference between them was that the younger – who seemed about Tonino's age – had a large bulging forehead, which made her face even primmer than her sister's. It was possible that one of them was the famous Angelica, who had turned Old Guido green.

The boys stared at them, trying to decide which it might be, until they encountered the prim, derisive stare of the elder girl. It was clear she thought they looked ridiculous. But Paolo and Tonino knew they still looked smart – they felt so uncomfortable – so they took no notice.

After they had waited a while, both parties began to talk quietly among themselves, as if the others were not there. Tonino murmured to Paolo, "Which one is Angelica?"

"I don't know," Paolo whispered.

"Didn't you see them at the Old Bridge then?"

"I didn't see any of them. They were all down the other—"

Part of the red hanging swung aside and a lady hurried in. "I'm so sorry," she said. "My husband has been delayed."

Everyone in the room bent their heads and murmured "Your Grace" because this was the Duchess. But Paolo and

Tonino kept their eyes on her while they bent their heads, wanting to know what she was like. She had a stiff greyish dress on, which put them in mind of a statue of a saint, and her face might almost have been part of the same statue. It was a statue-pale face, almost waxy, as if the Duchess were carved out of slightly soapy marble. But Tonino was not sure the Duchess was really like a saint. Her eyebrows were set in a strong sarcastic arch, and her mouth was tight with what looked like impatience. For a second, Tonino thought he felt that impatience – and a number of other unsaintly feelings – pouring into the room from behind the Duchess's waxy mask like a strong rank smell.

The Duchess smiled at Old Niccolo. "Signor Niccolo Montana?" There was no scrap of impatience, only stateliness. Tonino thought to himself, I've been reading too many books. Rather ashamed, he watched Old Niccolo bow and introduce them all. The Duchess nodded graciously and turned to the Petrocchis. "Signor Guido Petrocchi?"

The red-bearded man bowed in a rough, brusque way. He was nothing like as courtly as Old Niccolo. "Your Grace. With me are my great-uncle Dr Luigi Petrocchi, my elder daughter Renata, and my younger daughter Angelica."

Paolo and Tonino stared at the younger girl, from her bulge of forehead to her thin white legs. So *this* was Angelica. She did not look capable of doing anything wrong, or interesting.

The Duchess said, "I believe you understand why—"

The red curtains were once more swept aside. A bulky excited-looking man raced in with his head down, and took the Duchess by one arm. "Lucrezia, you must come! The scenery looks a treat!"

The Duchess turned as a statue might turn, all one piece. Her eyebrows were very high and her mouth pinched. "My lord Duke!" she said freezingly.

Tonino stared at the bulky man. He was now wearing slightly shabby green velvet with big brass buttons. Otherwise, he was exactly the same as the big damp Mr Glister who had interrupted the Punch and Judy show that time. So he had been the Duke of Caprona after all! And he was not in the least put off by the Duchess's frigid look. "You must come and look!" he said, tugging at her arm, as excited as ever. He turned to the Montanas and the Petrocchis as if he expected them to help him pull the Duchess out of the room – and then seemed to realise that they were not courtiers. "Who are you?"

"These," said the Duchess – her eyebrows were still higher and her voice was strong with patience – "these are the Petrocchis and the Montanas awaiting your pleasure, my lord."

The Duke slapped a large, damp-looking hand to his shiny forehead. "Well I'm blessed! The people who make spells! I was thinking of sending for you. Have you come about this enchanter-fellow who's got his knife into Caprona?" he asked Old Niccolo.

"My lord!" said the Duchess, her face rigid.

But the Duke broke away from her, beaming and gleaming, and dived on the Petrocchis. He shook Old Guido's hand hugely, and then the girl Renata's. After that, he dived round and did the same to Old Niccolo and Paolo. Paolo had to rub his hand secretly on his trousers after he let go. He was wet. "And they say the young ones are as clever as the old ones," the Duke said happily. "Amazing families! Just the people I need for my play – my pantomime, you know. We're putting it on here for Christmas and I could do with some special effects."

The Duchess gave a sigh. Paolo looked at her rigid face and thought that it must be hard, dealing with someone like the Duke.

The Duke dived on Domenico. "Can you arrange for a flight of cupids blowing trumpets?" he asked him eagerly. Domenico swallowed and managed to whisper the word "illusion". "Oh good!" said the Duke, and dived at Angelica Petrocchi. "And you'll love my collection of Punch and Judys," he said. "I've got hundreds!"

"How nice," Angelica answered primly.

"My lord," said the Duchess, "these good people did not come here to discuss the theatre."

"Maybe, maybe," the Duke said, with an impatient, eager wave of his large hand. "But while they're here, I might as well ask them about that too. Mightn't I?" he said, diving at Old Niccolo.

Old Niccolo showed great presence of mind. He smiled.

"Of course, Your Grace. No trouble at all. After we've discussed the State business we came for, we shall be happy to take orders for any stage effects you want."

"So will we," said Guido Petrocchi, with a sour glance at the air over Old Niccolo.

The Duchess smiled graciously at Old Niccolo for backing her up, which made Old Guido look sourer than ever, and fixed the Duke with a meaning look.

It seemed to get through to the Duke at last. "Yes, yes," he said. "Better get down to business. It's like this, you see—"

The Duchess interrupted, with a gentle fixed smile. "Refreshments are laid out in the small Conference Room. If you and the adults like to hold your discussion there, I will arrange something for the children here."

Guido Petrocchi saw a chance to get even with Old Niccolo. "Your Grace," he barked stiffly, "my daughters are as loyal to Caprona as the rest of my house. I have no secrets from them."

The Duke flashed him a glistening smile. "Quite right! But they won't be half as bored if they stay here, will they?"

Quite suddenly, everyone except Paolo and Tonino and the two Petrocchi girls was crowding away through another door behind the red hangings. The Duke leaned back, beaming. "I tell you what," he said, "you must come to my pantomime, all of you. You'll love it! I'll send you tickets. Coming, Lucrezia."

The four children were left standing under the ceiling full of wrestling angels.

After a moment, the Petrocchi girls walked to the chairs against the wall and sat down. Paolo and Tonino looked at one another. They marched to the chairs on the opposite side of the room and sat down there. It seemed a safe distance. From there, the Petrocchi girls were dark blurs with thin white legs and foxy blobs for heads.

"I wish I'd brought my book," said Tonino.

They sat with their heels hooked into the rungs of their chairs, trying to feel patient. "I think the Duchess must be a saint," said Paolo, "to be so patient with the Duke."

Tonino was surprised Paolo should think that. He knew the Duke did not behave much like a duke should, while the Duchess was every inch a duchess. But he was not sure it was right, the way she let them know how patient she was being. "Mother dashes about like that," he said, "and Father doesn't mind. It stops him looking worried."

"Father's not a Duchess," said Paolo.

Tonino did not argue because, at that moment, two footmen appeared, pushing a most interesting trolley. Tonino's mouth fell open. He had never seen so many cakes together in his life before. Across the room, there were black gaps in the faces of the Petrocchi girls. Evidently they had never seen so many cakes either. Tonino shut his mouth quickly and tried to look as if he saw such sights every day.

The footmen served the Petrocchi girls first. They were

very cool and seemed to take hours choosing. When the trolley was finally wheeled across to Paolo and Tonino, they found it hard to seem as composed. There were twenty different kinds of cake. They took ten each, with greedy speed, so that they had one of every kind between them and could swap if necessary. When the trolley was wheeled away, Tonino just managed to spare a glance from his plate to see how the Petrocchis were doing. Each girl had her white knees hooked up to carry a plate big enough to hold ten cakes.

They were rich cakes. By the time Paolo reached the tenth, he was going slowly, wondering if he really cared for meringue as much as he had thought, and Tonino was only on his sixth. By the time Paolo had put his plate neatly under his chair and cleaned himself with his handkerchief, Tonino, sticky with jam, smeared with chocolate and cream and infested with crumbs, was still doggedly ploughing through his eighth. And this was the moment the Duchess chose to sit smiling down beside Paolo.

"I won't interrupt your brother," she said, laughing. "Tell me about yourself, Paolo." Paolo did not know what to answer. All he could think of was the mess Tonino looked. "For instance," the Duchess asked helpfully, "does spell-making come easily to you? Do you find it hard to learn?"

"Oh no, Your Grace," Paolo said proudly. "I learn very easily." Then he was afraid this might upset Tonino. He looked quickly at Tonino's pastry-plastered face and found Tonino staring gravely at the Duchess. Paolo felt ashamed and responsible. He wanted the Duchess to know that Tonino was not just a messy staring little boy. "Tonino learns slowly," he said, "but he reads all the time. He's read all the books in the Library. He's almost as learned as Uncle Umberto."

"How remarkable," smiled the Duchess.

There was just a trace of disbelief in the arch of her eyebrows. Tonino was so embarrassed that he took a big bite out of his ninth cake. It was a great pastry puff. The instant his mouth closed round it, Tonino knew that, if he opened his mouth again, even to breathe, pastry would blow out of it like a hailstorm, all over Paolo and the Duchess. He clamped his lips together and chewed valiantly.

And, to Paolo's embarrassment, he went on staring at the Duchess. He was wishing Benvenuto was there to tell him about the Duchess. She muddled him. As she bent smiling over Paolo, she did not look like the haughty, rigid lady who had been so patient with the Duke. And yet, perhaps because she was not being patient, Tonino felt the rank strength of the unsaintly thoughts behind her waxy smile, stronger than ever.

Paolo willed Tonino to stop chewing and goggling. But Tonino went on, and the disbelief in the Duchess's eyebrows was so obvious, that he blurted out, "And Tonino's the only one who can talk to Benvenuto. He's our boss cat, Your—"

He remembered the Duchess did not like cats. "Er – you don't like cats, Your Grace."

The Duchess laughed. "But I don't mind hearing about them. What about Benvenuto?"

To Paolo's relief, Tonino turned his goggle eyes from the Duchess to him. So Paolo talked on. "You see, Your Grace, spells work much better and stronger if a cat's around, and particularly if Benvenuto is. Besides Benvenuto knows all sorts of things—"

He was interrupted by a thick noise from Tonino. Tonino was trying to speak without opening his mouth. It was clear there was going to be a pastry-storm any second. Paolo snatched out his jammy, creamy handkerchief and held it ready.

The Duchess stood up, rather hastily. "I think I'd better see how my other guests are getting on," she said, and went swiftly gliding across to the Petrocchi girls.

The Petrocchi girls, Paolo noticed resentfully, were ready to receive her. Their handkerchiefs had been busy while the Duchess talked to Paolo, and now their plates were neatly pushed under their chairs too. Each had left at least three cakes. This much encouraged Tonino. He was feeling rather unwell. He put the rest of the ninth cake back beside the tenth and laid the plate carefully on the next chair. By this time, he had managed to swallow his mouthful.

"You shouldn't have told her about Benvenuto," he said, hauling out his handkerchief. "He's a family secret."

"Then you should have said something yourself instead of staring like a dummy," Paolo retorted. To his mortification both Petrocchi girls were talking merrily to the Duchess. The bulge-headed Angelica was laughing. It so annoyed Paolo that he said, "Look at the way those girls are sucking up to the Duchess!"

"I didn't do that," Tonino pointed out.

As Paolo wanted to say he wished Tonino had, he found himself unable to say anything at all. He sat sourly watching the Duchess talking to the girls across the room, until she got up and went gliding away. She remembered to smile and wave at Paolo and Tonino as she went. Paolo thought that was good of her, considering the asses they had made of themselves.

Very soon after that, the curtains swung aside and Old Niccolo came back, walking slowly beside Guido Petrocchi. After them came the two gowned great-uncles, and Domenico came after that. It was like a procession. Everyone looked straight ahead, and it was plain they had a lot on their minds. All four children stood up, brushed crumbs off, and followed the procession. Paolo found he was walking beside the elder girl, but he was careful not to look at her. In utter silence, they marched to the great Palace door, where the carriages were moving along to receive them.

The Petrocchi carriage came first, with its black horses patched and beaded with rain. Tonino took another look at its coachman, rather hoping he had made a mistake. It was still raining and the man's clothes were soaked. His red Petrocchi hair was brown with wet under his wet hat. He was shivering as he leant down, and there was a questioning look on his pale face, as if he was anxious to be told what the Duke had said. No, he was real all right. The Montana coachman behind stared into space, ignoring the rain and his passengers equally. Tonino felt that the Petrocchis had definitely come out best.

CHAPTER FOUR

✳

When the coach was moving, Old Niccolo leaned back and said, "Well, the Duke is very good-natured, I'll say that. Perhaps he's not such a fool as he seems."

Uncle Umberto answered, with deepest gloom, "When my father was a boy, *his* father went to the Palace once a week. He was received as a friend."

Domenico said timidly, "At least we sold some stage effects."

"That," said Uncle Umberto crushingly, "is just what I'm complaining of."

Tonino and Paolo looked from one to the other,

wondering what had depressed them so.

Old Niccolo noticed them looking. "Guido Petrocchi wished those disgusting daughters of his to be present while we conferred with the Duke," he said. "I shall not—"

"Oh good Lord!" muttered Uncle Umberto. "One doesn't listen to a Petrocchi."

"No, but one trusts one's grandsons," said Old Niccolo. "Boys, old Caprona's in a bad way, it seems. The States of Florence, Pisa and Siena have now united against her. The Duke suspects they are paying an enchanter to—"

"Huh!" said Uncle Umberto. "Paying the Petrocchis."

Domenico, who had been rendered surprisingly bold by something, said, "Uncle, I could *see* the Petrocchis were no more traitors than we are!"

Both old men turned to look at him. He crumpled.

"The fact is," Old Niccolo continued, "Caprona is not the great State she once was. There are many reasons, no doubt. But we know, and the Duke knows – even Domenico knows – that each year we set the usual charms for the defence of Caprona, and each year we set them stronger, and each year they have less effect. Something – or someone – is definitely sapping our strength. So the Duke asks what else we can do. And—"

Domenico interrupted with a squawk of laughter. "And we said we'd find the words to the *Angel of Caprona*!"

Paolo and Tonino expected Domenico to be crushed again, but the two old men simply looked gloomy. Their heads

56

nodded mournfully. "But I don't understand," said Tonino. "The *Angel of Caprona*'s got words. We sing them at school."

"Hasn't your mother taught you—?" Old Niccolo began angrily. "Ah, no. I forgot. Your mother is English."

"One more reason for careful marriages," Uncle Umberto said dismally.

By this time, what with the rain ceaselessly pattering down as well, both boys were thoroughly depressed and alarmed. Domenico seemed to find them funny. He gave another squawk of laughter.

"Be quiet," said Old Niccolo. "This is the last time I take you where brandy is served. No, boys, the *Angel* has not got the right words. The words you sing are a makeshift. Some people say that the glorious Angel took the words back to Heaven after the White Devil was vanquished, leaving only the tune. Or the words have been lost since. But everyone knows that Caprona cannot be truly great until the words are found."

"In other words," Uncle Umberto said irritably, "the *Angel of Caprona* is a spell like any other spell. And without the proper words, any spell is only at half force, even if it is of divine origin." He gathered up his gown as the coach jerked to a stop outside the University. "And we – like idiots – have pledged ourselves to complete what God left unfinished," he said. "The presumption of man!" He climbed out of the coach, calling to Old Niccolo, "I'll look in every manuscript I can think of. There must be a clue somewhere. Oh this confounded rain!"

The door slammed and the coach jerked on again.

Paolo asked, "Have the Petrocchis said they'll find the words too?"

Old Niccolo's mouth bunched angrily. "They have. And I should die of shame if they did it before we did. I—" He stopped as the coach lurched round the corner into the Corso. It lurched again, and jerked. Sprays of water flew past the windows.

Domenico leaned forward. "Not driving so well, is he?"

"Quiet!" said Old Niccolo, and Paolo bit his tongue in a whole succession of jerks. Something was wrong. The coach was not making the right noise.

"I can't hear the horses' hooves," Tonino said, puzzled.

"I thought that was it!" Old Niccolo snapped. "It's the rain." He let down the window with a bang, bringing in a gust of watery wind, and, regardless of faces staring up at him from under wet umbrellas, he leaned out and bellowed the words of a spell. "And drive quickly, coachman! There," he said, as he pulled the window up again, "that should get us home before the horses turn to pulp. What a blessing this didn't happen before Umberto got out!"

The noise of the horses' hooves sounded again, clopping over the cobbles of the Corso. It seemed that the new spell was working. But, as they turned into the Via Cardinale, the noise changed to a spongy *thump-thump*, and when they came to the Via Magica the hooves made hardly a sound. And the lurching and jerking began again, worse than ever. As they turned to enter the gate of the Casa Montana, there came the most brutal jerk of all. The coach tipped forward, and there was a crash as the pole hit the cobbles. Paolo got his window open in time to see the limp paper figure of the coachman flop off the box into a puddle. Beyond him, two wet cardboard horses were draped over their traces.

"That spell," said Old Niccolo, "lasted for days in my grandfather's time."

"Do you mean it's that enchanter?" Paolo asked. "Is he spoiling all our spells?"

Old Niccolo stared at him, full-eyed, like a baby about to burst into tears. "No, lad. I fancy not. The truth is, the Casa Montana is in as bad a way as Caprona. The old virtue is fading. It has faded generation by generation, and now it is almost gone. I am ashamed that you should learn it like this. Let's get out, boys, and start dragging."

It was a wretched humiliation. Since the rest of the family were all either asleep or at work on the Old Bridge, there was no one to help them pull the coach through the gate. And Domenico was no use. He confessed afterwards that he could not remember getting home. They left him asleep in the coach and dragged it in, just the three of them. Even Benvenuto dashing through the rain did not cheer Tonino much.

"One consolation," panted their grandfather. "The rain. There is no one about to see Old Niccolo dragging his own coach."

Paolo and Tonino did not find much consolation in that. Now they understood the growing unease in the Casa, and it was not pleasant. They understood why everyone was so anxious about the Old Bridge, and so delighted when, just before Christmas, it was mended at last. They understood, too, the worry about a husband for Rosa. As soon as the bridge was repaired, everyone went back to discussing that. And Paolo and Tonino knew why everyone agreed that the young man Rosa must choose, must have, if he had nothing else, a strong talent for spells.

"To improve the breed, you mean?" said Rosa. She was very sarcastic and independent about it. "Very well, dear Uncle Lorenzo, I shall only fall in love with men who can make paper horses waterproof."

Uncle Lorenzo blushed angrily. The whole family felt humiliated by those horses. But Elizabeth was trying not to laugh. Elizabeth certainly encouraged Rosa in her independent attitude. Benvenuto informed Tonino it was the English way. Cats liked English people, he added.

"Have we really lost our virtue?" Tonino asked Benvenuto anxiously. He thought it was probably the explanation for his slowness.

Benvenuto said that he did not know what it was like in the old days, but he knew there was enough magic about now to make his coat spark. It seemed like a lot. But he sometimes wondered if it was being applied properly.

Around this time, twice as many newspapers found their

way into the Casa. There were journals from Rome and magazines from Genoa and Milan, as well as the usual Caprona papers. Everyone read them eagerly and talked in mutters about the attitude of Florence, movements in Pisa and opinion hardening in Siena. Out of the worried murmurs, the word *War* began to sound, more and more frequently. And, instead of the usual Christmas songs, the only tune heard in the Casa Montana, night and day, was the *Angel of Caprona*.

The tune was sung in bass, tenor and soprano. It was played slowly on flutes, picked out on guitars and lilted on violins. Every one of the Montanas lived in hope that he or she would be the person to find the true words. Rinaldo had a new idea. He procured a drum and sat on the edge of his bed beating out the rhythm, until Aunt Francesca implored him to stop. And even that did not help. Not one of the Montanas could begin to set the right words to the tune. Antonio looked so worried that Paolo could scarcely bear to look at him.

With so much to worry about, it was hardly surprising that Paolo and Tonino looked forward daily to being invited to the Duke's pantomime. It was the one bright spot. But Antonio and Rinaldo went to the Palace – on foot – to deliver the special effects, and came back without a word of invitation. Christmas came. The entire Montana family went to church, in the beautiful marble-fronted Church of Sant' Angelo, and behaved with great devotion. Usually it was only Aunt Anna and Aunt Maria who were notably religious, but now everyone felt they had something to pray for. It was only when the time came to sing the *Angel of Caprona* that the Montana devotion slackened. An absent-minded look came over their faces, from Old Niccolo to the smallest cousin. They sang:

> *"Merrily his music ringing,*
> *See an Angel cometh singing,*
> *Words of peace and comfort bringing*
> > *To Caprona's city fair.*
>
> *Victory that faileth never,*
> *Friendship that no strife can sever,*
> *Lasting strength and peace for ever,*
> > *For Caprona's city fair.*
>
> *See the Devil flee astounded!*
> *In Caprona now is founded*
> *Virtue strong and peace unbounded—*
> > *In Caprona's city fair."*

Every one of them was wondering what the real words were.

They came home for the family celebrations, and there was still no word from the Duke. Then Christmas was over. New Year drew on and passed too, and the boys were forced to realise that there would be no invitation after all. Each told himself he had *known* the Duke was like that. They did not speak of it to one another. But they were both bitterly disappointed.

They were roused from their gloom by Lucia racing along the gallery, screaming, "Come and look at Rosa's young man!"

"What?" said Antonio, raising his worried face from a book about the Angel of Caprona. "What? Nothing's decided yet."

Lucia leapt from foot to foot. She was pink with excitement. "Rosa's decided for herself! I knew she would. Come and see!"

Led by Lucia, Antonio, Paolo, Tonino and Benvenuto raced along the gallery and down the stone stairs at the end. People and cats were streaming through the courtyard from all directions, hurrying to the room called the Saloon, beyond the dining room.

Rosa was standing near the windows, looking happy but defiant, with both hands clasped round the arm of an embarrassed-looking young man with ginger hair. A bright ring winked on Rosa's finger. Elizabeth was with them, looking as happy as Rosa and almost as defiant. When the young man saw the family streaming through the door and crowding towards him, his face became bright pink and his hand went up to loosen his smart tie. But, in spite of that, it was plain to everyone that, underneath, the young man was as happy as Rosa. And Rosa was so happy that she seemed to shine, like the

Angel over the gate. This made everyone stare, marvelling. Which, of course, made the young man more embarrassed than ever.

Old Niccolo cleared his throat. "Now look here," he said. Then he stopped. This was Antonio's business. He looked at Antonio.

Paolo and Tonino noticed that their father looked at their mother first. Elizabeth's happy look seemed to reassure him a little. "Now, just who are you?" he said to the young man. "How did you meet my Rosa?"

"He was one of the contractors on the Old Bridge, Father," said Rosa.

"And he has enormous natural talent, Antonio," said Elizabeth, "and a beautiful singing voice."

"All right, all right," said Antonio. "Let the boy speak for himself, women."

The young man swallowed, and helped the swallow down with a shake of his tie. His face was now very pale. "My name is Marco Andretti," he said in a pleasant, if husky, voice. "I – I think you met my brother at the bridge, sir. I was on the other shift. That's how I came to meet Rosa." The way he smiled down at Rosa left everybody hoping that he would be fit to become a Montana.

"It'll break their hearts if Father says no," Lucia whispered to Paolo. Paolo nodded. He could see that.

Antonio was pulling his lip, which was a thing he did when his face could hold no more worry than it did already.

64

"Yes," he said. "I've met Mario Andretti, of course. A very respectable family." He made that sound not altogether a good thing. "But I'm sure you're aware, Signor Andretti, that ours is a special family. We have to be careful who we marry. First, what do you think of the Petrocchis?"

Marco's pale face went fiery red. He answered with a violence which surprised the Montanas, "I hate their guts, Signor Montana!"

He seemed so upset that Rosa pulled his arm down and patted it soothingly.

"Marco has personal family reasons, Father," she said.

"Which I'd prefer not to go into," Marco said.

"We – well, I'll not press you for them," Antonio said, and continued to pull his lip. "But, you see, our family must marry someone with at least some talent for magic. Have you any ability there, Signor Andretti?"

Marco Andretti seemed to relax at this. He smiled, and gently took Rosa's hands off his sleeve. Then he sang. Elizabeth had been right about his voice. It was a golden tenor. Uncle Lorenzo was heard to rumble that he could not think what a voice like that was doing outside the Milan Opera.

"*A golden tree there grows, a tree*
Whose golden branches bud with green..."

sang Marco. As he sang, the tree came into being, rooted in the carpet between Rosa and Antonio, first as a faint gold shadow, then as a rattling metal shape, dazzling gold in the shafts of sunlight from the windows. The Montanas nodded their appreciation. The trunk and each branch, even the smallest twig, was indeed pure gold.

But Marco sang on, and as he sang, the gold twigs put out buds, pale and fist-shaped at first, then bright and pointed. Instants later, the tree was in leaf. It was moving and rattling constantly to Marco's singing. It put out pink and white flowers in clusters, which budded, expanded and dropped, as quickly as flames in a firework. The room was full of scent, then of petals fluttering like confetti. Marco still sang, and the tree still moved. Before the last petal had fallen, pointed green fruit was swelling where the flowers had been. The fruit grew brownish and swelled, and swelled and turned bulging and yellow, until the tree drooped under the weight of a heavy crop of big yellow pears.

"...*With golden fruit for everyone,*"

Marco concluded. He put up a hand, picked one of the pears and held it, rather diffidently, out to Antonio.

There were murmurs of appreciation from the rest of the family. Antonio took the pear and sniffed it. And he smiled, to Marco's evident relief. "Good fruit," he said. "That was very elegantly done, Signor Andretti. But there is one more thing I must ask you. Would you agree to change your name to Montana? That is our custom, you see."

"Yes, Rosa told me," said Marco. "And – and this is a difficulty. My brother needs me in his firm, and he too wants to keep his family name. Would it be all right if I'm known as Montana when I'm here, and as – as Andretti when I'm at home with my brother?"

"You mean you and Rosa wouldn't live here?" Antonio asked, astonished.

"Not all the time. No," said Marco. From the way he said it, it was clear he was not going to change his mind.

This was serious. Antonio looked at Old Niccolo. And there were grave faces all round at the thought of the family being broken up.

"I don't see why they shouldn't," said Elizabeth.

"Well – my great-uncle did it," Old Niccolo said. "But it was not a success. His wife ran off to Sicily with a greasy little warlock."

"That doesn't mean *I'm* going to!" Rosa said.

The family wavered, with the tree gently rattling in their midst. Everyone loved Rosa. Marco was clearly nice. Nobody wanted to break their hearts. But this idea of living away from the Casa—!

Aunt Francesca heaved herself forward, saying, "I side with Elizabeth. Our Rosa has found herself a nice boy with more talent and a better voice than I've seen outside our family for years. Let them get married."

Antonio looked dreadfully worried at this, but he did not pull his lip. He seemed to be relaxing, ready to agree, when

Rinaldo set the tree rattling furiously by pushing his way underneath it.

"Just a moment. Aren't we all being a bit trustful? Who *is* this fellow, after all? Why haven't we come across him and his talents before?"

Paolo hung his head and watched Rinaldo under his hair. This was Rinaldo in the mood he least admired. Rinaldo loud and aggressive, with an unpleasant twist to his mouth. Rinaldo was still a little pale from the cut on his head, but this went rather well with the black clothes and the red brigand's scarf. Rinaldo knew it did. He flung up his head with an air, and contemptuously brushed off a petal that had fallen on his black sleeve. And he looked at Marco, challenging him to answer.

The way Marco looked back showed that he was quite ready to stand up to Rinaldo. "I've been at college in Rome until recently," he said. "If that's what you mean."

Rinaldo swung round to face the family. "So he says," he said. "He's done a pretty trick for us, and said all the right things – but so would anyone in his place." He swung round on Marco. It was so dramatic that Tonino winced and even Paolo felt a little unhappy. "I don't trust you," said Rinaldo. "I've seen your face before somewhere."

"At the Old Bridge," said Marco.

"No, not there. It was somewhere else," said Rinaldo.

And this must be true, Tonino realised. Marco did have a familiar look. And Tonino could not have seen him at the Old Bridge, because Tonino had never been there.

"Do you want me to fetch my brother, or my priest, to vouch for me?" asked Marco.

"No," said Rinaldo rudely. "I want the truth."

Marco took a deep breath. "I don't want to be unfriendly," he said. The arm Rosa was not holding bent, and so did the fist on the end of it. Rinaldo gave it a look as if he welcomed it, and swaggered a step nearer.

"Please!" Rosa said uselessly.

Benvenuto moved in Tonino's arms. Into Tonino's head came a picture of a large stripy tomcat swaggering on the Casa roof – Benvenuto's roof. Tonino nearly laughed. Benvenuto's muscular back legs pushed him backwards into Paolo as Benvenuto took off. Benvenuto landed between Rinaldo and Marco. There was a gentle "Ah!" from the rest of the family. They knew Benvenuto would settle it.

Benvenuto deliberately ignored Rinaldo. Arching himself tall, with his tail straight up like a cypress tree, he minced to Marco's legs and rubbed himself round them. Marco undoubled his fist and bent to hold his hand out to Benvenuto. "Hallo," he said. "What's your name?" He paused, for Benvenuto to tell him. "I'm pleased to meet you, Benvenuto," he said.

The "Ah!" from the family was loud and long this time. It was followed by cries of, "Get out of it, Rinaldo! Don't make a fool of yourself! Leave Marco alone!"

Though Rinaldo was nothing like as easily crushed as Domenico, even he could not stand up to the whole family.

When he looked at Old Niccolo and saw Old Niccolo waving him angrily aside, he gave up and shoved his way out of the room.

"Rosa and Marco," said Antonio, "I give my provisional consent to your marriage."

Upon that, everyone hugged everyone else, shook hands with Marco and kissed Rosa. Very flushed and happy, Marco plucked pear after pear from the golden tree and gave them to everyone, even the newest baby. They were delicious pears, ripe to perfection. They melted in mouths and dribbled down chins.

"I don't want to be a spoilsport," Aunt Maria said, slurping juice in Paolo's ear, "but a tree in the Saloon is going to be a nuisance."

But Marco had thought of that. As soon as the last pear was picked, the tree began to fade. Soon it was a clattering golden glitter, a vanishing shadow-tree, and then it was not there at all. Everyone applauded. Aunt Gina and Aunt Anna fetched bottles of wine and glasses, and the Casa drank to the health of Rosa and Marco.

"Thank goodness!" Tonino heard Elizabeth say. "I was so nervous for her!"

On the other side of Elizabeth, Old Niccolo was telling Uncle Lorenzo that Marco was a real acquisition, because he could understand cats. Tonino felt a little wistful at this. He went outside into the chilly yard. As he had expected, Benvenuto was now curled up in the sunny patch on the gallery steps. He undulated his tail in annoyance at Tonino. He had just settled down for a sleep.

But Marco could *not* understand cats, Benvenuto said irritably. He knew Benvenuto's name, because Rosa had told him, but he had no idea what Benvenuto had actually said to him. Benvenuto had told him that he and Rinaldo would get thoroughly scratched if they started a fight in the Casa – neither of them was boss cat here. Now, if Tonino would go away, a cat could get some sleep.

This was a great relief to Tonino. He now felt free to like Marco as much as Paolo did. Marco was fun. He was never in the Casa for very long, because he and his brother were building a villa out beyond the New Bridge, but he was one of the few people Tonino laid down his book to talk to. And that, Lucia told Rosa, was a compliment indeed.

Rosa and Marco were to be married in the spring. They laughed about it constantly as they swept in and out of the Casa together. Antonio and Uncle Lorenzo walked out to the villa where Mario Andretti lived, and arranged it all. Mario Andretti came to the Casa to settle the details. He was a large fat man – who drove a shrewd bargain, Aunt Francesca said – and quite different from Marco. The most notable thing about him was the long white motor car he came in.

Old Niccolo looked at that car reflectively. "It smells," he said. "But it looks more reliable than a cardboard horse." He sighed. He still felt deeply humiliated. All the same, after Mario Andretti had driven away, Tonino was very interested to be sent out to the post with two letters. One was addressed to Ferrari, the other to Rolls-Royce in England.

In the normal way, the talk in the Casa would have been all about that car and those two letters. But they passed unnoticed in the anxious murmurs about Florence, Siena and Pisa. The only topic able to drown out the talk of war was Rosa's wedding dress. Should it be long or short? With a train, or not? And what kind of veil? Rosa was quite as independent about that as she had been over Marco.

"I suppose I have no say in it at all," she said. "I shall have it knee-length one side and a train ten feet long on the other, I think. And no veil. Just a black mask."

This thoroughly offended Aunt Maria and Aunt Gina, who were the chief arguers. What with the noise they made, and the twanging the other side of the room, where Antonio had roped Marco in to help find the words to the *Angel*, Tonino was unable to concentrate on his book. He took it along the gallery to the library, hoping for peace there.

But Rinaldo was leaning on the gallery rail outside the library, looking remarkably sinister, and he stopped Tonino. "That Marco," he said. "I *wish* I could remember where I saw him. I've seen him in the Art Gallery with Rosa, but it wasn't there. I know it was somewhere much more damaging than that."

Tonino had no doubt that Rinaldo knew all sorts of damaging places. He took his book into the library, hoping that Rinaldo would not remember the place, and settled down in the chilly mustiness to read.

The next moment, Benvenuto landed on his book with a thump.

"Oh get off!" said Tonino. "I start school tomorrow, and I want to finish this first."

No, said Benvenuto. Tonino was to go to Old Niccolo *at once*. A flurry of scrips, spells, yellow parchment rolls and then a row of huge red books passed behind Tonino's eyes. It was followed by a storm of enormous images. Giants were running, banging, smoking and burning, and they all wore red and gold. But not yet. They were preparing to fight, marching in great huge boots. Benvenuto was so urgent that it took all Tonino's skill to sort out what he meant.

"All right," said Tonino. "I'll tell him." He got up and pelted round the gallery, past Rinaldo, who said, "What's the hurry?" to Old Niccolo's quarters. Old Niccolo was just coming out.

"Please," said Tonino, "Benvenuto says to get out the war-spells. The Duke is calling up the Reserves."

Old Niccolo stood so very quiet and wide-eyed that Tonino thought he did not believe it. Old Niccolo was feeling for the door-frame. He seemed to think it was missing.

"You did hear me, did you?" Tonino asked.

"Yes," said Old Niccolo. "Yes, I heard. It's just so soon – so sudden. I wish the Duke had warned us. So war is coming. Pray God our strength is still enough."

73

CHAPTER FIVE

*B*envenuto's news caused a stampede in the Casa Montana. The older cousins raced to the Scriptorium and began packing away all the usual spells, inks and pens. The aunts fetched out the special inks for use in war-spells. The uncles staggered under reams of fresh paper and parchment. Antonio, Old Niccolo and Rinaldo went to the library and fetched the giant red volumes, with *WAR* stamped on their spines, while Elizabeth raced to the music room with all the children to put away the ordinary music and set out the tunes and instruments of war.

Meanwhile, Rosa, Marco and Domenico raced out into the

Via Magica and came back with newspapers. Everyone at once left what they were doing and crowded into the dining room to see what the papers said.

They made a pile of people, all craning over the table. Rinaldo was standing on a chair, leaning over three aunts. Marco was underneath, craning anxiously sideways, head to head with Old Niccolo, as Rosa flipped over the pages. There were so many other people packed in and leaning over that Lucia, Paolo and Tonino were forced to squat with their chins on the table, in order to see at all.

"No, nothing," Rosa said, flipping over the second paper.

"Wait," said Marco. "Look at the Stop Press."

Everyone swayed towards it, pushing Marco further sideways. Then Tonino almost knew where he had seen Marco before.

"There it is," said Antonio.

All the bodies came upright, with their faces very serious.

"Reserve mobilised, right enough," said Rosa. "Oh, Marco!"

"What's the matter?" Rinaldo asked jeeringly from his chair. "Is Marco a Reservist?"

"No," said Marco. "My – my brother got me out of it."

Rinaldo laughed. "What a patriot!"

Marco looked up at him. "I'm a Final Reservist," he said, "and I hope you are too. If you aren't, it will be a pleasure to take you round to the Army Office in the Arsenal this moment."

The two glared at one another. Once again there were shouts to Rinaldo to stop making a fool of himself. Sulkily, Rinaldo climbed down and stalked out.

"Rinaldo *is* a Final Reservist," Paolo assured Marco.

"I thought he must be," Marco said. "Look, I must go. I – I must tell my brother. Rosa, I'll see you tomorrow if I can."

When Tonino fell asleep that night, the room next door to him was full of people talking of war and the *Angel of Caprona*, with occasional digressions about Rosa's wedding dress. Tonino's head was so full of these things that he was quite surprised, when he went to school, not to hear them talked of there. But no one seemed to have noticed there might be a war. True, some of the teachers looked grave, but that might have been just their natural feelings at the start of a new term.

Consequently, Tonino came home that afternoon thinking that maybe things were not so bad after all. As usual, Benvenuto leapt off the water butt and sprang into his arms. Tonino was rubbing his face against Benvenuto's nearest ragged ear, when he heard a carriage draw up behind him. Benvenuto promptly squirmed out of Tonino's arms. Tonino, very surprised, looked round to find him trotting, gently and politely, with his tail well up, towards a tall man who was just coming in through the Casa gate.

Benvenuto stood, his brush of tail waving slightly at the tip, his hind legs canted slightly apart under his fluffy drawers, staring gravely at the tall man. Tonino thought peevishly that, from behind, Benvenuto often looked pretty silly. The man looked almost as bad. He was wearing an exceedingly expensive coat with a fur collar and a tweed travelling cap with daft earflaps. And he bowed to Benvenuto.

"Good afternoon, Benvenuto," he said, as grave as Benvenuto himself. "I'm glad to see you so well. Yes, I'm very well thank you."

Benvenuto advanced to rub himself round the stranger's legs.

"No," said the man. "I beg you. Your hairs come off."

And Benvenuto stopped, without abating an ounce of his uncommon politeness.

By this time, Tonino was extremely resentful. This was the first time for years that Benvenuto had behaved as if anyone mattered more than Tonino. He raised his eyes accusingly to the stranger's. He met eyes even darker than his own, which seemed to spill brilliance over the rest of the man's smooth dark face. They gave Tonino a jolt, worse than the time the horses turned back to cardboard. He knew, beyond a shadow of doubt, that he was looking at a powerful enchanter.

"How do you do?" said the man. "No, despite your accusing glare, young man, I have never been able to understand cats – or not more than in the most general way. I wonder if you would be kind enough to translate for me what Benvenuto is saying."

Tonino listened to Benvenuto. "He says he's very pleased to see you again and welcome to the Casa Montana, sir." The *sir* was from Benvenuto, not Tonino. Tonino was not sure he cared for strange enchanters who walked into the Casa and took up Benvenuto's attention.

"Thank you, Benvenuto," said the enchanter. "I'm very pleased to be back. Though, frankly, I've seldom had such a difficult journey. Did you know your borders with Florence and Pisa were closed?" he asked Tonino. "I had to come in by sea from Genoa in the end."

"Did you?" Tonino said, wondering if the man thought it was his fault. "Where did you come from then?"

"Oh, England," said the man.

Tonino warmed to that. This then could not be the enchanter the Duke had talked about. Or could he? Tonino was not sure how far away enchanters could work from.

"Makes you feel better?" asked the man.

"Mother's English," Tonino admitted, feeling he was giving altogether too much away.

"Ah!" said the enchanter. "Now I know who you are. You're Antonio the Younger, aren't you? You were a baby when I saw you last, Tonino."

Since there is no reply to that kind of remark, Tonino was glad to see Old Niccolo hastening across the yard, followed by Aunt Francesca and Uncle Lorenzo, with Antonio and several more of the family hurrying behind them. They closed round the enchanter, leaving Tonino and Benvenuto beyond, by the gate.

"Yes, I've just come from the Casa Petrocc. heard the stranger say. To his surprise, everyone accepted if it were the most natural thing for the stranger to have done – as natural as the way he took off his ridiculous English hat to Aunt Francesca.

"But you'll stay the night with us," said Aunt Francesca.

"If it's not too much trouble," the stranger said.

In the distance, as if they already knew – as they unquestionably did in a place like the Casa Montana – Aunt Maria and Aunt Anna went clambering up the gallery steps to prepare the guest room above. Aunt Gina emerged from the kitchen, held her hands up to Heaven, and dashed indoors again. Thoughtfully, Tonino gathered up Benvenuto and asked exactly who this stranger was.

Chrestomanci, of course, he was told. The most powerful enchanter in the world.

"Is he the one who's spoiling our spells?" Tonino asked suspiciously.

Chrestomanci, he was told – impatiently, because Benvenuto evidently thought Tonino was being very stupid – is always on our side.

Tonino looked at the stranger again – or rather, at his smooth dark head sticking out from among the shorter Montanas – and understood that Chrestomanci's coming meant there was a crisis indeed.

The stranger must have said something about him. Tonino

found them all looking at him, his family smiling lovingly. He smiled back shyly.

"Oh, he's a good boy," said Aunt Francesca.

Then they all surged, talking, across the yard. "What makes it particularly difficult," Tonino heard Chrestomanci saying, "is that I am, first and foremost, an employee of the British Government. And Britain is keeping out of Italian affairs. But luckily I have a fairly wide brief."

Almost at once, Aunt Gina shot out of the kitchen again. She had cancelled the ordinary supper and started on a new one in honour of Chrestomanci. Six people were sent out at once for cakes and fruit, and two more for lettuce and cheese. Paolo, Corinna and Lucia were caught as they came in chatting from school and told to go at once to the butcher's. But, at this point, Rinaldo erupted furiously from the Scriptorium.

"What do you mean, sending all the kids off like this!" he bawled from the gallery. "We're up to our ears in war-spells here. I need copiers!"

Aunt Gina put her hands on her hips and bawled back at him. "And I need steak! Don't you stand up there cheeking me, Rinaldo Montana! English people always eat steak, so steak I must have!"

"Then cut pieces off the cats!" screamed Rinaldo. "I need Corinna and Lucia up here!"

"I tell you they are going to run after *me* for once!" yelled Aunt Gina.

"Dear me," said Chrestomanci, wandering into the yard.

"What a very Italian scene! Can I help in any way?" He nodded and smiled from Aunt Gina to Rinaldo. Both of them smiled back, Rinaldo at his most charming.

"You would agree I need copiers, sir, wouldn't you?" he said.

"Bah!" said Aunt Gina. "Rinaldo turns on the charm and I get left to struggle alone! As usual! All right. Because it's war-spells, Paolo and Tonino can go for the steak. But wait while I write you a note, or you'll come back with something no one can chew."

"So glad to be of service," Chrestomanci murmured, and turned away to greet Elizabeth, who came racing down from the gallery waving a sheaf of music and fell into his arms. The heads of the five little cousins Elizabeth had been teaching stared wonderingly over the gallery rail. "Elizabeth!" said Chrestomanci. "Looking younger than ever!" Tonino stared as wonderingly as his cousins. His mother was laughing and crying at once. He could not follow the torrent of English speech. "Virtue," he heard, and "war" and, before long, the inevitable *Angel of Caprona*. He was still staring when Aunt Gina stuck her note into his hand and told him to make haste.

As they hurried to the butcher's, Tonino said to Paolo, "I didn't know Mother knew anyone like Chrestomanci."

"Neither did I," Paolo confessed. He was only a year older than Tonino, after all, and it seemed that Chrestomanci had last been in Caprona a very long time ago. "Perhaps he's come to find the words to the *Angel*," Paolo suggested. "I hope so. I don't want Rinaldo to have to go away and fight."

"Or Marco," Tonino agreed. "Or Carlo or Luigi or even Domenico."

Because of Aunt Gina's note, the butcher treated them with great respect. "Tell her this is the last good steak she'll see, if war is declared," he said, and he passed them each a heavy, squashy pink armload.

They arrived back with their armfuls just as a cab set down Uncle Umberto, puffing and panting, outside the Casa gate. "I am right, Chrestomanci *is* here? Eh, Paolo?" Uncle Umberto asked Tonino.

Both boys nodded. It seemed easier than explaining that Paolo was Tonino.

"Good, good!" exclaimed Uncle Umberto and surged into the Casa, where he found Chrestomanci just crossing the yard. "The *Angel of Caprona*," Uncle Umberto said to him eagerly. "Could you—?"

"My dear Umberto," said Chrestomanci, shaking his hand warmly, "everyone here is asking me that. For that matter, so was everyone in the Casa Petrocchi too. And I'm afraid I know no more than you do. But I shall think about it, don't worry."

"If you could find just a line, to get us started," Uncle Umberto said pleadingly.

"I *will* do my best!" Chrestomanci was saying, when, with a great clattering of heels, Rosa shot past. From the look on her face, she had seen Marco arriving. "I promise you that,"

Chrestomanci said, as his head turned to see what Rosa was running for.

Marco came through the gate and stopped so dead, staring at Chrestomanci, that Rosa charged into him and nearly knocked him over. Marco staggered a bit, put his arms round Rosa, and went on staring at Chrestomanci. Tonino found himself holding his breath. Rinaldo was right. There *was* something about Marco. Chrestomanci knew it, and Marco knew he knew. From the look on Marco's face, he expected Chrestomanci to say what it was.

Chrestomanci indeed opened his mouth to say something, but he shut it again and pursed his lips in a sort of whistle instead. Marco looked at him uncertainly.

"Oh," said Uncle Umberto, "may I introduce—" He stopped and thought. Rosa he usually remembered, because of her fair hair, but he could not place Marco. "Corinna's fiancé," he suggested.

"I'm Rosa," said Rosa. "This is Marco Andretti."

"How do you do?" Chrestomanci said politely. Marco seemed to relax. Chrestomanci's eyes turned to Paolo and Tonino, standing staring. "Good heavens!" he said. "Everyone here seems to live such exciting lives. What have you boys killed?"

Paolo and Tonino looked down in consternation, to find that the steak was leaking on to their shoes. Two or three cats were approaching meaningly.

Aunt Gina appeared in the kitchen doorway. "*Where's my steak?*"

Paolo and Tonino sped towards her, leaving a pattering trail. "What was all that about?" Paolo panted to Tonino.

"I don't know," said Tonino, because he didn't, and because he liked Marco.

Aunt Gina shortly became very sharp and passionate about the steak. The leaking trail attracted every cat in the Casa. They were underfoot in the kitchen all evening, mewing pitifully. Benvenuto was also present, at a wary distance from Aunt Gina, and he made good use of his time. Aunt Gina erupted into the yard again, trumpeting.

"Tonino! *Ton-in-ooh!*"

Tonino laid down his book and hurried outside. "Yes, Aunt Gina?"

"That cat of yours has stolen a whole pound of steak!" Aunt Gina trumpeted, flinging a dramatic arm skyward.

Tonino looked, and there, sure enough, Benvenuto was, crouched on the pantiles of the roof, with one paw holding down quite a large lump of meat. "Oh dear," he said. "I don't think I can make him give it back, Aunt Gina."

"I don't want it back. Look where it's been!" screamed Aunt Gina. "Tell him from me that I shall wring his evil neck if he comes near me again!"

"My goodness, you do seem to be at the centre of everything," Chrestomanci remarked, appearing beside Tonino in the yard. "Are you always in such demand?"

"I shall have hysterics," declared Aunt Gina. "And no one will get any supper."

Elizabeth and Aunt Maria and Cousins Claudia and Teresa immediately came to her assistance and led her tenderly back indoors.

"Thank the Lord!" said Chrestomanci. "I'm not sure I could stand hysterics and starvation at once. How did you know I was an enchanter, Tonino? From Benvenuto?"

"No. I just knew when I looked at you," said Tonino.

"I see," said Chrestomanci. "This is interesting. Most people find it impossible to tell. It makes me wonder if Old Niccolo is right, when he talks of the virtue leaving your house. Would you be able to tell another enchanter when you looked at him, do you think?"

Tonino screwed up his face and wondered. "I might. It's the eyes. You mean, would I know the enchanter who's spoiling our spells?"

"I think I mean that," said Chrestomanci. "I'm beginning to believe there is someone. I'm sure, at least, that the spells on the Old Bridge were deliberately broken. Would it interfere with your plans too much, if I asked your grandfather to take you with him whenever he has to meet strangers?"

"I haven't got any plans," said Tonino. Then he thought, and he laughed. "I think you make jokes all the time."

"I aim to please," Chrestomanci said.

However, when Tonino next saw Chrestomanci, it was at supper – which was magnificent, despite Benvenuto and the hysterics – and Chrestomanci was very serious indeed. "My dear Niccolo," he said, "my mission *has* to concern the misuse of magic, not the balance of power in Italy. There would be no end of trouble if I was caught trying to stop a war."

Old Niccolo had his look of a baby about to cry. Aunt Francesca said, "We're not asking this personally—"

"But, my dear," said Chrestomanci, "don't you see that I can only do something like this as a personal matter? Please ask me personally. I shan't let the strict terms of my mission interfere with what I owe my friends." He smiled then, and his eyes swept round everyone gathered at the great table, very affectionately. He did not seem to exclude Marco. "So," he said, "I think my best plan for the moment is to go on to Rome. I know certain quarters there, where I can get impartial information, which should enable me to pin down this enchanter. At the moment, all we know is that he exists. If I'm lucky, I can prove whether Florence, or Siena, or Pisa is paying him – in which case, they and he can be indicted at the Court of Europe. And if, while I'm at it, I can get Rome, or Naples, to move on Caprona's behalf, be very sure I shall do it."

"Thank you," said Old Niccolo.

For the rest of supper, they discussed how Chrestomanci could best get to Rome. He would have to go by sea. It seemed that the last stretch of border, between Caprona and Siena, was now closed.

Much later that night, when Paolo and Tonino were on their way to bed, they saw lights in the Scriptorium. They tiptoed along to investigate. Chrestomanci was there with Antonio, Rinaldo and Aunt Francesca, going through spells in the big red books. Everyone was speaking in mutters, but they heard Chrestomanci say, "This is a sound combination, but it'll need new words." And on another page, "Get Elizabeth to put this in English, as a surprise factor." And again, "Ignore the tune. The only tune which is going to be any use to you at the moment is the *Angel*. He can't block that."

"Why just those three?" Tonino whispered.

"They're best at making new spells," Paolo whispered back. "We need new war-spells. It sounds as if the other enchanter knows the old ones."

They crept to bed with an excited, urgent feeling, and neither of them found it easy to sleep.

Chrestomanci left the next morning before the children went to school. Benvenuto and Old Niccolo escorted him to the gate, one on either side, and the entire Casa gathered to wave him off. Things felt both flat and worrying once he was gone. That day, there was a great deal of talk of war at school. The teachers whispered together. Two had left, to join the Reserves. Rumours went round the classes. Someone told Tonino that war would be declared next Sunday, so that it would be a Holy War. Someone else told Paolo that all the Reserves had been issued with two left boots, so that they would not be able to fight. There was no truth in these things. It was just that everyone now knew that war was coming.

The boys hurried home, anxious for some real news. As

usual, Benvenuto leapt off his water butt. While Tonino was enjoying Benvenuto's undivided attention again, Elizabeth called from the gallery, "Tonino! Someone's sent you a parcel."

Tonino and Benvenuto sprang for the gallery stairs, highly excited. Tonino had never had a parcel before. But before he got anywhere near it, he was seized on by Aunt Maria, Rosa and Uncle Lorenzo. They seized on all the children who could write and hurried them to the dining room. This had been set up as another Scriptorium. By each chair was a special pen, a bottle of red war-ink and a pile of strips of paper. There the children were kept busy fully two hours, copying the same war-charm, again and again. Tonino had never been so frustrated in his life. He did not even know what shape his parcel was. He was not the only one to feel frustrated.

"Oh, why?" complained Lucia, Paolo and young Cousin Lena.

"I know," said Aunt Maria. "Like school again. Start writing."

"It's exploiting children, that's what we're doing," Rosa said cheerfully. "There are probably laws against it, so do complain."

"Don't worry, I will," said Lucia. "I am doing."

"As long as you write while you grumble," said Rosa.

"It's a new spell-scrip for the Army," Uncle Lorenzo explained. "It's very urgent."

"It's hard. It's all new words," Paolo grumbled.

"Your father made it last night," said Aunt Maria. "Get writing. We'll be watching for mistakes."

When finally, stiff-necked and with red splodges on their fingers, they were let out into the yard, Tonino discovered that he had barely time to unwrap the parcel before supper. Supper was early that night, so that the elder Montanas could put in another shift on the army-spells before bedtime.

"It's worse than working on the Old Bridge," said Lucia. "What's that, Tonino? Who sent it?"

The parcel was promisingly book-shaped. It bore the stamp and the arms of the University of Caprona. This was the only indication Tonino had that Uncle Umberto had sent it, for, when he wrenched off the thick brown paper, there was no letter, not even a card. There was only a new shiny book. Tonino's face beamed. At least Uncle Umberto knew this much about him. He turned the book lovingly over. It was called *The Boy Who Saved His Country*, and the cover was the same shiny, pimpled red leather as the great volumes of war-spells.

"Is Uncle Umberto trying to give you a hint, or something?" Paolo asked, amused. He and Lucia and Corinna leant over Tonino while he flipped through the pages. There were pictures, to Tonino's delight. Soldiers rode horses, soldiers rode machines; a boy hung from a rope and scrambled up the frowning wall of a fortress; and, most exciting of all, a boy stood on a rock with a flag, confronting a whole troop of ferocious-looking dragoons. Sighing with anticipation, Tonino turned to Chapter One: *How Giorgio Uncovered an Enemy Plot.*

"*Supper!*" howled Aunt Gina from the yard. "Oh I shall go mad! Nobody attends to me!"

Tonino was forced to shut the lovely book again and hurry down to the dining room. He watched Aunt Gina anxiously as she doled out minestrone. She looked so hectic that he was convinced Benvenuto must have been at work in the kitchen again.

"It's all right," Rosa said. "It's just she thought she'd got a line from the *Angel of Caprona*. Then the soup boiled over and she forgot it again."

Aunt Gina was distinctly tearful. "With so much to do, my memory is like a sieve," she kept saying. "Now I've let you all down."

"Of course you haven't, Gina my dear," said Old Niccolo. "This is nothing to worry about. It will come back to you."

"But I can't even remember what language it was in!" wailed Aunt Gina.

Everyone tried to console her. They sprinkled grated cheese on their soup and slurped it with special relish, to show Aunt Gina how much they appreciated her, but Aunt Gina continued to sniff and accuse herself. Then Rinaldo thought of pointing out that she had got further than anyone else in the Casa Montana. "None of the rest of us has any of the *Angel of Caprona* to forget," he said, giving Aunt Gina his best smile.

"Bah!" said Aunt Gina. "Turning on the charm, Rinaldo Montana!" But she seemed a good deal more cheerful after that.

Tonino was glad Benvenuto had nothing to do with it this time. He looked round for Benvenuto. Benvenuto usually took up a good position for stealing scraps, near the serving table. But tonight he was nowhere to be seen. Nor, for that matter, was Marco.

"Where's Marco?" Paolo asked Rosa.

Rosa smiled. She seemed quite cheerful about it. "He has to help his brother," she said, "with fortifications."

That brought home to Paolo and Tonino the fact that there was going to be a war. They looked at one another nervously. Neither of them was quite sure whether you behaved in the usual way in wartime, or not. Tonino's mind shot to his beautiful new book, *The Boy Who Saved His Country*. He slurped the title through his mind, just as he was slurping his soup. Had Uncle Umberto meant to say to him, find the words to the *Angel of Caprona* and save your country, Tonino? It would indeed be the most marvellous thing if he, Tonino Montana, could find the words and save his country. He could hardly wait to see how the boy in the book had done it.

As soon as supper was over, he sprang up, ready to dash off and start reading. And once again he was prevented. This time it was because the children were told to wash up supper. Tonino groaned. And, again, he was not the only one.

"It isn't fair!" Corinna said passionately. "We slave all afternoon at spells, and we slave all evening at washing-up! I know there's going to be a war, but I still have to do my exams. How am I ever going to do my homework?" The way she flung out an impassioned arm made Paolo and Tonino think that Aunt Gina's manner must be catching.

Rather unexpectedly, Lucia sympathised with Corinna. "I think you're too old to be one of us children," she said. "Why don't you go away and do your homework and let me organise the kids?"

Corinna looked at her uncertainly. "What about your homework?"

"I've not got much. I'm not aiming for the University like you," Lucia said kindly. "Run along." And she pushed Corinna out of the dining room. As soon as the door was shut, she turned briskly to the other children. "Come on. What are you lot standing gooping for? Everyone take a pile of plates to the kitchen. Quick march, Tonino. Move, Lena and Bernardo. Paolo, you take the big bowls."

With Lucia standing over them like a sergeant major, Tonino had no chance to slip away. He trudged to the kitchen with everyone else, where, to his surprise, Lucia ordered everyone to lay the plates and cutlery out in rows on the floor. Then she made them stand in a row themselves, facing the rows of greasy dishes.

Lucia was very pleased with herself. "Now," she said, "this is something I've always wanted to try. This is washing-up-made-easy, by Lucia Montana's patent method. I'll tell you the words. They go to the *Angel of Caprona*. And you're all to sing after me—"

"Are you sure we should?" asked Lena, who was a very law-abiding cousin.

Lucia gave her a look of scalding contempt. "If some people," she remarked to the whitewashed beams of the ceiling, "don't know true intelligence when they see it, they are quite at liberty to go and live with the Petrocchis."

"I only asked," Lena said, crushed.

"Well, don't," said Lucia. "This is the spell…"

Shortly, they were all singing lustily:

"Angel, clean our knives and dishes,
Clean our spoons and salad-bowls,
Wash our saucepans, hear our wishes,
Angel, make our forks quite clean."

At first, nothing seemed to happen. Then it became clear that the orange grease was certainly slowly clearing from the plates. Then the lengths of spaghetti stuck to the bottom of the largest saucepan started unwinding and wriggling like worms. Up over the edge of the saucepan they wriggled, and over the stone floor, to ooze themselves into the waste-cans. The orange grease and the salad oil travelled after them, in rivulets. And the singing faltered a little, as people broke off to laugh.

"Sing, *sing*!" shouted Lucia. So they sang.

Unfortunately for Lucia, the noise penetrated to the Scriptorium. The plates were still pale pink and rather greasy, and the last of the spaghetti was still wriggling across the floor, when Elizabeth and Aunt Maria burst into the kitchen.

"Lucia!" said Elizabeth.

"You irreligious brats!" said Aunt Maria.

"I don't see what's so wrong," said Lucia.

"She doesn't see – Elizabeth, words fail!" said Aunt Maria. "How can I have taught her so little and so badly? Lucia, a spell is not *instead* of a thing. It is only to *help* that thing. And on top of that, you go and use the *Angel of Caprona*, as if it was any old tune, and not the most powerful song in all Italy! I – I could box your ears, Lucia!"

"So could I," said Elizabeth. "Don't you understand we need all our virtue – the whole combined strength of the Casa Montana – to put into the war-charms? And here you go frittering it away in the kitchen!"

"Put those plates in the sink, Paolo," ordered Aunt Maria. "Tonino, pick up those saucepans. The rest of you pick up the cutlery. And now you'll wash them properly."

Very chastened, everyone obeyed. Lucia was angry as well as chastened. When Lena whispered, "I *told* you so!" Lucia broke a plate and jumped on the pieces.

"Lucia!" snapped Aunt Maria, glaring at her. It was the first time any of the children had seen her look likely to slap someone.

"Well, how was I to know?" Lucia stormed. "Nobody

ever explained – nobody *told* me spells were like that!"

"Yes, but you knew perfectly well you were doing something you shouldn't," Elizabeth told her, "even if you didn't know why. The rest of you, stop sniggering. Lena, you can learn from this too."

All through doing the washing-up properly – which took nearly an hour – Tonino was saying to himself, "And *then* I can read my book at last."

When it was finally done, he sped out into the yard. And there was Old Niccolo hurrying down the steps to meet him in the dark.

"Tonino, may I have Benvenuto for a while, please?"

But Benvenuto was still not to be found. Tonino began to think he would die of book-frustration. All the children joined in hunting and calling, but there was still no Benvenuto. Soon, most of the grown-ups were looking for him too, and still Benvenuto did not appear. Antonio was so exasperated that he seized Tonino's arm and shook him.

"It's too bad, Tonino! You must have known we'd need Benvenuto. Why did you let him go?"

"I didn't! You *know* what Benvenuto's like!" Tonino protested, equally exasperated.

"Now, now, now," said Old Niccolo, taking each of them by a shoulder. "It is quite plain by now that Benvenuto is on the other side of town, making vile noises on a roof somewhere. All we can do is hope someone empties a jug of water on him soon. It's not Tonino's fault, Antonio."

Antonio let go Tonino's arm and rubbed both hands on his face. He looked very tired. "I'm sorry, Tonino," he said. "Forgive me. Let us know as soon as Benvenuto comes back, won't you?"

He and Old Niccolo hurried back to the Scriptorium. As they passed under the light, their faces were stiff with worry. "I don't think I like war, Tonino," Paolo said. "Let's go and play table-tennis in the dining room."

"I'm going to read my book," Tonino said firmly. He thought he would get like Aunt Gina if anything else happened to stop him.

CHAPTER SIX

*T*onino read half the night. With all the grown-ups hard at work in the Scriptorium, there was no one to tell him to go to bed. Corinna tried, when she had finished her homework, but Tonino was too deep in the book even to hear her. And Corinna went respectfully away, thinking that, as the book had come from Uncle Umberto, it was probably very learned.

It was not in the least learned. It was the most gripping story Tonino had ever read. It started with the boy, Giorgio, going along a mysterious alleyway near the docks on his way home from school. There was a peeling blue house at the end of the alley and, just as Giorgio passed it, a scrap of paper fluttered from one of its windows. It contained a mysterious message, which led Giorgio at once into a set of adventures with the enemies of his country. Each one was more exciting than the last.

Well after midnight, when Giorgio was holding a pass single-handed against the enemy, Tonino happened to hear his father and mother coming to bed. He was forced to leave Giorgio lying wounded and dive into bed himself. All night he dreamt of notes fluttering from the windows of peeling blue houses, of Giorgio – who was sometimes Tonino himself and sometimes Paolo – and of villainous enemies – most of whom seemed to have red beards and black hair, like Guido Petrocchi – and, as the sun rose, he was too excited to stay asleep. He woke up and went on reading.

When the rest of the Casa Montana began to stir, Tonino had finished the book. Giorgio had saved his country. Tonino was quivering with excitement and exhaustion. He wished the book was twice as long. If it had not been time to get up, he would have gone straight back to the beginning and started reading the book again.

And the beauty of it, he thought, eating breakfast without noticing, was that Giorgio had saved his country, not only single-handed, but without a spell coming into it anywhere. If Tonino was going to save Caprona, that was the way he would like to do it.

Around Tonino, everyone else was complaining and Lucia

was sulking. The washing-up spell was still about in the kitchen. Every cup and plate was covered with a thin layer of orange spaghetti grease, and the butter tasted of soap.

"What did she *use*, in Heaven's name?" groaned Uncle Lorenzo. "This coffee tastes of tomato."

"Her own words to the *Angel of Caprona*," Aunt Maria said, and shuddered as she picked up her greasy cup.

"Lucia, you fool!" said Rinaldo. "That's the strongest tune there is."

"All right, all right. Stop going on at me. I'm sorry!" Lucia said angrily.

"So are the rest of us, unfortunately," sighed Uncle Lorenzo.

If only I could be like Giorgio, Tonino thought, as he got up from the table. I suppose what I should have to do is to find the words to the *Angel*. He went to school without seeing anything on the way, wondering how he could manage to do that, when the rest of his family had failed. He was realistic enough to know that he was simply not good enough at spells to make up the words in the ordinary way. It made him sigh heavily.

"Cheer up," said Paolo, as they went into school.

"I'm all right," Tonino said. He was surprised Paolo should think he was miserable. He was not miserable at all. He was wrapped in delightful dreams. Maybe I can do it by accident, he thought.

He sat in class composing strings of gibberish to the tune of the *Angel*, in hopes that some of it might be right. But that did not seem satisfactory, somehow. Then, in a lesson that was probably History – for he did not hear a word of it – it struck him, like a blinding light, what he had to do. He had to *find* the words, of course. The First Duke must have had them written down somewhere and lost the paper. Tonino was the boy whose mission it was to discover that lost paper. No nonsense about making up words, just straight detective work. And Tonino was positive that the book had been a clue. He must find a peeling blue house, and the paper with the words on would be somewhere near.

"Tonino," asked the teacher, for the fourth time, "where did Marco Polo journey to?"

Tonino did not hear the question, but he realised he was being asked something. "The Angel of Caprona," he said.

Nobody at school got much sense out of Tonino that day. He was full of the wonder of his discovery. It did not occur to him that Uncle Umberto had looked in every piece of writing in the University Library and not found the words to the *Angel*. Tonino knew.

After school, he avoided Paolo and his cousins. As soon as they were safely headed for the Casa Montana, Tonino set off in the opposite direction, towards the docks and quays by the New Bridge.

An hour later, Rosa said to Paolo, "What's the matter with Benvenuto? Look at him."

Paolo leant over the gallery rail beside her. Benvenuto, looking surprisingly small and piteous, was running backwards and forwards just inside the gate, mewing frantically. Every so often, as if he was too distracted to know what he was doing, he sat down, shot out a hind leg, and licked it madly. Then he leapt up and ran about again.

Paolo had never seen Benvenuto behave like this. He called out, "Benvenuto, what's the matter?"

Benvenuto swung round, crouching low on the ground, and stared urgently up at him. His eyes were like two yellow beacons of distress. He gave a string of mews, so penetrating and so demanding that Paolo felt his stomach turn uneasily.

"What *is* it, Benvenuto?" called Rosa.

Benvenuto's tail flapped in exasperation. He gave a great leap and vanished somewhere out of sight. Rosa and Paolo hung by their midriffs over the rail and craned after him. Benvenuto was now standing on the water butt, with his tail slashing. As soon as he knew they could see him, he stared fixedly at them again and uttered a truly appalling noise.

Wong wong wong wong-wong-wong!

Paolo and Rosa, without more ado, swung towards the stairs and clattered down them. Benvenuto's wails had already attracted all the other cats in the Casa. They were running across the yard and dropping from roofs before Paolo and Rosa were halfway down the stairs. They were forced to step carefully to the water butt among smooth furry bodies and staring, anxious green or yellow eyes.

"*Mee-ow-ow!*" Benvenuto said peremptorily, when they reached him.

He was thinner and browner than Paolo had ever seen him. There was a new rent in his left ear, and his coat was in ragged spikes. He looked truly wretched. "Mee-ow-ow!" he reiterated, from a wide pink mouth.

"Something's wrong," Paolo said uneasily. "He's trying to say something." Guiltily, he wished he had kept his resolution to learn to understand Benvenuto. But when Tonino could do it so easily, it had never been worth the bother. Now here was Benvenuto with an urgent message – perhaps word from Chrestomanci – and he could not understand it. "We'd better get Tonino," he said.

Benvenuto's tail slashed again. "Mee-ow-ow!" he said, with tremendous force and meaning. Around Paolo and Rosa, the pink mouths of all the other cats opened too. "MEE-OW-OW!" It was deafening. Paolo stared helplessly.

It was Rosa who tumbled to their meaning. "Tonino!" she exclaimed. "They're saying *Tonino*! Paolo, where's Tonino?"

With a jolt of worry, Paolo realised he had not seen Tonino since breakfast. And as soon as he realised that, Rosa knew it too. And, such was the nature of the Casa Montana, that the alarm was given then and there. Aunt Gina shot out of the kitchen, holding a pair of kitchen tongs in one hand and a ladle in the other. Domenico and Aunt Maria came out of the Saloon, and Elizabeth appeared in the gallery outside the Music Room with the five little cousins. The door of the

Scriptorium opened, filled with anxious faces.

Benvenuto gave a whisk of his tail and leapt for the gallery steps. He bounded up them, followed by the other cats; and Paolo and Rosa hurried up too, in a sort of shoal of leaping black and white bodies. Everyone converged on Antonio's rooms. People poured out of the Scriptorium, Elizabeth raced round the gallery, and Aunt Maria and Aunt Gina clambered up the steps by the kitchen quicker than either had ever climbed in her life. The Casa filled with the sound of hollow running feet.

The whole family jammed themselves after Rosa and Paolo into the room where Tonino was usually to be found reading. There was no Tonino, only the red book lying on the windowsill. It was no longer shiny. The pages were thick at the edges and the red cover was curling upwards, as if the book was wet.

Benvenuto, with his jagged brown coat up in a ridge along his back and his tail fluffed like a fox's brush, landed on the sill beside the book and rashly put his nose forward to sniff at it. He leapt back again, shaking his head, crouching, and growling like a dog. Smoke poured up from the book. People coughed and cats sneezed. The book curled and writhed on the sill, amid clouds of smoke, exactly as if it were on fire. But instead of turning black, it turned pale grey-blue where it smoked, and looked slimy. The room filled with a smell of rotting.

"Ugh!" said everybody.

Old Niccolo barged members of his family right and left to get near it. He stood over it and sang, in a strong tenor voice almost as good as Marco's, three strange words. He sang them twice before he had to break off coughing. "Sing!" he croaked, with tears pouring down his face. "All of you."

All the Montanas obediently broke into song, three long notes in unison. And again. And again. After that, quite a number of them had to cough, though the smoke was distinctly less. Old Niccolo recovered and waved his arms, like the conductor of a choir. All who could, sang once more. It took ten repetitions to halt the decay of the book. By that time, it was a shrivelled triangle, about half the size it had been. Gingerly, Antonio leant over and opened the window beyond it, to let out the last of the smoke.

"What was it?" he asked Old Niccolo. "Someone trying to suffocate us all?"

"I thought it came from Umberto," Elizabeth faltered. "I never would have—"

Old Niccolo shook his head. "This thing never came from Umberto. And I don't think it was meant to kill. Let's see what kind of spell it is." He snapped his fingers and held out a hand, rather like a surgeon performing an operation. Without needing to be told, Aunt Gina put her kitchen tongs into his hand. Carefully, gently, Old Niccolo used the tongs to open the cover of the book.

"A good pair of tongs ruined," Aunt Gina said.

"Ssh!" said Old Niccolo. The shrivelled pages of the book

had stuck into a gummy block. He snapped his fingers and held out his hand again. This time, Rinaldo put the pen he was carrying in it.

"And a good pen," he said, with a grimace at Aunt Gina.

With the pen as well as the tongs, Old Niccolo was able to pry the pages of the book apart without touching them and peel them over, one by one. Chins rested on both Paolo's shoulders as everyone craned to see, and there were chins on the shoulders of those with the chins. There was no sound but the sound of breathing.

On nearly every page, the printing had melted away, leaving a slimy, leathery surface quite unlike paper, with only a mark or so left in the middle. Old Niccolo looked closely at each mark and grunted. He grunted again at the first picture, which had faded like the print, but left a clearer mark. After that, though there was no print on any of the pages, the remaining mark was steadily clearer, up to the centre of the book, when it began to become more faded again, until the mark was barely visible on the back page.

Old Niccolo laid down the pen and the tongs in terrible silence. "Right through," he said at length. People shifted and someone coughed, but nobody said anything. "I do not know," said Old Niccolo, "the substance this object is made of, but I know a calling-charm when I see one. Tonino must have been like one hypnotised, if he had read all this."

"He *was* a bit strange at breakfast," Paolo whispered.

"I am sure he was," said his grandfather. He looked

reflectively at the shrivelled stump of the book and then round at the crowded faces of his family. "Now who," he asked softly, "would want to set a strong calling-charm on Tonino Montana? Who would be mean enough to pick on a child? Who would—?" He turned suddenly on Benvenuto, crouched beside the book, and Benvenuto cowered right down, quivering, with his ragged ears flat against his flat head. "Where were you last night, Benvenuto?" he asked, more softly still.

No one understood the reply Benvenuto gave as he cowered, but everyone knew the answer. It was in Antonio and Elizabeth's harrowed faces, in the set of Rinaldo's chin, in Aunt Francesca's narrowed eyes, narrowed almost out of existence, and in the way Aunt Maria looked at Uncle Lorenzo; but most of all, it was in the way Benvenuto threw himself down on his side, with his back to the room, the picture of a cat in despair.

Old Niccolo looked up. "Now isn't that odd?" he said gently. "Benvenuto spent last night chasing a white she-cat – over the roofs of the Casa Petrocchi." He paused to let that sink in. "So Benvenuto," he said, "who knows a bad spell when he sees one, was not around to warn Tonino."

"But *why*?" Elizabeth asked despairingly.

Old Niccolo went, if possible, quieter still. "I can only conclude, my dear, that the Petrocchis are being paid by Florence, Siena, or Pisa."

There was another silence, thick and meaningful. Antonio

broke it. "Well," he said, in such a subdued, grim way that Paolo stared at him. "Well? Are we going?"

"Of course," said Old Niccolo. "Domenico, fetch me my small black spell-book."

Everyone left the room, so suddenly, quietly and purposefully that Paolo was left behind, not clear what was going on. He turned uncertainly to go to the door, and realised that Rosa had been left behind too. She was sitting on Tonino's bed, with one hand to her head, white as Tonino's sheets.

"Paolo," she said, "tell Claudia I'll have the baby, if she wants to go. I'll have all the little ones."

She looked up at Paolo as she said it, and she looked so strange that Paolo was suddenly frightened. He ran gladly out into the gallery. The family was gathering, still quiet and grim, in the yard. Paolo ran down there and gave his message. Protesting little ones were pushed up the steps to Rosa, but Paolo did not help. He found Elizabeth and Lucia and pushed close to them. Elizabeth put an arm round him and an arm round Lucia.

"Keep close to me, loves," she said. "I'll keep you safe." Paolo looked across her at Lucia and saw that Lucia was not frightened at all. She was excited. She winked at him. Paolo winked back and felt better.

A minute later, Old Niccolo took his place at the head of the family and they all hurried to the gate. Paolo had just forced his way through, jostling his mother on one side and Domenico on the other, when a carriage drew up in the road, and Uncle Umberto scrambled out of it. He came up to Old Niccolo in that grim, quiet way in which everyone seemed to be moving.

"Who is kidnapped? Bernardo? Domenico?"

"Tonino," replied Old Niccolo. "A book, with the University arms on the wrapping."

Uncle Umberto answered, "Luigi Petrocchi is also a member of the University."

"I bear that in mind," said Old Niccolo.

"I shall come with you to the Casa Petrocchi," said Uncle Umberto. He waved at the cab driver to tell him to go. The man was only too ready to. He nearly pulled his horses over on their sides, trying to turn them too quickly. The sight of the entire Casa Montana grimly streaming into the street seemed altogether too much for him.

That pleased Paolo. He looked back and forth as they swung down the Via Magica, and pride grew in him. There were such a lot of them. And they were so single-minded. The same intent look was in every face. And though children pattered and young men strode, though the ladies clattered on the cobbles in elegant shoes, though Old Niccolo's steps were short and bustling, and Antonio, because he could not wait to come at the Petrocchis, walked with long lunging steps, the common purpose gave the whole family a common rhythm. Paolo could almost believe they were marching in step.

The concourse crowded down the Via Sant' Angelo and swept round the corner into the Corso, with the Cathedral at their backs. People out shopping hastily gave them room. But Old Niccolo was too angry to use the pavement like a mere pedestrian. He led the family into the middle of the road and they marched there like a vengeful army, forcing cars and carriages to draw into the kerbs, with Old Niccolo stepping proudly at their head. It was hard to believe that a fat old man with a baby's face could look so warlike.

The Corso bends slightly beyond the Archbishop's Palace. Then it runs straight again by the shops, past the columns of the Art Gallery on one side and the gilded doors of the Arsenal on the other. They swung round that bend. There, approaching from the opposite direction, was another similar crowd, also walking in the road. The Petrocchis were on the march too.

"Extraordinary!" muttered Uncle Umberto.

"Perfect!" spat Old Niccolo.

The two families advanced on one another. There was utter silence now, except for the cloppering of feet. Every ordinary citizen, as soon as they saw the entire Casa Montana advancing on the entire Casa Petrocchi, made haste to get off the street. People knocked on the doors of perfect strangers and were let in without question. The manager of Grossi's, the biggest shop in Caprona, threw open his plate-glass doors and sent his assistants out to fetch in everyone nearby. After which he clapped the doors shut and locked a steel grille down in front of them. From between the bars, white faces stared out at the oncoming spell-makers. And a troop of Reservists, newly called up and sloppily marching in crumpled new uniforms, were horrified to find themselves caught between the two parties. They broke and ran, as one crumpled Reservist, and sought frantic shelter in the Arsenal. The great gilt doors clanged shut on them just as Old Niccolo halted, face to face with Guido Petrocchi.

"Well?" said Old Niccolo, his baby eyes glaring.

"Well?" retorted Guido, his red beard jutting.

"Was it," asked Old Niccolo, "Florence or Pisa that paid you to kidnap my grandson Tonino?"

Guido Petrocchi gave a bark of contemptuous laughter. "You mean," he said, "was it Pisa or Siena who paid *you* to kidnap my daughter Angelica?"

"Do you imagine," said Old Niccolo, "that saying that makes it any less obvious that you are a baby snatcher?"

"Do you," asked Guido, "accuse me of lying?"

"*Yes!*" roared the Casa Montana. "*Liar!*"

"*And the same to you!*" howled the Casa Petrocchi, crowding up behind Guido, lean and ferocious, many of them red-haired. "*Filthy liars!*"

The fighting began while they were still shouting. There was no knowing who started it. The roars on either side were mixed with singing and muttering. Scrips fluttered in many hands. And the air was suddenly full of flying eggs. Paolo received one, a very greasy fried egg, right across the mouth, and it made him so angry that he began to shout egg-spells too, at the top of his voice. Eggs splattered down, fried eggs, poached eggs, scrambled eggs, new-laid eggs, and eggs so horribly bad that they were like bombs when they burst. Everyone slithered on the eggy cobbles. Egg streamed off the ends of people's hair and spattered everyone's clothes.

Then somebody varied it with a bad tomato or so. Immediately, all manner of unpleasant things were flying about the Corso: cold spaghetti and cowpats – though these may have been Rinaldo's idea in the first place, they were very quickly coming from both sides – and cabbages; squirts of oil and showers of ice; dead rats and chicken livers.

It was no wonder that the ordinary people kept out of the way. Egg and tomato ran down the grilles over Grossi's windows and splashed the white columns of the Art Gallery. There were loud clangs as rotten cabbages hit the brass doors of the Arsenal.

This was the first, disorganised phase of the battle, with everyone venting his fury separately. But, by the time everyone was filthy and sticky, their fury took shape a little. Both sides began on a more organised chant. It grew, and became two strong rhythmic choruses.

The result was that the objects flying about the Corso rose up into the air and began to rain down as much more harmful things. Paolo looked up to see a cloud of transparent, glittering, frozen-looking pieces tumbling out of the sky at him. He thought it was snow at first, until a piece hit his arm and cut it.

"Vicious beasts!" Lucia screamed beside him. "It's broken glass!"

Before the main body of the glass came down, Old Niccolo's penetrating tenor voice soared above the yells and the chanting. "Testudo!"

Antonio's full bass backed him up: "Testudo!" and so did Uncle Lorenzo's baritone. Feet tramped. Paolo knew this one. He bowed over, tramping regularly, and kept up the charm with them. The whole family did it. *Tramp, tramp, tramp.* "Testudo, testudo, testudo!" Over their bent heads, the glass splinters bounced and showered harmlessly off an invisible barrier. "Testudo." From the middle of the bowed backs, Elizabeth's voice rang up sweetly in yet another spell. She was joined by Aunt Anna, Aunt Maria and Corinna. It was like a soprano descant over a rhythmic tramping chorus.

Paolo knew without being told that he must keep up the shield-charm while Elizabeth worked her spell. So did everyone else. It was extraordinary, exciting, amazing, he thought. Each Montana picked up the slightest hint and acted on it as if it were orders.

He risked glancing up and saw that the descant spell was working. Every glass splinter, as it hit the unseen shield Paolo was helping to make, turned into an angry hornet and buzzed back at the Petrocchis. But the Petrocchis simply turned them into glass splinters again and hurled them back. At the same time, Paolo could tell from the rhythm of their singing that some of them were working to destroy the shield-charm.

Paolo sang and tramped harder than ever.

Meanwhile, Rinaldo's voice and his father's were singing gently, deeply, at work on something yet again. More of the ladies joined in the hornet-song so that the Petrocchis would not guess. And all the while, the tramp, tramp of the shield-charm was kept up by everyone else. It could have been the grandest chorus in the grandest opera ever, except that it all had a different purpose. The purpose came with a perfect roar of voices. The Petrocchis threw up their arms and staggered. The cobbles beneath them heaved and the solid Corso began to give way into a pit. Their instant reply was another huge sung chord, with discords innumerable. And the Montanas suddenly found themselves inside a wall of flame.

There was total confusion. Paolo staggered for safety, with his hair singed, over cobbles that quaked and heaved under his shoes. "Voltava!" he sang frantically. "Voltava!" Behind him, the flames hissed. Clouds of steam blotted out even the tall Art Gallery as the river answered the charm and came swirling up the Corso. Water was knee-deep round Paolo, up to his waist, and still rising. There was too much water. Someone had sung out of tune, and Paolo rather thought it was him. He saw his cousin Lena almost up to her chin in water and grabbed her. Towing Lena, he staggered through the current, over the heaving road, trying to make for the Arsenal steps.

Someone must have had the sense to work a cancel-spell. Everything suddenly cleared, steam, water and smoke together. Paolo found himself on the steps of the Art Gallery, not by the Arsenal at all. Behind him, the Corso was a mass of loose cobbles, shiny with mud and littered with cowpats, tomatoes and fried eggs. There could hardly have been more mess if Caprona had been invaded by the armies of Florence, Pisa and Siena.

Paolo felt he had had enough. Lena was crying. She was too young. She should have been left with Rosa. He could see his mother picking Lucia out of the mud, and Rinaldo helping Aunt Gina up.

"Let's go home, Paolo," whimpered Lena.

But the battle was not really finished. Montanas and Petrocchis were up and down the Corso in little angry, muddy groups, shouting abuse at one another.

"I'll give you broken glass!"

"You started it!"

"You lying Petrocchi swine! Kidnapper!"

"Swine yourself! Spell-bungler! Traitor!"

Aunt Gina and Rinaldo slithered over to what looked like a muddy boulder in the street and heaved at it. The vast bulk of Aunt Francesca arose, covered with mud and angrier than Paolo had ever seen her.

"You filthy Petrocchis! I demand single combat!" she screamed. Her voice scraped like a great saw-blade and filled the Corso.

CHAPTER SEVEN

✴

*A*unt Francesca's challenge seemed to rally both sides. A female Petrocchi voice screamed, "We agree!" and all the muddy groups hastened towards the middle of the Corso again.

Paolo reached his family to hear Old Niccolo saying, "Don't be a fool, Francesca!" He looked more like a muddy goblin than the head of a famous family. He was almost too breathless to speak.

"They have insulted us and fought us!" said Aunt Francesca. "They deserve to be disgraced and drummed out of Caprona. And I shall do it! I'm more than a match for a

115

Petrocchi!" She looked it, vast and muddy as she was, with her huge black dress in tatters and her grey hair half undone and streaming over one shoulder.

But the other Montanas knew Aunt Francesca was an old woman. There was a chorus of protest. Uncle Lorenzo and Rinaldo both offered to take on the Petrocchi champion in her place.

"No," said Old Niccolo. "Rinaldo, you were wounded—"

He was interrupted by catcalls from the Petrocchis. "Cowards! We want single combat!"

Old Niccolo's muddy face screwed up with anger. "Very well, they shall have their single combat," he said. "Antonio, I appoint you. Step forward."

Paolo felt a gush of pride. So his father was, as he had always thought, the best spell-maker in the Casa Montana. But the pride became mixed with alarm, when Paolo saw the way his mother clutched Antonio's arm, and the worried, reluctant look on his father's mud-streaked face.

"Go on!" Old Niccolo said crossly.

Slowly, Antonio advanced into the space between the two families, stumbling a little among the loose cobbles. "I'm ready," he called to the Petrocchis. "Who's your champion?"

It was clear that there was some indecision among the Petrocchis. A dismayed voice said, "It's *Antonio*!" This was followed by a babble of talk. From the turning of heads and the uncertain heaving about, Paolo thought they were looking for a Petrocchi who was unaccountably missing. But the fuss died away, and Guido Petrocchi himself stepped forward. Paolo could see several Petrocchis looking as alarmed as Elizabeth.

"I'm ready too," said Guido, baring his teeth angrily. Since his face was plastered with mud, it made him look quite savage. He was also large and sturdy. He made Antonio look small, gentle and fragile. "And I demand an unlimited contest!" snarled Guido. He seemed even angrier than Old Niccolo.

"Very well," Antonio said. There could have been the least shake in his voice. "You're aware that means a fight to the finish, are you?"

"Suits me perfectly," said Guido. He was like a giant saying "Fee-fi-fo-fum". Paolo was suddenly very frightened.

It was at this moment that the Ducal Police arrived. They had come in, quietly and cunningly, riding bicycles along the pavements. No one noticed them until the Chief of Police and his lieutenant were standing beside the two champions.

"Guido Petrocchi and Antonio Montana," said the lieutenant, "I arrest you—"

Both champions jumped, and turned to find blue braided uniforms on either side of them.

"Oh go away," said Old Niccolo, hastening forward. "What do you have to interfere for?"

"Yes, go away," said Guido. "We're busy."

The lieutenant flinched at Guido's face, but the Chief of Police was a bold and dashing man with a handsome moustache, and he had his reputation to keep up as a bold and dashing man. He bowed to Old Niccolo. "These two are under arrest," he said. "The rest of you I order to sink your differences and remember there is about to be a war."

"We're at war already," said Old Niccolo. "Go away."

"I regret," said the Chief of Police, "that that is impossible."

"Then don't say you weren't warned," said Guido.

There was a short burst of song from the adults of both families. Paolo wished he knew that spell. It sounded useful. As soon as it was over, Rinaldo and a swarthy young Petrocchi came over to the two policemen and towed them away backwards. They were as stiff as the tailor's dummies in the barred windows of Grossi's. Rinaldo and the other young man laid them against the steps of the Art Gallery and returned each to his family, without looking at one another. As for the rest of the Ducal Police, they seemed to have vanished, bicycles and all.

"Ready now?" said Guido.

"Ready," said Antonio.

And the single combat commenced.

Looking back on it afterwards, Paolo realised that it could not have lasted more than three minutes, though it seemed endless at the time. For, in that time, the strength, skill and speed of both champions was tried to the utmost. The first, and probably the longest, part was when the two were testing one another for an opening, and comparatively little seemed to happen. Both stood, leaning slightly forward, muttering, humming, occasionally flicking a hand.

Paolo stared at his father's strained face and wondered just what was going on. Then, momentarily, Guido was a man-shaped red-and-white check duster. Someone gasped. But Antonio almost simultaneously became a cardboard man covered with green triangles. Then both flicked back to themselves again.

The speed of it astounded Paolo. A spell had not only been cast on both sides, but also a counter-spell, and a spell counter to that, all in the time it took someone to gasp. Both combatants were panting and looking warily at each other. It was clear they were very evenly matched.

Again there was a space when nothing seemed to happen, except a sort of flickering on both sides. Then suddenly Antonio struck, and struck so hard that it was plain he had all the time been building a strong spell, beneath the flicker of trivial spells designed to keep Guido occupied. Guido gave a shout and dissolved into dust, which swept away backwards in a spiral. But, somehow, as he dissolved, he threw *his* strong spell at Antonio. Antonio broke into a thousand little pieces, like a spilt jigsaw puzzle.

For an ageless time, the swirl of dust and the pile of broken Antonio hung in mid-air. Both were struggling to stay together and not to patter down on the uprooted cobbles of the Corso. In fact, they were still struggling to make spells too. When, at last, Antonio staggered forward in one piece, holding some kind of red fruit in his right hand, he had barely time to dodge. Guido was a leopard in mid-spring.

Elizabeth screamed.

Antonio threw himself to one side, heaved a breath and sang. "*Oliphans!*" His usually silky voice was rough and ragged, but he hit the right notes. A gigantic elephant, with tusks longer than Paolo was tall, cut off the low sun and shook the Corso as it advanced, ears spread, to trample the attacking leopard. It was hard to believe the great beast was indeed worried, thin Antonio Montana.

For a shadow of a second, the leopard was Guido Petrocchi, very white in the face and luridly red in the beard, gabbling a frantic song. "*Hickory-dickory-muggery-mus!*" And he must have hit the right notes too. He seemed to vanish.

The Montanas were raising a cheer at Guido's cowardice, when the elephant panicked. Paolo had the merest glimpse of a little tiny mouse scampering aggressively at the great front feet of the elephant, before he was running for his life. The shrill trumpeting of Antonio seemed to tear his ears apart. Behind him, Paolo knew that the elephant was stark, staring mad, trampling this way and that among terrified Montanas. Lucia ran past him, carrying Lena clutched backwards against her front. Paolo grabbed little Bernardo by one arm and ran with him, wincing at the horrible brazen, braying squeal from his father.

Elephants are afraid of mice, horribly afraid. And there are very few people who can shift shape without taking the nature of the shape they shift to. It seemed that Guido Petrocchi had not only won, but got most of the Montanas trampled to death into the bargain.

But when Paolo next looked, Elizabeth was standing in the elephant's path, staring up at its wild little eyes. "Antonio!" she shouted. "*Antonio*, control yourself!" She looked so tiny and the elephant was coming so fast that Paolo shut his eyes.

He opened them in time to see the elephant in the act of swinging his mother up on its back. Tears of relief so clouded Paolo's eyes that he almost failed to see Guido's next attack. He was simply aware of a shattering noise, a horrible smell, and a sort of moving tower. He saw the elephant swing round, and Elizabeth crouch down on its back. It was now being confronted by a vast iron machine, even larger than itself, throbbing with mechanical power and filling the Corso with nasty blue smoke. This thing ground slowly towards Antonio on huge moving tracks. As it came, a gun in its front swung down to aim between the elephant's eyes.

On the spur of the moment, Antonio became another machine. He was in such a hurry, and he knew so little about machines, that it was a very bizarre machine indeed. It was pale duck-egg blue, with enormous rubber wheels. In fact, it was probably made of rubber all through, because the bullet from Guido's machine bounced off it and crashed into the steps of the Arsenal. Most people threw themselves flat.

"Mother's *inside* that thing!" Lucia screamed to Paolo, above the noise.

Paolo realised she must be. Antonio had had no time to put

Elizabeth down. And now he was barging recklessly at Guido, *bang*-bounce, *bang*-bounce. It must have been horrible for Elizabeth. Luckily, it only lasted a second. Elizabeth and Antonio suddenly appeared in their own shapes, almost under the mighty tracks of the Guido-machine. Elizabeth ran – Paolo had not known she could run so fast – like the wind towards the Arsenal. And it may have been Petrocchi viciousness, or perhaps simple confusion, but the great Guido-tank swung its gun down to point at Elizabeth.

Antonio called Guido a very bad name, and threw the tomato he still had in his hand. The red fruit hit, and splashed, and ran down the iron side. Paolo was just wondering what use that was, when the tank was not there any more. Nor was Guido. In his place was a giant tomato. It was about the size of a pumpkin. And it simply sat in the road and did not move.

That was the winning stroke. Paolo could tell it was from the look on Antonio's face as he walked up to the tomato. Disgusted and weary, Antonio bent down to pick up the tomato. There were scattered groans from the Petrocchis, and cheers, not quite certain and even more scattered, from the Montanas.

Then somebody cast yet another spell.

This time, it was a thick wet fog. No doubt, at the beginning, it would not have seemed so terrible, but, after all the rest, just when the fight was over, Paolo felt it was the last straw. All he could see, in front of his eyes, was thick whiteness. After he had taken a breath or so, he was coughing.

He could hear coughing all round, and far off into the distance, which was the only thing which showed him he was not entirely alone. He turned his head from trying to see who else was coughing, and found he could not see Lucia. Nor could he find Bernardo, and he knew he had been holding Bernardo's arm a second before. As soon as he realised that, he found he had lost his sense of direction too. He was all alone, coughing and shivering, in cold white emptiness.

"I am *not* going to lose my head," Paolo told himself sternly. "My father didn't, and so I shan't. I shall find somewhere to shelter until this beastly spell is over. Then I shall go home. I don't care if Tonino *is* still missing—" He stopped then, because a thought came to him, like an astonishing discovery. "We're never going to find Tonino this way, anyway," he said. And he knew it was true.

With his hands stretched out in front of him and his eyes spread very wide in hopes of seeing something – which was unlikely, since they were streaming from the fog, and so was his nose – Paolo coughed and sniffed and shuffled his way forward until his toes came up against stone. Paolo looked down, but he could not see what it was. He tried lifting one foot, with his toes scraping against the obstruction. And, after a few inches, the obstruction stopped and his foot shot forward. It was a ledge, then. Probably the kerb. He had been near the edge of the road when he ran away from the elephant. He got both feet on the kerb and shuffled forward six inches – then he fell upstairs over what seemed to be a body.

It gave Paolo such a shock that he dared not move at first. But he soon realised the body beneath him was shivering, as he was, and trying to cough and mutter at the same time. "Holy Mary—" Paolo heard, in a hoarse blurred voice. Very puzzled, Paolo put out a careful hand and felt the body. His fingers met cold metal buttons, uniform braid, and, a little above that, a warm face – which gave a croak as Paolo's cold hand met its mouth – and a large furry moustache beneath the nose.

Angel of Caprona! Paolo thought. It's the Chief of Police!

Paolo got himself to his knees on what must be the steps of the Art Gallery. There was no one around he could ask, but it did not seem fair to leave someone lying helpless in the fog. It was bad enough if you could move. So hoping he was doing the right thing, Paolo knelt and sang, very softly, the most general cancel-spell he could think of. It had no effect on the fog – that was evidently very strong magic – but he heard the Chief of Police roll over on his side and groan. Boots scraped as he tested his legs. "*Mamma mia!*" Paolo heard him moan.

He sounded as if he wanted to be alone. Paolo left him and crawled his way up the Gallery steps. He had no idea he had reached the top, until he hit his elbow on a pillar and drove his head into Lucia's stomach at the same moment. Both of them said some extremely unpleasant things.

"When you've quite finished swearing," Lucia said at

length, "you can get between these pillars with me and keep me warm." She coughed and shivered. "Isn't this awful? Who did it?" She coughed again. The fog had made her hoarse.

"It wasn't us," said Paolo. "We'd have known. Ow, my elbow!" He took hold of her for a guide and wedged himself down beside her. He felt better like that.

"The pigs," said Lucia. "I call this a mean trick. It's funny – you spend your life being told what pigs they are, and thinking they *can't* be, really. Then you meet them, and they're worse than you were told. Was it you singing just now?"

"I fell over the Chief of Police on the steps," said Paolo.

Lucia laughed. "I fell over the other one. I sang a cancel-spell too. He was lying on all the corners of the stairs and it must have bruised him all over when I fell on him."

"It's bad enough when you can move," Paolo agreed. "Like being blind."

"Horrible," said Lucia. "That blind beggar in the Via Sant' Angelo – I shall give him some money tomorrow."

"The one with white eyes?" said Paolo. "Yes, so shall I. And I never want to see another spell."

"To tell you the truth," said Lucia, "I was wishing I dared burn the Library and the Scriptorium down. It came to me like a blinding flash – just before I fell over that policeman – that no amount of spells are going to work on those beastly kidnappers."

"That's just what I thought!" exclaimed Paolo. "I know the only way to find Tonino—"

"Hang on," said Lucia. "I think the fog's getting thinner."

She was right. When Paolo leant forward, he could see two dark lumps below, where the Chief of Police and his lieutenant were sitting on the steps with their heads in their hands. He could see quite a stretch of the Corso beyond them – cobbles which were dark and wet-looking, but, to his surprise, neither muddy nor out of place.

"Someone's put it all back!" said Lucia.

The fog thinned further. They could see the glimmering doors of the Arsenal now, and the entire foggy width of the Corso, with every cobblestone back where it should be. Somewhere about the middle of it, Antonio and Guido Petrocchi were standing facing one another.

"Oh, they're not going to begin again, are they?" wailed Paolo.

But, almost at once, Antonio and Guido swung round and walked away from one another.

"Thank goodness!" said Lucia. She and Paolo turned to one another, smiling with relief.

Except that it was not Lucia. Paolo found himself staring into a white pointed face, and eyes darker, larger and shrewder than Lucia's. Surrounding the face were draggled dark red curls. The smile died from the face and horror replaced it as Paolo stared. He felt his own face behaving the same way. He had been huddling up against a Petrocchi! He knew which one, too. It was the elder of the two who had been at the palace. Renata, that was her name. And she knew him too.

"You're that blue-eyed Montana boy!" she exclaimed. She made it sound quite disgusting.

Both of them got up. Renata backed into the pillars, as if she was trying to get inside the stone, and Paolo backed away along the steps.

"I thought you were my sister Lucia," he said.

"I thought you were my cousin Claudio," Renata retorted.

Somehow, they both made it sound as if it was the other one's fault.

"It wasn't my fault!" Paolo said angrily. "Blame the person who made the fog, not me. There's an enemy enchanter."

"I know. Chrestomanci said," said Renata.

Paolo felt he hated Chrestomanci. He had no business to go and say the same things to the Petrocchis as he said to the Montanas. But he hated the enemy enchanter even more. He had been responsible for the most embarrassing thing which had ever happened to Paolo. Muttering with shame, Paolo turned to run away.

"No, stop! *Wait!*" Renata said. She said it so commandingly that Paolo stopped without thinking, and gave Renata time to snatch hold of his arm. Instead of pulling away, Paolo stood quite still and attempted to behave with the dignity becoming to a Montana. He looked at his arm, and at Renata's hand holding it, as if both had become one composite slimy toad. But Renata hung on. "Look all you like," she said. "I don't care. I'm not letting go until you tell me what your family has done with Angelica."

"Nothing," Paolo said contemptuously. "We wouldn't touch one of you with a barge-pole. What have you lot done with Tonino?"

An odd little frown wrinkled Renata's white forehead. "Is that your brother? Is he really missing?"

"He was sent a book with a calling-spell in it," said Paolo.

"A book," said Renata slowly, "got Angelica too. We only realised when it shrivelled away."

She let go of Paolo's arm. They stared at one another in the blowing remains of the fog.

"It must be the enemy enchanter," said Paolo.

"Trying to take our minds off the war," said Renata. "Tell your family, won't you?"

"If you tell yours," said Paolo.

"Of course I will. What do you take me for?" said Renata.

In spite of everything, Paolo found himself laughing. "I think you're a Petrocchi!" he said.

But when Renata began to laugh too, Paolo realised it was too much. He turned to run away, and found himself facing the Chief of Police. The Chief of Police had evidently recovered his dignity. "Now then, you children. Move along," he said.

Renata fled, without more ado, red in the face with the shame of being caught talking to a Montana. Paolo hung on. It seemed to him that he ought to report that Tonino was missing.

"I said move along!" repeated the Chief of Police, and he

pulled down his jacket with a most threatening jerk.

Paolo's nerve broke. After all, an ordinary policeman was not going to be much help against an enchanter. He ran.

He ran all the way to the Casa Montana. The fog and the wetness did not extend beyond the Corso. As soon as he turned into a side road, Paolo found himself in the bleak shadows and low red sun of a winter evening. It was like being shot back into another world – a world where things happened as they should, where one's father did not turn into a mad elephant, where, above all, one's sister did not turn out to be a Petrocchi.

Paolo's face fired with shame as he ran. Of all the awful things to happen!

The Casa Montana came in sight, with the familiar Angel safely over the gate. Paolo shot in under it, and ran into his father. Antonio was standing under the archway, panting as if he too had run all the way home.

"Who!? Oh, Paolo," said Antonio. "Stay where you are."

"Why?" asked Paolo. He wanted to get in, where it was safe, and perhaps eat a large lump of bread and honey. He was surprised his father did not feel the same. Antonio looked tired out, and his clothes were torn and muddy rags. The arm he stretched out to keep Paolo in the gateway was half bare and covered with scratches. Paolo was going to protest, when he saw that something was indeed wrong. Most of the cats were in the gateway too, crouching around with their ears flattened. Benvenuto was patrolling the entrance to the yard, like a lean brown ferret. Paolo could hear him growling.

Antonio's scratched hand took Paolo by the shoulder and pulled him forward so that he could see into the yard. "Look."

Paolo found himself blinking at foot-high letters, which seemed to hang in the air in the middle of the yard. In the fading light, they were glowing an unpleasant, sick yellow.

STOP ALL SPELLS OR YOUR CHILD SUFFERS.
CASA PETROCCHI

The name was in sicker and brighter letters. They were meant to make no mistake about who had sent the message.

After what Renata had said, Paolo knew it was wrong. "It *wasn't* the Petrocchis," he said. "It's that enchanter Chrestomanci told us about."

"Yes, to be sure," said Antonio.

Paolo looked up at him and saw that his father did not believe him – probably had not even attended to him. "But it's true!" he said. "He wants us to stop making war-spells."

Antonio sighed, and drew himself together to explain to Paolo. "Paolo," he said, "nobody but Chrestomanci believes in this enchanter. In magic, as in everything else, the simplest explanation is always best. In other words, why invent an unknown enchanter, when you have a known enemy with known reasons for hating you? Why shouldn't it be the Petrocchis?"

Paolo wanted to protest, but he was still too embarrassed about Renata to say that Angelica Petrocchi was missing too. He was struggling to find something that he *could* say, which might convince his father, when a square of light sprang up in the gallery as a door there opened.

"Rosa!" shouted Antonio. His voice cracked with anxiety.

The shape of Rosa appeared in the light, carrying Cousin Claudia's baby. The light itself was so orange and so bright, beside the sick glow of the letters floating in the yard, that Paolo was flooded with relief.

Behind Rosa, there was Marco, carrying another little one.

"Praised be!" said Antonio. He shouted, "Are you all right, Rosa? How did those words come here?"

"We don't know," Rosa called back. "They just appeared. We've been trying to get rid of them, but we can't."

Marco leant over the rails and called, "It's not true, Antonio. The Petrocchis wouldn't do a thing like this."

Antonio called back, "Don't go around saying that, Marco." He said it so forbiddingly that Paolo knew nothing he said was going to be believed. If he had had a chance of convincing Antonio, he had now lost it.

CHAPTER EIGHT

When Tonino came to his senses – at, incidentally, the precise moment when the enchanted book began to shrivel away – he had, at first, a nightmare feeling that he was shut in a cardboard box. He rolled his head sideways on his arms. He seemed to be lying on his face on a hard but faintly furry floor. In the far distance, he could blurrily see someone else, leaning up against a wall like a doll, but he felt too queer to be very interested in that. He rolled his head round the other way and saw the panels of a wall quite near. That told him he was in a fairly long room. He rolled his head to stare down at the furry floor. It was patterned, in a pattern too big for his eyes to grasp, and he supposed it was a carpet of some kind. He shut his blurry eyes and tried to think what had happened.

He remembered going down near the New Bridge. He had been full of excitement. He had read a book which he thought was telling him how to save Caprona. He knew he had to find an alleyway with a peeling blue house at the end of it. It seemed a bit silly now. Tonino knew things never happened the way they did in books. Even then, he had been rather amazed to find that there *was* an alleyway with, really and truly, a peeling blue house at the end of it. And, to his huge excitement, there was a scrap of paper fluttering down at his feet. The book was coming true. Tonino had bent down and picked up the paper.

And, after that, he had known nothing till this moment.

That was really true. Tonino took himself through what had happened several times, but each time his memories stopped in exactly the same place – with himself picking up the scrap of paper. After that, it was all a vague sense of nightmare. By this time, he was fairly sure he had been the victim of a spell. He began to feel ashamed of himself. So he sat up.

He saw at once why he had seemed to dream he was shut up in a cardboard box. The room he was in was long and low, almost exactly the shape of a shoebox. The walls and ceiling were painted cream-colour – a sort of whitish cardboard-colour, in fact – but they seemed to be wood, because there were carvings picked out in gold paint on them. There was a crystal chandelier hanging from the ceiling, although the light came from four long windows in one of the longer walls; a rich carpet on the floor, and a very elegant dining-table and chairs by the wall opposite the windows. There were two silver candlesticks on the table. Altogether the place was extremely elegant – and wrong, somehow.

Tonino sat trying to puzzle out just what was wrong. The room was awfully bare. But that was not quite it. There was something strange about the daylight coming through the four long windows, as if the sun was somehow further away than it should be. But that was not quite it either. Tonino's eyes went to the four bands of too-faded sunlight falling through the windows on to the carpet, and then travelled along the carpet. At the end, he came to the person leaning up against the wall. It was Angelica Petrocchi, who had been at the Palace. Her eyes were closed beneath her bulge of forehead, and she looked ill. So she had been caught too.

Tonino looked back at the carpet. That was an odd thing. It was not really a carpet. It had been painted on the slightly furry substance of the floor. Tonino could see the brush-strokes in the sprawling pattern. And the reason he had thought the pattern was too big, was because it *was* too big. It was the wrong size for the rest of the room.

More puzzled than ever, Tonino struggled to his feet. He felt a little wobbly, so he put a hand on the gilded panels of the wall to steady himself. That felt furry too, except where it was gold. The gold was flat, but not quite hard, like – Tonino thought, but no other likeness came to him – like paint. He ran his hand over the apparently carved panel. It was a total cheat. It was not even wood, and the carving was painted on, in lines of brown, blue and gold. Whoever had caught him was trying to seem richer than they were, but doing it very badly.

There were movements at the other end of the room. Angelica Petrocchi was wavering to her feet, and she too was running her hand over the painted carving. Very anxiously and cautiously, she turned and looked at Tonino.

"Will you let me go now, please?" she said.

There was a little wobble in her voice that showed Tonino she was very frightened. So was he, now he came to think of it. "I can't let you go," he said. "I didn't catch you. Neither of us can go. There isn't a door."

That was the wrong thing he had been trying not to notice. And as soon as he said it, he wished he had kept his mouth shut. Angelica screamed. And the sound sent Tonino into a panic too. There was no door! He was shut into a cardboard box with a Petrocchi child!

Tonino may have screamed as well – he was not sure. When he caught up with himself, he had one of the elegant chairs in his hands and was battering at the nearest window with it. That was more frightening than ever. The glass did not break. It was made of some slightly rubbery stuff, and the chair bounced off. Beyond him, the Petrocchi girl was banging away at another window with one of the silver candlesticks, screaming all the time. Outside the window, Tonino could clearly see the smug spire-shape of a little cypress tree, lit by afternoon sun. So they were in one of those rich villas near the Palace, were they? Just let him get *out*! He lifted the chair and smashed it against the window with all his strength.

He made no impression on the window, but the chair came to pieces. Two ill-glued legs fell off it, and the rest crumpled to splintery matchwood. Tonino thought it was disgustingly badly made. He threw it to the painted carpet and fetched another chair. This time, for variety, he attacked the wall beside the window. Pieces of that chair came away and flew about, and Tonino was left with its painted seat – painted to look like embroidery, just as the floor was painted to look like carpet. He drove it into the wall, again and again. It made large brown dents. Better still, the wall shook and leapt about, sounding muffled and hollow, as if it were made of something very cheap. Tonino beat at it and yelled. Angelica beat at the wall and the window impartially with her candlestick, and went on screaming.

They were stopped by a terrible hammering. Someone seemed to be dealing hundreds of thunderous blows on the ceiling. The room was like the inside of a drum. It was too loud to bear. The Petrocchi girl dropped her candlestick and rolled on the floor. Tonino found himself crouching down, with his hands to his ears, looking up at the chandelier jiggling overhead. He thought his head would burst.

The pounding stopped. There was no sound except a whimper, which Tonino rather thought came from him.

A great huge voice spoke through the ceiling. "That's better. Now be quiet, or you won't get any food. And if you try any more tricks, you'll be punished. Understand?"

Tonino and Angelica both sat up. "*Let us out!*" they screamed.

There was no answer, only a distant shuffling. The owner of the huge voice seemed to be going away.

"A mean trick with an amplifying spell," Angelica said. She picked up the candlestick and looked at it with disgust. The branched part was bent at right-angles to the base. "What *is* this place?" she said. "Everything's so shoddy."

They got up and went to the windows again, in hopes of a clue. Several little spire-shaped trees were clearly to be seen, just outside, and a sort of terrace beyond that. But, peer as they might, all they could make out further off was queer blue distance, with one or two square-shaped mountains catching the sun on a glossy corner or so. There seemed to be no sky.

"It's a spell," said Angelica. Her voice suggested she might be going to panic again. "A spell to stop us knowing where we are."

Tonino supposed it must be. There was no other way of accounting for the strange absence of view. "But I'm sure I know," he said, "by those trees. We're in one of those rich villas by the Palace."

"You're right," agreed Angelica. The panic had left her voice. "I shall never envy those people again. Their lives are all show."

137

They turned from the windows and discovered that the vast banging had dislodged one of the wall panels behind the dining-table. It hung open like a door. They shoved one another out of the way to reach it first. But there was only a cupboard-sized bathroom, without a window.

"Good," said Angelica. "I was wondering what we'd do. And at least we'll have water." She reached out to one of the taps over the small washbasin. It came away in her hand. Under it was a blob of glue on white china. It was clear the tap had never been meant to be used. Angelica stared at it with such a ridiculous look of bewilderment that Tonino laughed. She drew herself up at that. "Don't you laugh at me, you beastly Montana!" She stalked out into the main room and threw the useless tap on to the table with a clump. Then she sat in one of the two remaining chairs and rested her elbows gloomily on the table.

After a while, Tonino did the same. The chair creaked under him. So did the table. Though its surface was painted to look like smooth mahogany, close to, it was all blobs of varnish and huge splinters. "There's nothing that's not shoddy," he said.

"Including you, Whatyoumecall Montana!" Angelica said. She was still angry.

"My name's Tonino," Tonino said.

"It's the last twist of the knife, being shut up with a Montana!" Angelica said. "Whatever your name is. I shall have to put up with all your filthy habits."

"Well, I've got to put up with yours," Tonino said irritably. It suddenly struck him that he was all alone, far from the friendly bustle of the Casa Montana. Even when he was hidden in a corner of the Casa with a book, he knew the rest of the family was all round him. And Benvenuto would be purring and pricking him, to remind him he was not alone. Dear old Benvenuto. Tonino was afraid he was going to cry – in front of a Petrocchi too. "How did they catch you?" he said, to take his mind off it.

"With a book." A slight, woeful smile appeared on Angelica's tight white face. "It was called *The Girl Who Saved Her Country*, and I thought it was from Great-Uncle Luigi. I still think it was a good story." She looked defiantly at Tonino.

Tonino was annoyed. It was not pleasant to think he had been caught by the same spell as a Petrocchi. "Me too," he said gruffly.

"And *I* haven't got any filthy habits!" snapped Angelica.

"Yes you have. All the Petrocchis have," said Tonino. "But I expect you don't realise because they're normal to you."

"I like that!" Angelica picked up the broken tap, as if she had half a mind to throw it.

"I don't care about your habits," said Tonino. Nor did he. All he wanted to do was find some way out of this nightmare room and go home. "How shall we get out of here?"

"Through the ceiling," Angelica said sarcastically.

Tonino looked upwards. There was that chandelier. If they

could give it a pull, it might well rip a hole in the shoddy ceiling.

"Don't be stupid," said Angelica. "If there's a spell out in front, there's bound to be one up there to stop us getting out."

Tonino feared she was right, but it was worth a try. He climbed from his chair on to the table. He thought he could reach the chandelier from there if he stood up. There was a violent creaking. Before Tonino could begin to stand up, the table swayed away sideways, as if all four of its legs were loose.

"Get down!" said Angelica.

Tonino got down. It was clear the table would fall to pieces if he stayed on it. Gloomily he pushed the crooked legs straight again. "So that's no good," he said.

"Unless," said Angelica, suddenly bright and pert, "we steady it with a spell."

Tonino transferred his miserable look from the table legs to her sharp little face. He sighed. The subject had been bound to come up. "You'll have to do the spell," he said. Angelica stared at him. He could feel his face heating up. "I hardly know any spells," he said. "I – I'm slow."

He had expected Angelica to laugh, and she did. But he thought she need not have laughed in such a mean, exultant way, nor keep saying, "Oh that's good!" like that.

"What's so funny?" he said. "You can laugh! I know all about you turning your father green. You're no better than me!"

"Want to bet?" said Angelica, still laughing.

"No," said Tonino. "Just make the spell."

"I can't," said Angelica. It was Tonino's turn to stare, and Angelica's turn to blush. A thin bright pink spread right up the bulge of her forehead, and she put her chin up defiantly. "I'm hopeless at spells," she said. "I've never got a spell right in my life." Seeing Tonino still staring, she said, "It's a pity you didn't bet. I'm *much* worse than you are."

Tonino could not credit it. "How?" he said. "Why? Can't you learn spells either, then?"

"Oh, I can *learn* them all right." Angelica took up the broken tap again and scribbled angrily with it, great yellow scratches in the varnished top of the table. "I know hundreds of spells," she said, "but I always get them wrong. For a start, I'm tone-deaf. I can't sing a tune right to save my life. Like now." Carefully, as if she was a craftsman doing a fine carving, she peeled up a long yellow curl of varnish from the table, using the tap as a gouge. "But it's not only that," she said angrily, following her work intently. "I get words wrong too – everything wrong. And my spells always work, that's the worst of it. I've turned all my family all colours of the rainbow. I've turned the baby's bath into wine, and the wine into gravy. I turned my own head back to front once. I'm much worse than you. I *daren't* do spells. About all I'm good for is understanding cats. And I even turned my cat purple too."

Tonino watched her working away with the tap, with rather mixed feelings. If you looked at it practically, this was the worst possible news. Neither of them had a hope against the powerful spell-maker who had caught them. On the other hand, he had never met anyone who was worse at spells than he was. He thought, a little smugly, that at least he had never made a mistake in a spell, and that made him feel good. He wondered how the Casa Montana would feel if he kept turning them all colours of the rainbow. He imagined the stern Petrocchis must hate it. "Doesn't your family mind?" he asked.

"Not much," Angelica said, surprisingly. "They don't mind it half as much as I do. Everyone has a good laugh every time I make a new mistake – but they don't let anyone talk about it outside the Casa. Papa says I'm notorious enough for turning him green, and he doesn't like me to be even *seen* anywhere until I've grown out of it."

"But you went to the Palace," said Tonino. He thought Angelica must be exaggerating.

"Only because Cousin Monica was having her baby and everyone was so busy on the Old Bridge," said Angelica. "He had to take Renata off her shift and get my brother out of bed to drive the coach, in order to have enough of us."

"There were five of us," Tonino said, smugly.

"Our horses collapsed in the rain." Angelica turned from her gouging and looked at Tonino keenly. "So my brother said yours were bound to have collapsed too, because *you* only had a cardboard coachman."

Uncomfortably, Tonino knew Angelica had scored a point. "Our coachman collapsed too," he admitted.

"I thought so," said Angelica, "from the look on your face." She went back to scraping the table, conscious of victory.

"It wasn't our fault!" Tonino protested. "Chrestomanci says there's an enemy enchanter."

Angelica took such a slice out of the varnish that the table swooped sideways and Tonino had to push it straight. "And he's got us now," she said. "And he's taken care to get the two who are no good at spells. So how do we get out of here and spite him, Tonino Montana? Any ideas?"

Tonino sat with his chin in his hands and thought. He had read enough books, for goodness' sake. People were always being kidnapped in books. And in his favourite books – this was like a bad joke – they escaped without using magic of any kind. But there was no door. That was what made it seem impossible. Wait a moment! The vast voice had promised them food. "If they think we're behaving," he said, "they'll bring us supper probably. And they've got to bring the food in somehow. If we watch where it comes in, we ought to be able to get out the same way."

"There's bound to be a spell on the entrance," Angelica said gloomily.

"Do stop bleating away about spells," said Tonino. "Don't you Petrocchis ever talk about anything else?"

Angelica did not reply, but simply scraped away with her

tap. Tonino sat wanly in his creaking chair thinking over the few spells he really knew. The most useful seemed to be a simple cancel-spell.

"A cancel-spell," Angelica said irritatingly, scratching carefully with the tap. The floor round her feet was heaped with yellow curls of varnish. "That might hold the entrance open. Or isn't a cancel-spell one of the ones you know?"

"I know a cancel-spell," said Tonino.

"So does my baby brother," said Angelica. "He'd probably be more use."

Their supper arrived. It appeared, without warning, on a tray, floating towards them from the windows. It took Tonino completely by surprise.

"*Spell!*" Angelica squawked at him. "Don't just stare!"

Tonino sang the spell. Hurried and surprised though he was, he was *sure* he got it right. But it was the tray the spell worked on. The tray, and the food on it, began to grow. Within seconds, it was bigger than the table-top. And it still floated towards the table, growing as it came. Tonino found himself backing away from two steaming bath-sized bowls of soup and two great orange thickets of spaghetti, all of which were getting steadily vaster the nearer they came. By now, there was not much room round the edges of the tray. Tonino backed against the end wall, wondering if Angelica's trouble with spells was catching. Angelica herself was squashed against the bathroom door. Both of them were in danger of being cut in two.

"Get down on the floor!" Tonino shouted.

They slithered hurriedly down the wall, underneath the tray, which hung over them like a too-low ceiling. The huge odour of spaghetti was quite oppressive.

"What have you done?" Angelica said, coming towards Tonino on hands and knees. "You didn't get it right."

"Yes, but if it gets much bigger, it might break the room open," said Tonino.

Angelica sank back on her knees and looked at him with what was nearly respect. "That's almost a good idea."

But it was only almost. The tray certainly met all four walls. They heard it thump against them. There was a deal of swaying, creaking and squeezing, from the tray and from the walls, but the walls did not give. After a moment it was clear that the tray was not being allowed to get any bigger.

"There *is* a spell on this room," Angelica said. It was not meant to be I-told-you-so. She was miserable.

Tonino gave up and sang the cancel-spell, carefully and correctly. The tray shrank at once. They were left kneeling on the floor looking at a reasonable-sized supper laid neatly in the centre of the table. "We might as well eat it," he said.

Angelica annoyed him thoroughly again by saying, as she picked up her spoon, "Well, I'm glad to know I'm not the only person who gets my spells wrong."

"I know I got it right," Tonino muttered into his spoon, but Angelica chose not to hear.

After a while, he was even more annoyed to find, every

time he looked up, that Angelica was staring at him curiously. "What's the matter now?" he said at last, quite exasperated.

"I was waiting to see your filthy eating habits," she said. "But I think you must be on your best behaviour."

"I always eat like this!" Tonino saw that he had wound far too much spaghetti on his fork. He hurriedly unwound it.

The bulge of Angelica's forehead was wavy with frown-lines. "No you don't. Montanas always eat disgustingly because of the way Old Ricardo Petrocchi made them eat their words."

"Don't talk nonsense," said Tonino. "Anyway, it was Old Francesco Montana who made the Petrocchis eat *their* words."

"It was not!" Angelica said heatedly. "It was the first story I ever learnt. The Petrocchis made the Montanas eat their spells disguised as spaghetti."

"No they didn't. It was the other way round!" said Tonino. "It was the first story I ever learnt too."

Somehow, neither of them felt like finishing their spaghetti. They laid their forks down and went on arguing.

"And because of eating those spells," said Angelica, "the Montanas went quite disgusting and started eating their uncles and aunts when they died."

"We do not!" said Tonino. "You eat babies."

"How dare you!" said Angelica. "You eat cowpats for pizzas, and you can smell the Casa Montana right on the Corso."

"The Casa Petrocchi smells all down the Via Sant' Angelo," said Tonino, "and you can hear the flies buzzing from the New Bridge. You have babies like kittens and—"

"That's a lie!" shrieked Angelica. "You just put that about because you don't want people to know that the Montanas never get married properly!"

"Yes we do!" bawled Tonino. "It's you who don't!"

"I like that!" yelled Angelica. "I'll have you know, my brother got married, in church, just after Christmas. So there!"

"I don't believe you," said Tonino. "And my sister's going to get married in Spring, so—"

"I was a *bridesmaid*!" screamed Angelica.

While they argued, the tray quietly floated off the table and vanished somewhere near the windows. Tonino and Angelica looked irritably round for it, extremely annoyed that they had once again missed noticing how it got in and out.

"Now look what you've done!" said Angelica.

"It's your fault for telling lies about my family," said Tonino.

CHAPTER NINE

✳

"If you're not careful," said Angelica, glowering under the bulge of her forehead, "I shall sing the first spell that comes into my head. And I hope it turns you into a slug."

That was a threat indeed. Tonino quailed a little. But the honour of the Montanas was at stake. "Take back what you said about my family," he said.

"Only if you take back what you said about mine," said Angelica. "Swear by the Angel of Caprona that none of those dreadful lies are true. Look. I've got the Angel here. Come and swear." Her pink finger jabbed down at the table top. She reminded Tonino of his school teacher on a bad day.

He left his creaking chair and leant over to see what she was pointing at. Angelica fussily dusted away a shower of yellow varnish to show him that she indeed had the Angel, scratched with the useless tap into the top of the table. It was quite a good drawing, considering that the tap was not a good gouge and had shown a tendency to slip about. But Tonino was not prepared to admire it. "You've forgotten the scroll," he said.

Angelica jumped up, and her flimsy chair crashed over backwards. "That does it! You've asked for it!" She marched over to the empty space by the windows and took up a position of power. From there, with her hands raised, she looked at Tonino to see if he was going to relent. Tonino would have liked to relent. He did not want to be a slug. He sought about in his mind for some way of giving in which did not look like cowardice. But, as with everything, he was too slow. Angelica flounced round, so that her arms were no longer at quite the right angle.

"Right," she said. "I shall make it a cancel-spell, to cancel you out." And she began to sing.

Angelica's voice was horrible, sharp and flat by turns, and wandering from key to key. Tonino would have liked to interrupt her, or at least distract her by making noises, but he did not quite dare. That might only make things worse.

He waited while Angelica squawked out a couple of verses of a spell which seemed to centre round the words *turn the spell round, break the spell off*. Since he was a boy and not a spell, Tonino rather hoped it would not do anything to him.

Angelica raised her arms higher for the third verse and changed key for the sixth time. "Turn the spell off, break the spell round—"

"That's wrong," said Tonino.

"Don't you dare put me off!" snapped Angelica, and turned round to say it, which sent the angle of her arms more thoroughly wrong than ever. One hand was now pointing at a window. "I command the unbinding of that which was bound," she sang, cross and shrill.

Tonino looked quickly down at himself, but he seemed to be still there, and the usual colour. He told himself that he had known all along that such a bungled spell could not possibly work.

There came a great creaking from the ceiling, just above the windows. The whole room swayed. Then, to Tonino's amazement, the entire front wall of the room, windows and all, split away from the side walls and the ceiling, and fell outwards with a soft clatter – a curiously soft sound for the whole side of a house. A draught of musty-smelling air blew in through the open space.

Angelica was quite as astonished as Tonino. But that did not prevent her turning to him with a smug and triumphant smile. "See? My spells always work."

"Let's get out," said Tonino. "Quick. Before somebody comes."

They ran out across the painted panels between the windows, across the marks Tonino had made with the chair. They stepped down off the surprisingly clean, straight edge, where the wall had joined the ceiling, on to the terrace in front of the house. It appeared to be made of wood, not of stone as Tonino had expected. And beyond that—

They stopped, just in time, at the edge of a huge cliff. Both of them swayed forward, and caught at one another. The cliff went down sheer, into murky darkness. They could not see the bottom. Nor could they see much more when they looked straight ahead. There was a blaze of red-gold sunlight there, dazzling them.

"There's still a spell on the view," said Tonino.

"In that case," said Angelica, "let's just keep walking. There must be a road or a garden that we can't see."

There certainly should have been something of the kind, but it neither felt nor looked like that. Tonino was sure he could sense vast hollow spaces below the cliff. There were no city sounds, and only a strangely musty smell.

"Coward!" said Angelica.

"You go," said Tonino.

"Only if you go too," she said.

They hovered, glaring at one another. And, as they hovered, the blaze of sunlight was cut off by an immense black shape. "*Naughty!*" said a vast voice. "Bad children shall be punished."

A force almost too strong to feel swept them away on to the fallen wall. The fallen wall rose briskly back into its place, sweeping Angelica and Tonino with it, helplessly sliding and rolling, until they thumped on to the painted carpet. By that time, Tonino was so breathless and dizzy that he hardly heard the wall snap back into place with a click.

After that, the dizziness grew worse. Tonino knew he was in the grip of another spell. He struggled against it furiously, but whoever was casting it was immensely strong. He felt surging and bumping. The light from the windows changed, and changed again. Almost he could have sworn, the room was being *carried*. It stopped with a jolt. He heard Angelica's voice gabbling a prayer to Our Lady, and he did not blame her. Then there was a mystifying gap in what Tonino knew.

He came to himself because whoever was casting the spell wanted him to. Tonino was quite sure of that. The punishment would not be so much fun, unless Tonino knew about it.

He was in a confusion of light and noise – there was a huge blur of it to one side – and he was racing up and down a narrow wooden platform, dragging (of all things!) a string of sausages. He was wearing a bright red nightgown and there was a heaviness on the front of his face. Each time he reached one end of the wooden platform, he found a white cardboard dog there, with a frill round its neck. The dog's cardboard mouth opened and shut. It was making feeble cardboard attempts to get the sausages.

The noise was terrific. Tonino seemed to be making some

of it himself. "What a clever fellow! What a clever fellow!" he heard himself squawking, in a voice quite unlike his own. It was like the noise you make singing into paper over a comb. The rest of the noise was coming from the lighted space to one side. Vast voices were roaring and laughing, mixed with tinny music.

"This is a dream!" Tonino told himself. But he knew it was not. He had a fair idea what was happening, though his head still felt muzzy and his eyes were blurred. As he raced back down the little platform, he turned his bleary eyes inwards, towards the heaviness on his face. Sure enough, blurred and doubled, he could see a great red and pink nose there. He was Mr Punch.

Naturally, then, he tried to dig in his heels and stop racing up and down, and to lift his hand and wrench off the huge pink nose. He could not do either. More than that, whoever was making him be Mr Punch promptly took mean pleasure in making him run faster and whirl the sausages about harder.

"Oh, very good!" yelled someone from the lighted space.

Tonino thought he knew that voice. He sped toward the cardboard Dog Toby again, whirled the sausages away from its cardboard jaws and waited for his head and eyes to stop feeling so fuzzy. He was sure they would. The mean person wanted him conscious. "What a clever fellow!" he squawked. As he raced down the stage the other way, he snatched a look across his huge nose towards the lighted space, but it was a blur. So he snatched a look towards the other side.

153

He saw the wall of a golden villa there, with four long windows. Beside each window stood a little dark cypress tree. Now he knew why the strange room had seemed so shoddy. It was only meant as scenery. The door on the outside wall was painted on. Between the villa and the stage was a hole. The person who was working the puppets ought to have been down there, but Tonino could only see empty blackness. It was all being done by magic.

Just then he was distracted by a cardboard person diving upwards from the hole, squawking that Mr Punch had stolen his sausages. Tonino was forced to stand still and squawk back. He was glad of a rest by then. Meanwhile, the cardboard dog seized the sausages and dived out of sight with them. The audience clapped and shouted, "Look at Dog Toby!" The cardboard person sped past Tonino squawking that he would fetch the police.

Once again, Tonino tried to look out at the audience. This time, he could dimly see a brightly lit room and black bulky shapes sitting in chairs, but it was like trying to see something against the sun. His eyes watered. A tear ran down the pink beak on his face. And Tonino could feel that the mean person was delighted to see that. He thought Tonino was crying. Tonino was annoyed, but also rather pleased; it looked as if the person could be fooled by his own mean thoughts. He stared out, in spite of the dazzle, trying to see the mean person, but all he could clearly see was a carving up near the roof of the lighted room. It was the

Angel of Caprona, one hand held out in blessing, the other holding the scroll.

Then he was jumped round to face Judy. On the other side of him, the wall had gone from the front of the villa. The scene was the room he knew only too well, with the chandelier artistically alight.

Judy was coming along the stage holding the white rolled-up shape of the baby. Judy wore a blue nightdress and a blue cap. Her face was mauve, with a nose in the middle of it nearly as large and red as Tonino's. But the eyes on either side of it were Angelica's, alternately blinking and wide with terror. She blinked beseechingly at Tonino as she squawked, "I have to go out, Mr Punch. Mind you mind the baby!"

"Don't want to mind the baby!" he squawked.

All through the long silly conversation, he could see Angelica's eyes blinking at him, imploring him to think of a spell to stop this. But of course Tonino could not. He did not think Rinaldo, or even Antonio, could stop anything as powerful as this. Angel of Caprona! he thought. Help us! That made him feel better, although nothing stopped the spell. Angelica planted the baby in his arms and dived out of sight.

The baby started to cry. Tonino first squawked abuse at it, then took it by the end of its long white dress and beat its brains out on the platform. The baby was much more realistic than Dog Toby. It may have been only cardboard, but it wriggled and waved its arms and cried most horribly. Tonino could almost have believed it was Cousin Claudia's baby. It so horrified him that he found he was repeating the words of the *Angel of Caprona* as he swung the baby up and down. And those might not have been the right words, but he could feel they were doing something. When he finally flung the white bundle over the front of the stage, he could see the shiny floor the baby fell on, away below. And when he looked up at the clapping spectators, he could see them too, equally clearly.

The first person he saw was the Duke of Caprona. He was sitting on a gilded chair, in a glitter of buttons, laughing gigantically. Tonino wondered how he could laugh like that at something so horrible, until he remembered that he had stood himself, a score of times, and laughed himself sick, at just the same thing. But those had been only puppets. Then it dawned on Tonino that the Duke thought they *were* puppets. He was laughing at the skill of the showman.

"What a clever fellow!" squawked Tonino, and was made to dance about gleefully, without wanting to in the least. But as he danced, he looked sharply at the rest of the audience, to see who it was who knew he was not a puppet.

To his terror, a good half of them knew. Tonino met a knowing look on the faces of the three grave men surrounding the Duke, and the same on the elegantly made-up faces of the two ladies with the Duchess. And the Duchess – as soon as Tonino saw the amused arch of the Duchess's eyebrows and the little, secret smile on her mouth, he knew she was the one doing it. He looked her in the eyes. Yes, she was an enchantress. That was what had so troubled him about her when he saw her before. And the Duchess saw him look, and smiled less secretly, because Tonino could do nothing about it.

That really frightened Tonino. But Angelica came swooping upwards again, with a large stick clutched in her arms, and he had no time to think.

"What have you done with the baby?" squawked Angelica. And she belaboured Tonino with the stick. It really hurt. It knocked him to his knees and went on bashing at him. Tonino could see Angelica's lips moving. Though her silly squeaky voice kept saying, "I'll teach you to kill the baby!" her mouth was forming the words of the *Angel of Caprona*. That was because she knew what came next.

Tonino said the words of the *Angel* too and tried to stay crouched on the floor. But it was no good. He was made to spring up, wrest the stick from Judy and beat Angelica with it. He could see the Duke laughing, and the courtiers smiling. The Duchess's smile was very broad now, because, of course, Tonino was going to have to beat Angelica to death.

Tonino tried to hold the stick so that it would only hit Angelica lightly. She might be a Petrocchi and a thoroughly irritating girl, but she had not deserved this. But the stick leapt up and down of its own accord, and Tonino's arms went with it. Angelica fell on her knees and then on her face. Her squawks redoubled, as Tonino smote away at her back, and then her voice stopped. She lay with her head hanging down from the front of the platform, looking just like a puppet. Tonino found himself having to kick her down the empty space between the false villa and the stage. He heard the distant *flop* as she fell. And then he was forced to skip and cackle with glee, while the Duchess threw back her head and laughed as heartily as the Duke.

Tonino hated her. He was so angry and so miserable that he did not mind at all when a cardboard policeman appeared and he chased him with the stick too. He laid into the policeman as if he was the Duchess and not a cardboard doll at all.

"Are you all right, Lucrezia?" he heard the Duke say.

Tonino looked sideways as he dealt another mighty swipe at the policeman's cardboard helmet. He saw the Duchess wince as the stick landed. He was not surprised when the policeman was immediately whisked away and he himself forced into a violent capering and even louder squawking. He let himself do it. He felt truly gleeful as he squawked, "What a clever fellow!" for what felt like the thousandth time. For he understood what had happened. The Duchess *was* the policeman, in a sort of way. She was putting some of herself into all the puppets to make them work. But he must not let her know he knew. Tonino capered and chortled, doing his best to seem terrified, and kept his eyes on that carving of the Angel, high up over the door of the room.

And now the hooded Hangman-puppet appeared, dragging a little wooden gibbet with a string noose dangling from it. Tonino capered cautiously. This was where the Duchess did for him unless he was very careful. On the other hand, if this Punch and Judy show went as it should, he might just do for the Duchess.

The silly scene began. Tonino had never worked so hard at anything in his life. He kept repeating the words of the *Angel* in his head, both as a kind of prayer and as a smoke-screen, so that the Duchess would not understand what he was trying to do. At the same time, he thought, fiercely and vengefully, that the Hangman was not just a puppet – it was the Duchess herself. And, also at the same time, he attended to Mr Punch's conversation with all his might. This had to go right.

"Come along, Mr Punch," croaked the Hangman. "Just put your head in this noose."

"How do I do that?" asked Mr Punch and Tonino, both pretending hard to be stupid.

"You put your head in here," croaked the Hangman, putting one hand through the noose.

Mr Punch and Tonino, both of them quivering with cunning, put his head first one side of the noose, then the other. "Is this right? Is this?" Then, pretending even harder to be stupid, "I can't see how to do it. You'll have to show me."

Either the Duchess was wanting to play with Tonino's

feelings, or she was trying the same cunning. They went through this several times. Each time, the Hangman put his hand through the noose to show Mr Punch what to do. Tonino did not dare look at the Duchess. He looked at the Hangman and kept thinking, That's the Duchess, and reciting the *Angel* for all he was worth. At last, to his relief, the Duke became restive.

"Come on, Mr Punch!" he shouted.

"You'll have to put your head in and show me," Mr Punch and Tonino said, as persuasively as he knew how.

"Oh well," croaked the Hangman. "Since you're so stupid." And he put his cardboard head through the noose.

Mr Punch and Tonino promptly pulled the rope and hanged him. But Tonino thought, This is the *Duchess*! and went as limp and heavy as he could. For just a second, his full puppet's weight swung on the end of the rope.

It only lasted that second. Tonino had a glimpse of the Duchess on her feet with her hands to her throat. He felt real triumph. Then he was thrown, flat on his face, across the stage, unable to move at all. There he was forced to lie. His head hung down from the front of the stage, so that he could see very little. But he gathered that the Duchess was being led tenderly away, with the Duke fussing round her.

I think I feel as pleased as Punch, he thought.

CHAPTER TEN

✳

Paolo never wanted to remember that night afterwards. He was still staring at the sick yellow message in the yard, when the rest of the family arrived. He was crowded aside to let Old Niccolo and Aunt Francesca through, but Benvenuto spat at them like hot fat hitting fire and would not let them pass.

"Let be, old boy," Old Niccolo said. "You've done your best." He turned to Aunt Francesca. "I shall never forgive the Petrocchis," he said. "Never."

Paolo was once again struck by how wretched and goblin-like his grandfather looked. He had thought Old

Niccolo was helping vast, panting, muddy Aunt Francesca along, but he now wondered if it was not the other way round.

"Well. Let's get rid of this horrible message," Old Niccolo said irritably to the rest of them.

He raised his arms to start the family on the spell and collapsed. His hands went to his chest. He slid to his knees, and his face was a strange colour. Paolo thought he was dead until he saw him breathing, in uneven jerks. Elizabeth, Uncle Lorenzo and Aunt Maria rushed to him.

"Heart attack," Uncle Lorenzo said, nodding over at Antonio. "Get that spell going. We've got to get him indoors."

"Paolo, run for the doctor," said Elizabeth.

As Paolo ran, he heard the burst of singing behind him. When he came back with the doctor, the message had vanished and Old Niccolo had been carried up to bed. Aunt Francesca, still muddy, with her hair hanging down one side, was roving up and down the yard like a moving mountain, crying and wringing her hands.

"Spells are forbidden," she called out to Paolo. "I've stopped everything."

"And a good thing too!" the doctor said sourly. "A man of Niccolo Montana's age has no business to be brawling in the streets. And make your great-aunt lie down," he said to Paolo. "She'll be in bed next."

Aunt Francesca would only go to the Saloon, where she refused even to sit down. She raged up and down, wailing about Old Niccolo, weeping about Tonino, declaring that the virtue had gone from the Casa Montana for good, and uttering terrible threats against the Petrocchis. Nobody else was much better. The children cried with tiredness. Elizabeth and the aunts worried about Old Niccolo, and then about Aunt Francesca. In the Scriptorium, among all the abandoned spells, Antonio and the uncles sat rigid with worry, and the rest of the Casa was full of older cousins wandering about and cursing the Petrocchis.

Paolo found Rinaldo leaning moodily on the gallery rail, in spite of it being dark now and really quite cold. "Curse those Petrocchis," he said gloomily to Paolo. "We can't even earn a living now, let alone help if there's a war."

Paolo, in spite of his misery, was very flattered that Rinaldo seemed to think him old enough to talk family business to. He said, "Yes, it's awful," and tried to lean on the rail in the same elegant attitude as Rinaldo. It was not easy, since Paolo was not nearly tall enough, but he leant and prepared the arguments he would use to persuade Rinaldo that Tonino was in the hands of an enemy enchanter. That was not easy either. Paolo knew that Rinaldo would not listen to him if he dropped the least small hint that he had talked to a Petrocchi – and besides, he would have died rather than told his cousin. But he knew that, if he persuaded Rinaldo, Rinaldo would rescue Tonino in five dashing minutes. Rinaldo was a true Montana.

While he thought, Rinaldo said angrily, "What possessed that stupid brat Tonino to read that blessed book? I shall give him something to think about when we get him back!"

Paolo shivered in the cold. "Tonino always reads books." Then he shifted a bit – the elegant attitude was not at all comfortable – and asked timidly, "How shall we get him back?"

This was not at all what he had planned to say. He was annoyed with himself.

"What's the use?" Rinaldo said. "We know where he is – in the Casa Petrocchi. And if he's uncomfortable there, it's his own fault!"

"But he's not!" Paolo protested. As far as he could see in the light from the yard lamp, Rinaldo turned and looked at him jeeringly. The discussion seemed to be getting further from the way he had planned it every second. "An enemy enchanter's got him," he said. "The one Chrestomanci talked about."

Rinaldo laughed. "Load of old crab-apples, Paolo. Our friend had been talking to the Petrocchis. He invented his convenient enchanter because he wanted us all working for Caprona. Most of us saw through it at once."

"Then who made that mist on the Corso?" Paolo said. "It wasn't us, and it wasn't them."

But Rinaldo only said, "Who said it wasn't them?"

As Paolo could not say it was Renata Petrocchi, he could not answer. Instead, he said rather desperately, "Come with me to the Casa Petrocchi. If you used a finding-spell, you could *prove* Tonino isn't there."

"What?" Rinaldo seemed astounded. "What kind of fool do you take me for, Paolo? I'm not going to take on a whole family of spell-makers single-handed. And if I go there and use a spell, and they do something to Tonino, everyone's going to blame me, aren't they? For something we know anyway. It's not worth it, Paolo. But I tell you what—"

He was interrupted by Aunt Gina trumpeting below in the yard. "Notti's is the only chemist open by now. Tell him it's for Niccolo Montana!"

With some relief, Paolo dropped the elegant attitude entirely and leant over the rail to watch Lucia and Corinna hurry through the yard with the doctor's prescription. The sight gave his stomach a wrench of worry. "Do you think Old Niccolo's going to die, Rinaldo?"

Rinaldo shrugged. "Could be. He's pretty old. It's about time the old idiot gave up anyway. I shall be one step closer to being head of the Casa Montana then."

A peculiar thing happened inside Paolo's head then. He had never given much thought to who might follow Antonio – for it was clear his father would follow Old Niccolo – as head of the Casa Montana. But he had never, for some reason, thought it might be Rinaldo. Now he tried to imagine Rinaldo doing the things Old Niccolo did. And as soon as he did, he saw Rinaldo was quite unsuitable. Rinaldo was vain, and selfish – and cowardly, provided he could be a coward and still keep up a good appearance. It was as if Rinaldo had said a powerful spell to clear Paolo's eyes.

It never occurred to Rinaldo, expert spell-maker though he was, that a few ordinary words could make such a difference. He bent towards Paolo and dropped his voice to a melodious murmur. "I was going to tell you, Paolo. I'm going round enlisting all the young ones. We're going to swear to work a secret revenge on the Petrocchis. We'll do something worse than make them eat their words. Are you with me? Will you swear to join the plan?"

Maybe he was in earnest. It would suit Rinaldo to work in secret, with lots of willing helpers. But Paolo was sure that this plan was a step in Rinaldo's plans to be head of the Casa. Paolo sidled away along the rail.

"Are you game?" Rinaldo whispered, laughing a little.

Paolo sidled beyond grabbing-distance. "Tell you later." He turned and scudded away. Rinaldo laughed and did not try to catch him. He thought Paolo was scared.

Paolo went down into the yard, feeling more lonely than he had felt in his life. Tonino was not there. Tonino was not vain, or selfish, or cowardly. And nobody would help him find Tonino. Paolo had not noticed until now how much he depended on Tonino. They did everything important together. Even if Paolo was busy on his own, he knew Tonino was there somewhere, sitting reading, ready to put his book down if Paolo needed him. Now there seemed to be nothing for Paolo to do. And the whole Casa reeked of worry.

He went to the kitchen, where there seemed, at last, to be something happening. All his small cousins were there. Rosa and Marco were trying to make soup for them.

"Come in and help, Paolo," Rosa said. "We're going to put them to bed after soup, but we're having a bit of trouble."

Both she and Marco were looking tired and flustered. Most of the little ones were grizzling, including the baby. The trouble was Lucia's spell. Paolo understood this because Marco dumped the baby in his arms. Its wrapper was covered with orange grease. "Yuk!" said Paolo.

"I know," said Rosa. "Well, Marco, better try again. Clean saucepan. Clean water. The very last packet of soup-powder – don't make that face, Paolo. We've got through all the vegetables. They just sail away to the waste-bins, and they're mouldy before they get there."

Paolo looked nervously at the door, wondering if the enemy enchanter was powerful enough to overhear him. "Try a cancel-spell," he whispered.

"Aunt Gina went through them all this afternoon," said Rosa. "No good. Little Lucia used the *Angel of Caprona*, you see. We're trying Marco's way now. Ready, Marco?"

Rosa opened the packet of soup and held it over the saucepan. As the dry pink powder poured into the water, Marco leant over the saucepan and sang furiously. Paolo watched them nervously. This was just what the message told them not to do, he was sure. When all the powder was in the water, Rosa and Marco peered anxiously into the saucepan. "Have we done it?" asked Marco.

"I think—" Rosa began, and ended in a yell of exasperation. "Oh *no*!" The little pasta shells in the powder had turned into real sea-shells, little grey ones. "With *creatures* in!" Rosa said despairingly, dipping a spoonful out. "Where *is* Lucia?" she said. "Bring her here. Tell her I— No, don't. Just fetch her, Paolo."

"She's gone to the chemist," said Paolo.

There was shouting in the yard. Paolo passed the greasy baby to the nearest cousin and shot outside, dreading another sick yellow message about Tonino. Or there was just a chance the noise was Lucia.

It was neither. It was Rinaldo. The uncles must have left the Scriptorium, for Rinaldo was making a bonfire of spells in the middle of the yard. Domenico, Carlo and Luigi were busily carrying armfuls of scrips, envelopes and scrolls down from the gallery. Paolo recognised, already curling among the flames, the army-charms he and the other children had spent such a time copying. It was a shocking waste of work.

"This is what the Petrocchis have forced us to!" shouted Rinaldo, striking an attitude beside the flames. It was evidently part of his plan to enlist the young ones.

Paolo was glad to see Antonio and Uncle Lorenzo hurry out of the Saloon.

"Rinaldo!" shouted Antonio. "Rinaldo, we're worried about Umberto. We want you to go to the University and enquire."

"Send Domenico," said Rinaldo, and turned back to the flames.

"No," said Antonio. "You go." There was something about the way he said it that caused Rinaldo to back away from him.

"I'll go," said Rinaldo. He held up one hand, laughing. "I was only joking, Uncle Antonio."

He left at once. "Take those spells back," Uncle Lorenzo said to the other three cousins. "I hate to see good work wasted." Domenico, Carlo and Luigi obeyed without a word. Antonio and Uncle Lorenzo went to the bonfire and tried to stamp out the flames, but they were burning too strongly. Paolo saw them look at one another, rather guiltily, and then lean forward and whisper a spell over the fire. It flicked out as if it had been turned off with a switch. Paolo sighed worriedly. It was plain that no one in the Casa Montana could drop the habit of using spells. He wondered how long it would be before the enemy enchanter noticed.

"Fetch a light!" Antonio shouted to Domenico. "And sort out the ones that aren't burnt."

Paolo went back to the kitchen before they asked him to help. The bonfire had given him an idea.

"There is quite a bit of mince," Rosa was saying. "Dare we try with that?"

"Why don't you," said Paolo, "take the food to the dining room? I'll light a fire there, and you can cook it on that."

"The boy's a genius!" said Marco.

They did that. Rosa cooked by relays and Marco made

cocoa. The children were fed first, Paolo included. Paolo sat on one of the long benches, thinking it was almost enjoyable – except if he thought of Tonino, or Old Niccolo in bed upstairs. He was very pleased and surprised when a sudden bundle of claw and warm-iron muscle landed on his knee. Benvenuto was missing Tonino too. He rubbed against Paolo with a kind of desperation, but he would not purr.

Rosa and Marco were getting up to put the young ones to bed, when there was a sudden great clanging, outside in the night.

"Good Heavens!" said Rosa, and opened the yard door.

The noise flooded in, an uneven metal sound, hasty and huge. The nearest – *clang-clang-clang* – was so near that it could only be the bell of Sant' Angelo's. Behind it, the bell of the Cathedral tolled. And beyond that, now near, now faint and tinny, every bell in every church in Caprona beat and boomed and clashed and chimed. Corinna and Lucia came racing in, their faces bright with cold excitement.

"We're at war! The Duke's declared war!"

Marco said he thought he had better go. "Oh no, don't!" Rosa cried out. "Not yet. By the way, Lucia—"

Lucia took a quick look at the cooking in the hearth. "I'll go and take Aunt Gina the prescription," she said, and prudently ran away.

Marco and Rosa looked at one another. "Three States against us and no spells to fight with," said Marco. "We're not likely to have a long and happy marriage, are we?"

"Mr Notti says the Final Reserve is being called up tomorrow," Corinna said encouragingly. She caught Rosa's eye. "Come on, you kids," she said to four cousins at random. "Bedtime."

While the young ones were being put to bed, Paolo sat nursing Benvenuto, feeling more dismal than ever. He wondered if there would be soldiers from Florence and Pisa and Siena in Caprona by tomorrow. Would guns fire in the streets? He thought of big marble chips shot off the Cathedral, the New Bridge broken, despite all the spells in it, and swarthy enemy soldiers dragging Rosa off screaming. And he saw that all this could really have happened by the end of the week.

Here, he became quite certain that Benvenuto was trying to tell him something. He could tell from the accusing stare of Benvenuto's yellow eyes. But he simply could not understand.

"I'll try," he said to Benvenuto. "I really will try."

He had, fleetingly, the feeling that Benvenuto was glad. Encouraged by this, Paolo bent his head and stared at Benvenuto's urgent face. But it did no good. All that Paolo could get out of it was a picture in his mind – a picture of somewhere with a coloured marble front, very large and beautiful.

"The Church of Sant' Angelo?" he said doubtfully.

While Benvenuto's tail was still lashing with annoyance, Rosa and Marco came back. "Oh dear!" Rosa said to Marco. "There's Paolo taking all the troubles of the Casa on his shoulders again!"

Paolo looked up in surprise.

Marco said, "You look just like Antonio sometimes."

"I can't understand Benvenuto," Paolo said despairingly.

Marco sat on the table beside him. "Then he'll have to find some other way of telling us what he wants," he said. "He's a clever cat – the cleverest I've ever known. He'll do it."

He put out a hand and Benvenuto let him stroke his head. "Your ears," said Marco, "Sir Cat, are like sea-holly without the prickles."

Rosa perched on the table too, on the other side of Paolo. "What is it, Paolo? Tonino?"

Paolo nodded. "Nobody will believe me that the enemy enchanter's got him."

"We do," said Marco.

Rosa said, "Paolo, it's just as well he's got Tonino and not you. Tonino'll take it much more calmly."

Paolo was a little bewildered. "Why do you two believe in the enchanter and no one else does?"

"What makes you think he exists?" Marco countered.

Even to Rosa and Marco, Paolo could not bring himself to tell of his embarrassing encounter with a Petrocchi. "There was a horrible fog at the end of the fight," he said.

Rosa and Marco jumped round delightedly. Their hands met with a smack over Paolo's head. "It worked! It worked!" And Marco added, "We were hoping someone would mention a certain fog! Did there seem to have been a large-scale cancel-spell with it, by any chance?"

"Yes," said Paolo.

"*We* made that fog," Rosa said. "Marco and me. We were hoping to stop the fighting, but it took us ages to make it, because all the magic in Caprona was going into the fight."

Paolo digested this. That took care of the one piece of proof that did not depend on the word of a Petrocchi. Perhaps the enchanter did not exist after all. Perhaps Tonino really was at the Casa Petrocchi. He remembered that Renata had not said Angelica was missing until the fog cleared and she knew who he was. "Look," he said. "Will you two come to the Casa Petrocchi with me and see if Tonino's there?"

He was aware that Rosa and Marco were exchanging some kind of look above his head.

"Why?" said Rosa.

"Because," said Paolo. "Because." The need to persuade them cleared his wits at last. "Because Guido Petrocchi said Angelica Petrocchi was missing too."

"I'm afraid we can't," Marco said, with what sounded like real regret. "You'd understand, if you knew how pressing our reasons are, believe me!"

Paolo did not understand. He knew that, with these two, it was not cowardice, or pride, or anything like that. That only made it more maddening. "Oh, nobody will help!" he cried out.

Rosa put her arm around him. "Paolo! You're just like

Father. You think you have to do everything yourself. There is one thing we can do."

"Call Chrestomanci?" said Marco.

Paolo felt Rosa nod. "But he's in Rome," he objected.

"It doesn't matter," said Marco. "He's that kind of enchanter. If he's near enough and you need him enough, he comes when you call."

"I must cook!" said Rosa, jumping off the table.

Just before the second supper was ready, Rinaldo came back, in great good spirits. Uncle Umberto and old Luigi Petrocchi had had another fight, in the dining-hall of the University. That was why Uncle Umberto had not turned up to see how Old Niccolo was. He and Luigi were both in bed, prostrated with exhaustion. Rinaldo had been drinking wine with some students who told him all about the fight. The students' supper had been ruined. Cutlets and pasta had flown about, followed by chairs, tables and benches. Umberto had tried to drown Luigi in a soup tureen, and Luigi had replied by hurling the whole of the Doctors' supper at Umberto. The students were going on strike. They did not mind the fight, but Luigi had shown them that the Doctors' food was better than theirs.

Paolo listened without truly attending. He was thinking about Tonino and wondering if he dared depend on the word of a Petrocchi.

CHAPTER ELEVEN

✳

*A*fter a while, someone came and picked Tonino up. That
was unpleasant. His legs and arms dragged and dangled
in all directions, and he could not do anything about it. He was
plunged somewhere much darker. Then he was left to lie amid
a great deal of bumping and scraping, as if he were in a box
which was being pushed across a floor. When it stopped, he
found he could move. He sat up, trembling all over.

He was in the same room as before, but it seemed to be
much smaller. He could tell that, if he stood up, his head would
brush the little lighted chandelier in the ceiling. So he was
larger now; where he had been three inches tall before, he must

now be more like nine. The puppets must be too big for their scenery, and the false villa meant to look as if it was some distance away. And, with the Duchess suddenly taken ill, none of her helpers had bothered what size Tonino was. They had simply made sure he was shut up again.

"Tonino," whispered Angelica.

Tonino whirled round. Half the room was full of a pile of lax puppet bodies. He scanned the cardboard head of the policeman, then his enemy the Hangman, and the white sausage of the baby, and came upon Angelica's face halfway up the pile. It was her own face, though swollen and tearstained. Tonino clapped his hand to his nose. To his relief, the red beak was gone, though he still seemed to be wearing Mr Punch's scarlet nightgown.

"I'm sorry," he said. His teeth seemed to be chattering. "I tried not to hurt you. Are your bones broken?"

"No—o," said Angelica. She did not sound too sure. "Tonino, what happened?"

"I hanged the Duchess," Tonino said, and he felt some vicious triumph as he said it. "I didn't kill her though," he added regretfully.

Angelica laughed. She laughed until the heap of puppets was shaking and sliding about. But Tonino could not find it funny. He burst into tears, even though he was crying in front of a Petrocchi.

"Oh dear," said Angelica. "Tonino, stop it! Tonino – please!" She struggled out from among the puppets and hobbled looming through the room. Her head banged the chandelier and sent it tinkling and casting mad shadows over them as she knelt down beside Tonino. "Tonino, please stop. She'll be furious as soon as she feels better."

Angelica was wearing Judy's blue cap and Judy's blue dress still. She took off the blue cap and held it out to Tonino. "Here. Blow on that. I used the baby's dress. It made me feel better." She tried to smile at him, but the smile went hopelessly crooked in her swollen face. Angelica's large forehead must have hit the floor first. It was now enlarged by a huge red bump. Under it, the grin looked grotesque.

Tonino understood it was meant for a smile and smiled back, as well as he could for his chattering teeth.

"Here." Angelica loomed back through the room to the pile of puppets and heaved at the Hangman. She returned with his black felt cape. "Put this on."

Tonino wrapped himself in the cape and blew his nose on the blue cap and felt better.

Angelica heaved more puppets about. "I'm going to wear the policeman's jacket," she said. "Tonino – have you thought?"

"Not really," said Tonino. "I sort of know."

He had known from the moment he looked at the Duchess. She was the enchanter who was sapping the strength of Caprona and spoiling the spells of the Casa Montana. Tonino was not sure about the Duke – probably he was too stupid to count. But in spite of the Duchess's enchantments, the spells of the Casa Montana – and the Casa Petrocchi – must still be strong enough to be a nuisance to her. So he and Angelica had been kidnapped to blackmail both houses into stopping making spells. And if they stopped, Caprona would be defeated. The frightening part was that Tonino and Angelica were the only two people who knew, and the Duchess did not care that they knew. It was not only that even someone as clever as Paolo would never think of looking in the Palace, inside a Punch and Judy show: it must mean that the two of them would be dead before anyone found them.

"We absolutely have to get away," said Angelica. "Before she's better from being hanged."

"She'll have thought of that," said Tonino.

"I'm not sure," said Angelica. "I could tell everyone was startled to death. They let me see you being put through the floor, and I think we could get out that way. It will be easier now we're bigger."

Tonino fastened the cape round him and struggled to his feet, though he felt almost too tired and bruised to bother. His head hit the chandelier too. Huge flickering shadows fled round the room, and made the heap of puppets look as if they were squirming about. "Where did they put me through?" he said.

"Just where you're standing," said Angelica.

Tonino backed against the windows and looked at the place. He would not have known there was any opening. But, now Angelica had told him, he could see, disguised by the painted swirls of the carpet and confused by the swinging light, the faintest black line. The outline made an oblong about the size of the shoddy dining-table. The tray of supper must have come through that way too.

"Sing an opening spell," Angelica commanded him.

"I don't know one," Tonino was forced to confess.

He could tell by the stiff way Angelica stood that she was trying not to say a number of nasty things. "Well, I don't dare," she said. "You saw what happened last time. If I do anything, they'll catch us again and punish us by making us be puppets. And I couldn't bear another time."

Tonino was not sure he could bear it either, even though, now he thought about it, he was not sure it had been a punishment. The Duchess had probably intended to make them perform anyway. She was quite mean enough. On the other hand, he was not sure he could stand another of Angelica's botched spells, either. "Well, it's only a trap-door," he said. "It must be held up by one of those little hooks. Let's try bashing at it with the candlesticks."

"And if there's a spell on it?" said Angelica. "Oh, come on. Let's try."

They seized a candlestick each and knelt beside the windows, knocking diligently at the scarcely-seen black line. The cardboard was tough and pulpy. The candlesticks shortly looked like metal weeping-willow trees. But they succeeded in making a crumbly hollow in the middle of one edge of the hidden door. Tonino thought he could see a glimmer of metal showing. He raised his bent candlestick high to deliver a mighty blow.

"*Stop!*" hissed Angelica.

There were large shuffling footsteps somewhere. Tonino lowered the candlestick by gentle fractions and scarcely dared breathe. A distant voice grumbled... "Mice then" ... "Nothing here..." It was suddenly very much darker. Someone had switched off a light, leaving them only with the bluish glimmer of the little chandelier. The footsteps shuffled. A door bumped, and there was silence.

Angelica laid her candlestick down and began trying to tear at the cardboard with her fingers. Tonino got up and wandered away. It was no good. Someone was going to hear them, whatever they did. The Palace was full of footmen and soldiers. Tonino would have given up then and waited for the Duchess to do her worst. Only now he was standing up, the cardboard room seemed so small. Half of it was filled with the puppets. There was hardly room to move. Tonino wanted to hurl himself at the walls and scream. He did make a movement, and knocked the table. Because he was so much bigger and heavier now, the table swayed and creaked.

"I know!" he said. "Finish drawing the Angel."

The bump on Angelica's forehead turned up to him. "I'm not in the mood for doodling."

"Not a doodle, a spell," Tonino explained. "And then pull the table over us while we make a hole in the trap door."

Angelica did not need telling that the Angel was the most

potent spell in Caprona. She threw the candlestick aside and scrambled up. "That might just work," she said. "You know, for a Montana, you have very good ideas." Her head hit the chandelier again. In the confusion of swinging shadows, they could not find the tap Angelica had been drawing with. Tonino had to jam his head and arm into the tiny bathroom and pull off the other useless tap.

Even when the shadows stopped swinging, the Angel scratched on the table was hard to see. It now looked faint and small.

"He needs his scroll," said Angelica. "And I'd better put in a halo to make sure he's holy."

Angelica was now so much bigger and stronger that she kept dropping the tap. The halo, when she had scratched it in, was too big, and the scroll would not go right. The table swayed this way and that, the tap ploughed and skidded, and there was a danger the Angel would end up a complete mess.

"It's so fiddly!" said Angelica. "Will that do?"

"No," said Tonino. "It needs the scroll more unrolled. Some of the words show on our Angel."

Because he was quite right, Angelica lost her temper. "All right! Do it yourself, if you're so clever, you horrible Montana!"

She held the tap out to Tonino and he snatched it from her, quite as angry. "Here," he said, ploughing up a long curl of varnish. "Here's the hanging bit. And the words go sideways. You can see *Carmen pa, Venit ang, Cap* and a lot more, but there won't be room for it."

"Our Angel," said Angelica, "says *cis saeculare, elus cantare* and *virtus data* near the end." Tonino scratched away and took no notice. It was hard enough shaping tiny letters with a thing like a tap, without listening to Angelica arguing. "Well it *does*!" said Angelica. "I've often wondered why it's not the words we sing—"

The same idea came to both of them. They stared at one another, nose to nose across the scratched varnish.

"*Finding* the words means *looking* for them," said Tonino.

"And they were over our gates all the time! Oh how *stupid*!" exclaimed Angelica. "Come on. We *must* get out now!"

Tonino left the scroll with *Carmen* scraped on it. There was really no room for any more. They dragged the creaking, swaying table across the hole they had made in the floor and set to work underneath it, hacking lumps out of the painted floor.

Shortly, they could see a bar of silvery metal stretching from the trap door to the floor underneath them. Tonino forced the end of his candlestick down between the battered cardboard edges and heaved sideways at the metal.

"There's a spell on it," he said.

"Angel of Caprona," Angelica said at the same moment.

And the bar slipped sideways. A big oblong piece of the

floor dropped away from in front of their knees and swung, leaving a very deep dark hole.

"Let's get the Hangman's rope," said Angelica.

They edged along to the pile of puppets and disentangled the string from the little gibbet. Tonino tied it to the table leg.

"It's a long way down," he said dubiously.

"It's only a few feet *really*," Angelica said. "And we're not heavy enough to hurt. I went all floppy when you kicked me off the stage and – well – I didn't break anything anyway."

Tonino let Angelica go first, swinging down into the dark space like an energetic blue monkey. *Crunch* went the shoddy table. *Creeeak*. And it swayed towards the leg where the rope was tied.

"Angel of Caprona!" Tonino whispered.

The table plunged, one corner first, down into the space. The cardboard room rattled. And, with a rending and creaking of wood, the table stuck, mostly in the hole, but with one corner out and wedged against the sides. There was a thump from below. Tonino was fairly sure he was stuck in the room for good now.

"I'm down," Angelica whispered up. "You can pull the rope up. It nearly reaches the floor."

Tonino leaned over and fumbled the string up from the table leg. He was sure there had been a miracle. That leg ought to have broken off, or the table ought to have gone down the hole. He whispered, "Angel of Caprona!" again as he slid down under the table into the dark.

The table creaked hideously, but it held together. The string burnt Tonino's hands as he slid, and then it was suddenly not there. His feet hit the floor almost at once.

"Oof!" he went. His feet felt as if they had been knocked up through his legs.

Down there, they were standing on the shiny floor of a Palace room. The towering walls of the Punch and Judy show were on three sides of them. Instead of a back wall, there was a curtain, intended to hide the puppet-master, and very dim light was coming in round its edges. They pulled one end of the curtain aside. It felt coarse and heavy, like a sack. Behind it was the wall of the room. The puppet show had evidently been simply pushed away to one side. There was just space for Angelica and Tonino to squeeze past the ends of the show, into a large room lit by moonlight falling in strong silver blocks across its shiny floor.

It was the same room where the court had watched the Punch and Judy show. The puppet show had not been put away. Tonino thought of the time he and Angelica had tottered on the edge of the stage, looking into nothingness. They could have been killed. That seemed another miracle. Then, they must have been in some kind of storeroom. But, when the Duchess was so mysteriously taken ill, no one had bothered to put them back there.

The moonlight glittered on the polished face of the Angel, high up on the other side of the room, leaning out over some big double doors. There were other doors, but Tonino and

Angelica set out, without hesitation, towards the Angel. Both of them took it for a guide.

"Oh bother!" said Angelica, before they reached the first block of moonlight. "We're still small. I thought we'd be the right size as soon as we got out, didn't you?"

Tonino's one idea was to get out, whatever his size. "It'll be easier to hide like this," he said. "Someone in your Casa can easily turn you back." He pulled the Hangman's cloak round him and shivered. It was colder out in the big room. He could see the moon through the big windows, riding high and cold in a wintry dark blue sky. It was not going to be fun running through the streets in a red nightgown.

"But I *hate* being this small!" Angelica complained. "We'll never be able to get down stairs."

She was right to complain, as Tonino soon discovered. It seemed a mile across the polished floor. When they reached the double doors, they were tired out. High above them, the carved Angel dangled a scroll they could not possibly read, and no longer looked so friendly. But the doors were open a crack. They managed to push the crack wider by leaning their backs against the edge of both doors. It was maddening to think they could have opened them with one hand if only they had been the proper size.

Beyond was an even bigger room. This one was full of chairs and small tables. The only advantage of being doll-sized was that they could walk under every piece of furniture in a straight line to the far-too-distant door. It was like trudging through a golden moonlit forest, where every tree had an elegant swan-bend to its trunk. The floor seemed to be marble.

Before they reached the door, they were quarrelling again from sheer tiredness.

"It's going to take all *night* to get out of here!" Angelica grumbled.

"Oh shut up!" said Tonino. "You make more fuss about things than my Aunt Gina!"

"Is your Aunt Gina bruised all over because you hit her?" Angelica demanded.

When they came to the half-open door at last, there was only another room, slightly smaller. This one had a carpet. Gilded sofas stood about like Dutch barns, and large frilly armchairs. Angelica gave a wail of despair.

Tonino stood on tiptoe. There seemed to be cushions on some of the seats. "Suppose we hid under a cushion for the night?" he suggested, trying to make peace.

Angelica turned on him furiously. "Stupid! No wonder you're slow at spells! We may be small, but they'll find us *because* of that. We must *stink* of magic. Even my baby brother could find us, and he may be a baby but he's cleverer than you!"

Tonino was too angry to answer. He simply marched away into the carpet. At first it was a relief to his sore feet, but it soon became another trial. It was like walking through long, tufty grass – and anyone who has done that for a mile or so will know how tiring that can be. On top of that, they had to keep going round puffy armchairs that seemed as big as houses, frilly footstools and screens as big as hoardings. Some of these things would have made good hiding-places, but they were both too angry and frightened to suggest it.

Then, when they reached the door at last, it was shut. They threw themselves against the hard wood. It did not even shake.

"Now what?" said Tonino, leaning his back against it. The moon was going down by now. The carpet was in darkness. The bars of moonlight from the far-off windows only touched the tops of armchairs, or picked out the gold on the sofa backs, or the glitter from a shelf of coloured glass vases. It would be quite dark soon.

"There's an Angel over there," Angelica said wearily.

She was right. Tonino could just see it, as coloured flickers on wood, lit by moonlight reflected off the shelf of glass vases. There was another door under the Angel, or rather a dark space, because that door was wide open. Too tired even to speak, Tonino set off again, across another mile of tufty carpet, past beetling cliffs of furniture, to the other side of the room.

By the time they reached that open door, they were so tired that nothing seemed real any more. There were four steps down beyond the door. Very well. They went down them somehow. At the bottom was an even more brutally tufted carpet. It was quite dark.

Angelica sniffed the darkness. "Cigars."

It could have been scillas for all Tonino cared. All he wanted was the next door. He set off, feeling round the walls for it, with Angelica stumbling after. They bumped into one huge piece of furniture, felt their way round it, and banged into another, which stuck even further into the room. And so they went, stumbling and banging, climbing across two rounded metal bars, wading in carpet, until they arrived at the four steps again. It was quite a small room – for the Palace – and it had only one door. Tonino felt for the first step, as high as his head, and did not think he had the strength to get up them again. The Angel had not been a guide after all.

"That part that stuck out," said Angelica. "I don't know what it was, but it was hollow, like a box. Shall we risk hiding in it?"

"Let's find it," said Tonino.

They found it, or something like it, by walking into it. It was a steep-sided box which came up to their armpits. There was a large piece of metal, like a very wide door-knocker, hung on the front of it. When they felt inside, they felt sheets of stiff leather, and crisper stuff that was possibly paper.

"I think it's an open drawer," said Tonino.

Angelica did not answer. She simply climbed in. Tonino heard her flapping and crackling among the paper – if it was paper. Well! he thought. And it was Angelica who said they smelt of magic. But he was so tired that he climbed in too, and fell into a warm crumply nest where Angelica was already asleep. Tonino was almost too tired by now to care if they were found or not. But he had the sense to drag a piece of parchment over them both before he went to sleep too.

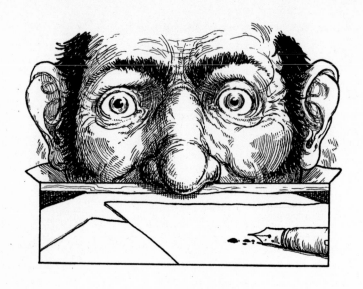

Chapter Twelve

✳

*T*onino woke up feeling chilly and puzzled. The light was pale and yellow because his sheet seemed to be over his face. Tonino gazed up at it, thinking it was a surprisingly flat, stiff sheet. It had large black letters on it too. His eyes travelled along the letters. *DECLARATION OF WAR (Duplicate Copy)*, he read.

Then he knew, with a jump, that he was nine inches high and lying in a drawer in the Palace. And it was light! Someone would find them. In fact, someone nearly had. That was what had woken him. He could hear someone moving about the room, making obscure thumps and shuffles, and occasionally whistling a snatch of the *Angel of Caprona*.

Whoever it was had reached the drawer now. Tonino could hear the floor creak under him and a dress rustling, loud and near. He moved his head, gently and stiffly, and found Angelica's frightened face resting on crumpled paper an inch or so away. The rustling dress proved the person was a woman. It must be the Duchess looking for them.

"That Duke!" said the person, in a voice no Duchess would use. "There never was such an untidy man!" Her breathing came suddenly nearer. Before either Tonino or Angelica could think what to do, the drawer moved. Helplessly, they were shunted inwards, feet first into darkness, and the drawer shut with a bang behind their heads.

"Help!" whispered Angelica.

"Ssh!"

The maid was still in the room. They could hear her move something, and then a tinkle of notes as she dusted a piano. Then a bump. And finally nothing. When they were quite sure she was gone, Angelica whispered, "What do we do now?"

There was room to sit up in the drawer, but not much else. Above their heads was a slit of light where the drawer met the desk, or whatever it was, and no way of opening it. But they could see quite well. Light was coming in at the back, beyond their feet. They tried bracing their hands against the wood overhead and heaving, but the drawer was made of solid, spicy-smelling wood and they could not budge it.

"We keep being shut in places without doors!" Angelica cried out. And she went floundering through the papers to the back of the drawer, where the light came in. Tonino crawled after her.

As soon as they got there, they realised this was the way out. The end of the drawer was lower than the front, and it did not reach the back of the wooden desk it was part of. There was quite a big gap there. When they put their heads into the space, they could see the ends of the other drawers above theirs going up like a ladder, and a slit of daylight at the top.

They squeezed through into the gap and climbed, side by side. It was as easy as climbing a ladder. They were one drawer away from the slit of daylight – which was going to be a tight squeeze – when they heard someone else in the room.

"They came down here, madam," said a lady's voice.

"Then we've caught them," replied the Duchess. "Look very carefully."

Tonino and Angelica hung from the back of the drawers by their fingers and toes, not daring to move. Silk dresses rustled as the Duchess and her lady moved round the room. "There's nothing this end at all, madam."

"And I swear this window hasn't been opened," said the Duchess. "Open all the drawers in the desk."

There was a sharp rumble above Tonino's head. Dusty white light flooded down from the open top drawer. Papers were loudly tossed over. "Nothing," said the lady. The top drawer slammed in again. Tonino and Angelica had been hanging on to the second drawer. They climbed down to the next as fast and quietly as they could. The second drawer rumbled open, and slammed shut, nearly deafening them. The drawer they were on jerked. Luckily, it was stiff. The lady tugged and rattled at it, and that gave Tonino and Angelica just time to climb frantically up to the second drawer again and cling there. And there they hung, in the dark narrow space, while the lady opened the third drawer, slammed it shut, and pulled out the bottom drawer. They craned over their arms and watched the white light flood in from below.

"Look at this!" cried the lady. "They've been here! It's like a mouse-nest!"

Silks rustled as the Duchess hurried over. "Curse it!" she said. "Not long ago too! I can smell them even through the cigars. Quick! They can't be far away. They must have got out before the room was cleaned."

The drawer rumbled in, bringing dusty darkness with it. There was a flurry of silks as the two women hurried away up the steps to the room with the armchairs, and the quiet, firm *clap* of the door closing.

"Do you think it's a trap?" Angelica whispered.

"No," said Tonino. He was sure the Duchess had not guessed where they were. But they were shut in this room now, by the sound, and he had no idea how they would get the door open.

All the same, even a shut room was great open spaces

compared with the narrow slit at the back of the drawers. Angelica and Tonino pushed and squeezed and forced themselves through the narrow daylight slit, and finally crawled out on the top of a writing-desk. Before their eyes had got used to the light, Tonino stubbed his toe on a vast pen like a telegraph pole and then tripped over a paper-knife like an ivory plank. Angelica bumped into a china ornament standing at the back of the desk. It swayed. She swayed. She flung her arms round it. When her eyes stopped watering, she found she was hugging a china Mr Punch, nose, red nightgown and all, about the same height as she was. There was a china Judy standing at the other end of the desk.

"We can't get away from these things!" she said.

The desk was covered in smooth red leather, very easy on the feet, and held a huge white blotter, which was even more comfortable to walk on. A chair with a matching red seat stood in front of the desk. Tonino saw they could easily jump down on to it. Even more easily, they could climb down the handles of the drawers. On the other hand, the piano the maid had dusted stood right beside the desk, and the window was round the corner from the piano. To reach the window was only a long stride from the piano. Though the window was shut, it had quite an easy-looking catch, if only they could reach it.

"Look!" said Angelica, pointing disgustedly.

A whole row of Punch and Judys stood along the top of the piano. Two were puppets on stands, very old and valuable by the look of them; two more were actually made of gold; and two others were rather arty clay models, which made Punch look like a leering ordinary man and Judy uncomfortably like the Duchess. And the music which was open on the piano was headed *Arnolfini – Punch and Judy Suite*.

"I think this is the Duke's study," said Angelica. And both of them got the giggles.

Still giggling, Tonino stepped on to the piano and started to walk to the window. *Do – ti – so – fa*, went the piano.

"Come back!" Angelica laughed.

Tonino came back – *fa – so – ti – do* – nearly in hysterics.

The door of the room opened and someone hurried down the steps. Angelica and Tonino could think of nothing better to do than stand stiffly where they were, hoping to be taken for more Punch and Judys. And, luckily, the man who came in was busy and worried. He slapped a pile of papers on the desk, without so much as glancing at the two new puppets, and hurried out again, gently closing the door behind him.

"Phew!" said Angelica.

They walked round to the front of the papers and looked at them curiously. The top one said:

Report of Campaign at 08.00 hours. Summary:
Troops advancing on all fronts to repel invasion.
Heavy Artillery and Reservists moving up in support.
Pisan front reports heavy losses. Fleet sighted –
Pisan? – steaming for mouth of Voltava.

"We're at war!" said Tonino. "Why?"

"Because the Duchess has got us, of course," said Angelica. "And our families daren't make war-spells. Tonino, we must get *out*. We must tell them where the words to the *Angel* are!"

"But why does the Duchess want Caprona beaten?" Tonino said.

"I don't know," said Angelica. "There's something wrong about her, I know that. Aunt Bella said there was an awful fuss when the Duke decided to marry her. Nobody likes her."

"Let's see if we can open the window," said Tonino. He set off along the piano again. **Do-ti-so-*fa-me-re*—**

"Quiet!" said Angelica.

Tonino discovered that, if he put each foot down very slowly, the notes did not sound. He was halfway along the keyboard, and Angelica had one foot stretched out to follow, when they heard someone opening the door again. There was no time to be careful. Angelica fled back to the desk. Tonino, with a terrible discord, scrambled across the black notes and squeezed behind the music on the stand.

He was only just in time. When he looked – he was standing with his feet and head sideways, like an Ancient Egyptian – the Duke of Caprona himself was standing in front of the desk. Tonino thought the Duke seemed both puzzled and sad. He was tapping the *Report of Campaign* against his teeth and did not seem to notice Angelica standing between the Punch and Judy on his desk, although Angelica's eyes were blinking against the glitter from the Duke's buttons.

"But I didn't declare war!" the Duke said to himself. "I was watching that puppet-show. How could I—?" He sighed and bit the *Report* worriedly between two rows of big shiny teeth. "Is my mind going?" he asked. He seemed to be talking to Angelica. She had the sense not to answer.

"I must go and ask Lucrezia," the Duke said. He flung the *Report* down at Angelica's feet and hurried out of the study.

Tonino slid cautiously down the piano-lid on to the keys again – *ker-pling*. Angelica was now standing at the end of the piano, pointing at the window. She was speechless with horror.

Tonino looked – and for a moment he was as frightened as Angelica. There was a brown monster glaring at him through the glass, wide-faced, wide-eyed and shaggy. The thing had eyes like yellow lamps.

Faintly, through the glass, came a slightly irritable request to pull himself together and open the window.

"Benvenuto!" shouted Tonino.

"Oh – it's only a cat," Angelica quavered. "How terrible it must feel to be a mouse!"

"Just a cat!" Tonino said scornfully. "That's Benvenuto." He tried to explain to Benvenuto that it was not easy to open windows when you were nine inches high.

Benvenuto's impatient answer was to shove Tonino's latest magic exercise book in front of Tonino's mind's eye, open at almost the first page.

"Oh, thanks," Tonino said, rather ashamed. There were three opening-spells on that page, and none of them had stuck in his head. He chose the easiest, shut his eyes so that he could read the imaginary page more clearly, and sang the spell.

Gently and easily, the window swung open, letting in a gust of cold wind. And Benvenuto came in with the wind, almost as lightly. As Benvenuto trod gently up the scale towards him, Tonino had another moment when he knew how mice felt. Then he forgot it in the gladness of seeing Benvenuto. He stretched his arms wide to rub behind Benvenuto's horny ears.

Benvenuto put his sticky black nose to Tonino's face, and they both stood, delighted, holding down a long humming discord on the piano.

Benvenuto said that Paolo was not quick enough; he could not make him understand where Tonino was. Tonino must send Paolo a message. Could Tonino write this size?

"There's a pen on the desk here," Angelica called. And Tonino remembered her saying she could understand cats.

Rather anxiously, Benvenuto wanted to know if Tonino minded him talking to a Petrocchi.

The question astonished Tonino for a moment. He had clean forgotten that he and Angelica were supposed to hate one another. It seemed a waste of time, when they were both in such trouble. "Not at all," he said.

"Do get off that piano, both of you," said Angelica. "The humming's horrible."

Benvenuto obliged, with one great flowing leap. Tonino

struggled after him with his elbows hooked over the piano-lid, pushing himself along against the black notes. By the time he reached the desk, Benvenuto and Angelica had exchanged formal introductions, and Benvenuto was advising them not to try getting out of the window. The room was three floors up. The stonework was crumbling, and even a cat had some trouble keeping his feet. If they would wait, Benvenuto would fetch help.

"But the Duchess—" said Tonino.

"And the Duke," said Angelica. "This is the Duke's study."

Benvenuto considered the Duke harmless on his own. He thought they were in the safest place in the Palace. They were to stay hidden and write him a note small enough to carry in his mouth.

"Wouldn't it be better if we tied it round your neck?" Angelica asked.

Benvenuto had never submitted to anything round his neck, and he was not going to start now. Anyway, someone in the Palace might see the message.

So Tonino put one foot on the *Report of Campaign* and succeeded, by heaving with both hands, in tearing off a corner of it. Angelica passed him the huge pen, which he had to hold in both hands, with the end resting on his shoulder. Then she stood on the paper to keep it steady while Tonino wielded the pen. It was such hard work, that he kept the message as short as possible. *In Duke's Palace. Duchess enchantress. T.M. &*

"Tell them about the words to the *Angel*," said Angelica. "Just in case."

Tonino turned the paper over and wrote *Words to* Angel *on* Angel *over gate. T & A.* Then, exhausted with heaving the pen up and down, he folded the piece of paper with that message inside and the first one outside, and trod it flat. Benvenuto opened his mouth. Angelica winced at that pink cavern with its arched wrinkly roof and its row of white fangs, and let Tonino place the message across Benvenuto's prickly tongue. Benvenuto gave Tonino a loving glare and sprang away. He struck one ringing chord from the piano, around middle C, made the slightest thump on the windowsill, and vanished.

Tonino and Angelica were staring after him and did not notice, until it was too late, that the Duke had come back.

"Funny," said the Duke. "There's a new Punch now, as well as a new Judy."

Tonino and Angelica stood stiff as posts, one on each end of the blotter, in agonisingly uncomfortable attitudes.

Fortunately, the Duke noticed the open window. "Blessed maids and their fresh air!" he grumbled, and went over to shut it. Tonino seized the opportunity to stand on both feet, Angelica to uncrick her neck. Then they both jumped. An unmistakable gunshot cracked out, from somewhere below. And another. The Duke bent out of the window and seemed to be watching something. "Poor pussy," he said. He sounded sad and resigned. "Why couldn't you keep away, puss? She hates cats. And they make such a din, too, shooting them."

Another shot cracked out, and then several more. The Duke stood up, shaking his head sadly. "Ah well," he said, as he shut the window. "I suppose they do eat birds."

He came back across the study. Tonino and Angelica could not have moved if they tried. They were both too stricken.

The Duke's face folded into shiny wrinkles. He had noticed the corner torn from the *Report*. "I've been eating paper now!" he said. His sad, puzzled face turned towards Tonino and Angelica. "I think I do forget things," he said. "I talk to myself. That's a bad sign. But I really don't remember you two at all. At least, I remember the new Judy, but," he said to Tonino, "I don't remember you at all. How did you get here?"

Tonino was far too upset about Benvenuto to think. After all, the Duke really was speaking to him. "Please, sir," he said, "I'll explain—"

"Shut *up*!" snapped Angelica. "I'll say a spell!"

"—only please tell me if they shot my cat," said Tonino.

"I think so," said the Duke. "It looked as if they got it." Here he took a deep breath and turned his eyes carefully to the ceiling, before he looked at Tonino and Angelica again. Neither of them moved. Angelica was glaring at Tonino, promising him spells unimaginable if he said another word. And Tonino knew he had been an utter idiot anyway. Benvenuto was dead and there was no point in moving – no point in anything.

The Duke, meanwhile, slowly pulled a large handkerchief out of his pocket. A slightly crumpled cigar came out with it and flopped on the desk. The Duke picked it up and put it absent-mindedly between his glistening teeth. And then he had to take it out again to wipe his shiny face. "Both of you spoke," he said, putting the handkerchief away and fetching out a gold lighter. "You know that?" he said, putting the cigar back into his mouth. He gave a furtive look round, clicked the lighter, and lit the cigar. "You are looking," he said, "at a poor dotty Duke." Smoke rolled out with his words, as much smoke as if the Duke had been a dragon.

Angelica sneezed. Tonino thought he was going to sneeze. He drew a deep breath to stop himself and burst out coughing.

"Ahah!" cried the Duke. "Got you!" His large wet hands pounced, and seized each of them round the legs. Holding them like that, firmly pinned to the blotter, he sat down in the chair and bent his triumphant shiny face until it was level with theirs. The cigar, cocked out of one side of his mouth, continued to roll smoke over them. They flailed their arms for balance and coughed and coughed. "Now what are you?" said the Duke. "Another of her fiendish devices for making me think I'm potty? Eh?"

"No we're not!" coughed Tonino, and Angelica coughed, "Oh, please stop that smoke!"

The Duke laughed. "The old Chinese cigar-torture," he said gleefully, "guaranteed to bring statues to life." But his right hand moved Tonino, stumbling and swaying, across the blotter to Angelica, where his left hand gathered him in. His right hand took the cigar out of his mouth and laid it on the edge of the desk. "Now," he said. "Let's have a look at you."

They scrubbed their streaming eyes and looked fearfully up at his great grinning face. It was impossible to look at all of it at once. Angelica settled for his left eye, Tonino for his right eye. Both eyes bulged at them, round and innocent, like Old Niccolo's.

"Bless me!" said the Duke. "You're the spell-makers' children who were supposed to come to my pantomime! Why didn't you come?"

"We never got an invitation, Your Grace," Angelica said. "Did you?" she asked Tonino.

"No," Tonino said mournfully.

The Duke's face sagged. "So that's why it was. I wrote them myself too. That's my life in a nutshell. None of the orders I give ever get carried out, and an awful lot of things get done that I never ordered at all." He opened his hand slowly. The big warm fingers peeled damply off their legs. "You feel funny wriggling about in my hand," he said. "There, if I let you go, will you tell me how you got here?"

They told him, with one or two forced pauses when he took a puff at his cigar and set them coughing again. He listened wonderingly. It was not like explaining things to a huge grown-up Duke. Tonino felt as if he was telling a made-up story to his small cousins. From the way the Duke's eyes popped, and the way he kept saying "Go on!" Tonino was sure the Duke was believing it no more than the little Montanas believed the story of Giovanni the Giant Killer.

Yet, when they had finished, the Duke said, "That Punch and Judy show started at eight-thirty and went on till nine-fifteen. I know, because there was a clock just over you. They say I declared war at nine o'clock last night. Did either of you notice me declaring war?"

"No," they said. "Though," Angelica added sourly, "I was being beaten to death at the time and I might not have noticed."

"My apologies," said the Duke. "But did either of you hear gunfire? No. But firing started around eleven and went on all night. It's still going on. You can see it, but not hear it, from the tower over this study. Which means another damn spell, I suppose. And I think I'm supposed to sit here and not notice Caprona being blown to pieces around me." He put his chin in his hands and stared at them miserably. "I know I'm a fool," he said, "but just because I love plays and puppet-theatres, I'm not an idiot. The question is, how do we get you two out of here without Lucrezia knowing?"

Tonino and Angelica were almost too surprised and grateful to speak. And while they were still trying to say thank you, the Duke jumped upright, staring pop-eyed.

"She's coming! I've got an instinct. Quick! Get in my pockets!"

He turned round sideways to the desk and held one pocket of his coat stretched against it, between two fingers. Angelica hastily lifted the pocket-flap and slid down between the two layers of cloth. The Duke stubbed out his cigar on the edge of the desk and popped it in after her. Then he turned round and held the other pocket open for Tonino. As Tonino crouched down in fuzzy darkness, he heard the door open and the voice of the Duchess.

"My lord, you've been smoking cigars in here again."

CHAPTER THIRTEEN

✳

*P*aolo woke up that morning knowing that he was going to have to look for Tonino himself. If his father, and Rinaldo, and then Rosa and Marco, all refused to try, then there was no use asking anyone else.

He sat up and realised that the Casa was full of unusual noises. Below in the yard, the gate was open. He could hear the voices of Elizabeth, Aunt Anna, Aunt Maria and Cousin Claudia, who were bringing the day's bread.

"Just look at the Angel!" he heard his mother say. "Now what did that?"

"It's because we've stopped our spells," said Cousin Claudia.

Following that came a single note of song from Aunt Anna, cut off short with a squeak.

Aunt Maria said angrily, "No spells, Anna! Think of Tonino!"

This was intriguing, but what really interested Paolo were the noises behind the voices: marching feet, orders being shouted, a drum beating, horses' hooves, heavy rumbling and some cursing. Paolo shot out of bed. It must be the army.

"Hundreds of them," he heard Aunt Anna say.

"Most of them younger than my Domenico," said Aunt Maria. "Claudia, take this basket while I shut the gate. All going to face three armies without a war-scrip between them. I could cry!"

Paolo shot along the gallery, pulling on his jacket, and hurried down the steps into the cold yellow sunlight. He was too late. The gate was barred and the war-noises shut out. The ladies were crossing the yard with their baskets.

"Where do you think you're going?" Elizabeth called to him. "No one's going out today. There's going to be fighting. The schools are all closed."

They put down their baskets to open the kitchen door. Paolo saw them recoil, with cries of dismay.

"Good Lord!" said Elizabeth.

"Don't anyone tell Gina!" said Aunt Maria.

At the same moment, someone knocked heavily at the Casa gate.

"See who that is, Paolo," called Aunt Anna.

Paolo went under the archway and undid the flap of the peephole. He was pleased to have this chance to see the army, and pleased that the schools were shut. He had not intended to go to school today anyway.

There was a man in uniform outside, who shouted, "Open and receive this, in the name of the Duke!" Behind him, Paolo caught glimpses of shiny marching boots and more uniforms. He unbarred the gate.

Meanwhile, it became plain that Aunt Gina was not to be kept away from the kitchen. Her feet clattered on the stairs. There was a stunned pause. Then the whole Casa filled with her voice.

"Oh my God! Mother of God! *Insects!*" It even drowned the noise of the military band that was marching past as Paolo opened the gate.

The man outside thrust a sheet of paper at Paolo and darted off to hammer on the next door. Paolo looked at it. He had a mad idea that he had just been handed the words to the *Angel*. After that, he went on staring, oblivious alike of Aunt Gina – who was now screaming what she was going to do to Lucia – and of the great gun that went rumbling past, pulled by four straining horses.

State of Caprona, Paolo read, *Form FR3 Call Up of Final Reservists. The following to report to the Arsenal for immediate duty at 03.00 hrs, January 14th, 1979: Antonio Montana, Lorenzo Montana, Piero Montana, Ricardo Montana, Arturo Montana (ne Notti), Carlo Montana, Luigi*

Montana, Angelo Montana, Luca Montana, Giovanni Montana, Piero Iacopo Montana, Rinaldo Montana, Domenico Montana, Francesco Montana.

That was everyone! Paolo had not realised that even his father was a Final Reservist.

"Shut the gate, Paolo!" shrieked Aunt Maria.

Paolo was about to obey, when he remembered that he had not yet looked at the Angel. He dodged outside and stared up, while half a regiment of infantry marched past behind him. It looked as if, in the night, every pigeon in Caprona had chosen to sit on that one golden carving. It was plastered with bird-droppings. They were particularly thick, not unnaturally, on the outstretched arm holding the scroll, and the scroll was a crusty white mass. Paolo shuddered. It seemed like an omen. He did not notice one of the marching soldiers detach himself from the column and come up behind him.

"I should close the gate, if I were you," said Chrestomanci.

Paolo looked up at him and wondered why people looked so different in uniform. He pulled himself together and dragged the two halves of the gate shut. Chrestomanci helped him slot the big iron bars in to lock it. As he did, he said, "I was at the Casa Petrocchi around dawn, so there's no great need for explanations. But I would like to know what's the matter in the kitchen this time."

Paolo looked. Eight baskets piled high with round tan-coloured loaves stood outside the kitchen. There were agitated noises from inside it, and a curious long droning-sound. "I think it's Lucia's spell again," he said.

He and Chrestomanci set off across the yard. Before they had gone three steps, the aunts burst out of the kitchen and rushed towards him. Antonio and the uncles hurried down from the gallery, and cousins arrived from everywhere else.

Aunt Francesca surged out of the Saloon. She had spent the night there, and looked as if she had. Chrestomanci was soon in the middle of a crowd and holding several conversations at once.

"You were quite right to call me," he said to Rosa, and to Aunt Francesca, "Old Niccolo is good for years yet, but you should rest." To Elizabeth and Antonio, he said, "I know about Tonino," and to Rinaldo, "This is my fourth uniform today. There's heavy fighting in the hills and I had to get through somehow. What possessed the Duke," he asked the uncles, "to declare war so soon? I could have got help from Rome if he'd waited." None of them knew, and they all told him so at once. "I know," said Chrestomanci. "I know. No war-spells. I think our enemy enchanter has made a mistake over Tonino and Angelica. If it does nothing else, it allows me a free hand." Then, as the clamour showed no sign of abating, he said, "By the way, the Final Reserve has been called up," and nodded to Paolo to give the paper to Antonio.

In the sober hush that this produced, Chrestomanci pushed his way to the kitchen and put his head inside. "My goodness me!" Paolo heard him murmur.

Paolo ducked under all the people crowding round Antonio and looked into the kitchen under Chrestomanci's elbow. He looked into a wall of insects. The place was black with them, and glittering, and crawling, and dense with different humming. Flies of all kinds, mosquitoes, wasps and midges filled the air-space. Beetles, ants, moths and a hundred other crawling things occupied the floor and shelves and sink.

Peering through the buzzing clouds, Paolo was almost sure he saw a swarm of locusts on the cooking-stove. It was even worse than he had imagined the Petrocchi kitchen when he was little.

Chrestomanci drew a deep breath. Paolo suspected he was trying not to laugh. They both looked round for Lucia, who was standing on one leg among the breadbaskets, wondering whether to run away. "I am sure," Chrestomanci said to her – he *was* trying not to laugh; he had to start again. "I am sure people have talked to you about misusing spells. But – just out of interest – what did you use?"

"She used her own words to the *Angel of Caprona*!" Aunt Maria said, bursting angrily out of the crowd. "Gina's nearly out of her mind!"

"All the children did it," Lucia said defiantly. "It wasn't only me."

Chrestomanci looked at Paolo, and Paolo nodded. "A considerable tribute to the powers of the younger Montanas," said Chrestomanci. He turned and snapped his fingers into the buzzing, crawling kitchen. Not much happened. The air

211

cleared enough for Paolo to see that it was indeed locusts on the cooker, but that was all. Chrestomanci's eyebrows went up a little. He tried again. This time nothing happened at all. He retreated from the buzzing, looking thoughtful.

"With all due respect," he said to Paolo and Lucia, "to the *Angel of Caprona*, it should not be this powerful on its own. I'm afraid this spell will just have to wear itself out." And he said to Aunt Maria, "No wonder the enemy enchanter is so much afraid of the Casa Montana. Does this mean there won't be any breakfast?"

"No, no. We'll make it in the dining-room," Aunt Maria said, looking very flustered.

"Good," said Chrestomanci. "There's something I have to say to everyone, when they're all there."

And when everyone was gathered round the tables to eat plain rolls and drink black coffee made over the dining-room fire, Chrestomanci stood in front of the fire, holding a coffee cup, and said, "I know few of you believe Tonino is not in the Casa Petrocchi, but I swear to you he is not, and that Angelica Petrocchi is also missing. I think you are quite right to stop making spells until they are found, but I want to say this: even if I found Tonino and Angelica this minute, all the spells of the Casa Montana and the Casa Petrocchi are not going to save Caprona now. There are three armies, and the fleet of Pisa, closing in on her. The *only thing* which is going to help you is the true words to the *Angel of Caprona*. Have you all understood?"

They all had. Everyone was silent. Nobody spoke for some time. Then Uncle Lorenzo began grumbling. Moths had got into his Reservist uniform. "Someone took the spell out," he complained. "I shan't be fit to be seen."

"Does it matter?" asked Rinaldo. His face was very white and he was not having anything but coffee. "You'll only be seen dead anyway."

"But that's just it!" said Uncle Lorenzo. "I don't want to be seen dead in it!"

"Oh be quiet!" Domenico snapped at him. Uncle Lorenzo was so surprised that he stopped talking. Breakfast finished in gloomy murmurs.

Paolo got up and slid behind the bench where Chrestomanci was sitting. "Excuse me, sir. Do you know where Tonino is?"

"I wish I did," said Chrestomanci. "This enchanter is good. So far, I have only two clues. Last night, when I was coming up through Siena, somebody worked two very strange spells somewhere ahead of me."

"Tonino?" Paolo said eagerly.

Chrestomanci shook his head. "The first one was definitely Angelica. She has what you might call an individual style. But the other one baffled me. Do you think your brother is capable of working anything strong enough to get through an enchanter's spells? Angelica did it through sheer weirdness. Could Tonino, do you think?"

"I shouldn't think so," said Paolo. "He doesn't know many

spells, but he always gets them right and they work—"

"Then it remains a mystery," said Chrestomanci. He sighed. Paolo thought he looked tired.

"Thanks," he said, and slipped off, carefully thinking careless thoughts about what he would do now school was closed. He did not want anyone to notice what he meant to do.

He slipped through the coach-house, past the crumpled horses and coachman, past the coach, and opened the little door in the wall at the back. He was half through it, when Rosa said doubtfully, at the front of the coach-house, "Paolo? Are you in there?"

No, I'm not, Paolo thought, and shut the little door after him as gently as he knew how. Then he ran.

By this time, there were hardly any soldiers in the streets, and hardly anyone else either. Paolo ran past yellow houses, heavily shuttered, in a quiet broken by the uneasy ringing of bells. From time to time, he thought he could hear a dull, distant noise – a sort of booming, with a clatter in its midst. Wherever the houses opened out and Paolo could see the hills, he saw soldiers – not as soldiers, but as crawling, twinkling lines, winding upwards – and some puffs of smoke. He knew Chrestomanci was right. The fighting was very near.

He was the only person about in the Via Cantello. The Casa Petrocchi was as shuttered and barred as the Casa Montana. And their Angel was covered with bird-lime too. Like the Montanas, they had stopped making spells. Which showed, thought Paolo, that Chrestomanci was right about

Angelica too. He was much encouraged by that as he hammered on the rough old gate.

There was no sound from inside, but, after a second or so, a white cat jumped to the top of the gate, and crouched in the gap under the archway, looking down with eyes even bluer than Paolo's.

Those eyes reminded Paolo that his own eyes were likely to give him away. He did not think he dared disguise them with a spell, in case the Petrocchis noticed. So he swallowed, told himself that he had to find the one person who was likely to help him look for Tonino, and said to the cat, "Renata. Could I speak to Renata?"

The white cat stared. Maybe it made some remark. Then it jumped down inside the Casa, leaving Paolo with an uncomfortable feeling that it knew who he was. But he waited. Before he had quite decided to go away again, the peephole was unlatched. To his relief, it was Renata's pointed face that looked through the bars at him.

"Whoops!" she said. "I see why Vittoria fetched *me*. What a relief you came!"

"Come and help find Tonino and Angelica," said Paolo. "Nobody will listen."

"Ung." Renata pulled a strip of her red hair into her mouth and bit it. "We're forbidden to go out. Think of an excuse."

"Your teacher's ill and scared of the war and wants us to sit with her," said Paolo.

"That might do," said Renata. "Come in while I ask."

Paolo heard the gate being unbarred. "Her name's Mrs Grimaldi," Renata whispered, holding the gate open for him. "She lives in the Via Sant' Angelo and she's ever so ugly, in case they ask. Come in."

Considerably to his amazement, Paolo entered the Casa Petrocchi, and was even more amazed not to be particularly frightened. He felt as if he was about to do an exam, keyed up, and knowing he was in for it, but that was all.

He saw a yard and a gallery so like his own that he could almost have believed he had been magically whisked back home. There were differences, of course. The gallery railings were fancy wrought-iron, with iron leopards in them at intervals. The cats that sat sunning themselves on the water butts were mostly ginger or tabby – whereas in the Casa Montana, Benvenuto had left his mark, and the cats were either black or black and white. And there was a gush of smell from the kitchen – frying onions – the like of which Paolo had not smelt since Lucia cast her unlucky spell.

"Mother!" shouted Renata.

But the first person who appeared was Marco. Marco was galloping down the steps from the gallery with a pair of long shiny boots in one hand, and a crumpled red uniform over his arm. "Mother!" Marco bellowed, in the free and easy way people always bellow for their mothers. "Mother! There's moth in my uniform! Who took the spell out of it?"

"Stupid!" Renata said to him. "We put every single spell

away last night." And she said to Paolo, "That's my brother Marco."

Marco turned indignantly to Renata. "But moths take months—!" And he saw Paolo. It was hard to tell which of them was more dismayed.

At that moment, a red-haired, worried-looking lady came across the yard, carrying a little boy. The baby had black hair and the same bulging forehead as Angelica. "I don't know, Marco," she said. "Get Rosa to mend it. What is it, Renata?"

Marco interrupted. "Rosa," he said, looking fixedly at Paolo, "is with her *sister*. Who's your friend, Renata?"

Paolo could not resist. "I'm Paolo Andretti," he said wickedly. Marco rewarded him with a look which dared him to say another word.

Renata was relieved, because she now knew what to call Paolo. "Paolo wants me to come and help look after Mrs Grimaldi. She's ill in bed, Mother."

Paolo could see by the way Marco's eyes went first wide and then almost to slits, that Marco was extremely alarmed by this and determined to stop Renata. But Paolo could not see how Marco could do anything. He could not give away that he knew who Paolo was without giving away himself and Rosa too. It made him want to laugh.

"Oh poor Mrs Grimaldi!" said Mrs Petrocchi. "But, Renata, I don't think—"

"Doesn't Mrs Grimaldi realise there's a war on?" Marco said. "Did Paolo tell you she was ill?"

"Yes," Paolo said glibly. "My mother's great friends with Mrs Grimaldi. She's sorry for her because she's so ugly."

"And of course she knows about the war." Renata said. "I kept telling you, Marco, how she dives under her desk if she hears a bang. She's scared stiff of guns."

"And it's all been too much for her, Mother says," Paolo added artistically.

Marco tried another tack. "But why does Mrs Grimaldi want *you*, Renata? Since when have you been teacher's pet?"

Renata, who was obviously as quick as Paolo, said, "Oh, I'm not. She just wants me to amuse her with some spells—"

At this, Mrs Petrocchi and Marco said, "You're not to use spells! Angelica—"

"—but of course I won't," Renata continued smoothly. "I'll just sing songs. She likes me to sing. And Paolo's going to read to her out of the Bible. Do say we can go, Mother. She's lying in bed all on her own."

"Well—" said Mrs Petrocchi.

"The streets aren't safe," said Marco.

"There was no one about at all," Paolo said, giving Marco a look to make him watch it. Two could play at that.

"Mother," said Renata, "you *are* going to mend Marco's uniform, aren't you?"

"Yes, yes, of course," said Mrs Petrocchi.

Renata at once took this as permission to go with Paolo. "Come on, Paolo," she said, and raced under Marco's nose to what was obviously the coach-house. Paolo whizzed after her.

Marco, however, was not defeated. Before Renata's hand was on the latch of the big door, an obvious uncle was leaning over the gallery. "Renata! Be a good girl and find me my tobacco." An obvious aunt shot out of the kitchen. She looked like Aunt Gina with red hair, and she hooted in the same way. "Renata! Have you taken my good knife?" Two young cousins shot out of another door. "Renata, you said you'd play dressing-up!" and Mrs Petrocchi, looking anxious and undecided, was holding the baby boy out, saying, "Renata, you'll have to mind Roberto while I'm sewing."

"I can't stop now!" Renata shouted back. "Poor Mrs Grimaldi!" She wrenched open the big door and pushed Paolo inside. "What's going on?" she whispered.

It was obvious to Paolo what was going on. It was so like the Casa Montana. Marco had broadcast – not an alarm, because he dared not – a sort of general uneasiness about Renata. "Marco's trying to stop us," he said.

"I know *that*," Renata said, hurrying him past the sleek Petrocchi coach and – to Paolo's interest – past four black cardboard horses as crumpled and muddy as the Casa Montana ones. "*Why* is he? How does he know?"

Behind them was a perfect clamour of Petrocchi voices, all wanting Renata. "He just does," Paolo said. "Be quick!"

The small door to the street had a big stiff key. Renata took it in both hands and struggled to turn it. "Does he know *you*?" she said sharply.

Like an answer, Marco's voice sounded from behind the

coach. "Renata!" Then, much more softly, "Paolo – Paolo Montana, come here!"

The door came open. "Run, if you're coming!" Paolo said. They shot out into the street, both running hard. Marco came to the door and shouted something, but he did not seem to be following. Nevertheless, Paolo kept on running, which forced Renata to run too. He did not want to talk. He wanted to absorb the shock of Marco. Marco Andretti was really Marco Petrocchi – he must be Guido's eldest son! Rosa Montana and Marco Petrocchi. How did they do it? How ever did they *manage* it? he kept wondering. And also – more soberly – How ever will they get away with it?

"All right. That will do," Renata panted. By this time they had crossed the Corso and were down beside the river, trotting along empty quaysides towards the New Bridge. Renata slowed down, and Paolo did too, quite breathless. "Now," she said, "tell me how Marco knew you, or I won't come a step further."

Paolo looked at her warily. He had already discovered that Renata was, as Aunt Gina would say, sharp enough to cut herself, and he did not like the way she was looking at him. "He saw me at the Palace of course," Paolo said.

"No he didn't," said Renata. "He drove the coach. He knows your name *and* he knows why you came, doesn't he? How?"

"I think he must have been standing behind us on the Art Gallery steps, and we didn't see him in the fog," said Paolo.

Renata's shrewd eyes continued the look Paolo did not like.

"Good try," she said. Paolo tried to break off the look by turning and sauntering on along the quays. Renata followed him, saying, "And I was meant to get all embarrassed and not ask any more. You're sharp enough to cut yourself, Mr Montana. But what a pity. Marco wasn't in the fight. They wanted him for the single combat, that's how I know, and he wasn't there, so Papa had to do it. And I can tell that you don't want me to know how Marco knows you. And I can tell Marco doesn't, or he'd have stopped me going by saying who you were. So—"

"You're the one who's going to cut yourself," Paolo said over his shoulder, "by being too clever. I don't know how Marco knew me, but he was being kind not say—" He stopped. He sniffed. He was level with an alleyway, where a peeling blue house bulged out on to the jetty. Paolo felt the air round that alley with a sense he hardly knew he had, inborn over generations of spellmaking. A spell had been set here – a strong spell, not long ago.

Renata came up behind. "You're not going to wriggle out—" She stopped too. "Someone made a spell here!"

"Was it Angelica? Can you tell?" Paolo asked.

"Why?" said Renata.

Paolo told her what Chrestomanci had said. Her face went red, and she prodded with her toe at a mooring-chain in the path. "Individual style!" she said. "Him and his jokes! It's not

Angelica's fault. She was born that way. And it's not everyone who can get a spell to work by doing everything wrong. I think she's a sort of back-to-front genius, and I told the Duchess of Caprona so when she laughed, too!"

"But is the spell hers?" asked Paolo. He could hear gunfire, from somewhere down the river, mixed with the dull booming from the hills. It was a blunt, bonking *clomp, clomp*, like a giant chopping wood. His head went up to listen as he said, "I know it's not Tonino. His feel careful."

"No," said Renata, and her head was up too. "It's a bit stale, isn't it? And it doesn't feel very nice. The war sounds awfully close. I think we ought to get off the quays."

She was probably right. Paolo hesitated. He was sure they were hot on the trail. The stale spell had a slight sick feeling to it, which reminded him of the message in the yard last night.

And while he hesitated, the war seemed suddenly right on top of them. It was deafening, brazen, horrible. Paolo thought of someone holding one end of an acre of sheet metal and flapping it, or of gigantic alarm clocks. But that did not do justice to the noise. Nor did it account for some huge metallic screeches. He and Renata ducked and put their hands to their ears, and enormous things whirled above them. They went on, whatever they were, out above the river. Paolo and Renata crouched on the quay, staring at them.

They flapped across in a group – there were at least eight of them – gonging and screeching. Paolo thought first of flying machines and then of the Montana winged horse. There seemed to be legs dangling beneath the great black bodies, and their metal wings were whirling furiously. Some of them were not flying so well. One lost height, despite madly clanging with its wings, and dropped into the river with a splash that threw water all over the New Bridge and spattered Renata and Paolo. Another one lost height and whirled its iron tail for balance. Paolo recognised it as one of the iron griffins from the Piazza Nuova, as it, too, fell into a spout of water.

Renata began to laugh. "Now that *is* Angelica!" she said. "I'd know her spells anywhere."

They leapt up and raced for the long flight of stairs up to the Piazza Nuova. The din from the griffins was still drowning all but the nearest gunfire. Renata and Paolo ran up the steps, turning round at every landing to see what was happening to the rest of the griffins. Two more came down in the river. A further two plunged into the gardens of rich villas. But the last two were going well. When Paolo next looked, they seemed to be struggling to gain altitude in order to get over the hills beyond the Palace. The distant clanging was fast and furious, and the metal wings a blur.

Paolo and Renata turned and climbed again.

"What is it? A call for help?" panted Paolo.

"Must be," gasped Renata. "Angelica's spells – always – mad kind of reasonableness."

An echoing clang brought them whirling round. Another griffin was down, but they did not see where. Fascinated, they watched the efforts of the last one. It had now reached the marble front of the Duke's Palace, and it was not high enough to clear it. The griffin seemed to know. It put out its claws and seemed to be clutching at the zig-zag marble battlements. But that did no good. They saw it, a distant black blot, go sliding down the coloured marble facade – they could even hear the grinding – down and down, until it crashed on to the roof of the marble gateway, where it drooped and lay still. Above it, even from here, they could see two long lines of scratches, all down the front of the Palace.

"Wow!" said Paolo.

He and Renata climbed up into the strangely bare Piazza Nuova. It was now nothing but a big paved platform surrounded by a low wall. At intervals round the wall were the snapped-off stumps of the griffins' pedestals, each with a broken green or crimson plaque lying beside it. In the middle, what had been a tangled griffin-fountain was now a jet of water from a broken pipe.

"Just look at all these spells she's broken!" exclaimed Renata. "I didn't think she could do anything this strong!"

Paolo looked across at the scratched Palace, rather enviously. There were spells in the marble to stop that kind of thing. Angelica must have broken them all. The odd thing was that he could not feel the spell. The Piazza Nuova ought to have reeked of magic, but it just felt empty. He stared round, puzzled. And there, trotting slowly and wearily along the low wall, was a familiar brown shape with a trailing bush of a tail.

"Benvenuto!" he said.

For a moment, it looked as if Benvenuto was going to walk straight past Paolo, as he so often did. But that must have been because he was tired. He stopped. He glared urgently at Paolo. Then he carefully opened his mouth and spat out a small folded scrap of paper. After that, he lay down and lost interest in the world. Paolo could see his brown sides heaving when he picked up the paper.

Renata looked over Paolo's shoulder as Paolo – rather disgustedly, because it was wet – unfolded the paper. The writing was definitely Tonino's, though it was far too small. And, though Paolo did not know it, not much of Tonino's message had survived. He and Renata read:

ords to Angel on Angel over

It was small wonder that Paolo and Renata misunderstood. From the Piazza Nuova, now the griffins were gone, an Angel was clearly visible. It stood, golden and serene, guarding a Caprona which was already surrounded in the smoke from gunfire, on top of the great dome of the Cathedral.

"Do you think we can get up there?" said Paolo.

Renata's face was white. "We'd better try. But I warn you, I'm no good at heights."

They hurried down among the red roofs and golden walls, leaving Benvenuto asleep on the wall. After a while, Benvenuto picked himself up and trotted away, restored. It took more than a few ill-aimed rifles to finish Benvenuto.

When Paolo and Renata reached the cobbled square in front of the Cathedral, the great bell in the bell-tower beside it was tolling. People were gathering into the church to pray for Caprona, and the Archbishop of Caprona himself was standing by the door blessing everyone who entered. Renata and Paolo joined the line. It seemed the easiest way to get in. They had nearly reached the door, when Marco dashed into the square towing Rosa. Rosa saw Renata's hair and pointed. She was too blown to speak. Marco grinned. "Your spell wins," he said.

CHAPTER FOURTEEN

✳

*T*he warm pocket holding Tonino swayed and swooped as the Duke stood up. "Of course I smoked a cigar," he said to the Duchess, injured. "Anyone would smoke a cigar, if they found they'd declared war without knowing they had, and knew they were bound to be beaten." His voice came rumbling to Tonino's ears through his body, more than from outside.

"I've told you it's bad for your health," said the Duchess. "Where are you going?"

"Me? Oh," said the Duke. The pockets swooped, then swooped again, as he climbed the steps to the door. "Off to the kitchens. I feel peckish."

"You could send for food," said the Duchess, but she did not sound displeased. Tonino knew she had guessed they had been in the study all along and wanted the Duke out of it while she found them.

He heard the door shut. The pocket swung rhythmically as the Duke walked. It was not too bad once Tonino was used to it. It was a large pocket. There was almost room in it for Tonino, and the Duke's lighter, and his handkerchief, and another cigar, and some string, and some money, and a rosary, and some dice. Tonino made himself comfortable with the handkerchief as a cushion and wished the Duke would not keep patting at him to see if he was there.

"Are you all right in there?" the Duke rumbled at last. "Nobody about. You can stick your heads out. I thought of the kitchens because you didn't seem to have had any breakfast."

"You are kind," Angelica's voice came faintly. Tonino worked himself to his feet and put his head out under the flap of the pocket. He still could not see Angelica – the Duke's generous middle was in the way – but he heard her say, "You keep rather a lot of things in your pockets, don't you? Do you happen to know what I've got stuck to my foot?"

"Er – toffee, I suspect," said the Duke. "Please oblige me by eating it."

"Thanks," Angelica said doubtfully.

"I say," said Tonino. "Why didn't the Duchess know we were in your pockets? She could smell us before."

The Duke's loud laugh rumbled through him. The gilded wall Tonino could see began to jolt upward, and upward, and upward. The Duke was walking downstairs. "Cigars, lad!" the Duke said. "Why do you think I smoke them? She can't smell anything through them, and she hates that. She tried setting a spell on me to make me stop once, but I got so bad-tempered she had to take it off."

"Excuse me, sir," came Angelica's voice from the other side of the Duke. "Won't someone notice if you walk downstairs talking to yourself?"

The Duke laughed again. "Not a soul! I talk to myself all the time – and laugh, too, if something amuses me. They all think I'm potty anyway. Now, have you two thought of a way to get you out of here? The safest way would be to fetch your families here. Then I could hand you over in secret, and she'd be none the wiser."

"Can't you just send for them?" Tonino suggested. "Say you need them to help in the war."

"She'd smell a rat," said the Duke. "She says your war-charms are all washed-up anyway. Think of something that's nothing to do with the war."

"Special effects for another pantomime," Tonino suggested, rather hopelessly. But he could see that even the Duke was not likely to produce a play while Caprona was being invaded.

"I know," said Angelica. "I shall cast a spell."

"No!" said Tonino. "Anything might happen!"

"That doesn't matter," said Angelica. "My family would know it's me, and they'd come here like a shot."

"But you might turn the Duke green!" said Tonino.

"I really wouldn't mind," the Duke put in mildly.

He came to the bottom of the stairs and went with long, charging strides through rooms and corridors of the Palace. Angelica and Tonino each held on to an edge of their pockets and shouted arguments round him.

"But you could help me," said Angelica, "and your part would go right. Suppose we made it a calling-charm to fetch all the rats and mice in Caprona to the Palace. If you did the calling, we'd fetch something."

"Yes, but what would it be?" said Tonino.

"We could make it in honour of Benvenuto," shouted Angelica, hoping to please him.

But Tonino thought of Benvenuto lying somewhere on a Palace roof and became more obstinate than ever. He shouted that he was not going to do anything so disrespectful.

"Are you telling me you can't do a calling-spell?" shrieked Angelica. "Even my baby brother—"

They were shouting so loudly that the Duke had to tell them to shush twice. The military man hurrying up to the Duke stared slightly. "No need to stare, Major," the Duke said to him. "I said Shush and I meant Shush. Your boots squeak. What is it?"

"I'm afraid the forces of Caprona are in retreat in the south, Your Grace," said the soldier. "And our coastal batteries have fallen to the Pisan fleet."

Both pockets drooped as the Duke's shoulders slumped. "Thank you," he said. "Report to me personally next time you have news." The Major saluted and went, glancing at the Duke once or twice over his shoulder. The Duke sighed. "There goes another one who thinks I'm mad. Didn't you two say you were the only ones who knew where to find the words to the *Angel*?"

Tonino and Angelica put their heads out of his pockets again. "Yes," they said.

"Then," said the Duke, "will you please agree on a spell. You really must get out and get those words while there's still some of Caprona left."

"All right," said Tonino. "Let's call mice." He had not seen it was so urgent.

So the Duke stood in a wide window-bay and lit the cigar stub from under Angelica with the lighter from under Tonino, to cover up the spell. Tonino leant out of his pocket and sang, slowly and carefully, the only calling-spell he knew.

Angelica stood in the other pocket with her arms upraised and spoke, quickly, confidently and – quite certainly – wrong. Afterwards, she swore it was because she nearly laughed.

Another man approached. Tonino thought it was one of the courtiers who had watched the puppet show, but he was never sure, because the Duke flipped his pocket-flaps down over their heads and began singing himself.

"Merrily his music ringing,
See an Angel cometh singing…"

roared the Duke. Even Angelica did not sing so much out of
tune. Tonino had the greatest difficulty in keeping up his own
song. And it was certainly around then that the spell seemed to
go wrong. Tonino had the sudden feeling that his words were
pulling a great weight.

The Duke broke off his abominable singing to say, "Ah,
Pollio, there's nothing like a good song while Caprona burns!
Nero did it, and now me."

"Yes, Your Grace," the man said feebly. They heard him
scuttle away.

"And he's *sure* I'm mad," said the Duke. "Finished?"

Just then, Tonino's words came loose, with a sort of jerk,
and he knew the spell had worked in some way or another.
"Yes," he said.

But nothing seemed to happen. The Duke said
philosophically that it would take a mouse quite a while to run
from the Corso to the Palace, and strode on to the kitchens.
They thought he was mad there, too, Tonino could tell. The
Duke asked for two bread rolls and two pats of butter and
solemnly put one into each pocket. No doubt they thought he
was madder still when he remarked to no one: "There's a cigar
cutter in my right pocket that spreads butter quite well."

"Indeed, Your Grace?" they heard someone say dubiously.

Just then, someone rushed in screaming about the griffins

from the Piazza Nuova. They were flying across the river, straight for the Palace. There was a general panic. Everyone screamed and yammered and said it was an omen of defeat. Then someone else rushed in yelling that one griffin had actually reached the Palace and was sliding down the marble front. There was more outcry. The next thing, everyone said, the great gold Angel from the Cathedral would fly away too.

Tonino was taking advantage of the confusion to bash a piece off his roll with the Duke's lighter, when the Duke bellowed, "*Nonsense!*" There was sudden quiet. Tonino dared not move, because everyone was certainly looking at the Duke.

"Don't you see?" said the Duke. "It's just an enemy trick. But we in Caprona don't frighten that easily, do we? Here – you – go and fetch the Montanas. And you go and get the Petrocchis. Tell them it's urgent. Tell as many of them to come as possible. I shall be in the North gallery." And he went striding off there, while Angelica and Tonino jigged against bread and tried not to tread in the butter.

When he got to the gallery, the Duke sat down on a window-seat. Angelica and Tonino stood half out of his pockets and managed to eat their bread and butter. The Duke amiably handed the cigar-cutter from one to the other and, in between whiles, seemed lost in thought, staring at the white puffs of shells bursting on the hills behind Caprona.

Angelica was inclined to be smug. "I told you," she said to Tonino, "my spells always work."

"Iron griffins," said Tonino, "aren't mice."

"No, but I've never done anything as big as that before," said Angelica. "I'm glad it didn't knock the Palace down."

The Duke said gloomily, "The guns of Pisa are going to do that soon. I can see gunboats on the river, and I'm sure they aren't ours. I wish your families would be quick."

But it was half an hour before a polite footman came up to the Duke, causing him to flip his pocket-flaps down and scatter buttery crumbs in all directions.

"Your Grace, members of the Montana and Petrocchi families are awaiting you in the Large Reception Saloon."

"Good!" said the Duke. He leapt up and ran so fast that Tonino and Angelica had to brace their feet on the seams of his pockets and hang on hard to the edges. They lost their footing several times, even though the Duke tried to help them by holding his pockets as he ran. They felt him clatter to a stop. "Blast!" he said. "This is always happening!"

"What?" asked Tonino breathlessly. He felt jerked out of shape.

"They've told me the wrong room!" said the Duke and set off again on another swaying, jolting run. They felt him dive forward through a doorway. His pockets swung. Then they swung the other way as he slid and stopped. "Lucrezia, this is too bad! Is this why you always tell me the wrong room?"

"My lord," came the coldest voice of the Duchess from some way off, "I can't answer for the slackness of the footmen. What is the matter?"

"This," said the Duke. "These—" They felt him shaking. "Those were the Montanas and the Petrocchis, weren't they? Don't fob me off, Lucrezia. I sent for them. I know."

"And what if they were?" said the Duchess, rather nearer. "Do you wish to join them, my lord?"

They felt the Duke backing away. "No. No indeed! My dear, your will is always my pleasure. I – I just want to know why. They only came about some griffins."

The Duchess's voice moved away again as she answered. "Because, if you must know, Antonio Montana recognised me."

"But – but—" said the Duke, laughing uneasily, "everyone knows you, my dear. You're the Duchess of Caprona."

"I mean, he recognised me for what I am," said the Duchess from the distance. The sound of a door shutting followed.

"Look!" said the Duke in a shaky whisper. "Just look!" While he was still saying it, Angelica and Tonino were bracing their feet on the seams of his pockets and pushing their heads out from under the flaps.

They saw the same polished room where they had once waited and eaten cakes, the same gilded chairs and angelic ceiling. But this time the polished floor was littered with puppets. Puppets lay all over it, limp grotesque things, scattered this way and that as people might lie if they had suddenly fallen. They were in two groups. Otherwise there was no way of telling which puppet was who. There were Punches, Judys, Hangmen, Sausage-men, Policemen, and an odd Devil or so, over and over again. From the numbers, it looked as if both families had realised that Tonino and Angelica were behind the mysterious griffins and had sent nearly every grown-up in the Casas.

Tonino could not speak. Angelica said, "That hateful woman! Her mind seems to run on puppets."

"She sees people that way," the Duke said miserably. "I'm sorry, both of you. She's been too many for us. Terrible female! I can't think why I married her – but I suppose that was a spell too."

"Do you think she suspects you've got us?" Tonino asked. "She must be wondering where we are."

"Maybe, maybe," said the Duke. He marched up and down the room, while they leant out of his pockets and looked down at the crowd of strewn floppy puppets. "She doesn't care now, of course," he said. "She's done for both families anyway. Oh, I am a fool!"

"It's not your fault," said Angelica.

"Oh, but it *is*," said the Duke. "I never show the slightest resolution. I always take the easiest way— What is it?" Darkness descended as he flipped his pocket-flaps down.

"Your Grace," said the Major whose boots squeaked, "the Pisan fleet is landing men down beyond the New Quays. And our troops to the south are being rolled back into the suburbs."

They felt the Duke droop. "Almost done, in fact," he said. "Thanks— No, wait. Major! Could you be a good fellow and go to the stables and order out my coach? The lackeys have all run away, you know. Ask for it at the door in five minutes."

"But, Your Grace—" said the Major.

"I intend to go down into the city and speak with the people," said the Duke. "Give them what's-it-called. Moral support."

"A very fine aim, sir," said the Major, with a great deal more warmth. "In five minutes, sir." His boots went squeaking swiftly off.

"Did you hear that?" said the Duke. "He called me 'sir'! Poor fellow. I told him a set of whoppers and he couldn't take his eyes off all those puppets, but he called me 'sir', and he'll get that coach and he won't tell *her*. Cardboard box!"

The hangings whipped by as the Duke charged through a doorway into another room. This one had a long table down the middle. "Ah!" said the Duke, and charged towards a stack of boxes by the wall. The boxes proved to have wine-glasses in them, which the Duke proceeded feverishly to unload on to the table.

"I don't understand," Tonino said.

"Box," said the Duke. "We can't leave your families behind, for her to revenge herself on. I'm going to be resolute for once. I'm going to get in the coach and go, and dare her to stop me." So saying, he stormed back to the reception room with the empty box and knelt down to collect the puppets. Angelica was bounced on the floor as his coat swung. "Sorry," said the Duke.

"Pick them up gently," said Tonino. "It hurts if you don't."

Tenderly and hastily, using both hands for each puppet, the Duke packed the puppets in layers in the cardboard box. In the process, Montanas got very thoroughly mixed with Petrocchis, but there was no way of preventing that. All three of them were expecting the Duchess to come in any moment. The Duke kept looking nervously round and then muttering to himself "Resolute!" He was still muttering it when he set off awkwardly carrying the cardboard box in his arms. "Funny to think," he remarked, "that I'm carrying almost every spell-maker in Caprona at the moment."

Boots squeaked towards them. "Your coach is waiting, sir," said the voice of the Major.

"Resolute," said the Duke. "I mean, thank you. I shall think of you in heaven, Major, since I'm sure that's where most of us are going soon. Meanwhile, can you do two more things for me?"

"Sir?" said the Major alertly.

"First, when you think of the Angel of Caprona, what do you think of?"

"The song or the figure, sir?" the Major asked, more wary now than alert.

"The figure."

"Why—" The Major was becoming sure that the Duke was mad again. "I – I think of the golden Angel on the Cathedral, Your Grace."

"Good man!" the Duke cried out. "So do I! The other

thing is, can you take this box and stow it in my coach for me?" Neither Tonino nor Angelica could resist peeping out to see how the Major took this request. Unfortunately, his face was hidden behind the box as the Duke thrust it at him. They felt they had missed a rare sight. "If anyone asks," the Duke said, "it's gifts for the war-weary people."

"Yes, Your Grace." The Major sounded amused and indulgent, humouring the Duke in his madness, but they heard his boots squeaking briskly off.

"Thank the lord!" said the Duke. "I'm not going to be caught with them. I can feel her coming."

Thanks to the Duke's charging run, it was some minutes before the Duchess caught up with them. Tonino, squinting out under the flap, could see the great marble entrance hall when the Duke skidded to a stop. He dropped the flap hastily when he heard the cold voice of the Duchess. She sounded out of breath but triumphant.

"The enemy is by the New Bridge, my lord. You'll be killed if you go out now."

"And I'll be killed if I stay here too," said the Duke. He waited for the Duchess to deny this, but she said nothing. They heard the Duke swallow. But his resolution held. "I'm going," he said, a mite squeakily, "to drive down among my people and comfort their remaining hours."

"Sentimental fool," said the Duchess. She was not angry. It was what she thought the Duke was.

This made the Duke bluster. "I may not be a good ruler,"

he said, "but this is what a good ruler should do. I shall – I shall pat the heads of children and join in the singing of the choir."

The Duchess laughed. "And much good may it do you, particularly if you sing," she said. "Very well. You can get killed down there instead of up here. Run along and pat heads."

"Thank you, my dear," the Duke said humbly. He surged forward again, *thump, thump, thump,* down marble steps. They heard the sound of hooves on gravel and felt the Duke shaking. "Let's go, Carlo," he said. "What is it? What are you pointing—? Oh yes. So it is a griffin. How remarkable. Drive on, can't you?" He surged upwards. Coach springs creaked and a door clapped shut. The Duke surged down. They heard him say "Oh good!" as he sat, and the rather-too-familiar sound of cardboard being hit, as he patted the box on the seat beside him. Then the coach started, with a shrilling of wheels on gravel and a battering of hooves. They felt the Duke sigh with relief. It made them bounce. "You can come out now," said the Duke.

They climbed cautiously out on to his wide knees. The Duke kindly moved over to the window so that they could see out. And the first thing that met their eyes was an iron griffin, very crumpled and bent, lying in quite a large crater in the Palace yard.

"You know," said the Duke, "if my Palace wasn't going to be broken up anyway by Pisans, or Sienese, or Florentines, I'd get damages off you two. The other griffin has scraped two great ditches all down my facade." He laughed and patted at his glossy face with his handkerchief. He was still very nervous.

As the coach rolled out of the yard on to the road, they heard gunfire. Some of it sounded near, a rattle of shots from below by the river. Most of it was far and huge, a long grumble from the hills. The bangs were so close together that the sound was nearly continuous, but every so often, out of the grumble, came a very much nearer *clap-clap-clap*. It made all three of them jump each time.

"We *are* taking a pounding," the Duke said unhappily.

The coach slowed down. They could hear the prim voice of the coachman among the other noise. "I fear the New Bridge is under fire, Your Grace. Where exactly are we bound?"

The Duke pushed down the window. The noise doubled. "The Cathedral. Go upriver and see if we can cross by the Old Bridge." He pushed the window shut. "Phew! I don't envy Carlo up there on the box!"

"Why are we going to the Cathedral?" Angelica asked anxiously. "We want to look at the Angels on our Casas."

"No," said the Duke. "She'll have thought of those. That's why I asked the Major. It seems to me that the one place where those words are always safe and always invisible *must* be on the Cathedral Angel. You think of it at once, but it's up there and far away, so you forget it."

"But it's *miles* up!" said Angelica.

"It's got a scroll, though," said Tonino. "And the scroll

looks to be more unrolled than the ones on our Angels."

"I'm afraid it's bound to be about the only place she might have forgotten," said the Duke.

They rattled along briskly, except for one place, where there was a shell crater in the road. Somehow, Carlo got them round it.

"Good man, Carlo," said the Duke. "About the one good man she hasn't got rid of."

The noise diminished a little as the coach went down to the river and the Piazza Martia – at least, Angelica and Tonino guessed that was where it was; they found they were too small to see any great distance. They could tell they were on the Old Bridge, by the rumble under the wheels and the little shuttered houses on either side. The Duke several times craned round, whistled and shook his head, but they could not see why. They recognised the Cathedral, when the coach wheeled towards it across the cobbles, because it was so huge and snowy white. Its great bell was still tolling. A large crowd, mostly of women and children, was slowly moving towards its door. As the coach drew up, it was near enough for Tonino and Angelica to see the Archbishop of Caprona in his spreading robes, standing at the door, sprinkling each person with holy water and murmuring a blessing.

"Now there's a brave man," said the Duke. "I wish I could do as well. Look, I'll pop you two out of this door and then get out of the other one and keep everyone busy while you get up on the dome. Will that do?" He had the door nearest the Cathedral open as he spoke.

Tonino and Angelica felt lost and helpless. "But what shall we do?"

"Climb up there and read out those words," said the Duke. He leant down, encircled them with his warm wet hands, and planted them out on the cold cobbles. They stood shivering under the vast hoop of the coach-wheel. "Be sensible," he whispered down to them. "If I ask the Archbishop to put up ladders, she'll guess." That of course was quite true. They heard him surge to the other door and that door crash open.

"He always does everything so *hugely*," Angelica said.

"People of Caprona!" shouted the Duke. "I've come here to be with you in your hour of sorrow. Believe me, I didn't choose what has happened today—"

There was a mutter from the crowd, even a scatter of cheering. "He's doing it quite well," said Angelica.

"We'd better do our bit," said Tonino. "There's only us left now."

Chapter Fifteen

*T*onino and Angelica pattered over to the vast marble cliff of the Cathedral and doubtfully approached a long, sloping buttress. That was the only thing they could see which gave them some chance of climbing up. Once they were close to it, they saw it was not difficult at all. The marble looked smooth, but, to people as small as they were, it was rough enough to give a grip to their hands and feet.

They went up like monkeys, with the cold air reviving them. The truth was that, though they had had an eventful morning, it had also been a restful and stuffy one. They were full of energy and they weighed no more than a few ounces.

They were scarcely panting as they scampered up the long cold slope of the lowest dome. But there the rest of the Cathedral rose before them, a complicated glacier of white and rose and green marble. They could not see the Angel at all.

Neither of them knew which way to climb next. They hung on to a golden cross and stared up. And there, brown-black hair and white fur hurtled up to them. Gold eyes glared and blue eyes gazed. A black nose and a pink nose dabbed at them.

"Benvenuto!" shouted Tonino. "Did you—?"

"Vittoria!" cried Angelica, and threw her arms round the neck of the white cat.

But the cats were hasty and very worried. Things tumbled into their heads, muddled, troubled things about Paolo and Renata, Marco and Rosa. Would Tonino and Angelica please come on, and *hurry*!

They began an upward scamper which they would never have believed possible. With the cats to guide them, they raced up long lead groins, and over rainbow buttresses, like dizzy bridges, to higher domes. Always the cats implored them to hurry, and always they were there if the footing was difficult. With his hand on Benvenuto's wiry back, Tonino went gaily up marble glacis and through tiny drain-holes hanging over huge drops, and raced up high curving surfaces, where the green marble ribs of a dome seemed as tall as a wall beside him. Even when they began the long toil up the slope of the great dome itself, neither of them was troubled. Once, Angelica stumbled and saved herself by catching hold of Vittoria's silky tail; and once Benvenuto took Tonino's red nightgown in his teeth and heaved him aside from a deep drain. But up here it was rounded and remote. Tonino felt as if he was on the surface of the moon, in spite of the pale winter sky overhead and the wind singing. The rumble of guns was almost beyond the scope of his small ears.

At last, they scrambled between fat marble pillars on to the platform at the very top of the dome. And there was the golden Angel above them. The Angel's tremendous feet rested on a golden pedestal rather higher than Tonino's normal height. There was a design round the pedestal, which Tonino absently took in, of golden leopards entwined with winged horses. But he was looking up beyond, to the Angel's flowing robes, the enormous wings outspread to a width of twenty feet or more, the huge hand high above his head, raised in blessing, and the other hand flung out against the sky, further away still, holding the great unrolled scroll. Far above that again, shone the Angel's vast and tranquil face, unheedingly beaming its blessing over Caprona.

"He's enormous!" Angelica said. "We'll never get up to that scroll, if we try all day!"

The cats, however, were nudging and hustling at them, to come to a place further round the platform. Wondering, they trotted round, almost under the Angel's scroll. And there was Paolo's head above the balustrade, with his hair blown back in a tuft and his face exceedingly pale. He had one arm clutched over the marble railing. The other stretched away downward. Tonino peered between the marble pillars to see why. And there was the miserable humped huddle of Renata hanging on to Paolo.

"But she's terrified of heights!" said Angelica. "How *did* she get this high?"

Vittoria told Angelica she was to get Renata up at once.

Angelica stuck her upper half out between the pillars. Being small certainly had its advantages. Distances which were mercilessly huge to Renata and Paolo were too far away to worry Angelica. The dome was like a whole small world to her.

Paolo said, carefully patient, "I can't hold on much longer. Do you think you can have another try?" The answer from Renata was a sobbing shudder.

"Renata!" shouted Angelica.

Renata's scared face turned slowly up. "Something's happened to my eyes now! You look tiny."

"I *am* tiny!" yelled Angelica.

"Both of them are!" Paolo said, staring at Tonino's head.

"Pull me up quick," said Renata. The size of Angelica and Tonino so worried Renata and Paolo that both of them forgot they were hundreds of feet in the air. Paolo heaved on Renata and Renata shoved at Paolo, and they scrambled over the marble rail in a second. But there, Renata looked up at the immense golden Angel and had an instant relapse. "Oh – oh!"

she wailed and sank down in a heap against the golden pedestal.

Tonino and Angelica huddled behind her. The warmth of climbing had worn off. They were feeling the wind keenly through their scanty nightshirts.

Benvenuto leapt across Renata to them. Something else had to be done, and done quickly.

Tonino went again and looked through the marble pillars, where the dome curved away and down like an ice-field with ribs of green and gold. There, coming into view over the curve, was a bright red uniform, making Marco's carroty hair look faded and sallow against it. The uniform went with Marco's hair even less well than the crimson he had worn as a coachman. Tonino knew who Marco was in that instant. But that bothered him less than seeing Marco flattened to the surface and looking backwards, which Tonino was sure was a mistake. Beyond Marco's boots, fair hair was wildly blowing. Rosa's flushed face came into sight.

"I'm all *right*. Look after yourself," Rosa said.

Benvenuto was beside Tonino. They were to come up quicker than that. It was important.

"Get Rosa and Marco up here quickly!" Tonino shrieked to Paolo. He did not know if he had caught the feeling from the cats or not, but he was sure Rosa and Marco were in danger.

Paolo went unwillingly to the railing and flinched at the height. "They've been following us and shouting the whole way," he said. "Get up here quickly!" he shouted.

"Thank you very much!" Marco shouted back. "Whose fault is it we're up here anyway?"

"Is Renata all right?" Rosa yelled.

Angelica and Tonino pushed themselves between the pillars. "Hurry up!" they screamed.

The sight of them worked on Rosa and Marco as it had done on Renata and Paolo. They stared at the two tiny figures, and got to their feet as they stared. Then, stooping over, with their hands hanging, they came racing up the last of the curve for a closer look. Marco tumbled over the rail and said, as he was pulling Rosa over, "I couldn't believe my eyes at first! We'd better do a growing-spell before—"

"Get down!" said Paolo. Benvenuto's message was so urgent that he had caught it too. Both cats were crouching, still and low, and even Benvenuto's flat ears were flattened. Rosa stooped down. Marco grudgingly went on one knee.

"Look here, Paolo—" he began.

A savage gale hit the dome. Freezing wind shrieked across the platform, howled in the spaces between the marble pillars, and scoured across the curve of the dome below. The Angel's wings thrummed with it. It brought stabs of rain and needles of ice, hurling so hard that Tonino was thrown flat on his face. He could hear ice rattling on the Angel and spitting on the dome. Paolo snatched him into shelter behind himself. Renata feebly scrabbled about until she found Angelica and dragged her into shelter by one arm. Marco and Rosa bowed over. It was quite clear that anyone climbing the dome would have been blown off.

The wind passed, wailing like a wolf. They raised their heads into the sun.

The Duchess was standing on the platform in front of them. She had melting ice winking and trickling from her hair and from every fold of her marble-grey dress. The smile on her waxy face was not pleasant.

"Oh no," she said. "The Angel is not going to help anyone this time. Did you think I'd forgotten?"

Marco and Rosa looked up at the Angel's golden arm holding the great scroll above them. If they had not understood before, they knew now. From their suddenly thoughtful faces, Tonino knew they were finding spells to use on the Duchess.

"Don't!" squeaked Angelica. "She's an enchantress!"

The Duchess's lips pursed in another unpleasant little smile. "More than that," she said. She pointed up at the Angel. "Let the words be removed from the scroll," she said.

There was a click from the huge golden statue, followed by a grating sound, as if a spring had been released. The arm holding the scroll began to move, gently and steadily downwards, making the slightest grinding noise as it moved. They could hear it easily, in spite of a sudden clatter of gunfire from the houses beyond the river. Downwards and inwards, travelled the Angel's arm, until it stopped with a small *clunk*. The scroll now hung, flashing in the sun, between them and the Duchess. There were large raised letters on it. *Angelus*, they saw. *Capronensi populo*. It was as if the Angel were holding it out for them to read.

"Exactly," said the Duchess, though Tonino thought, from the surprised arch of her eyebrows, that this was not at all what she expected. She pointed again at the scroll, with a long white finger like a white wax pencil. "Erase," she said. "Word by word."

Their heads all tipped anxiously as they looked at the lines of writing. The first word read *Carmen*. And, sure enough, the golden capital C was sinking slowly away into the metal background. Paolo moved. He had to do something. The Duchess glanced at him, a contemptuous flick of the eyebrows. Paolo found he was twisted to the spot, with jabbing cramp in both legs.

But he could still speak, and he remembered what Marco and Rosa had said last night. Without daring to draw breath, he screamed as loud as he could. "*Chrestomanci!*"

There was more wind. This was one keen blaring gust. And Chrestomanci was there, beyond Renata and the cats. There was so little room on the platform that Chrestomanci rocked, and quickly took hold of the marble balustrade. He was still in uniform, but it was muddy and he looked extremely tired.

The Duchess whirled round and pointed her long finger at him. "You! I misled you!"

"Oh you did," Chrestomanci said. If the Duchess had hoped to catch him off balance, she was too late. Chrestomanci was steady now. "You led me a proper wild-goose-chase," he said, and put out one hand, palm forwards, towards her pointing finger. The long finger bent and began dripping white, as if it were wax indeed. The Duchess stared at it, and then looked up at Chrestomanci almost imploringly. "No," Chrestomanci said, sounding very tired. "I think you've done enough harm. Take your true form, please." He beckoned at her, like someone sick of waiting.

Instantly, the Duchess's body was seething out of shape. Her arms gathered inwards. Her face lengthened, and yet still remained the same waxy, sardonic face. Whiskers sprang from her upper lip, and her eyes lit red, like bulging lamps. Her marble skirts turned white, billowed and gathered soapily to her ankles, revealing her feet as long pink claws. And all the time, she was shrinking. Two teeth appeared at the end of her lengthened white face. A naked pink tail, marked in rings like an earthworm, snaked from behind the soapy bundle of her skirts and lashed the marble floor angrily. She shrank again.

Finally a huge white rat with eyes like red marbles, leapt to the marble railing and crouched, chittering and glaring with its humped back twitching.

"The White Devil," said Chrestomanci, "which the Angel was sent to expel from Caprona. Right, Benvenuto and Vittoria. She's all yours. Make sure she never comes back."

Benvenuto and Vittoria were already creeping forward. Their tails swept about and their eyes stared. They sprang.

The rat sprang too, off the parapet with a squeal, and went racing away down the dome. Benvenuto raced with it, long and low, keeping just beside the pink whip of its tail. Vittoria raced the other side, a snowy sliver making the great rat look yellow, running at the rat's shoulder. They saw the rat turn and try to bite her. And then, suddenly, the three were joined by a dozen smaller rats, all running and squealing. They only saw them for an instant, before the whole group ran over the slope of the dome and disappeared.

"Her helpers from the Palace," said Chrestomanci.

"Will Vittoria be safe?" said Angelica.

"She's the best ratter in Caprona, isn't she?" said Chrestomanci. "Apart from Benvenuto, that is. And by the time the Devil and her friends get to the ground, they'll have every cat in Caprona after them. Now—"

Tonino found he was the right size again. He clung to Rosa's hand. Beyond Rosa, he could see Angelica, also the right size, shivering and pulling her flimsy blue dress down over her knees, before she grabbed for Marco's hand. The wind was far worse on a larger body. But what made Tonino grab at Rosa was not that. The dome was not world-sized any more. It was a white hummock wheeling in a grey-brown landscape. The hills round Caprona were pitilessly clear. He could see flashes of flame and running figures which seemed to be almost beside him, or just above him, as if the tiny white dome had reeled over on its side. Yet the houses of Caprona were immeasurably deep below, and the river seemed to stand up out of them. The New Bridge appeared almost overhead, suffused in clouds of smoke. Smoke rolled in the hills and swirled giddily out of the downside-upside houses beyond the Old Bridge, and, worst of all, the boom and clap, the rattle and yammer of guns was now nearly deafening. Tonino no longer wondered what had scared Renata and Paolo so. He felt as if he was spinning to his death.

He clung to Rosa's hand and looked desperately up at the Angel. That at least was still huge. The scroll, which it still held patiently towards them, was almost as big as the side of a house.

"—Now," said Chrestomanci, "the best thing you can do, all of you, is to sing those words, quickly."

"What? Me too?" said Angelica.

"Yes, all of you," said Chrestomanci.

They gathered, the six of them, against the marble parapet, facing the golden scroll, with the New Bridge behind them, and began, somewhat uncertainly, to fit those words to the tune of the *Angel of Caprona*. They matched like a glove. As soon as they realised this, everyone sang lustily. Angelica and Renata stopped shivering. Tonino let go of Rosa's hand, and Rosa put her arm over his shoulders instead. And they sang as if they had always known those words. It was only a version of the usual words in Latin, but it was what the tune had always asked for.

"Carmen pacis saeculare
Venit Angelus cantare,
Et deorsum pacem dare
  Capronensi populo.

Dabit pacem eternalem,
Sine morbo immortalem,
Sine pugna triumphalem,
  Capronensi populo.

En diabola albata
De Caprona expulsata,
Missa pax et virtus data
  Capronensi populo."

When they had finished, there was silence. There was not a sound from the hills, or the New Bridge, or the streets below. Every noise had stopped. So they were all the more startled at the tinny slithering with which the Angel slowly rolled up the scroll. The shining outstretched wings bent and settled against the Angel's golden shoulders, where the Angel gave them a shake to order the feathers. And that noise was not the sound of metal, but the softer rattling of real pinions. It brought with it a scent of such sweetness that there was a moment when they were not aware of anything else.

In that moment, the Angel was in flight. As the huge golden

wings passed over them, the scent came again and, with it, the sound of singing. It seemed like hundreds of voices, singing tune, harmony and descant to the *Angel of Caprona*. They had no idea if it was the Angel alone, or something else. They looked up and watched the golden figure wheel and soar and wheel, until it was only a golden glint in the sky. And there was still utter silence, except for the singing.

Rosa sighed. "I suppose we'd better climb down." Renata began to shiver again at the thought.

Chrestomanci sighed too. "Don't worry about that."

They were suddenly down again, on solid cobbles, in the Cathedral forecourt. The Cathedral was once more a great white building, the houses were high, the hills were away beyond, and the people surrounding them were anything but quiet. Everyone was running to where they could see the Angel, flashing in the sun as he soared. The Archbishop was in tears, and so was the Duke. They were wringing one another's hands beside the Duke's coach.

And Chrestomanci had brought them to earth in time to see another miracle. The coach began to work and bounce on its springs. Both doors burst open. Aunt Francesca squeezed out of one, and Guido Petrocchi fell out after her. From the other door tumbled Rinaldo and the red-haired Petrocchi aunt. After them came mingled Montanas and Petrocchis, more and more and more, until anyone could see that the coach could not possibly have held that number. People stopped crowding to see the Angel and crowded to look at the Duke's coach instead.

Rosa and Marco looked at one another and began to back away among the spectators. But Chrestomanci took them each by a shoulder. "It'll be all right," he said. "And if it isn't, I'll set you up in a spell-house in Venice."

Antonio disentangled himself from a Petrocchi uncle and hurried with Guido towards Tonino and Angelica. "Are you all right?" both of them said. "Was it you who fetched the griffins—?" They broke off to stare coldly at one another.

"Yes," said Tonino. "I'm sorry you were turned into puppets."

"She was too clever for us," said Angelica. "But be thankful you got your proper clothes back afterwards. Look at us. We—"

They were pulled apart then by aunts and cousins, fearing they were contaminating one another, and hurriedly given coats and sweaters by uncles. Paolo was swept away from Renata too, by Aunt Maria. "Don't go near her, my love!"

"Oh well," said Renata, as she was pulled away too. "Thanks for helping me up the dome, anyway."

"Just a moment!" Chrestomanci said loudly. Everyone turned to him, respectful but irritable. "If each spell-house," he said, "insists on regarding the other as monsters, I can promise you that Caprona will shortly fall again." They stared at him, Montanas and Petrocchis, equally indignant. The Archbishop looked at the Duke, and both of them began to edge towards the shelter of the Cathedral porch.

"What are you talking about?" Rinaldo said aggressively. His dignity was damaged by being a puppet anyway. The look in his eye seemed to promise cowpats for everyone – with the largest share for Chrestomanci.

"I'm talking about the Angel of Caprona," said Chrestomanci. "When the Angel alighted on the Cathedral, in the time of the First Duke of Caprona, bearing the safety of Caprona with him, history clearly states that the Duke appointed two men – Antonio Petrocchi and Piero Montana – to be keepers of the words of the Angel and therefore keepers of the safety of Caprona. In memory of this, each Casa has an Angel over its gate, and the great Angel stands on a pedestal showing the Petrocchi leopard entwined with the Montana winged horse." Chrestomanci pointed upwards. "If you don't believe me, ask for ladders and go and see. Antonio Petrocchi and Piero Montana were fast friends, and so were their families after them. There were frequent marriages between the two Casas. And Caprona became a great city and a strong State. Its decline dates from that ridiculous quarrel between Ricardo and Francesco."

There were murmurs from Montanas and Petrocchis alike, here, that the quarrel was *not* ridiculous.

"Of course it was," said Chrestomanci. "You've all been deceived from your cradles up. You've let Ricardo and Francesco fool you for two centuries. What they really quarrelled about we shall never know, but I know they both told their families the same lies. And you have all gone on believing their lies and getting deeper and deeper divided, until the White Devil was actually able to enter Caprona again."

Again there were murmurs. Antonio said, "The Duchess *was* the White Devil, but—"

"Yes," said Chrestomanci. "And she has gone for the moment, because the words were found and the Angel awakened by members of both families. I suspect it could only have been done by Montanas and Petrocchis united. The rest of you could have sung the right words separately, until you were all blue in the face, and nothing would have happened. The Angel respects only friendship. The young ones of both families are luckily less bigoted than the rest of you. Marco and Rosa have even had the courage to fall in love and get married—"

Up till then, both families had listened – restively, it was true, because it was not pleasant to be lectured in front of a crowd of fellow citizens, not to speak of the Duke and the Archbishop – but they had listened. But at this, pandemonium broke out.

"*Married!*" screamed the Montanas. "She's a *Montana*!" screamed the Petrocchis. Insults were yelled at Rosa and at Marco. Anyone who wished to count would have found no less than ten aunts in tears at once, and all cursing as they wept.

Rosa and Marco were both white. It needed only Rinaldo to step up to Marco, glowering, and he did. "This scum," he said to Rosa, "knocked me down and cut my head open. And you marry it!"

Chrestomanci made haste to get between Marco and Rinaldo. "I'd hoped someone would see reason," he said to Rosa. He seemed very tired. "It had better be Venice."

"Get out of my way!" said Rinaldo. "You double-dealing sorcerer!"

"Please move, sir," said Marco. "I don't need to be shielded from an idiot like him."

"Marco," said Chrestomanci, "have you thought what two families of powerful magicians could do to you and Rosa?"

"Of course we have!" Marco said angrily, trying to push Chrestomanci aside.

But a strange silence fell again, the silence of the Angel. The Archbishop knelt down. Awed people crowded to one side or another of the Cathedral yard. The Angel was returning. He came from far off down the Corso, on foot now, with his wing-tips brushing the cobbles and the chorus of voices swelling as he approached. As he passed through the Cathedral court, it was seen that in every place where a feather had touched the stones there grew a cluster of small golden flowers. Scent gushed over everyone as the Angel drew near and halted by the Cathedral porch, towering and golden.

There he turned his remote smiling face to everyone present. His voice was like one voice singing above many. "Caprona is at peace. Keep our covenant."

At that he spread his wings, making them all dizzy with the

scent. And he was next seen moving upwards, over lesser domes and greater, to take his place once more on the great dome, guarding Caprona in the years to come.

This is really the end of the story, except for one or two explanations.

Marco and Rosa had to tell their story many times, at least as often as Tonino and Angelica told theirs. Among the first people they told it to was Old Niccolo, who was lying restlessly in bed and only kept there because Elizabeth sat beside him all the time. "But I'm quite well!" he kept saying.

So, in order to keep him there, Elizabeth had first Tonino and then Rosa and Marco come and tell him their stories.

Rosa and Marco had met when they were both working on the Old Bridge. Falling in love and deciding to marry had been the easiest part, over in minutes. The difficulty was that they had to provide themselves with a family each which had nothing to do with either Casa. Rosa contrived a family first. She pretended to be English. She became very friendly with the English girl at the Art Gallery – the same Jane Smith that Rinaldo fancied so much. Jane Smith thought it was a great joke to pretend to be Rosa's sister. She wrote long letters in English to Guido Petrocchi, supposed to be from Rosa's English father, and visited the Casa Petrocchi herself the day Rosa was introduced there.

Rosa and Marco planned the introductions carefully. They used the pear-tree spell – which they worked together – in both

Casas, to Jane's amusement. But the Petrocchis, though they liked the pear-tree, were not kind to Rosa at first. In fact, some of Marco's aunts were so unpleasant that Marco was quite disgusted with them. That was why Marco was able to tell Antonio so vehemently that he hated the Petrocchis. But the aunts became used to Rosa in time. Renata and Angelica became very fond of her. And the wedding was held just after Christmas.

All this time, Marco had been unable to find anyone to act as a family for him. He was in despair. Then, only a few days before the wedding, his father sent him with a message to the house of Mario Andretti, the builder. And Marco discovered that the Andrettis had a blind daughter. When Marco asked, Mario Andretti said he would do anything for anyone who cured his daughter.

"Even then, we hardly dared hope," said Marco. "We didn't know if we could cure her."

"And apart from that," said Rosa, "the only time we dared both go there was the night after the wedding."

So the wedding was held in the Casa Petrocchi. Jane Smith helped Rosa make her dress and was a bridesmaid for her, together with Renata, Angelica and one of Marco's cousins.

Jane thoroughly enjoyed the wedding and seemed, Rosa said dryly, to find Marco's cousin Alberto at least as attractive as Rinaldo, whereas Rosa and Marco could think of almost nothing but little Maria Andretti. They hurried to the Andrettis' house as soon as the celebrations were over.

"And I've never known anything so difficult," said Rosa. "We were at it all night!"

Elizabeth was unable to contain herself here. "And I never even knew you were out!" she said.

"We took good care you didn't," said Rosa. "Anyway, we hadn't done anything like that before, so we had to look up spells in the University. We tried seventeen and none of them worked. In the end we had to make up one of our own. And all the time, I was thinking: suppose this doesn't work on the poor child either, and we've played with the Andrettis' hopes."

"Not to speak of our own," said Marco. "Then our spell worked. Maria yelled out that the room was all colours and there were things like trees in it – she thought people looked like trees – and we all jumped about in the dawn, hugging one another. And Andretti was as good as his word, and did his brother-act so well here that I told him he ought to be on the stage."

"He took *me* in," Old Niccolo said, wonderingly.

"But someone was bound to find out in the end," said Elizabeth. "What did you mean to do then?"

"Just hoped," said Marco. "We thought perhaps people might get used to it—"

"In other words, you behaved like a couple of young idiots," said Old Niccolo. "What is that terrible stench?" And he leapt up and raced out on to the gallery to investigate, with

Elizabeth, Rosa and Marco racing after him to stop him.

The smell, of course, was the kitchen-spell again. The insects had vanished and a smell of drains had taken their place. All day long, the kitchen belched out stinks, which grew stronger towards evening. It was particularly unfortunate, because the whole of Caprona was preparing to feast and celebrate. Caprona was truly at peace. The troops from Florence, and Pisa and Siena, had all returned home – somewhat bewildered and wondering how they had been beaten – and the people of Caprona were dancing in the streets.

"And we can't even cook, let alone celebrate!" wailed Aunt Gina.

Then an invitation arrived from the Casa Petrocchi. Would the Casa Montana be pleased to join in the celebrations at the Casa Petrocchi? It was a trifle stiff, but the Casa Montana did please. What could be more fortunate? Tonino and Paolo suspected that it was Chrestomanci's doing.

The only difficulty was to stop Old Niccolo getting out of bed and going with the rest of them. Everyone said Elizabeth had done enough. Everyone, even Aunt Francesca, wanted to go.

Then, more fortunately still, Uncle Umberto turned up, and old Luigi Petrocchi with him. They said they would sit with Old Niccolo – and on him if necessary. They were too old for dancing.

So everyone else went to the Casa Petrocchi, and it proved a celebration to remember. The Duke was there, because Angelica had insisted on it. The Duke was so grateful to be invited that he had brought with him as much wine and as many cakes as his coach would hold, and six footmen in a second coach to serve it.

"The Palace is awful," he said. "No one in it but Punch and Judys. Somehow I don't fancy them like I used to."

What with the wine, the cakes, and the good food baked in the Casa Petrocchi kitchen, the evening became very merry. Somebody found a barrel-organ and everyone danced to it in the yard. And, if the six footmen forgot to serve cakes and danced with the rest, who was to blame them? After all, the Duke was dancing with Aunt Francesca – a truly formidable sight.

Tonino sat with Paolo and Renata beside a charcoal brazier, watching the dancing. And while they sat, Benvenuto suddenly emerged from the shadows and sat down by the brazier, where he proceeded to give himself a fierce and thorough wash.

They had done a fine, enjoyable job on that white rat, he informed Tonino, as he stuck one leg high above his gnarled head and subjected it to punishing tongue-work. She'd not be back again.

"But is Vittoria all right?" Renata wanted to know.

Fine, was Benvenuto's answer. She was resting. She was going to have kittens. They would be particularly good kittens because Benvenuto was the father. Tonino was to make sure to get one for the Casa Montana.

Tonino asked Renata for a kitten then and there, and Renata promised to ask Angelica. Whereupon, Benvenuto, having worked over both hind legs, wafted himself on to Tonino's knees, where he made himself into a tight brown mat and slept for an hour.

"I wish I could understand him," said Paolo. "He tried to tell me where you were, but all I did was see a picture of the front of the Palace."

"But that's how he always tells things!" said Tonino. He was surprised Paolo had not known. "You just have to read his pictures."

"What's he saying now?" Renata asked Paolo.

"Nothing," said Paolo. "Snore, snore." And they all laughed.

Sometime later, when Benvenuto had woken up and drifted off to try his luck in the kitchen, Tonino wandered in to a room nearby, without quite knowing why he did. As soon as he got inside, though, he knew it was no accident. Chrestomanci was there, with Angelica and Guido Petrocchi, and so was Antonio. Antonio was looking so worried that Tonino braced himself for trouble.

"We were discussing you, Tonino," said Chrestomanci. "You helped Angelica fetch the griffins, didn't you?"

"Yes," said Tonino. He remembered the damage they had done and felt alarmed.

"And you helped in the kitchen-spell?" asked Chrestomanci.

Tonino said "Yes" again. Now he was sure there was trouble.

"And when you hanged the Duchess," Chrestomanci said, to Tonino's confusion, "how did you do that?"

Tonino wondered how he could be in trouble over that too, but he answered, "By doing what the puppet show made me do. I couldn't get out of it, so I had to go along with it, you see."

"I do," said Chrestomanci, and he turned to Antonio rather triumphantly. "You see? And that was the White Devil! What interests me is that it was someone else's spell each time." Then before Tonino could be too puzzled, he turned back to him. "Tonino," he said, "it seems to me that you have a new and rather useful talent. You may not be able to work many spells on your own, but you seem to be able to turn other people's magic to your own use. I think if they had let you help on the Old Bridge, for instance, it would have been mended in half a day. I've been asking your father if he'd let you come back to England with me, so that we could find out just what you can do."

Tonino looked at his father's worried face. He hardly knew what to think. "Not for good?" he said.

Antonio smiled. "Only for a few weeks," he said. "If Chrestomanci's right, we'll need you here badly."

Tonino smiled too. "Then I don't mind," he said.

"But," said Angelica, "it was me who fetched the griffins really."

"What were you really fetching?" asked Guido.

Angelica hung her head. "Mice." She looked resigned when her father roared with laughter.

"I wanted to talk about you too," said Chrestomanci. He said to Guido, "Her spells always work, don't they? It occurs to me you might learn from Angelica."

Guido scratched his beard. "How to turn things green and get griffins, you mean?"

Chrestomanci picked up his glass of wine. "There are risks, of course, to Angelica's methods. But I meant she can show you that a thing need not be done in the same old way in order to work. I think, in time, she will make you a whole new set of spells. Both houses can learn from her." He raised his wine glass.

"Your health, Angelica. Tonino. The Duchess thought she was getting the weakest members of both Casas, and it turned out quite the opposite."

Antonio and Guido raised their glasses too. "I'll say this," said Guido. "But for you two, we wouldn't be celebrating tonight."

Angelica and Tonino looked at each other and made faces. They felt very shy and very, very pleased.More than a Story

Writing The Magicians of Caprona   3

More than a Story

✳

More than a story © HarperCollins Children's Books 2008
The Game excerpt © Diana Wynne Jones 2007
The Game illustration © Rob Ryan 2007
Other illustrations © Tim Stevens

When the idea for *The Magicians of Caprona* struck me — in the middle of one afternoon while I was trying to mend some cushions — it came all of a piece, because someone was playing a record, which had a tune on it that ought to have had words, but hadn't. The tune was obviously the *Angel of Caprona*.

Caprona came into my head, and all things Italian with it, together with the great spellhouses and the families that came with them. *Romeo and Juliet* was also in there, because of course Shakespeare set that play in Italy (he set a lot of his plays in Italy, but for some reason none of the others seemed to fit so well). After that, I had enormous fun thinking of all the ways spells could go wrong, starting with the way someone could

3

accidentally turn their father green, or infest a kitchen, right on to the way mice could become iron griffins by mistake.

Then I thought of all the other things spells might do. They could make a magicians' war; they could make a war between states. They could also turn people an inch or so high. I can't tell you what fun it was thinking of how it would *really* feel to be six inches high and trying to escape from a large palace. It all became totally real to me in a matter of minutes.

Then, to my surprise, I discovered later that at least some of it was real. I had a long, courteous letter from the elderly Count of Caprona himself. Caprona was a real small state, but it has not, in this world, ever been very large or important. The Count told me that his family was exiled from there some

4

time in the Fourteenth Century and that he now lived in Sweden. But they still kept the title, although Caprona nowadays was not much more than a small castle with a rather strange chapel attached.

He had discovered my book because his son had found it somehow and given it to him for Christmas, knowing that he was interested in everything about Caprona. Would you believe that! This is not just a book coming true on me: it is a book being true before I even wrote it.

Diana Wynne Jones

Spells Gone Wrong

Can you unravel these spell(ing)s to reveal the correct words? Clue: all of these magical mix-ups can be found in *The Magicians of Caprona*.

1. ARCANE FANG POOL (3 words)

2. CELIA NAG (1 word)

3. HECTIC SOAP ARC (2 words)

4. COCO DILLON (2 words)

5. AN INN ON TOMATO (2 words)

6. A CHIC MONSTER (1 word)

7. BE VET NOUN (1 word)

8. HAG SET TIP (1 word)

9. FIN FOR GIN SIR (2 words)

10. ACT HERALD (1 word)

Answers on page 16

All sorts of creatures are found linked with magic. Sometimes this is because they are, by nature, magical beasts – such as dragons and unicorns and griffins. Sometimes they are enchanted humans – frogs and toads, in the main. Sometimes they are ingredients – usually of the multi-legged, creepy-crawly variety, although the entire animal is not always required (e.g. hair, claws or whiskers). But the animals that crop up time and time again, and particularly in connection with witches, are cats.

One of the prime reasons cats are such magical creatures is because they have nine lives. As Chrestomanci *has* to be a nine-lifed enchanter, it stands to reason that any creature with the luck, gifts and abilities of nine is going to be far more magical than a creature with just one! Which means that all cats are magical, even though their owners are probably not.

Knowing this makes cats extremely confident and self-sufficient, and they put their magic to use all the time. How else could

7

they appear from nowhere whenever the fridge door is opened? Or make a human open a door or window for them when they have a perfectly good catflap of their own? Or seek out the one person in a room who hates cats and snuggle up to them?

Most of the time, cats don't waste their energy displaying their superiority to non-magical humans. Occasionally they will, however, try to communicate with them – perhaps by staring at their subject for a very long time, or by sitting/standing/sleeping on whatever book/newspaper/homework that person might be occupied with, or by massaging that person's leg/stomach/shoulder with very spiky claws while purring loudly.

Cats tend to behave in the same way regardless of whether they live in a world with a lot of magic or a world with none. But in worlds that use magic every day, cats can be extremely useful – if they can be persuaded to help at all. Of course, it's a great advantage if you can understand cats; not everyone can –

not even every magic user can. (In fact, we learn that not even Chrestomanci can understand cats in *The Magicians of Caprona* – although he knows how to communicate in the proper manner.) It's therefore not surprising Tonino Montana gains much respect from his friends and family when Benvenuto – boss cat of the Casa Montana – takes Tonino under his wing. Benvenuto knew that all Tonino needed was a bit of help in learning how to use his special kind of magic – and the fact that Tonino also knows exactly the right way to scratch a cat behind the ears is just a big feline bonus! No doubt similar reasons brought Angelica Petrocchi and Vittoria together in the rival Casa Petrocchi household.

In some worlds cats are so magical they are sacred. The Temple of Asheth in Series 10, for example, is positively swarming with magical cats. The Goddess usually adopts a favourite as a companion and to aid her in her reading of portents. In *The Lives of Christopher Chant*, the Goddess's cats were Bethi, succeeded by Proudfoot.

Asheth Temple cats all have exceptionally strong personalities – the strongest being that of Throgmorten. No cats suffer fools gladly, but Throgmorten is probably the least tolerant of all and has no hesitation about venting his feelings with his razor sharp claws, lethal fangs and lightning quick reflexes. Throgmorten is a very handy ally in a fight against a deadly foe, but is not averse to ambushing innocent bystanders if he doesn't like them!

Some cats are not what they appear to be. Fiddle, in *Charmed Life*, was actually once a violin (hence the name). But never make the mistake of thinking that an enchanted cat is any less important or magical than a cat that grew up from a kitten – he may well have a vital role to play as all magic happens for a reason.

If you've got a cat, I'm sure you've noticed that he does whatever he pleases, whenever he chooses and always, ALWAYS knows he's right. You may think you've shut him indoors for safety while you are out of the house, only to come home and find him sitting on the front step, demanding to be let inside. Or you may have been searching for hours and hours, only to discover him curled up in a drawer or on your pillow. It's unlikely you'll ever get to the bottom of mysterious goings-on like these, but it's worth considering that you might own a cat who can walk through walls. Nutcase in *The Pinhoe Egg* was a master of this skill, and it was a long time before Marianne got wise to his game.

Like all cats, Nutcase was also very curious. Curiosity, they say, killed the cat, but this happens very rarely. Curiosity mostly ensures that a cat will at some point end up in a few sticky situations!

The best advice for dealing with cats is:

- always greet them politely
- don't make an unnecessary fuss over them
- be on the alert for signs they want to communicate with you
- and never, ever laugh at them!

If you're lucky, you might just find that your cat will decide that you are a magical person worthy of attention. Or then again, maybe they'd just like some fish...

Famous Felines

Grimalkin

Gobbolino

Pyewacket

Salem

Rutterkin

Macavity

Puss in Boots

The Cheshire Cat

Carbonel

Orlando

Thomasina

The Cat that Walks by Himself

Magician Muddle

All the magicians have got mixed up! Can you sort the Montanas from the Petrocchis? And spot the odd one out?

Rosa

Angelica

Luigi

Renata

Lucia

Mario

Rinaldo

Ricardo

Tonino

Niccolo

Paolo

Gina

Guido

Marco

Answers on page 16.

If you like, you'll love...

If you liked reading *The Magicians of Caprona*, you'll enjoy these other books by Diana Wynne Jones.

❋ If you like **Tonino Montana**, you'll love *Mixed Magics*.
Four stories all set in the worlds of Chrestomanci, and all featuring the famous enchanter himself. Tonino appears in 'Stealer of Souls' along with another favourite, Cat Chant.

❋ If you like **cats**, you'll love *The Lives of Christopher Chant*.
Christopher Chant learns that he is no ordinary boy, but destined to be Chrestomanci when he grows up – something he is less than thrilled about!

❋ If you like **crazy families**, you'll love *The Game*.
When Hayley is sent to live in Ireland with a whole host of cousins she never knew she had, she is introduced to the secret and mysterious Game, which takes her to the forbidden "mythosphere".

14

✳ If you like **mysteries**, you'll love *The Merlin Conspiracy*. Roddy Hyde and Nick Mallory are from two different worlds – literally. But when a murder plot is uncovered, it's only by teaming up that they can get to the bottom of it.

✳ If you like **feuding clans**, you'll love *Power of Three*. Ayna, Ceri and Gair live on the Moor, overcrowded and worried. Their enemies, the Dorig, are a constant threat, and the Giants are behaving strangely too…

✳ If you like **disguise spells**, you'll love *Howl's Moving Castle*. When Sophie falls under a curse, she seeks help from the fearsome Wizard Howl, whose appetite, they say, is satisfied only by the hearts of young girls…

Have you ever wondered?

✴ *The Magicians of Caprona* contains a very amusing story about how spaghetti was invented. Can you make up a funny and magical history for pizza?

✴ If you woke up and discovered you were as tiny as a puppet, how would this change the way you got ready for the day ahead?

✴ What songs and rhymes do you know that have words that could make good spells? What sort of spells would they be? How might they go wrong?

Answers

Spells Gone Wrong
1. Angel of Caprona   2. Angelica   3. Casa Petrocchi   4. Old Niccolo
5. Tonino Montana   6. Chrestomanci   7. Benvenuto   8. Spaghetti
9. Iron griffins   10. Cathedral

Magician Muddle
Montanas: Paolo, Tonino, Rinaldo, Rosa, Lucia, Gina, Niccolo
Petrocchis: Angelica, Guido, Luigi, Marco, Renata, Ricardo
Odd one out: Mario

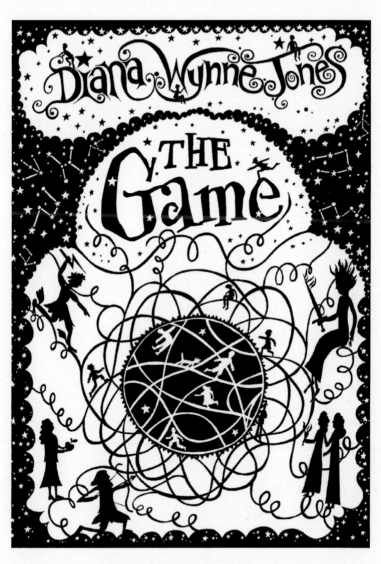

Sneak preview...

Grandpa was sitting massively in front of a screen, carefully following something on it with a light-pen. Hayley tiptoed up to look over his shoulder. It was a picture of Earth, slowly spinning in dark blue emptiness. She saw Africa rotating past as she arrived. But Africa was quite hard to see because it and the whole globe was swathed in a soft, multicoloured mist. The mist seemed to be made up of thousands of tiny pale threads, all of them moving and swirling outwards. Each thread shone as it moved, gentle and pearly, so the effect was as if Earth spun in a luminous rainbow veil. While Hayley watched, some of the threads wrapped themselves together into a shining skein and this grew on outwards, growing brighter and harder-looking as it grew, and then got thrown gently sideways with the turning of the world, so that it became a silver red spiral. There were dozens of these skeins, when Hayley looked closely, in dozens of silvery colours. But underneath these were thousands of other shining threads which busily drifted and wove and plaited close to Earth.

"That's *beautiful*!" Hayley said. "What are they?"

"Are your hands clean?" Grandpa answered absently. His light-pen steadily picked out a gold gleaming set of threads underneath the spirals and followed it in and out, here and there, through the gauzy mass. He seemed to take it for granted that Hayley had washed her hands because he went on, "This is the mythosphere. It's made up of all the stories, theories and beliefs, legends, myths and hopes, that are generated here on Earth. As you can see, it's constantly growing and moving as people invent new tales to tell or find new things to believe. The older strands move out to become these spirals, where things tend to become quite crude and dangerous. They've hardened off, you see."

"Are they real, the same as atoms and planets?" Hayley asked.

18

"Quite as real – even realler in some ways," Grandpa replied.

Hayley said the name of it to herself, in order not to forget it. "The mythosphere. And what are you doing with it?"

"Tracing the golden apples," Grandpa said. "Wondering why they've never become a spiral of their own. They mix into other strands all the time. Look." He did something to the keyboard to make Earth turn about and spread itself into a flat plain with continents slowly twirling across it. Golden threads rose from India, from the flatness north of the mountains, from the Mediterranean and from Sweden, Norway and Britain. "See here." Grandpa's big hairy hand pointed the light-pen this way and that as the threads arose. "This thread mingles with three different dragon stories. And this..." the line of light moved southward "...mixes with two quite different stories here. This one's the judgement of Paris and here we have Atalanta, the girl who was distracted from winning a race by some golden apples. And there are hundreds of folktales..." The pen moved northwards to golden threads growing like grass over Europe and Asia. Grandpa shook his head. "Golden apples all over. They cause death and eternal life and danger and choices. They *must* be important. But none of them combine. None of them spiral and harden. I don't know why."

"If they're real," Hayley said, "can a person go and walk in them, or are they like germs and atoms and too small to see?"

"Oh, yes," Grandpa said, frowning at the threads. "Only I don't advocate walking in the spirals. Everything gets pretty fierce out there."

"But nearer in. Do you walk or float?" Hayley wanted to know.

19

"You could take a boat if you want," Grandpa said, "or even a car sometimes. But I prefer to walk myself. It's—"

But here Grandma came storming in and seized Hayley by one arm. "Really! Honest to goodness, Tas!" she said, dragging Hayley away from the screen. "You ought to know better than to let Hayley in among this stuff!"

"It's not doing her any harm!" Grandpa protested.

"On the contrary. It could do immense harm – to us and Hayley too, if Jolyon gets to hear of it!" Grandma retorted. She dragged Hayley out of the room and shut the door with a bang. "Hayley, you are not to have anything to do with the mythosphere *ever* again!" she said. "Forget you ever saw it!"